D0229026

79 682 652 1

NIGHT
HERON

NIGHT HERON

Adam Brookes

sphere

SPHERE

First published in Great Britain in 2014 by Sphere

A CIP catalogue record for this book
is available from the British Library.

ISBN HB 978-0-7515-5248-5
ISBN CF 978-0-7515-5249-2

Typeset in Garamond by M Rules
Printed and bound in Great Britain by
Clays Ltd, St Ives plc

Papers used by Sphere are from well-managed forests
and other responsible sources.

MIX
Paper from
responsible sources
FSC® C104740

Sphere
An imprint of
Little, Brown Book Group
100 Victoria Embankment
London EC4Y 0DY

An Hachette UK Company
www.hachette.co.uk

www.littlebrown.co.uk

For my parents,
Jill and Michael Brookes

It may be that, like the military-industrial complex, the existence of the espionage-industrial complex has become a foregone conclusion, so deeply entrenched, and so vital, for all its shortcomings, to the nation's security, that it can never be undone.

'Privatized Spying: the Emerging Intelligence Industry' by Patrick R. Keefe
in *The Oxford Handbook of National Security Intelligence*, p. 307.

PART ONE

The Contact.

1

Qinghai Province, western China
The recent past

1.37 a.m.

Prisoner 5995 was where he should not be, and fear was congealing in his mouth.

Any second now.

The thought flickered across his mind, sent adrenalin thrumming through his gut.

He stood in darkness. Beyond the barrack block an arc light saturated the prison camp with silvery light, turned the razor wire to coils of iridescence against the night sky.

Any second now. Any bitching second.

He flattened his bulk against the wall, the brick cool against his hands. He willed himself into shadow, willed himself to stillness. His breathing came fast. In his nostrils, the cool desert air, flecked with kerosene and dust. In his mouth, fear, a rancid, viscous paste.

Any second now.

And there the man was, lumbering along the dusty path

3

between the barracks, his grey uniform shapeless, his brown leather belt sagging with the weight of the dangling baton, peaked cap high on the back of the head, eyes down, a walkie-talkie in one hand, a cigarette in the other. The 1.30 patrol.

From the shadows, Prisoner 5995 watched the man shamble down the path. The inmates called them *leizi*, the slow-witted, venal imbeciles who constituted the prison guard. *Leizi*. Thunders. For their rumbling and coughing and incessant shouting. 5995 pulled back deeper into darkness. He caught a whiff of cigarette smoke and felt the craving like a kick to the throat.

The thunder had almost reached the block behind which Prisoner 5995 was concealed. 5995 could hear the thunder's boots scuffing the gravelly dust. The thunder should now, by all that was right and holy, walk past the block and turn to the right, his shadow shrinking beneath the fierce scrutiny of the arc light, the crunch of his footsteps receding. The thunder should disappear into the blank night, allowing the prisoner to continue unseen on his precarious way – to what? To freedom? To a firing squad? Or to lethal injection, sodium thiopental bubbling in the vein, in keeping with the times?

5995 waited for the footfalls to pass.

But, silence. The thunder had halted.

A crackle from the walkie-talkie and an electronic *pip* sound.

5995 sought to compress his sizeable girth, his thick thighs and neck, his bristled head and muscular hands, into invisibility, into stillness. A slow crunch of gravel, as if the thunder were turning or shifting his weight. Then a murmur, another crackle. *Pip.*

Silence.

5995 exhaled an iota, took a tiny breath. Still. Still. Stay still.

Then, slowly, the gravelly footsteps resumed. 5995 closed his eyes, felt a prickling of sweat on his scalp. The footsteps were getting closer.

The thunder was not turning away from 5995, as predicted by

months of routine and all the intelligence a practised operative like 5995 could gather. The thunder was confounding reason and walking directly towards 5995 and his grossly inadequate cover. Screw his mother. Had 5995, in his reconnoitring, missed a security camera? Or had the treacherous, conniving bitches with whom he had shared two decades of life in this labour reform facility turned him in already?

The footsteps came closer, boot on concrete, grit, particulate.

Fear stopped his breath, shredded his thoughts. He forced himself against the wall, crushed an overwhelming desire to bolt, to run, to *move*.

The thunder stepped off the path, out of the light, his back to 5995. From where he stood, an arc of scarlet light, then a scatter of sparks.

His cigarette.

The thunder seemed to be reaching for something in his clothing. Silence, then a liquid hiss and spatter, a whiff of ammonia and alcohol.

The man is pissing, thought 5995. He is pissing against the wall.

The spatter turned sporadic, and stopped. The thunder arranged himself and coughed, a shocking bark in the darkness. 5995 imagined himself encased in clay, eternally silent and still like some tomb warrior, buried, invisible since the days of Qin.

The thunder was yawning, feeling in his pocket. He pulled out a packet of cigarettes. 5995 heard its cellophane rustle. The thunder shook the packet, held it up to the arc light, made a pincer with his forefinger and thumb and drew from it a bent cigarette. He placed the cigarette between his lips. Now the lighter, its raspy *snick*. 5995 blinked at the flame and saw the thunder tilt his head back, inhale noisily. The thunder crumpled the empty packet in his hand, turned, raised his arm and hurled it into the shadows. It hit 5995 on the chin, causing him to jerk reflexively, as if he had been struck. The packet fell to the ground, and the thunder turned quickly and peered into the darkness. He cannot see me, thought 5995. He has no night vision. The thunder tilted his head, looked again. Very, very still now.

The walkie-talkie crackled.

The thunder looked down, pressed the talk key, and in a desultory movement brought the walkie-talkie to his mouth, mumbled, and let it fall. He sighed and turned away. His footsteps receded into the night.

1.42 a.m. Eighteen minutes until the next patrol.

Move.

Delicately, and with a degree of light-footedness and quiet surprising in such a big man, Prisoner 5995 ran through the savage arc light, across the path, to the windowless two-storey boiler house opposite. A grey door, which, thought 5995 as he ran, must be unlocked if I am to live. He slowed, reached for the handle.

The door gave. His momentum carried him through, and he was inside. A dim, cool interior, damp concrete under his feet, a sulphurous smell. He closed the door behind him gently, breathing heavily, allowed his eyes to readjust.

Before him he made out a pile of coal. Beyond it a doorway, through which came the hissing and ticking of the boiler. The boiler room was festooned with pipework, lit by a single bulb, water pooling on the floor. He stopped in the doorway, listened. Nothing. He passed the boiler soundlessly and pushed to one side a dense plastic curtain. A dingy corridor, in darkness. At its end double doors.

Move.

He inched the doors open, peered into a shadowy office space of six or seven desks, dull filing cabinets, a smell of old cardboard, cigarettes. He stood, collecting himself. He thought, Dear God, this might work. This might . . .

A hand on his shoulder.

Adrenalin like lightning in his muscles, anger and shock flickering in the brain, 5995 turned fast, reaching for anything, cloth, flesh, hair. He forced his weight forward, a shout strangled in his throat. The body before him gave, unresisting. 5995 slammed it into the wall. The body grunted with the impact, and then spoke, a quavering whisper.

'Bit less noise, if I were you.'

With one hand to its neck, the other raised to strike, 5995 regarded this creature, its flickering eyes.

'What, what in God's name are you doing here?' he whispered.

'I did everything you said.'

'I nearly killed you.'

'The locks, everything. And all the stuff is over there on the floor.'

'God in heaven.' 5995 let it go, this trembling scrap of humanity, in its labour reform grey, its cotton shoes. He rolled his head back, caught his breath.

'It's all there, you can check it,' said the man.

'Oh, I will.'

5995 turned. Between the desks lay a miserable pile of objects. He kneeled and rummaged through them, checking off each one. Two large plastic containers, of the sort that might have held cooking oil, with screw tops, filled with water and linked together by a length of green nylon cord. A carrier bag, containing a paper bag half-filled with corn bread and cooked greens, the grease rendering the paper bag translucent. Two bars of the atrocious chocolate they sold at the commissary. Nine packs of cigarettes. A lighter. A few yuan notes, barely enough to buy a bowl of noodles in the real world. A small clear polythene bag, cinched at the top with an elastic band, and what appeared to be a yellowed newspaper clipping inside. And a brick. That was it. His escape equipment. His plan.

'It's all there, isn't it?'

5995 looked at him hard.

'Yes, it's all there,' he said.

'Yes.'

'And why are you here?' said 5995.

'We have a deal, don't we? Peanut?'

That was what they called him. Peanut.

'Yes, we have a deal,' he said.

'You will stick to it, yes?' said the man.

'For God's sake, yes.' It was, in truth, less of a deal, and more, well, blackmail, Peanut reflected briefly. He had found this creature, a trusty with a job in the prison administration, behind the kitchen storage bins, eyes wide with panic, pants round ankles and manhood pointing to the stars, while the cookhouse thunder kneeled and gaped. Peanut had offered a careful bargain: his silence in exchange for access to the offices and the loading dock.

'You won't say anything, Peanut? About me, my mistakes. When you're ... out.'

5995 rolled his eyes.

'I will not tell anyone that you sold sexual favours in a labour reform facility.'

'That's a harsh way of putting it, Peanut. Unkind.'

'Screw unkind. Now lock the doors behind you and keep your mouth shut.'

The man sighed.

5995 shook his head, shoved the supplies in his pockets, draped the water bottles over his shoulder, picked up the brick. The man's eyes held his for a second, a half-smile.

'Good luck, Peanut.'

'Screw luck.'

And Prisoner 5995, alias Peanut, was gone.

*

The loading dock was flanked by seven-foot walls. Beyond the dock, a series of three locked gates and the road to the main prison complex, forty miles away.

On the other side of the seven-foot wall, nothing. No fences, no perimeter, no wire. Just two hundred miles of rocky desert plain. Not so hard to escape labour reform, but the desert? No one escaped the desert. No one tried.

The loading dock was in darkness. Peanut listened to the night. Nothing.

Three blue plastic crates of the sort that might have held beer bottles were in their prearranged position. Peanut set them one atop the other, quietly, next to the wall. Standing on the crates, he rested his elbows on the wall, into which some thoughtful comrade had cemented jagged chunks of broken glass. Peanut took off the stained blue tracksuit top that he wore. He laid it on the wall to cover a swathe of glass perhaps eighteen inches wide. He took the brick, felt its heft, and very gently, the tracksuit muffling the noise, chipped at the glass. Within minutes he had created a narrow, navigable pathway across the top of the wall.

He hauled himself up, kneeled on the wall, swaying for a moment, clutching the water bottles and the carrier bag. Then he jumped.

Stillness, he knew, was enemy to him.

So he ran.

He ran for hours in the night. The desert plain was strewn with sharp shale. It rattled and clinked beneath each footfall, and his cotton shoes were too thin, and the shale jutted and forced his ankles to odd angles and his feet were an agony. The two plastic water bottles grew heavier and swung and slapped against him, queering his movement, and the nylon cord that held them cut a welt in his shoulder. He longed to leave the water and go on unencumbered. But without it he'd die. Quickly. The air was cold in his throat and his breath came in gasps.

Ahead, low hills against the night sky.

He stopped in the dark, squatted, tried to calm his breathing and hold his balance. Faint starlight, the wind sharp. Could he risk a cigarette? He cupped his hands around the flare of the lighter. The tobacco stank in the clear air. They would smell it a mile away.

Screw them.

A deep, cold billow of fear.

You're exhausted, he thought. Fear is born of loneliness and exhaustion. Where had he read that?

Stillness is the enemy.

Move.

Up and running, stumbling over the jagged ground, the water bottles flailing, towards the dark hills. As he ran, a beautiful, stupid song from childhood shimmered in his head.

Er yue li lai ya! Hao chun guan! February's coming! A fine spring beckons! The families are at work in the fields! We hand grain to the troops!

How he loved that idiotic song. He'd sung it the day he got his red scarf, scrubbed raw and on parade outside the neighbourhood committee offices. Afterwards Father, walking stiffly by then, subdued, had taken him and his sister, Mei, to the park. It was 1969. They'd sat on a stone bench under a luminous willow, ice cream dripping from the stick, cicadas whirring in the still, thundery air.

He had about two hours until dawn, and the sirens and the dogs.

His absence had already been noted. Back in the barracks, Prisoner 7775, fraudster, rapist and light sleeper, was awake and contemplating the empty bunk above him. Peanut often got up in the night to piss. They'd fought about it for years. But this time Peanut had not reappeared. It had been a good hour and a half, and if the thunders came in at dawn and found Peanut gone, Prisoner 7775 was going to be asked about it, as was everyone else in Production Squad 20. Asked forcefully.

Prisoner 7775 turned the problem over in his mind. He liked his absent neighbour, which was rare, because in general 7775 didn't hold with the intellectuals and the politicals. He didn't trust them, all their bold words evaporating into the labour reform cringe at the first sign of trouble.

But Peanut was different. He was *resourceful*. While most of Production Squad 20 were skin and bone, laced with taut, wiry muscle, Peanut remained fleshy. While 7775 struggled to accumulate items of value in the prison economy – cigarettes, letter paper, antibiotics – Peanut seemed always to have a supply. Which he would share, sometimes.

Prisoner 7775 reflected on his acquaintance with his calculating companion. Their years together in labour reform were indistinguishable one from another, punctuated only by occasional, strange, memorable episodes. 7775 spooled them through his mind.

Once, years before, a weedy little political had arrived in the camp, trembling and weepy, eyes sunken. He was a lawyer of some sort, who'd tried too hard. On a work party up in the hills, he got knocked about because he was useless with a shovel, and because he had straggly hairs on his upper lip, and because it was raining. Nothing serious, but a couple of thunders joined in with their batons and his nose went and the blood was running down his chin, gobbets in it, and he was all weepy again. Peanut watched it unfold, and when it was over, stood the little political on his feet, helped him back to the barracks and cleaned him up.

And then Peanut told the little political to write a letter, to address it to 'foreign journalists'. In Beijing. There were lots of them, he said, and they lived in a big compound near Altar of the Sun Park. So the two prisoners composed a letter, and the little political, in spidery characters blotched with tears, told of the terror and degradation that was labour reform, spiced up a bit, and Peanut got it smuggled out in the laundry run and sent to Beijing. And some foreign newspaper printed it! Big exposé! *Horrors of China's Gulag!* And, soon after, inspection teams showed up, and the thunders' faces were a treat.

Now, as Peanut pointed out, the higher-ups did not care one whit about conditions in labour reform, or beatings, or whether the little political lived or died. But they cared that they had been humiliated by foreigners. And they were going to make everyone else in the Labour Reform Bureau care too. The little political was given a cushy job in the kitchen, and no one said a word, and Peanut just looked at the thunders with a knowing expression, an I-can-fuck-you-up-if-I-try expression.

How the hell did Peanut know about foreign journalists, anyway?

7775 lay in the fetid air of the barracks, the night pressing in on him, listening to the whispered breathing of the other prisoners. He clutched at his blanket and thought of a home he'd once had and a little girl in pigtails cracking sunflower seeds with her teeth. Her face was almost gone now. He pawed away the desperation.

7775 wouldn't turn Peanut in.

Not yet, anyway. Wait another hour.

He was on the slope now, heading into the hills, the ground less stony, a little easier. The darkness was holding, and it was colder, traces of snow on the ground. Exhaustion took his mind in discursive, pointless directions. He wondered idly if he was leaving scent, if they even had dogs. He'd never seen a dog in the camp. Any dog to come within range of Production Squad 20 would have been beaten to death and grilled with the cumin that 1414's mother sent. 1414 – *yao si yao si.* It wasn't his number; it just rhymed with *want to die, want to die*, which was what he shouted at night, and it stuck. Early on 1414 had been in the shackles, hands chained to the waist, and a wooden bar two feet long affixed each end to an ankle, so that when he walked each foot described a half-circle. A couple of the Christians had fed him and wiped his arse.

Peanut stopped, breathing heavily, and looked behind him. He was gaining height. He saw the lights of the prison camp across the plain, faint now, silver in the night. No sound, no activity, yet. No trucks. Of course no one escaped. Where the hell would anyone go? He looked up again, breathing hard. The slope would steepen, he knew, and then he'd almost be there. Move.

7775 pondered again the empty bunk above him, then sat up. Time now, Peanut. Sorry, but needs must. In the darkness he felt for the grey jacket hanging from the peg above him, the white stripes across the shoulders. He padded down the centre of the barracks, the concrete cold against his bare feet, biding his time. The next few hours would be tricky.

He leaned over the familiar sleeping form. 'Section Chief, wake up! Prisoner Number 7775 wishes to report.'

From the section chief, nothing, just the hiss of sleep. 7775 bit his lip, then shook a shoulder. 'Prisoner Number 7775 wishes to report.'

One baleful eye opened, grasping for meaning at this dead hour.

'Section Chief!' 7775 stood upright now. Better make it official, he thought. 'Prisoner Number 7775 wishes to report that Prisoner Number 5995 is absent.'

'What time is it?'

'Five, Section Chief.'

A yawn, a thick smell rising from the bedroll. 'What do you mean he's absent?'

'He's not there, Section Chief.'

'Well, where's he gone? Isn't it Peanut?'

'Prisoner Number 7775 does not know where Prisoner Number 5995 has gone, Section Chief.'

'Why are you talking like that? Have you been to look for him?'

'No, Section Chief.'

Over the section chief's sleep-sodden face, a shadow of real-isation spread slowly. He blinked and struggled out of his bedroll. Their balding, affable section chief, himself a prisoner – saboteur apparently, though no one knew of what – was oppres-sor and friend both. Now he was pulling on a vest and standing pot-bellied in the dark, rubbing his hand across his chin.

'So where's he gone?'

'I don't know where he's gone, Section Chief,' which got a direct look.

The section chief turned and looked out of the window at the dust and the glow from the arc lights, breath steaming the glass, fingers splayed against the pane, hopeful.

'What do we do?'

7775 opened his mouth, then shut it again.

'Yes? What?'

'7775 would suggest reporting to the duty guard officer, Section Chief.'

The section chief stared at him. 'But he must be somewhere.'

'It's been . . . a while.'

Panic flaring now.

'A while?'

The section chief was out of the barracks at a splay-footed run, heading towards the guard house, where the thunders were dozing in front of a Hong Kong movie in which brave monks chopped down the enemies of China.

*

Prisoner 5995 had a pain in his chest. The last half-hour had him stopping often, bent double, breath rasping, knees shaking. But now he looked down on a little flooded gravel pit, its black water a mirror for the stars.

You'd hardly know it was there. On three sides were jagged low cliffs, the track the only way in or out. He picked his way down to the water's edge. To the east the sky was just starting to lighten.

The water wasn't just cold. It was sickening. He was in up to his waist, his clothes in a bundle on his shoulder, the bottles around his neck. The cold crept up his spine, making him gag. Up to his chest now. The rock walls enclosing the water had gone from steep to sheer, and, there, a sapling clung on. Just there. Reaching up, he felt the lip of the blasting tunnel, eighteen inches above his head. His clothes went in first, then the water bottles. Bare feet scratching for purchase on the submerged rock face, fingertips clawing for grip, shoulders screaming, one elbow in and a desperate, horrible scrabble, and he was up, dripping and shaking.

The tunnel was narrower than he remembered, but deep. He'd noticed it years before, on a work party, and he'd stored away the details, as he was prone to doing. He dried off with his shirt, crouching, put the damp clothes back on, zipped up the blue tracksuit top, and shook some more. If he moved crabwise, backwards, he could disappear twenty feet into the rock.

This is where he would sit it out, the sirens and the dogs and the whatever, all the thunders buzzing around like flies in a shithouse, terrified of losing their bonuses. They must be looking by now, surely.

Heaven, he was hungry. The paper bag of crumbling cornmeal bread and greens looked tiny and woeful. What had he been thinking? Save it. Cigarette instead, then sleep.

Or maybe not. Maybe he should keep moving.

They'll be looking, he thought. He rubbed himself, blew on his hands.

Nobody escaped. Escapees died in the desert, miles from anywhere, their tongues engorged, their flesh like putty.

But then someone had built a railway.

The sky was lightening. The water was streaked red.

Thunders were stumbling out of the guard block, doing up their belts, working the slides on their AKs, shielding their eyes against the cool morning sun. Dust hung in the air. A jeep whined out of the front gate, the driver gesticulating, then stopped, then started again and headed out on to the plain.

7775 and the others were in ranks in front of the barracks. They'd been that way for forty minutes now. The section chief, wide-eyed and sweating, stood in front of them. Three times already 7775 had told the story they'd settled on.

'I woke and he was gone,' he'd said. 'It was five o'clock and I reported immediately.' Blurt it. Look contrite.

The commandant was murmuring into a mobile phone, affecting calm. The thunders looked confused and pissed off, a dangerous combination for Peanut when they found him. Which they would, 7775 was sure.

The sun was up.

He'd scraped his fingers raw clearing the tunnel floor of shale. He sat on a circle of exposed rock, dank and cold, his pathetic stores in a pile beside him.

Think of the cave as a cell, a scholar's cell, a writer's studio, he told himself, somewhere for reflection, for rediscovering intellectual purpose.

In the prison camp they called intellectuals 'shit-eaters'. The two terms, intellectual and shit-eater, sounded almost identical, *zhishifenzi/chishifenzi*, their confusion irresistible. The other inmates had pegged Peanut as a shit-eater the minute he stumbled through the front gate. His soft hands gave him away.

But when the inmates found out that Peanut's offence was not political, but was attempted murder, they backed off a little. The question of whom Peanut had attempted to murder, and why, preoccupied them. Over time it became known that Peanut's offence had been committed on the hot night of 3 June 1989, as gunfire rang through Beijing and the foundations of China's state shook. Peanut had, it was learned, in a moment of terror and fury, brought a lump of paving slab down upon the face of a little soldier who lay screaming at his feet. The little soldier had blinked and convulsed, and Peanut had seen the blood spatter on the asphalt. The inmates puzzled over this. How could a shit-eater, a professor, do such a thing?

So Peanut had lived the life of a hybrid: part criminal of unfathomable violence, part shit-eater. He had employed his bulk and his vengeful temperament to his advantage in dealing with the other inmates. And once he had carved out a tolerable space in the camp hierarchy, he turned his attention, over the years, to shoring up the identity bequeathed him by his parents and his classmates: one who created with the mind, who exercised an acute moral understanding of justice and power, an intellectual of China. He was, he told himself, much more than inmate; he was the wronged, exiled thinker of legend, a modern Qu Yuan, a dealer in truth reviled by the state, and never mind the paving slab.

He craned his neck and saw the gleaming water of the gravel pit.

Early on in his sentence he had decided that to preserve his sense of himself as intellectual/shit-eater, measures were required. A book. A prison memoir! Something desperate and devastating, to be smuggled out of the camp, published abroad, circulated illicitly at home. Something with a fancy, despairing title. *Superfluous Words from the Desert Chamber*, perhaps.

Over years, on thin, grainy, squared paper of the sort children use to practise their characters, Peanut observed and recorded. Every name, every routine; every load of wilting cabbage dumped on the loading dock, every ton of coal from the withered little mine; every rotation of young thunders, bumping in by truck, the grey dust in their hair; every square metre of dry grey desert picked clear of rock; every stint in the *xiaohao*, the punishment cell; every facet of this desiccated hive deep in the Qinghai desert, Peanut tallied it and noted it down. He did this in the latrine, late at night, and built an extended, minutely detailed narrative of incarceration in modern China that would, he was certain, shock the world's conscience and cement his place in history. He kept the pages in his bedroll, until the thunders found them.

The prison commandant was flummoxed, flimsy papers in his hands, some strewn across the floor of the barracks. Prisoner 5995, real name Li Huasheng, known as Peanut, stood, a thunder on each arm, his head forced downward, calculating.

'Prisoner 5995,' said the commandant. 'You do realise these are state secrets?'

Prisoner 5995, known as Peanut, stared at the floor, hard. The commandant handed the pages to a cadaverous deputy and licked his lips. He walked absently over to the prisoner and, one finger under the chin, forced Peanut's head up.

'Why are you gathering state secrets?'

Peanut said nothing.

'Are you spying on us?'

Peanut felt the world rock, kept his footing, just.

'Are you a spy?'

Well, strictly speaking, Commandant, the answer to that is complicated.

'I didn't understand these were state secrets, Commandant.' The words were thick in his dry mouth. 'I will confess all my mistakes.'

So he did.

First to a spiky little Labour Reform Bureau 'investigator', who made notes. They sat in an echoing concrete 'investigation' room next to the camp office. Peanut talked, searched for an angle, talked more. And when he stopped talking, a bored, overweight thunder standing behind him jammed an electric baton to his neck and sparked him up.

Then a drive to the main prison complex, forty miles shackled in a van with no windows. Peanut vomited on his trousers.

Followed by a surprise visit to his old friend, the *xiaohao* punishment cell. This one was nothing more than an iron cage on the floor in an empty brick barracks with broken windows. The cage was not quite tall enough to sit up in. He marvelled at his response, just as in the weeks after his arrest: a faint gratitude that they were, at least, leaving him alone for a few days. The thirst was very bad.

More confession, this time in a smart conference room with blond wood fittings and a window that looked out on parched poplars.

'I like to make lists, keep diaries, write. Sir.' He noticed a camera mounted on the wall, a bead of red light.

'Why would you keep lists?' This from a senior uniform, barking, the anger contrived.

Build walls, and hold them as long as you can. That was what they'd once told him. Did it apply now, here?

'It is just a way of keeping busy. Sir. Just lists, writing, observing. I confess my mistakes.'

'You were gathering state secrets.'

He stayed silent.

'If you confess you can expect leniency. If you do not confess your punishment will be severe.'

Words for the generations of China. Words for my father. Words for me.

'Yes. I confess my mistakes and my crimes,' he repeated.

A nod from the uniform, and Peanut was taken back to the *xiaohao*, where a plate of vegetable soup, still warm, awaited him.

The final act had come a week later. He was led, shackled, across a courtyard. A leathery old woman in a blue tunic splashed water on the concrete to keep the dust down. It was morning, late in the summer. In the air, behind the heat, a whisper of cold to come.

A jaundiced, balding judge asked cursory questions into a microphone, which stood on a table covered with green baize. A prosecutor mumbled.

He stood in the dock. To his left was a woman he had not seen before, with grey hair in a bun, who looked at her notes and said nothing. His defence lawyer, he realised. He leaned over and tried to speak to her. She pursed her lips and shook her head, a tight, definitive movement. *Stay away from me.* There was business about Article 32 of the State Secrets Law, and Article 111 of the Criminal Law, and they added five years to his sentence.

Back in the barracks, they'd showed him something approaching sympathy. 7775 had taken him out for a cigarette and laid a hand on his shoulder. Peanut had to stop himself laughing.

And then he'd walked off by himself, by the wall, as the dark came down. No shadowy celebrity for him, then. He watched a bat dip and flicker against the sky.

So fuck it. Once a spy, always a spy.

Day two, and panic. He had awoken at dawn, parched, to the sound of engines grinding up the track towards the gravel pit. He lay on his stomach, inched forward and peered from the mouth of the tunnel. Two jeeps, six thunders getting out of them, AKs slung. They spread out. One walked to the water's edge and kneeled, peering at the ground and looking across the water. Another walked down to join him and seemed to be asking what he was thinking because the first thunder gestured across the water and pointed at the ground. Peanut flattened himself against the rocky tunnel floor. The second thunder appeared to be considering, then walked back towards the jeep and waved the others into the vehicles. The jeeps started up, ground into gear, and turned back down the track. The manner of their departure suggested they were not finished here.

And later in the day they were back, with a dog that bounded from the back of the jeep, a big black and brown thing with pointed ears. Its handler was in military uniform, which Peanut construed as bad news, because military uniforms suggested competence. The handler ran with the dog along the edge of the water as if in play, the dog jumping and pawing at him. And then the handler got the dog's nose to the ground, and it began to scent. It moved this way and that, excited, turning, and whining, and looking back to its handler. Peanut slowly pushed backwards in the dark, as far as he could go. He heard the whining of the dog, some faint shouts – orders? – then nothing for a while. And then engines, moving off down the track.

The light was weakening at the mouth of the tunnel. He shifted from ham to ham on the damp floor. He was very hungry. Half of his water was gone, but the gravel pit was infested with liver fluke and undrinkable. He sat up and leaned forward, tried to touch his toes. In a little while, he would allow himself a bar of the awful chocolate. There had been no activity around the pit for six hours.

He had started, gingerly, to think about reaching the railway. In another twenty-four hours he would be getting weak, so it would have to be tonight. Twelve miles over hard ground, and no guarantees, just the freight cars lumbering down from Tibet on their way to Xining.

Who would he be, if he made it to the city, and on?

Over the years China's bureaucratic minds had imposed many identities upon Peanut. To each a name: student, class traitor, intellectual, dissenter, criminal, prisoner. To each a season, by turns exhilarating and terrifying.

But another identity lived in him, planted and nurtured by a different bureaucracy. Its season was brief and silent and long past. Its name he had never uttered out loud, even in the darkest hours of the *xiaohao* or under the electric baton. Yet the name remained, preserved, he knew, in a file, in a country he'd never seen.

Night heron.

He stripped awkwardly in the confined space, bundled his clothes, reached for the little paper bag and the water bottles, and shuffled up the tunnel towards the night. The water beckoned.

Move.

2

Beijing

The morning had begun – crisp, tinged with the acrid smell of Beijing's cold days – with a frenzy of phone calls to London and, for Mangan, a testing of the correspondent's powers of persuasion.

Mangan had been in the 'bureau', termed more accurately the front room of his Jianguomenwai flat, since six a.m. The bureau featured two chipped and musty desks, exposed phone wires that protruded from holes in the whitewashed walls, and a stained blue sofa. The tiled floor made the room clatter and echo.

When the London duty editor said she was not following the Jiangxi situation, Mangan expressed mild surprise, careful not to let the telephone amplify it into stark disbelief. She'd said wryly, educate me, Philip.

Well, they're cultists, he explained, and they've occupied a town. Thousands of them, apparently. They call themselves Followers. They believe their incantations lend them cosmic awareness and that their master will return and start a new dynasty. The police are blockading them and will soon move in and kick the crap out of them. It's a great story. We should go.

'Won't they try to stop you?' the duty editor asked, yawning. Well, yes, but we should go anyway.

Harvey was listening, shaking his head, fiddling with lenses.

Mangan and the duty editor haggled over cost. There were admonitions, and promises, and a dash to the airport. Now Mangan and Harvey sat in the back of a maroon taxi, four hours out of Nanchang in China's damp south, speeding east down route G316.

Mangan watched the towns slip by, brick factories, white-washed concrete blocks with orange tiled roofs, a market glossy with rain where a woman in blue sold ducks and young toughs leaned on their bicycles. On the walls the political slogan of the moment: *Wending yadao yiqie*. Stability overrides everything. After the towns, low, rippled green mountains swathed in cloud.

Dusk, and they stopped to eat noodles, steaming and peppery, from a stall by the side of the road. Mangan ate standing, the bowl in one hand, listening to the crickets in the wet air. They forged on, into the night, promising the mystified driver more money if he would keep going.

Mangan tried to remain inconspicuous, but he was six feet, red-haired, green-eyed. They'd picked the taxi for its darkened windows, but if Public Security stopped them, then, well, the usual.

Mangan's phone rang. The guide was waiting. They've set up roadblocks two miles out of town, the guide warned. Before you hit them, look for a torch at a turnoff. Mangan wondered how they would know they were going to hit the roadblocks before they hit them. They drove on in the dark.

Suddenly there it was, the torch, jiggling up and down at every passing car. Harvey spotted it. He pushed his sunglasses up on to his head and reached for the camera bag.

They pulled over, the driver complaining. *Here?*

The guide was a stooped, toothless old man in a black

waterproof and rubber boots. Harvey grinned and Mangan did the talking, struggling to understand the old man's sibilant southern speech. He took out the agreed-upon cash, but the man waved it away. Afterwards.

'Through the fields.' The man gestured. 'We'll skirt the roadblocks, but it'll be wet.'

The three of them set off in the darkness. Across the fields Mangan saw the flickering lights of police vehicles blocking the road. Their guide moved quickly through the high grass. Mangan stumbled, his trousers soaked and clinging, mud weighing on his shoes.

'Is he one of them?' Harvey's Australian stage whisper, famously audible from half a mile.

'No. He lives on the edge of the town.'

'How did you find him?'

Mangan had spent hours calling at random, attaching five digits to the area code and hoping. Most of his respondents were indignant. Those people! they'd complained. Sitting in the streets, chanting! Disrupting traffic! But this old man had been intrigued more than angry. They seem harmless enough, he'd said. Mangan asked if he would guide them into the town. Discreetly. For a sum.

The town was called Jinyi. Golden Rill. Mangan had looked at a satellite image. Flat grey sprawl around a cement works, a river. The guide took them to the river's bank, a path lined by dimly lit brick shanties. A dog barked. The river smelled of garbage and shit.

They went under a bridge and up stone steps into the street, Harvey first. Mangan saw him smoothly pulling off the backpack and reaching in for the little camera. He liked watching Harvey start to work, the sudden tension in him when the image presented itself.

And what an image. Under the light from the streetlamps the

Followers were sitting in rows, hundreds of them, cross-legged, their hands describing graceful arcs in front of them. A cassette player sat on an upturned crate, playing a rhythmic, undulating, repetitive chant punctuated with bells, turned up so loud it was distorting. They mouthed along to it, their eyes closed.

The guide tapped Mangan on the arm, then gestured, his eyes blank.

'That's her, the organiser. I'll go now.' He took the cash and disappeared into the dark.

Mangan saw her coming towards him, waving. She was forty years old perhaps, wearing a black jacket with a high collar, jeans and knee-length black boots. She was no more than five feet tall. From behind a fringe, she had a look that contrived at innocence, childishness.

'You must be Mr Mangan. I didn't think you would make it in. You must be very good at, well, evading.'

She was speaking English. Her accent was South China, clipped, heavily layered with America, trying for playfulness amid the tension. Mangan shook a minute, limp hand. She introduced herself as Shannon.

'I don't think we have very long,' he said.

'Well, whoever, you can talk to them. Get your pictures. This is important for us. The police will come in the morning, we think.' They stood outside a shuttered bakery.

'You're not from here,' Mangan said.

'Originally, yes, but Long Island now. I came back because the movement needs people who can speak for it, help organise.' She gestured to the seated, chanting rows.

Harvey was on one knee, the camera balanced on his thigh, working up a sequence of an elderly woman with a face like parchment, her bird-like hands fluttering and circling. She wore a purple rain jacket and mouthed silently.

'What are they chanting?' Mangan said.

'The Three Principles. Humanity, understanding, rebirth. You could call it a mantra. The Master tells us that to perfect ourselves and enlighten ourselves we must meditate on the Principles.'

'Is the Master coming here?'

'Well, that is why we're here. He was born here.'

And, Mangan knew, now lived in Scottsdale, Arizona, in a gated community.

'What are you hoping to achieve?'

She looked at him and folded her arms. The chanting had stopped, and now just the occasional chime came from the cassette player. The Followers sat silent and motionless under the streetlights.

'Do not speak to us as if we were some hopeless cause, Mr Mangan. We are changing China. We are not political, but we are part of an awakening that will see China return to her core beliefs, transmuted for a new era.'

Mangan knew it word for word. He had heard it from them in grimy backrooms in Beijing, on Tiananmen Square as they were dragged away by the buzzcut plainclothes men, in cold villages up north, the condensation running down the windows as whole families sat on the *kang* studying the Master's texts.

'But you understand why the Party sees you as a political threat, surely?'

'No. We are peaceful. We are not against the Communist Party. Do you know how many of us they have locked up now? Do you?' She looked at him, working up her righteous fury. 'Three million of us, at least.'

Mangan doubted the number was anything like that big, but kept silent. There had been, he knew, thousands of them in re-education camps. He'd seen some on a ghoulish press tour outside Shanghai. He remembered the reek of disinfectant as the camp staff waved them through, saying, you see? It's all quite humane. They'd entered a dining hall with a concrete floor where a hundred Followers sat on plastic chairs and stared fixedly at a television playing cartoons. When the press corps, cameras, microphones, white people in rustling, garish gear, shuffled in, their eyes didn't leave the screen. Mangan had been shocked and repulsed.

Harvey looked over his shoulder and winked. Mangan made his way over and Harvey handed him a microphone. The old woman in the purple jacket seemed to be looking past him. Mangan leaned towards her and went into Chinese.

'Can you tell me why you are here?'

'We have come to do the Master's bidding.' Her hands trembled, Mangan saw.

'And what is that?'

'We must meditate on the Three Principles and resist oppression. My husband was taken away, so I have come here with the others.'

'Is your husband a Follower of the Master?'

'Yes. They took him away. I can't see him.' Her words began to speed up, her voice turning shrill. 'They sent me a letter. He said he renounced his beliefs and that he thanked the state for freeing him. But they tortured him to say that.' Now tears spilled down her cheeks.

Mangan had seen it often, the blankness turning to uncontrolled emotion in seconds. Shannon raised her eyebrows. You see?

The chanting had started up again.

Harvey looked about, exhaled. 'I've got enough of that. What else?'

They filmed more interviews. Shannon hovered, then brought tea from a red thermos. Harvey paused and sipped from a steaming cup, and, for safety, took the memory card from the camera and backed up all the pictures on a slender laptop.

*

At three in the morning the first siren sounded, a whoop from a police car starting from the darkness and moving at speed down the main street towards them. Olive-green trucks, five or six of them, lumbered behind. Some of the Followers began to stand up, walking quickly away, ducking down alleyways. Shannon was on her mobile phone. The trucks came to a halt with a compressed air hiss. Green uniforms in riot helmets, with batons, jumped from the tailgates.

Harvey and Mangan ran for a nearby doorway and crouched in shadow. Harvey filmed. The uniforms – they were *wujing*, paramilitary police – jogged down the street and into the crowd in columns. They were, to start with, methodical. A sergeant yelled for everyone to stay where they were, and then walked over to the cassette player, which was still playing the weird, distorted chimes. He looked down at it for a minute, then dealt it an almighty kick, sending it bouncing across the street, broken plastic skittering off it.

Most of the Followers seemed to understand it was all over, and stood sullenly. The *wujing* pinned their arms and walked them to the trucks. They dragged those who refused to walk. Mangan watched them drag the old woman in the purple waterproof. One of her shoes had come off. She was still mouthing her chants. Mangan thought she was crying.

Harvey lowered the camera, shuffled backward into the shadow, and looked about him.

'I think we need to move,' he said.

Mangan gingerly stuck his head out into the street, searching for a way out. Nothing, just uniforms, blinding headlights. He ducked back into the doorway. Harvey ejected a second memory card from the camera, handed it to Mangan.

'That's the good stuff, so stick it where they won't find it,' he said.

Mangan worked quickly, tearing off a strip of gaffer tape with his teeth, reaching into his trousers and strapping the memory card to his thigh. He turned to the door behind them. It was wooden; the entrance to an apartment block? He rattled it. It was loose, but on a spring latch. Harvey reached into his pack, pulled out the stiff plastic card he used to white-balance the camera, and jammed it into the crack between door and jamb, jiggling it in and out, looking for the latch. Mangan watched. Implacable, confident Harvey. Then a *snick* and the door swung open. Harvey opened his mouth wide in a clown grin.

'Sometimes you amaze me,' said Mangan.

'I amaze myself.'

Six flights of concrete stairs brought them to a fire door and the roof. They stayed low, crawled to the edge and looked down on the street.

The scene was chaotic. *Wujing* ran at random down the street, grabbing Followers by their clothes and hair. Some worked with their batons, not hard, but not gently either. Mangan saw a young man with a ponytail, kneeling, his forehead split open, wiping blood from his eyes. Mangan tapped Harvey on the shoulder and pointed. Harvey framed and focused just as a *wujing* put his boot in the young man's back and he went down. Harvey lingered, let it play out. The boy tried to stand, hands raised in submission, but the *wujing* kept on putting him down, then changed his mind, grabbed the boy by his collar and forced him towards the trucks.

Harvey licked his lips, took a breath. 'That's strong.'

Then he stopped, looking over Mangan's shoulder, and winced. Mangan turned. The door on to the roof had opened and a tall man in a light-grey suit and open-necked shirt was coming through it, with two *wujing* behind him.

'Stop, please.' In English.

Mangan's stomach turned over.

'You stay, please.'

He was young, with neat parted hair. No buzzcut, this one. Very un-thuggish. Lean, athletic, but slender hands.

'Who are you, please?' The tone not impolite.

Mangan stayed in English. 'We are from Beijing.'

The man actually smiled. 'I see, from Beijing. And why are you here, please?'

Mangan said, 'We are journalists.' A little too fast.

'Journalists!' As if all were clear, *silly me.* 'So you must come with us, please.'

Mangan shook his head. 'No, we mustn't. We are entitled to report, to report freely in China.'

The man nodded. 'I'm very sorry.'

'Can I see your identification?' Mangan went into Chinese.

'No. Sorry. I am from the State Security Bureau. Please come with us.' Another smile and a shrug.

State Security? Mangan looked at Harvey, who raised his eyebrows.

'Are you detaining us?' said Mangan. *Juliu*, meaning: are you prepared to make this official?

'I hope we won't need to do that, but you will come with us now. Please.'

Mangan, for his own self-respect, held on a bit longer.

'We do not have to come with you.'

'It will get more complicated.' The man's gaze was quite level, and he had his hands in his pockets now. The two *wujing* – both big ones, Mangan noticed – shifted behind him.

Harvey got up and picked up his pack, signalling: let's get it over with.

Mangan stood too, relieved Harvey had made the move and not him. Grey Suit cocked his head to one side and gestured to the stairwell. They went back down into the street and to a black car.

The driver was the same species, different genus. Wiry, dark, a moustache, leather jacket. Still, bloodshot eyes. He smiled as he opened the rear door. They got in, holding their packs. The car smelled of cigarette smoke. Mangan tried the window but it wouldn't open. The driver started the engine, then paused and turned around to look straight at them. Here we all are, then, his look said. Grey Suit touched him on the arm and gestured. The driver faced the front and pulled away.

They sat alone on plastic chairs in the *Anquanju*, the local State Security bureau, a whitewashed office with barred windows, for twenty minutes before anyone spoke to them. Mangan looked for cameras but couldn't see any. He took the SIM cards out of their mobile phones. Harvey had a pocketknife. Mangan laid the cards on the table and sliced them up, crumbled the plastic and scattered it on the floor. He went through his notebook, tearing out the relevant pages – phone numbers, names – and solemnly put them in his mouth, chewing until the paper was mush. He stuck some more gaffer around the card strapped to his thigh. Harvey smirked and they waited. The sun was coming up.

When the door opened it was Grey Suit. With him was the taxi driver who had driven them to Jinyi, terrified. Grey Suit held the door open, gestured towards Harvey and Mangan, then looked quizzically at the driver. *Them?* The driver nodded.

Mangan stood up.

'He had nothing to do with it. He doesn't know us.'

Grey Suit looked amused and made a calming gesture with his palms. 'I know.'

'Then bloody well let him go.'

Grey Suit raised his eyebrows, then turned and closed the door. A few minutes later he was back, with a uniform, and a large green file.

'Please give me your mobile phones for a moment.' They handed over the phones.

Grey Suit slipped the backs off to find the SIM cards gone. A wry look and a shake of the head. He handed the phones to the uniform, who left the room.

For a while it was just ID, addresses and contact details. But then came a search through the bags. Grey Suit took the camera.

'I'll need all the footage, I'm afraid.'

Harvey gestured. 'Still in the camera.'

'Show me, please.' Harvey turned the machine on and rewound. The digital flicker showed the ponytailed boy with blood in his eyes, then the interviews and the rows of chanting Followers in the shadows.

'Is everything you filmed here?'

Harvey nodded.

'Please give me the memory card.'

'You have no right to confiscate our footage,' said Mangan.

Grey Suit sighed and ran his hands through his neatly parted hair.

'Please,' he said. 'I would rather you hand it to me than you force me to take it.'

Harvey sighed and ejected the memory card and handed it to him. Grey Suit regarded him, pursed his lips and nodded. Then, from the green file, he drew out two sheets of paper, on each a few typed sentences. He pushed them across the table towards Mangan.

'You'll have to sign these.'

Mangan squinted at the characters. It was the usual, a confession of sorts, and a get out of jail card: I, Philip Mangan, freelance journalist, holder of an accreditation from a reputable but crumbling British newspaper, indentured to a small television news agency, was in Jinyi illegally, filmed illegally, interviewed illegally and in general consorted with people who were entirely illegal. He translated the gist for Harvey. Grey Suit waited, arms folded. They signed. The forms went back into the green folder.

Business done, Grey Suit wanted to talk.

'What do you think of these people?' He appeared interested, his Mandarin deliberately slow and clear, little trace of Jiangxi in it. 'You've got some experience with them, I think.'

Mangan didn't know what to say. 'It's important to report what they do.'

'Yes, yes. But, we call them a cult. *Xiejiao*. An evil cult. Are we right, do you think?' Grey Suit appeared capable of earnestness.

'I don't understand why you – you the Communist Party, I mean – see them as a threat,' said Mangan. 'They seem naive, childish.' He could feel Harvey's eyes on him.

'Naive. I must say I hadn't thought of them like that.' Grey Suit paused. 'I'm sure you've read some Chinese history.'

'Yes, some.'

'We've seen these movements before, yes? They get danger-ous. Demagogues spouting religion. Peasants who think they're divine, hurling themselves on bayonets. Villages burning.'

Mangan shrugged.

'Those old ladies in the street tonight? I don't see that, I don't see some fiery rebellion. This isn't the nineteenth century.'

Grey Suit looked at him, weighing what he was saying. Then he reached out as if to shake hands, but stopped midway, and in a strange, operatic gesture, quavered his hand from side to side.

'I think, Mr Mangan, that we don't know who they are. I think we don't know.'

Harvey dozed for a while, leaning on the table, arms crossed. Mangan stared out of the window through the bars on to a con-crete parking lot. The green *wujing* trucks from the previous night stood in lines. A dark, wiry kid hosed them down, spray dripping from the canvas, the drab olive metal suddenly gleaming.

And then, in the breezy morning light, Mangan watched uni-forms walk a group of Followers – fifteen of them, perhaps –

across the concrete. They were cuffed, had their faces down and shuffled. No laces? They were all young men. The uniforms walked them to a truck. A sergeant dropped the tailgate. Two uniforms hoisted each Follower up on to the bed of the truck, which revved its engine, sending a black billow across the lot, pulled out, and was gone.

The wind had picked up and, in the silence, Mangan watched cloud shadow stipple the mountains.

'You can go,' said Grey Suit.

They caught an afternoon flight from Nanchang. Approaching Beijing, Mangan was tight and silent. Harvey drank Five Star beer. Beneath them the north China plain darkened from grey to purple. Beijing glistened in the early night as the aircraft banked and the engines hissed.

They were at Mangan's flat by ten to look at the pictures. They crashed through the front door, scattering equipment bags, to find Ting, wide-eyed and phone in hand, scolding. Mangan was brought round, her concern breaking his mood and calming him.

'I've been on the phone *all evening*,' she said. 'Where have you *been*?'

Mangan gestured to himself, as if he were making an entrance in fine attire.

'Here we are,' he said.

'She missed us,' said Harvey.

'She did,' said Mangan.

Ting waved her willowy, bare arms.

'I almost called London.'

She was done up for Beijing society: a slender dress in charcoal-grey silk, very short; Tibetan jewellery in exquisite dull silver. Her skin was Manchurian pale, the colour of ivory. She sat down hard, gave an exaggerated sigh and ran her hands through short spiky hair.

'Why didn't you call? I missed a gallery opening.'

'State Security ate my mobile,' said Harvey.

She put a hand to her mouth.

'Oh, no.'

Mangan smiled.

'We're okay. Really. It was okay.'

'And . . . we got the pictures,' said Harvey.

Mangan dropped his trousers and began picking away at the gaffer on his thigh, wincing theatrically, and they all laughed.

Mangan poured glasses of vodka, and Ting turned off the lights and the three of them sat on the shabby sofa and watched it all played back on Mangan's flatscreen television. The pictures were strong. They had the old woman in the purple rain jacket, with her quavering voice and weird stare. They had the chilling *wujing* images taken from the street, before they made their way to the roof. Harvey had silhouetted the *wujing* against the lights of the trucks, so they became anonymous, threatening shadows. And the arrests were very clear – the old woman dragged down the street, her feet juddering across the wet black asphalt. Mangan could feel the structure of the piece forming. It would tell well in straight chronology. This, then *this*.

But they had nothing from the roof. The worst of the violence – the ponytailed boy bleeding into the gutter – was all on the card confiscated by Grey Suit. The intensity, Mangan realised, built and came to not much. It would be a story without an end, he knew, a compromise.

He was bleeding. From where, though?

Peanut kneeled on the clinker, swaying. It was evening, he thought.

He wiped a hand across his mouth and the back of it came away smeared with blood. Was he bleeding from the nose? It seemed so. He was, he supposed, close to unconsciousness. A train passed a few feet from him, but the roar of the diesel, the *clack* of the wheels, seemed far away.

He began to crawl.

Far to his left, he could make out engine yards and beyond them the station. The darkening sky had to it the pale orange wash, not of sunset, but of a city's lights.

He had damaged himself when he jumped from the freight car, but he couldn't understand how. He crawled further away from the tracks, towards a low brick building with broken windows, weeds growing at the base of its walls. He was very cold and his tongue was thick in his mouth. For twenty-four hours, clinging to the coupling, he had eaten and drunk nothing. The wind chill had left him stunned.

He reached the brick building and slumped against the wall, from which, he now saw, a faucet protruded. He hauled himself to it and turned the tap. The faucet hissed and shook, and belched an intermittent spray of cold water. Peanut cupped his hands and drank, retched, drank more, and sluiced his face clean of blood.

His head began to clear. He flexed his limbs, rubbed his hands. Then, tentatively, he stood. He looked to the skyline, saw illuminated towers rising in the dark, flickering and silver. He'd never seen the like.

Xining. The city.

He looked up the tracks towards the station and saw flashlights, their beams dancing on the steel rails. He turned, felt in his pocket for the plastic bag cinched at the top with an elastic band, and found it between his fingers. Then he ran.

In an alley off the freight yards he stood and watched from the shadows. A girl sat in a doorway beneath a green neon light. She wore tight pink jeans. A man stood over her, murmuring to her with an expectant look. Or a greedy look, Peanut thought, as if he were contemplating some rich food. The man carried beneath his arm a small black bag with a loop for the wrist. The bag suggested its owner to be a man of business, a man of accoutrements. Peanut had seen such bags carried by visiting officials in the prison and had fixed upon them as the likely location of valuable items.

The man looked extremely valuable. He wore a blue jacket of a soft, slithery material, a striped shirt and cream slacks, and shoes that to Peanut's eye had the shine of polished wood. The man was balding and bulky and leaning over the girl, and she nodded and picked up a handbag that lay at her feet.

What did the valuable man think he was doing here at night in an alley off the freight yards, talking to girls in doorways?

Peanut stepped from the shadows and walked towards them. The man looked up and frowned. Seeing Peanut, in filthy green trousers, stained tracksuit top, he backed away a little. The girl sat very still and watched Peanut.

'What?' said the man.

Peanut held his hands open and moved closer to them.

'I just need a little help,' said Peanut.

'Piss off,' said the man. He sounded uncertain. Peanut made a regretful face. He stepped quickly to the man's left side in a feint. The man lashed out ineffectually with both arms. Peanut stepped in close and gripped his jaw and rammed his head against the wall. The man emitted a squeal. Peanut hit him hard on the chin and his knees gave way and down he went. The girl sat staring fixedly ahead, her hands splayed against the wall, as if steadying herself. Peanut said nothing, just leaned down and placed two fingers in a pinch on her throat. Her skin was very soft. He looked at her and raised his eyebrows in a questioning expression. She gave a tight shake of her head. He let go his grip, bent to pick up the black bag and walked shakily down the alley.

Xining bus station at night had the air of a transit camp, Peanut thought. Muslim families, the women in lace headscarves, sat on the floor amid orange peel and peanut shells cradling rose-cheeked children. Their men clutched mobile phones. Soldiers lounged and smoked. The tannoy clattered around the walls as the buses disappeared into the taut, dry night.

The toilets reeked of chemical perfume and urine. The floor was slippery with spit. Peanut squatted in a toilet stall, shivering, massaging the knuckles of his right hand. He was savagely hungry. Before him, the man's black bag.

Peanut unzipped the bag. He was dimly aware of the clatter of the paper towel dispenser, running water, a man hacking and spitting. He pulled the bag open carefully. As he did so, it emitted a sharp electronic whine. He flinched. The bag fell on to the slimy floor. The whine resolved into the marching favourite, 'Dang Bing De Ren', 'Those Who Join The Army'. The valuable man's mobile phone was ringing. Heart thumping, Peanut took it from the bag. The phone hummed and vibrated between his fingers and blinked blue. On a screen a single character flashed on and off. *Jia*. Home. Peanut stared at the device. He'd never held one before. *So now we'll turn it off. But how? Does one push a button?* Baffled, he stood up and dropped the phone into the squat toilet's dark aperture. The noise continued. Peanut flushed, and it stopped.

So, the contents of the bag. Cigarettes. A smart lighter. A diary – business meetings, something to do with property, phone numbers. And a black wallet. Within its folds five hundred and thirty-two yuan in a variety of notes, and the *shenfenzheng*, the laminated identity card. Its photograph showed the man aged about ten years younger, with a face less lined and less ample than the one that had crumpled before Peanut's fist. There was a likeness, perhaps, if you screwed up your eyes and hoped. Song Ping was the name, from Lanzhou.

So that's who he'd be. For now.

Peanut stood, opened the stall door and walked to the sinks.

He washed his hands with soap, scrubbing with his nails at the engine oil and blood. When he looked into the mirror, he wondered at what he saw. The skin was dark from the sun of the high desert, the hair short and bristled. In the eyes, something flickering between desperation and intention. He rolled his big shoulders, breathed.

The money and the identity card were in his pocket. He buried the clutch bag in a bin, walked out of the toilet, keeping to the wall, and pushed into the line for the long-distance ticket booth.

Where, to his horror, a policeman was checking documents. And another was standing back, just watching. Peanut looked down, patted his pockets, as if he had forgotten something, then stepped out of the line and walked quickly towards a fruit stall. He purchased a bag of oranges and without looking back walked out of the terminal to a stand of local buses. He chose one at random, boarded and paid full fare. He took a seat and looked back at the terminal. Four, no, five police cars had drawn up, and officers were moving through the long-distance terminal, trawling the crowd. For him? He sank low in the seat. The bus, half-empty, pulled out.

The bus was slow and anonymous. It took him south-east from Xining, meandering through grimy, dead towns.

Stillness is the enemy.

He savoured a dawn meal – dumplings of pork gristle and coriander, sluiced in black vinegar! – at a truck stop under a canvas tarpaulin in the rain. He took another bus, and then another, heading east. He spent a night in a scabrous hostel, one storey of crumbling concrete so filthy that, for an instant, he longed for the cleanliness of the prison. He spoke to no one, and moved, slowly, in the direction of Beijing.

3

Beijing

Harvey and Mangan cut the story the next morning. Beijing was grey with cold autumn rain. Harvey sat at the laptop, stringing together sequences. Ting, in a pink waterproof, brought coffee. She peered at the screen, at the *wujing* leaping from trucks.

'Bastards,' she said.

Harvey looked up.

'Temper,' he said.

She waved a hand. 'Really. They're thugs. We don't deserve them.'

Mangan, still in pyjamas, fought bravely with the script. London wanted the piece in at under three minutes, today. The state news agency, Xinhua, had run a terse five-line account of the mass arrests at Jinyi and the international wires were sniffing at it, so Mangan had to move fast. Harvey logged the pictures and built more sequences. Ting worked through the interviews, looking for the right grab, giving them options. But how to convey a sense of who the Followers *were*? A cult? A religion? Or vulnerable people so disoriented by life in modern

China that a levitating folk healer in Arizona looked like a hopeful prospect?

By mid-morning he was still struggling.

'They claim to be the denizens of a new order,' he told the microphone. 'An order based on ancient Chinese myth, remade in a bid to change China.' This over a mysterious, beautiful shot of the Followers' hands weaving in the air. A pause.

'But the Communist Party sees only the threat of rebellion.'

Harvey said, 'What is a denizen, for Pete's sake?'

'Look it up,' said Mangan.

'Shall we tell the viewers to do the same? And you said *in a bid*.'

Ting had the bureau dictionary. 'A denizen is an … inhabitant,' she said brightly.

Harvey folded his arms, downing tools. 'It's crap, Philip. It's clinical and full of cliché.' He swept his arm towards the screen. 'Just look at the pictures. Tell the story.'

Mangan sighed and deleted. Harvey was a ruthless picture editor – a side of him that Mangan at once valued and loathed.

Ting stood behind Mangan and gave his wide bony shoulders a mock massage.

'Come on, Philip. *Jia you*. Did you know the Master believes homosexuals are made of antimatter? Really, it's on his website.'

The streets from Liuliqiao long-distance bus station lead east towards the sacred centre of Beijing. On these streets it is common to see migrants from north-west China who have just alighted from their buses – here a Muslim man in a white skull-cap and a stringy beard, there a young woman in a headscarf from the tiny villages of yellow dust on the Loess Plateau. They stand in the middle of the pavement, looking up at the silvered sky-scrapers for the first time. They often look ill at ease, their poorly fitting clothes in brown and blue, their calloused hands, their dark skin. The pale *Beijing ren* sweep by the migrants on the street.

On this particular autumn morning, just after dawn, the casual observer might have noticed just such a migrant, a large man, with an ample midriff, make his way at moderate pace away from the bus station. He wore a blue tracksuit top and stained green trousers and a pair of newly purchased running shoes. A plastic carrier bag dangled at his side. He, too, seemed surprised by the power and scale of Beijing's new prosperity. He stopped and leaned back, admiring the sunrise reflected in the shimmering frontage of a bank. He looked this way and that, turning to appreciate some new perspective, some striking confluence of light and architecture. Now and again he stopped, turned about, sat for a moment.

Once, a security guard in a white belt strode out from behind hissing smoked glass doors and ordered him away. The rotund man bent at the waist, looked submissive, raised a hand.

'Sorry, Officer, at once, Officer,' he said, and continued on his way. At one point he ducked into a coffee shop only to emerge immediately. The casual observer might have seen a confused middle-aged migrant, his passage ponderous, a naif come to the brave new capital of China.

But a trained observer might have seen something different, a measure of watchfulness and purpose beneath the ponderousness. The trained observer might conclude that this bristle-haired fleshy character, in his stopping and starting and turning about and his smiling, quick-eyed appreciation of his new surroundings, was, in fact, conducting counter-surveillance. Rudimentary and unpractised, for sure, but counter-surveillance nonetheless. The tradecraft of those who live parallel, hidden lives. And such an observer might further conclude that this man was living such a life. Or perhaps practising to do so, or reminding himself how.

By early afternoon Mangan had coaxed a script into being, Harvey had laid the closing pictures, and they'd sent it. It was strong, but Mangan was not satisfied, picking over it in his mind.

The duty editor in London had sent back a *Thanks. Good work.* Which meant nothing.

The piece would run in an hour or two, perhaps even attract some attention. The agency supplied networks in odd places – South Africa, Lithuania. Often, carefully constructed stories were never heard of again. This time, though, the pictures were exclusive. Reuters had a story on the wire. *Baton-wielding paramilitary police detained hundreds of protesters in south China Wednesday, as a nationwide crackdown on religious sects continued.* The European and American networks would want to pick up the story. They'd pay the agency for Harvey's pictures, fillet them and revoice them using their own correspondent, who had neither been there to witness the brutality, nor spent the night in a State Security lockup, Mangan reflected. He sat at his desk, tried to turn his mind to a piece for the paper.

Ting was in the kitchen, spooning rice soup into a bowl, sprinkling it with spring onions. Mangan could see her silhouette against the window, watched her. She turned, holding the bowl gingerly, then caught his eye and gave him a questioning look.

'Anything I can do?'

'Write two thousand words for me,' he said.

'*Zuo meng, ni.*' You're dreaming.

'Where's Harv?'

'He said his work here was done and he was taking a long lunch.'

'I think I might join him.'

She placed the spoon carefully in the bowl and pointed sternly at his laptop.

'Write! Soon you won't be able to afford me.'

'Oh, no. What will you do?'

'Find a richer, less feckless western journalist and entrap him in marriage. Maybe a diplomat.'

He smiled. Ting's allegiances, he knew, were complex,

stretched between her wealthy, storied Party family, numerous suitors, and this dingy excuse for a bureau, with its pathetic salary and Mangan's quixotic journalism. Why did she stay? She looked at him.

'Tell me if you need anything. More quotes, anything,' she said.

'Oh, I will.'

He dropped his eyes to the blinking cursor. Exclusive from our China Correspondent. Should he write up his own arrest? The paper loved all that. *A tense night in the cells! Deep in the belly of China's security state!* Well, no. It would just bring more grief from the authorities. He rested his elbows on the desk. It was Ting's turn to watch him now, as she sat on the sofa, cross-legged, lithe, managing to eat hungrily but delicately at the same time. It was quiet but for the chink of spoon against bowl.

Mangan wrote, and by early evening the thing was done. A workable piece and not much more, but done. Ting was in the bathroom with unguents and lipstick. Harvey had reappeared in a rather sharp black suit, with a bottle of wine. Mangan wore a jacket in green tweed once raucous, now faded. He stood, rum-pled, holding out a glass in a spidery hand. Harvey regarded him with mock distaste, and poured. They eyed each other and drank fast. Harvey walked over and tapped on the bathroom door.

'Come on, empress. It's the embassy. Mustn't be late.'

The door opened and she did a fake sashay out. Crimson silk tonight. Very short, again. Harvey handed her a glass and they all drank. Mangan pointed to the door. Forward! And, tipsy, they ran across the clattering landing to the lift.

It was the ambassador's residence, a mansion on Guanghua Lu reeking of austere colonial purpose. From the windows, pools of golden light spilled into the smoky autumn evening.

At the wrought iron gates the three of them presented invitations through the bars to a smiling retainer, an elderly Chinese man in a bow tie. A British heavy in a blazer gave them the once-over, and they were buzzed in. Ting, excited, was up the steps to the front door, where more retainers fussed. Harvey took her arm, and she looked over her shoulder for Mangan and then the two of them glided into the reception, Mangan shambling in their wake.

The room glittered. Conversation clattered off walls hung with yellow silk and lustred oil paintings. A table of deep, glowing walnut bore silver chafing dishes. Here, a group of parliamentarians in from London, suited and bellowing. There, military attachés in tan serge, medal ribbons and braid. The Chinese guests – Party and National People's Congress, Mangan guessed – stood stolidly polite, as the diplomats worked them. Ting was deep in conversation with the press attaché, a freckled Welshman named Partridge who gazed at her. Harvey had found some Australians. A waiter in a white coat passed carrying a tray of drinks, and Mangan lunged for a gin and tonic, which, he found, was sparkling water. In his ear a sardonic voice.

'Don't look so mournful, Philip. It's only us.' Mangan turned to find Charteris, the political officer, his best – only – embassy contact.

'I thought this might be gin.' Mangan stared into his glass. 'What's this all in aid of, anyway?'

'Fifteen Labour and six Tories. All talking to each other in the corner. We get all these Party dignitaries to come to our reception and so far only the Honourable Member for Whitstable has had the manners to go and say hello.'

Charteris wore a navy blue suit and a signet ring. 'Saw your Jinyi piece,' he said.

Mangan looked up.

'Jiangxi provincial government is furious,' Charteris said.

'They've complained to *us*. The nerve. We pretended not to know you.'

'They've complained already?'

'Letter faxed to the press section.' Charteris sipped champagne, holding his glass by the stem, languid. He regarded Mangan. 'They're jolly angry. What did you do?'

'Got busted. Didn't give them the footage.'

Charteris smiled. 'You're more resourceful than you look, Philip Mangan. You deceive us all.'

Mangan shifted under the younger man's gaze. 'God almighty, that was quick. The complaint, I mean,' he said. 'Should I do anything?'

'Wait and see if they raise it with the Foreign Ministry, but I wouldn't worry. Don't go back to Jiangxi, perhaps.' Charteris watched the French ambassador and his retinue sidle up to an iron-faced member of the Central Committee. He turned back to Mangan.

'Any idea how many were arrested?'

Mangan thought. 'A hundred. More.' He thought of the young men, cuffed, in the parking lot. 'And they seemed to be separating out the boys, afterwards, taking them off in trucks.'

Charteris looked at him. Then paused, as if calculating whether he should say what he was going to say. 'Not from me, okay?'

'Of course.'

Charteris leaned in. 'You see, that's very interesting. Because we heard they were planning some sort of new programme aimed at the men. It's supposed to disrupt the leadership of the movement. Most of the Followers are still going into *laojiao*.' Re-education, the big detention camps for a year or two, no trial required. 'But we heard last month they were starting to corral the men and send them away somewhere. We're not quite sure what it's all about. But it's different.'

Mangan raised his eyebrows. 'You heard where?'

'That I cannot share. But you might try some of the families, no?'

Charteris downed the rest of his champagne. He has perennially golden skin, Mangan thought. He belongs on a yacht.

And now he was readying to move. 'Better go. The Central Committee seems plagued by frogs.' He turned away and then hesitated. 'Philip, it was a very good story. I'm glad someone's paying attention.' And with a mock-stern glance, Charteris eased away into the crowd.

Mangan knew the compliment for what it was – the polished work of a diplomat. But he enjoyed it, anyway.

4

Beijing

Peanut walked. He tried to stay with a crowd. He found the noise extraordinary. No shop was without an electronic wailing and tinkling, or the beat of music so loud he felt it in his stomach. The traffic roared, and every other pedestrian squealed into a mobile phone.

Twenty years of silence, of wind on the desert, now this.

He tried to watch his back, weaving an irregular course, retracing his steps.

He walked east, past the shining department stores whose messages and purposes, expressed in screeching primary colours, on flickering screens, he could not fathom. On one street, a parade of girls, dozens of them, thin as saplings in identical tight scarlet dresses, handed out leaflets. He reached for one, just to touch the glossy paper, but the girl ignored him so thoroughly it was as if she didn't even see him. Peanut found this both salutary and reassuring. Peanut did not wish to be seen.

Mid-morning found him on a detour. He crossed up into Beihai Park and walked by the lake. A weak autumn sun had broken through. On the lake, a lone pedal boat paddled by a woman in yellow and a child. He stopped, examined the contents of his carrier bag. Valuable man's funds were dwindling, only one hundred and fifteen yuan left. He extracted a crumpled note and purchased an ice cream and sat on a stone bench, before suddenly rising and moving off quickly as if the staying still had become too much to bear.

He sensed Tiananmen Square before he saw it. The noise diminished. The architecture reverted to state brutalism, looming over the vermilion walls of the Forbidden City. He took an underpass amid schoolchildren who chattered like starlings in a hissy southern dialect, and climbed the steps that would bring him out on the square.

As he emerged into the sunlight two men in polo shirts, static, attentive, looked straight at him. His stomach lurched. The children streamed past. Turn around? One of the two saw him hesitate, and gestured idly, a flip of the hand. Here, now.

Reflexively, Peanut turned to his cringe. The slight stoop, the falling shoulders, the bowed head, hands crossed in front of the body.

One of the two looked him up and down.

'*Lai zher ganma?*' What are you doing here?

'Just walking, Officer, some exercise.'

'What's in the bag?'

Peanut said nothing and opened the carrier bag. An apple, some underpants, some money. A newspaper clipping, wrapped in plastic. Polo Shirt peered in.

'No posters, no banners?'

Peanut affected shock. No, Officer. Absolutely not.

Polo Shirt heard the Beijing accent, but saw the hard hands, the banknotes. Something not right. Valuable man's identity card would not last a second here. Break his train of thought, now.

'And, Officer, if I may ask, what time would the flag-raising be tomorrow?'

Polo Shirt said nothing, just gave him a hard look.

'Only I have to bring my grandson, who's in from Harbin. And I'm not sure what time we should get here. For the flag-raising. Can you help me?'

Polo Shirt jerked his head towards the square. *Zou.* Go.

Peanut hurried away, his mouth dry, lost himself in the crowd.

On the square, families posed for snapshots with Chairman Mao's portrait behind them. So. The Great Helmsman's still here, he thought. A boy flew a kite. Peanut looked up, searching the sky for its flutter, but his gaze settled, in shock, on a lamppost, from which protruded a camera. No, multiple cameras. On every lamppost. Dear God. Dozens of them.

He looked down, tried to keep his pace slow, his body relaxed. He headed for the opposite corner of the square, to where another underpass would take him back on to Chang'an Avenue. You stupid, bitching idiot, he thought.

At the steps more polo shirts. But he was leaving the square now, and they paid him no attention. He clattered through the dark tunnel, back up on to the pavement, moved quickly away. Still, on each and every lamppost, cameras.

He took the first street that ran north off Chang'an, moving into the crowd. He was, he saw now, horribly conspicuous. The people on the pavement wore suits, sunglasses, fashionable shoes. They wore black. They were slim and smart. Peanut, the hulking, sweating migrant, needed to be among other sweating migrants as quickly as possible. He was shaken, badly. Move.

He turned east, and noticed, spray-painted on the wall of a shoe shop, a piece of graffiti, the stencilled face of a woman wearing a pair of absurd, protuberant goggles. Beneath her a single English word in capitals: THREATEN. The woman's delicate features were disfigured by the goggles. Peanut frowned at the image and walked on.

He was in back streets now, grey *hutongs*, which was comforting. The smell of coal smoke and frying allowed something of his past self to resurface. He stopped for a cigarette outside an old, familiar temple, Zhi Hua Si, the Temple of Wisdom Attained.

A little further on, he found what he had been searching for: the tall, beige, apartment blocks of the Jianguomenwai Foreign Diplomatic Compound. Near the Friendship Store. Where the foreign news agencies are. Or were.

He skirted the perimeter wall and noted the positions of the *wujing* guards on the gates. The blocks were, weirdly, just as he remembered. And they seemed still to house foreigners. He saw them coming and going as he wandered slowly past the north gate, a group of women in headscarves, a young man, a European perhaps, speaking into a mobile phone. He didn't linger.

Dusk fell as he walked along Guanghua Lu, past the foreign embassies. He slowed for a moment outside a mansion, from whose windows spilled golden light. A line of black limousines waited outside. He looked at the flag that hung limp in the autumn evening. Then he quickened his pace and was gone.

As darkness came he moved ever further east. The great buildings with their glistening frontages fell slowly away and the surroundings became meaner. Thunderous convoys of trucks were heading into the city, migrant workers in the back of them, sat atop piping and sand and breeze block. The building sites would churn all night. He walked past bleak auto repair shops and restaurants serving noodles in chipped bowls and glasses of the clear, blazing sorghum spirit, its odour fishy and sour. At a stall lit by a single bulb he bought *baozi* wrapped in paper, the pork mince leaking through the bread.

That first night he spent in a doorway, his hand on a piece of metal pipe he'd lifted from the side of the road. The cave, the desert shale and the freight car all seemed distant, half-imagined. He was, he realised, exhausted by feeling, by the working of memory.

He woke at dawn and stood in the half-light, calculating. He cut south down a filthy alleyway, its walls spray-painted with dozens of mobile phone numbers and tattered advertisements for venereal disease clinics.

The alley brought him out on to a narrow, shadowy thoroughfare, cluttered with shopfronts. A small state grain depot abutted a shoe repair shop, and a peeling café, the Elegant Blue Mountain Food Hall. Outside the Blue Mountain, the antithesis of elegance, was a chef in apron and white cap pulled low over the brow. The man's face was a cascade of loose flesh, lit by blue flame from a roaring gas stove before him. The chef gingerly dropped dough sticks into crackling oil, his jowls wobbling with concentration. After a moment he'd fish them out and add them to a glistening pile. A kettle steamed. Peanut walked over.

'I'll take three dough sticks. And some tea.'

The chef turned a pair of moist eyes on him.

'Good morning to you, too.'

Peanut stared at him. 'Sorry. Good morning. Now three of your dough sticks and some tea.' He reached into the carrier bag.

But the chef was looking straight at him. 'On the way to work, are we?'

'What's it to you?' said Peanut.

A sigh. 'Whatever happened to manners?' said the chef.

'They don't have those where I'm from,' said Peanut.

'Oh, yes? Where are you from, then?'

'Not your business.'

'You sound like you're from right here, in Beijing.'

Peanut looked at him again.

'Want sugar?' said the chef, unperturbed.

Peanut nodded. The chef dusted the dough sticks with powdered sugar, and then looked Peanut up and down.

'You can sit on the steps if you like.'

Peanut took the dough sticks and a scalding glass of tea and sat on the tiled steps in front of the Blue Mountain, and ate, the grease running down his chin. Then a slow, luscious cigarette, as the light came and the street began to stir. Chef was doing brisk business now, passing out the little bags of dough sticks, cups of *doujiang*, the sweet soy milk, and tea. A little boy handed over a few tiny coins for half a cup of *doujiang*. There was banter with a vigorous, permed matron. Peanut watched the chef. There was a living there, a life, on a little street somewhere.

But not yet.

'Ask you something,' said Peanut.

'Ask away,' said the chef.

'The migrants, where do they all live?'

The chef turned from the stove, eyebrows raised.

'Big hostels, fifteen to a room, if they can afford it. Others have built shanties further out to the east. But those places are rough, I warn you. Wretched people.'

He spat, and then grinned.

'But good for business,' he said.

Peanut probed.

'This your business, is it?'

'This place.' He gestured with his chin towards the Blue Mountain. 'And that one.'

Across the street stood the Blue Diamond Beauty Salon, its windows adorned with faded posters of lissom, pale girls. As if on cue, a steel shutter rattled and ran up, and out of the Blue Diamond stepped a girl teetering in red heels and tight black jeans. She held a mop and a bucket. Her hair was wet and hung long down her back. She set the bucket down and with tiny mincing steps began to work the mop ineffectually across the salon's tiled frontage.

Peanut stood up.

'I'll do that, if you like.'

Chef turned.

'I'll do your mopping if you let me use a bathroom for ten minutes,' said Peanut.

Chef considered. The girl looked at Peanut, expectantly, let the mop drop to her side. She was seventeen or so, toothy and wan. Even at this time of the morning she wore some sort of shimmering scarlet lipstick. Peanut attempted a jovial smile.

'Ten minutes, then, in the bathroom. And all the steps,' said Chef.

Peanut moved to walk across the street, but Chef placed a greasy hand on his arm. 'And no touching. You touch, you pay.'

Peanut waited a beat.

'Couldn't afford it,' he said.

So he mopped, reflecting that it was the first labour he had performed in two decades that would be rewarded in some way that he valued. A transaction. He worked for an hour. The steps gleamed. Peanut washed down the walls. He asked for some vinegar and newspaper, which Chef, bemused, gave him, and he began working the grime off the windows. From inside, the girls regarded him with puzzlement. The Blue Diamond, while not entirely losing its sordid air, regained the look, from the outside at least, of a hygienic establishment. Chef was amused.

'You may use the bathroom now,' he said.

The girl in the red heels took him inside. The trappings of a beauty salon were present: sinks, hairdryers, scissors. But the girl led him through a beaded curtain and down a dark corridor that smelled of disinfectant. On one side, doors with small glass panels through which Peanut could see beds and embroidered sheets.

'What's your name?'

She turned. 'Beautiful Peony.'

'For heaven's sake. What's your real name?'

She blinked. 'There's the bathroom.' And tottered away, her tiny frame silhouetted in the gloom.

Peanut locked the door and stripped and eased his bulk into a pink shower stall. The shower gave little more than a cool trickle, but he was content standing there. The water, grey with the dust of Qinghai and the filth from the train, seeped down the drain. He scrubbed out his underpants and shirt in the sink. He pulled a plastic razor from the carrier bag and began to work the grainy tablet of soap into a lather on his chin, then stopped.

From the salon, raised voices.

He turned off the tap and listened.

A scream?

Peanut pulled on his damp underpants and his running shoes, retrieved an item from the carrier bag, and made his way back down the corridor, stopping just before the beaded curtain.

Chef appeared to be having his hair washed. He was sat in a reclining hairdresser's chair, leaning back over a sink. But at his throat, well, that was a meat cleaver. Someone was screaming. The hand holding the meat cleaver belonged to a short, thickset kid. He wore a baseball cap with some sort of red design on it and a black leather jacket. He was looking towards another man, this one in a parka and sunglasses, a little older, wavy hair, tall, wiry. Peanut watched and listened.

'You're overdue.' It was Sunglasses talking. '*Shoubuliao.*' We can't have that.

Beautiful Peony was in a corner bent almost double with fright, clutching at another girl whose hair was dyed orange and who was crying. A woman, middle-aged, barrel-shaped – Chef's wife? The madam? – was trying to remonstrate with the two men. Let him go. We can pay.

The two men looked hard and quick, but young. Peanut hummed a little to himself. My good fortune today, he thought. He took a breath. And pushed through the beaded curtain.

After the reception at the residence they had gone out for a raucous dinner. Yunnanese food, complex mushroom dishes and a rice wine served in bamboo beakers that did early, serious damage. Harvey had found a lean Australian tennis coach from one of the big hotels and the two were drunk and bawdy. Milam from the *Los Angeles Times* was there, and the Reuters reporter, Mackenzie, the two of them rapturously attendant upon Ting, who sat sparkling-eyed between them. Mangan caught her eye, and she allowed her face to light up in a comical aren't-I-lucky expression, just for him. A dreamy French intern from one of the agencies dragged up a chair next to Mangan and sought advice about her career, which he failed to give. When they all pushed on to some new bar, Mangan slipped away and walked home alone to Jianguomenwai.

It was four in the morning when he was woken, irritated, by a soft, insistent pinging from his computer. He sat on the edge of his bed, chilled. The *ping* again, crisp and synthetic in the silence. He walked into the front room. The message icon was blinking.

TREEFROG: Dood!!!!!!!!
TREEFROG: You there bro
TREEFROG: WAKE UP BRO
TREEFROG: WAKE UP MANGMAN TALK TO DA FROG

Mangan rubbed his eyes and sat down. The kid was at a college somewhere on America's east coast. Was it a he? It sounded like a he.

Mangan had been introduced to Treefrog by a human rights activist. Treefrog, apparently, was a hacker of some repute. He had made it his personal business to map China in cyberspace. With a juvenile glee and, as far as Mangan could tell, a vicious precision, Treefrog felt out the digital borders of the Chinese state, and then penetrated them. For the hell of it, he said. For the LOLZ. But beneath the excruciating online patois, Mangan sensed seriousness. Treefrog had charted China's online attacks on the Followers for months. Denial of service attacks on Follower websites, poisoned emails, network incursions, Treefrog searched out their origins, published the addresses of the perpetrators, and maintained scrupulous records of what he had found. Mangan had quoted him in stories. *The notorious hacker, who is known in the cyber-underworld as Treefrog . . .*

ME: Here now.

TREEFROG: where you bin

ME: Asleep. It's 4am.

TREEFROG: THE FROG NEVER SLEEEPS. HIS ORANGE EYES SEE EEEEEVRYTHIGN

ME: Good for the frog. What do you want?

TREEFROG: Man you are AWWWWWWESOME. Your TV piece bro
Police pigs beatin on old follower dudes in that place
Sreious bro you nailed it

ME: Thanks.

TREEFROG: got sumpin for ya meet me at the place

Mangan clicked away to a secure chat room that Treefrog favoured and logged in.

TREEFROG: WO DERE. we got ourselves biiiiig ddos stinkin up
Followers main site last few hours so wot's new, know

wim sayin but there' other shit dalai lama offices got big
attack too. They network down, you should talk to em.

ME: Any sign who's doing the Dalai Lama attack?

TREEFROG: IP in west china, chengdu city. Guess on tech surv
units military but whoknows? Others too other places FROG
IS WORKIN THE ISSUE

ME: Good frog. tks

TREEFROG: nuttin of it dood. Also unclE sam is sniffin it out.

Mangan had been struck by Treefrog's awareness of the US government's cyber operations. He'd wondered if the hacker had some sort of link to the US security establishment.

ME: the feds? What are they chasing?

TREEFROG: stuff comin cross US servers that points to dalai
attack. Bots maybe. Counter intel busy busy Tell your US
doods to talk to em at DHS FBI. Could try corporate security
too see wat they knowin

ME: how do you know the feds are on it?

TREEFROG: froggy see froggy know

ME: OK OK. Let me know more, yes?

TREEFROG: you heard it from froggy

ME: I'll use your name.

TREEFROG: FROG OUT

The next morning he had woken late. Ting was already in the bureau, cross-legged on the couch with a pot of yoghurt, reading the *People's Daily*.

'Where did you go?' she said.

'Oh. You know.'

He turned on his computer. An email to the desk, first, on Treefrog's tip, then a call to the Dalai Lama's offices in India. But cyber-attacks, once a startling story, were becoming routine.

'The French one was cute,' said Ting.

'She was young. And earnest.'

She feigned reading the paper. 'Philip Mangan, you are the loneliest man alive.'

They all turned at once. An ample, middle-aged man, his face covered in soap, wearing only underpants and running shoes, was emerging slowly from behind a curtain of orange and blue beads. In his extended hand he proffered a wad of banknotes.

'You can take this.'

The man in sunglasses stared at him. Then looked back to the barrel-shaped woman.

'Who the fuck is he?'

The barrel-shaped woman opened her mouth and closed it again, and shook her head.

Peanut advanced tentatively towards Sunglasses.

'Go on, there's hundreds there. Take it.'

He inched forward. Chef, unmoving, the meat cleaver pressing on his throat, tried to watch what was happening from the corner of his eye.

Sunglasses reached out and snatched the wad.

On a small metal trolley to Peanut's right lay a hairdryer of the large, metal, professional kind. As Sunglasses looked down to inspect the notes, Peanut reached for the hairdryer. Sunglasses' head snapped up and he took half a step back. The kid with the meat cleaver shouted something incoherent. Peanut felt the weight of the hairdryer in his hand and in one flowing movement swept forward and brought it down on Sunglasses' temple. It was a glancing blow, but enough to stun. The sunglasses clattered to the floor and their owner grunted and raised both hands in front of his face. Peanut brought the hairdryer down again, deliberately catching the ends of the fingers, which brought a screech of pain. Then again, to the head, a swinging, arching blow just above the forehead that put the man on his knees. Two, three more, fast, this time around the face. The nose went with a sound like a ripe fruit shattering and the metallic surface of the hairdryer took on a bloody sheen. Peanut carried on working, breathing hard. The scalp had split and blood was pouring freely down the man's face. The meat cleaver kid was yelling about getting the others. Then he was gone, scampering out of the front of the salon.

Sunglasses was on the floor, still conscious, but barely. Blood was coming from his mouth. He held an arm half-raised.

Peanut stood up, nearly losing his footing on the bloody floor, grabbed a fistful of Sunglasses' hair and dragged him to the door and out on to the newly clean steps. Meat cleaver kid and two others were running up the street towards the Blue Diamond, but stopped when they saw Peanut holding their comrade, and then not holding him any more, so he fell limply down the steps and lay on the road.

Peanut faced them. 'Who's in charge?'

They pointed to Sunglasses, who lay unmoving.

'Tell him you don't touch this business any more. Others, do what you must, but not this one. Tell him, if he comes again I will break his back.'

They nodded dumbly. The meat cleaver kid tried to get Sunglasses to his feet. The man lolled and retched.

Peanut swept up broken glass and mopped up the blood. He had put on his stained green trousers, but was still shirtless. The inhabitants of the Blue Diamond sat and studied his smooth bulk. Eventually the barrel-shaped woman – they called her Dandan Mama – cleared her throat.

'I'm not sure if we should be grateful or fearful, frankly.'

Peanut leaned against the door jamb and lit a cigarette. Shaky again, but he didn't let them see it.

'How long had you been paying them off?'

'A couple of months.' She paused. 'Are we going to have to pay you off now?'

Peanut shook his head and exhaled. 'No payment. I could stay around if you want, though.'

Silence.

'Give me somewhere to sleep and I'll work for food and tips. Look after the place for a few weeks. Make sure they don't come back again.'

They emptied a storeroom at the back of the building and laid a mattress on the floor. Out of fear? Or am I useful? he wondered. He tipped the contents of the carrier bag into a small basket. Beautiful Peony brought him a flask of hot water, and a mug, and a packet of green tea.

'My name's Yin,' she said.

5

Beijing

So began his next incarnation, as assistant to the Blue Diamond Beauty Salon. In his mind it was cover and an operational base. He went into the street little, and spoke to no one beyond the salon and the restaurant.

The rhythm of his days took shape quickly. In the mornings he cleaned, and changed the stained sheets in the dim little back rooms. Dandan Mama found her sinks had a new shine and peeling paintwork had been smoothed and retouched.

He took to making the girls an early lunch, always the same, a big bowl of rice topped with vegetables in a spicy cumin broth, which they liked, and teased him about. So *exotic!* Where did you learn to cook with cumin? Where?

The afternoons were his own, before trade began picking up as the dark came down, and the migrant workers stumbled into the salon with beer and sorghum liquor on their breath. At night he sat on a stool next to the beaded curtain and smoked, and the girls felt safer, and the clients, their hands gritty from the building sites, were better behaved.

*

A week after his return to the capital Peanut took a bus that lumbered into the city. He got off at Jianguomenwai, close to the diplomatic compound, and waited near its north gate.

He struck up conversations with some of the women coming in and out, many of whom cooked and cleaned for diplomatic families. He was able, without too much trouble, to ascertain that the famous British newspaper retained its office, yes, in this very compound, indeed at the same address it always had. And for twenty yuan and some kind words, Peanut persuaded a simple-minded girl from Anhui, a nanny for a Pakistani diplomat's family, to describe the current occupant of the address. He was, she said, a tall red-headed Englishman, a journalist who was neighbour but one to the family for whom she worked, and who was polite to her, in good Mandarin, in the elevator. Peanut kept his expression level.

'Does he have a name?'

'Mang An. Something like that. I can never say their names.'

He called the old number, gave some rubbish about a delivery, Mr Mang An to sign. The nanny waited with him not far from the gate, just far enough that the *wujing* and the cameras would not notice. The street was flanked by a clothing warehouse, the pavement crowded with traders barking in Chinese and Russian. And after five or six minutes she pointed out the Englishman who walked out past the guard, in a tan raincoat, his breath just visible in the chill air, and stood and looked about him.

Peanut regarded the tall figure, its slight stoop, the hands dug deep in the pockets, the red hair so strong on the eye. A restlessness to him, an angularity to the shoulders and elbows that looked awkward and strong at once. He considered for a moment waiting, but the opportunity was before him.

Approaching the figure from the side, he started in his awful English.

'Mr Mang An. Journalist.'

The Englishman turned.

'Mr Mang An. You speak Chinese?'

The tall Englishman nodded.

Peanut stood back, hands down, palms out. The Englishman was looking at him with a questioning expression, not unfriendly, but with a level intelligence that Peanut could feel. Their strange, green eyes, he thought. He spoke in Mandarin.

'Mr Mang An. You represent the British newspaper?'

'Yes, I do.'

Peanut kept his expression neutral. 'I am an old friend of your newspaper.'

'Are you? We have not met, I think.'

'We have not met. But I will have information for you.'

'I see. Can you tell me what it is about?'

'Please tell your friends at the British Embassy.' He sensed the Englishman pull back.

'I do not work with the embassy.' A harder tone, but Peanut pushed on.

'This is very important, Mr Mang An, whether you work with them or not. Please tell them information is coming. And also, tell them one more thing.' And then in English, 'Tell them, the night heron is hunting.'

'I do not work with the embassy, and I do not want to hear any more of what you have to say. I am going to leave now.' The Englishman turned away.

Peanut called after him in English. 'The bird, Mr Mang An. The heron. Please tell them that.'

But the tall red-headed Englishman was striding quickly away, towards the gate.

Peanut watched him go, shivered, wondered what he had set in train.

6

Beijing

He woke long before dawn. The door to the storeroom was open, and there was Yin, silhouetted in the gloom. She shut the door and tiptoed across the concrete floor. She wore a long T-shirt, her legs bare. She bent and slipped under the quilt next to him on the threadbare little mattress. Peanut lay still, could feel her warmth. Soon her breathing was turning regular and shallow, sleep drawing her down. He nudged her.

'Will you do something for me?'

She smelled of some cream, something womanly.

'I've been doing it all night. Let me rest.'

'Not that.' He felt himself reddening, even in the darkness. 'Not *that*, you stupid girl.' He turned away from her, their backs touching now.

'What, then?'

'Take me shopping.'

They took a bus to a department store in Fangzhuang, Peanut clutching a week's tips and something extra from Dandan Mama.

Yin wore a black anorak with a fur hood. It was too big for her and she peered from its recesses, pale, but with a spark of pleasure that Peanut hadn't seen before. Blank little Yin, suddenly filled with purpose. He was watchful and ducked quickly into the store.

She steered him to the men's clothing and made him strip in a white changing stall. He wanted a blue jacket with gold buttons. Yin had to search to find one that coped with his girth. And a striped shirt and tan slacks. He settled on a pair of cheap shoes made of some indeterminate material, which shone the colour of chestnuts, and a plain black overcoat. He stood, labels dangling, under the neon, while Yin regarded him, hips cocked, arms folded.

'What's this for, anyway?'

For cover.

'I may have to meet someone and I want to look right,' said Peanut.

'Who may you have to meet?'

'Never mind.'

She smirked. 'But I do mind. When are you meeting her? Perhaps I'll follow you.'

Now he looked at her and spoke slowly. 'No. You won't.'

He tried hard, but the afternoon was broken after that. They rode the bus back to the Blue Diamond in silence.

That evening, as Yin and the other girls were getting down to work, he sat in the little storeroom under the dim light bulb, half an ear on the proceedings. He took from its plastic bag the faded, fragile newspaper clipping and looked intently at it for a long time.

A photograph in poor black and white print on yellowing paper.

A Party leader, wearing a suit with a scientist's white coat over the top. The leader is walking purposefully through what seems to be an aircraft hangar, his expression one of pride and resolution. Behind him a coterie of scientists, also in white coats, captured in mid-stride, keeping up, excited, gratified by this visit from the leadership. The caption: *Communist Party General Secretary and State President Jiang Zemin visits the Nanyuan Launch Vehicle Facility.* That's all. Among the scientists scurrying in the General Secretary's wake, one has his eyes down and carries a clipboard. Even through the smeary print, Peanut could make out the head of silver hair, long, touching the collar, and the fine bones in the face, a lean, sculpted look, ascetic if not for its handsomeness. The face of an intellectual whose great gifts are at the service of Party and Motherland. *Such important work!*

Peanut put the clipping back in its bag. He took out notepaper, and after some consideration wrote two letters. To whom it may concern. We were spies.

Mangan read the email from the agency. Meeting concurred, excellent work. Pix ran in major markets, strong network pickup. Well done and thanks to you and crew.

The paper was pleased, too, at Mangan's story. He'd thrashed the wire services. The piece ran high on the big news sites in Europe, the USA and Japan, but not in China. The Great Firewall blocked it.

Mangan looked out of the window, measuring the approval of his editors against his own sense of incompleteness. He could hear Ting as she wrestled with the story's fallout. She fielded a nasty call from the Jiangxi Provincial Foreign Affairs Bureau. And another one, more polite, but pointed, from the Foreign Ministry in Beijing, very close by, the purveyors of accreditation, all powerful.

'Would Mr Mangan come to discuss his recent trip to Jiangxi? There are some questions. When might be convenient?'

Nothing, mercifully, from State Security.

Ting did her best to calm the waters, and in good heart, but Mangan fretted. She was vulnerable. The more rules he and Harvey broke, the more vulnerable she became. They had talked about it, agreed that when the day came that she faced questioning because of his infractions, she'd play dumb as to Mangan's movements and contacts beyond the most inoffensive. Sometimes he kept things from her to protect her, and she pretended not to notice.

Two months earlier they'd had a horribly close call. Mangan had met a leathery old army colonel who had in his possession a copy of a very interesting letter. The letter, ten thousand characters in length, had circulated privately among Party stalwarts. It discussed, in florid terms, the challenges facing the Party: corruption, corruption and corruption in that order. A 'disease', it said, a 'betrayal'. The author of the letter was an octogenarian, well past his prime but still an inhabitant of the higher reaches of the political atmosphere. He bore a burnished, bloodied history that lent him authority. The letter was meant only for the Party's upper ranks, a warning, a plea, a final testament from a calloused old revolutionary. But word of its existence had leaked and the search for a copy became sport for the foreign correspondents.

Over lunch, the officer, fulminating at corrupt officialdom, the limousines, the perfumed whores, had agreed to give Mangan a copy. Mangan had returned to the bureau to find Ting, white-faced and tense, holding out a handwritten note. *The colonel called. There's a problem.*

The officer, it transpired, had faxed the thing. Only to find, forty minutes later, two representatives of State Security on his doorstep, asking: why, Colonel, are we faxing such material to foreigners? Why? The old man avoided arrest only by arguing that the letter itself had no secret designation, no *baomi*, no *juemi*. How was he to know? It had been a close-run thing. But then he'd called the bureau and insisted on telling Ting, over the bureau's utterly insecure phone, about the visit from State Security. Mangan had not written a story, instead burned the fax in the bathroom. Ting was frightened.

They really did listen. The fax really was unsafe. It really was.

And tonight, God, he'd almost forgotten, he was to meet Charteris. He left Ting in the bureau sorting through receipts and went from the compound in a dark, freezing drizzle. Jianwai Avenue was jammed, long lines of buses packed with office workers and shop girls, lumbering stop-start through the rain, the wet petroleum smell.

They met – it had become a reassuring habit – at Hot and Prickly, a small, clattering Sichuan place with plastic tablecloths and crackling red chillies strewn on the dishes. The legend in the window in red, haphazard English lettering read, 'Hot and Prickly Cuisine of West China', and the name had stuck.

Charteris was already there, still in his work suit, one arm draped across the back of the chair next to him, frowning at the menu.

'Tea-smoked duck, I think, Philip. And the *lazi ji ding.*' The diced chicken, in a sea of glistening chillies to shatter the sinuses. 'And the pea sprouts in garlic, yes?'

Mangan ordered cold mugs of beer, and they sat, quiet for a moment. The late autumn evening had people bustling into the restaurant blowing on their hands.

Charteris began.

'So, the Jiangxi trip a triumph?'

Mangan thought for a moment.

'On balance, yes. But we've used up some capital.'

'Ting okay? She's handling the flak, I assume.'

'She's handling it. I do worry.'

'You're right to. She's quite, exposed.'

'I know, I know. And she knows, too. But she sticks with it.'

70

'Why, do you think? Why does she stick with it?'

'Because she cares. Because she's too cautious to dissent openly, but she won't buy into the system. So working for me, well, she has distance, and perhaps it isn't entirely pointless. She feels she's finding things out and telling about them.'

Charteris paused, and the duck arrived. He stuffed a napkin in his collar to protect what looked to be a very good silk tie, and seemed suddenly Edwardian. Mangan smiled, and Charteris raised his eyebrows and clicked his chopsticks together. They ate, picking out the soft, pink flesh, the crispy, aromatic skin.

'I'm not trying to tell you how to run things, Philip, but they could use her to get at you.'

'That's true, but she can make her own decisions. Don't patronise her.'

'Patronise her? I think I'm in love with her.' Charteris put the back of his hand to his forehead, mock dramatic.

'You and the rest of expatriate Beijing,' Mangan said. They laughed, Mangan's laughter a touch forced, perhaps.

They talked about the fallout from the Jiangxi story and passed on political gossip, what to make of a recent Central Committee meeting, the new emphasis on stability in all the editorials. Occasionally Charteris asked something of Mangan, some detail, something he'd seen, and Mangan knew he was listening. And as they divided the bill Mangan dropped it in.

'Oh, and I think I've been dangled.'

Charteris, thumbing grimy yuan notes, looked up.

'Really? Very glamorous. How?'

'Yup. Grubby old man. Fat. No, big. Looked like a migrant, but sounded very Beijing. Just outside the compound. He said he was an old friend of the paper.'

And it was there, just for an instant, Mangan thought he saw something flicker through Charteris's eyes. Mangan pushed on.

'Said, in portentous fashion, that information was coming.'

Charteris was looking at the bill.

'Nothing I should worry about, right? Happens all the time.'

Charteris nodded. 'Yes. Yes, pretty common. If you're worried I can flag it in the embassy, with those who, um, *know*.'

'Who's doing it?'

'Well, not my trade. But probably MSS, State Security, just testing you. Wanting to see if you'll bite. Did he offer specific information? Documents or anything? Sometimes they do.'

'No, but he said one other thing, David. He talked about birds. Night herons. The night heron is hunting.'

Charteris smiled now, amused. 'My. Very mysterious. But don't forget, Philip, that chap at the *Los Angeles Times* had someone offering him bio-weapons secrets. So yours, I'm afraid, seems rather innocuous by comparison.'

Mangan, back in the cold apartment, left the lights off and stood by the window with a rare cigarette and a tumbler of vodka. He had a pair of binoculars, and sometimes scanned the windows of the Jianguomenwai apartments for activity in the dark. He did now. An Indian second secretary was being served dinner on a small metallic dish by his loving wife. The Colombian family opposite were hanging their washing to dry: trousers, a slip. Philip Mangan, observer of life from a distance, of small figures engaged in mundane tasks. He lay on the sofa, watched the orange light from Jianwai Avenue quiver on the ceiling. He called Milam of the *Los Angeles Times*.

'You didn't tell me you'd been dangled.'

'Dangled? Is that, like, a professional term?' Milam, the dark Californian, nonchalant, smart, on his mobile phone somewhere, the signal breaking into digital squelch; music, laughter in the background.

'What happened?' said Mangan.

'Actually, I'm not supposed to say.'

'What? You're a journalist. Of course you're supposed to bloody say.'

'Nope. The folks in Spook City told me.' Spook City. The brown windowless, concrete monstrosity on the old US Embassy grounds, widely assumed to be the home of the CIA, NSA, DIA and every other A. 'Say nothing, they said. So here I am, saying nothing.'

'But was it just once, or did it go on?'

'Few weeks. The guy kept turning up with all this secret shit.'

'And what did you tell him?'

'Fuck off, spook man.'

'Simple as that?'

'Sure.'

Charteris had waved Mangan off, hailed a taxi in the drizzle, then changed his mind. He crossed Jianwai Avenue and walked quickly north, back to the embassy. At the gate, a curt nod to the guard and he was buzzed through, leaving his mobile phone in the rack. Mid-evening, the building was silent now. An elevator, and at the end of the third-floor corridor, a heavy, silver steel door. A swipe and a punch code opened it with a click and a sigh.

Charteris entered the windowless space that was the exclusive domain of the Secret Intelligence Service.

The grey walls and blue carpet gave way to stranger features: a glass conference room slightly elevated from the floor with its own heavy door; computer screens that rested atop large metallic cases, a console of illuminated keys facing the user; telephones wired into the console; a server blinking in one corner, its hum against the deadening silence of the room; a row of black safes.

Charteris settled at a desk and turned on his screen.

The date. A reference number.

FM CX BEIJING

TO LONDON

TO TCI/29611

TO P/64815

FILE REF C/FE

FILE REF R/84459

FILE REF SB/38972

LEDGER UK S E C R E T

ROUTINE

/REPORT

1. BEI 2 met Philip MANGAN, UK journalist, Beijing-based. The meeting was pre-arranged and routine. MANGAN is well known to BEI 2, and, while freelance, holds a current accreditation and files regularly for a major London title and for a small television news agency.

2. MANGAN informed BEI 2 of what he suspected was an approach from BEI 72. MANGAN said he suspected he was being 'dangled'.

3. MANGAN described contact as middle-aged, male, heavily built, Beijing accent, but with the physical appearance of migrant, understood by BEI 2 to mean shabby, poorly dressed, down at heel. Contact approached MANGAN outside compound where MANGAN resides, gave no name, introduced himself as 'an old friend of the paper'. Contact told MANGAN 'information was coming'.

4. Contact used what appeared to be a recognition signal: 'THE NIGHT HERON IS HUNTING'.

5. Given the atypical nature of contact, the history of the title's Beijing bureau and its past affiliation with FU, BEI 2 recommends further action.

6. Grateful for traces on keywords: NIGHT, HERON/HERONS, HUNT/HUNTS/HUNTING.

/ENDS

Charteris saved the telegram and punched a series of keys on the console. Some red LEDs blinked on the server, and the telegram, encrypted, was gone.

The telegram arrived in London late afternoon ZULU, or UK time. Decrypted, it was directed to a section of the Secret Intelligence Service known as P/C, which stood for Production/China. In the P section the telegram was read by an Intelligence Officer, who sat straight-backed in a grey cubicle before two computer screens angled in such a way that the wandering gaze of a passing colleague might not see what was displayed upon them, and a computer tower that had been carefully modified to ensure no electromagnetic leakage.

Patterson marked the telegram for distribution and attention the following day. Then she read it again and sat back in her chair.

Curious, this one, she thought. Nothing here that fitted the protocols of any current or recent operation, or at least none she was aware of. And what's clever, sardonic Charteris doing tarting about with a journalist?

She stood and stretched to her full, considerable, height, flexed her shoulders.

Tomorrow. Tomorrow I'll do the traces.

She logged off, cleared her desk, slid her files into a black safe, and, to satisfy one of the Service's more absurd rules, double-checked that her worktop was clear of even a single scrap of paper.

She walked from the building into a cool, fine drizzle, a dull London twilight, quickly falling to darkness. She walked fast across Vauxhall Bridge, the rain beading on her wool coat, the river black beneath her.

The Tube was packed and leadenly slow and she stood the whole way, and changed carriages twice, just to make sure, as was her habit. She was alone.

At Archway, the little terraced house was silent, and she

climbed the stairs in darkness to her flat, let herself in. The place was cold. She turned the heating up and stood for a moment, looking from the kitchen window. London was spread out before her, bathing in its orange sodium glow. She dropped her bag, turned the light on, walked through to the bedroom. The flat was warming now, ticking and creaking. She stood in front of the mirror and took off her black business suit, the cropped jacket, the sensible trousers, and hung them up carefully. She pulled her halter top over her head, smoothed her hair, pulled it back off her forehead and crimped it tight into a bun, the way she'd worn it in the army, beneath her beret. In her underwear she surveyed herself, looked for failings, loss of muscle tone, slackening in those wide shoulders, creeping flab beneath the taut dark skin. Her army years had given her core and upper body a power that was hard to maintain now. The punishing pace of life as an Intelligence Officer of SIS did nothing to help, its unpredictability, its long hours in the glow of the screen, the jolts of stress from unexpected directions. She bent from the waist, tried to touch the palms of her hands to the floor, hung there exhaling, then dropped to front support position and attempted a few half-hearted press-ups. She had a sense of something leaking away from her, something to be gathered in, regained.

She showered and pulled on a blue towelling dressing gown, put a frozen quiche in the microwave, poured a glass of rioja to the brim. She ate standing in the kitchen, the fork rattling against the plastic tray. She reflected on her day. She had reviewed an approach by officers of Tokyo Station to a Chinese diplomat with a view to possible recruitment; she had distributed a brief report on the fate of a Chinese general found passing documents to Taiwanese intelligence: he was shot; and she had read the odd telegram from Beijing Station, which nagged at her.

7

Beijing

Peanut put on his jacket and shirt and slacks and shoes and over-coat and worried in front of the bathroom mirror. The clothes were new and synthetic against his weathered, fibrous skin. They looked unnatural. It was twenty-six days since he had emerged dripping from the gravel pit.

He proceeded down the corridor and through the beaded curtain that would, he knew, expose him to further examination. Sure enough, Dandan Mama and Chef were there, sat warming their hands around mugs of tea. It was a bright cold morning, the metallic surfaces of the salon gleamed in the sunlight and the steam rose from the mugs. Their eyes followed him through the salon as he headed for the door. Chef smirked, his rheumy eyes shining.

'Is it a wedding?'

Dandan Mama laughed. But he was through the front door and gone quickly. The street was uncomfortable and he kept his eyes down. Move.

A longish walk to a subway station, made longer by his cutting back on himself twice and stopping at a fast food joint, to see if anybody stopped with him. No one did, that he could tell. He moved with the morning crowd down the steps into the Metro station. At the kiosk he fumbled. Change? How much? Fare card? A few stares. A blowsy uniformed attendant with bright lipstick and tattooed eyebrows, frowning, jostled him to the turnstiles. Peanut sensed his own lack of congruence, the new clothes, the missing assurance, and knew others sensed it too.

He stepped on to the escalator, the slow, even descent, monitored, he now noticed, by a camera mounted on the ceiling, each and every face passing slowly through its field of vision. Look down? Too late.

Forty minutes on the subway. He changed carriages repeatedly.

At the Pingguoyuan terminus in the city's far west, he emerged into the cold, glistening morning, the Western Hills rising up in front of him. A rattletrap white minibus – FINE TOURISTIC AND BEAUTY TEMPLES stencilled in red on the door – for twelve yuan would drop him at the Jie Tai Temple, the driver beckoning from his window. But he took public bus 931, slower, less memorable.

By nine, he was climbing the stone steps into the temple complex. A weekday, and cold, so few visitors. Deep ochre pavilions amid gnarled trees, dank moss cascading down the walls, paths of flagstones sprouting weeds, but all in much better repair than he remembered. The last time he was here the temple was a curiosity, a place for picnics, a long bicycle ride from the university campus. He remembered *baozi* and warm beer from the bottle, the whirring cicadas of summer. Now, however, the temple seemed to be regaining its original purpose. He entered a dark pavilion. Inside, atop an altar, a golden Maitreya, pungent pink sticks of smouldering incense and some oranges. He stepped out into the courtyard. No one. Silence, wind in the trees.

On, to the north-west corner of the complex. Through a shadowed gateway, a glimpse of a huge marble altar. The Temple of the

Ordination Altar, he remembered, where monks of the Pure Land School had been ordained for centuries. And, good heavens, there was one now. Peanut caught a glimpse of an orange robe and a shaved head, half-running towards a shabby low brick structure by the temple wall, sandals flapping, clutching a styrofoam lunch box. He wondered at the return of monks, of belief.

He stood for a moment. In front of him was the rear gate. It led out into pine trees on the sloping rocky hillside. Peanut walked a way into the trees, and, not far from a soaring, ancient pine, sat down, lit a cigarette and waited.

He sat for an hour or so on the soft pine needles. Until, hurrying along the temple wall, just this side of furtive, came a man with a distinguished look, the billowing silver hair a little less fulsome now, perhaps, but still to the collar. Those finely drawn features, the delicate mouth, a mouth made for the expression of subtlety, for fine distinctions.

Perhaps twenty metres from Peanut, the man stopped and bent at the base of a pine. From his bag he removed a packet of incense sticks, some peaches, some packets of red spirit money and what appeared to be an entire roast duck. Peanut sat still and watched the man. Then, slowly, Peanut drew from his pocket the little plastic bag cinched at the top with a rubber band that he had carried all these years. He took out the yellowed newspaper clipping with its mottled, smeary image, as if to confirm what he already knew.

The man in the ancient photograph was now kneeling a short distance away from him, taking a lighter, igniting a fistful of incense sticks, planting them in the ground amid the pine needles. Beside the incense he placed the fruit, and next to the fruit, reverently, the duck. He clasped his hands before him and bowed three times. He mouthed something Peanut couldn't hear. He lit the spirit money, which burned and tumbled across the forest floor, the smoke acrid on the cold air. As the spirit money smouldered and died, the distinguished man sat back on his heels, a half-smile on his face. He looked reflective.

Now, thought Peanut. He stood.

'Wen Jinghan!' he called.

The distinguished man, startled, looked up, started to get to his feet. Peanut walked towards him, arms out in welcome, his best imitation of astonishment and gratification all over his face.

'Jinghan, you came.' Peanut kept moving forward. The distinguished man was looking hard at him, frowning, standing straight now, assertive.

'I'm sorry, who is it?'

'It's me. Li Huasheng.'

The distinguished man reeled, almost physically, but recovered fast.

'Huasheng! Good God. Is that you?'

'Yes! I knew I would find you here. Today.' Peanut grinned like a madman, gestured towards the incense, the duck.

'You remembered. My father.'

'Of course I remembered. I came here with you to scatter his ashes, didn't I? You said you'd always come. Every year. And here you are. I admire that, Jinghan, very much. You are truly a good son, a filial son.'

The silver-haired man was gathering himself, Peanut could see. They stood perhaps six feet apart, Peanut with his arms out, as if on the verge of attempting to embrace Professor Wen Jinghan, his old, treasured friend. Or perhaps to crush the life out of him. The distinguished man was tensed, ready to retreat fast.

'So you're ... *back*, Huasheng.'

'Yes, I am. Back.'

'Well. This is a surprise.' Peanut heard, behind the words, the rush of calculation. The distinguished man's eyes flickered up and down, took in the odd jacket, the cheap shoes. 'A wonderful surprise.'

'We've so much to talk about, Jinghan.' Peanut's face was a rictus, now.

Wen Jinghan looked levelly back at him, spoke quietly.

'It's so strange. I hadn't heard you'd . . . been released.'

'Well. That's quite a story.'

'Well, it must be. And one I want to hear.' Wen Jinghan nodded.

A pause. Peanut had harboured faint, ridiculous hopes that their long friendship might still have some life to it, but this was going nowhere. To hell with it.

'Well, do you know, it's probably a story I'm not going to tell you.' Peanut dropped his arms. And the smile. Wen Jinghan took a step back and slightly to the side.

'Listen carefully now, Jinghan. Because things are going to start moving fast. Are you still at the Launch Vehicle Academy?'

'I don't know what things you're talking about. And I suggest *you* listen carefully.'

Peanut spoke quietly. 'Answer the question.'

'Do you need help, Huasheng? I have resources. I can help you. But you will not threaten me.'

Peanut stepped forward and gripped the professor's arm. Hard. Wen Jinghan looked down, as if the power in Peanut's big hand made him fully cognizant of the differences that had grown between them.

Peanut spoke into his ear. 'Twenty years. In the desert. Twenty *years*. I never gave you up. I never gave anyone up. And yes, you will help me.'

Wen Jinghan licked his lips. 'This will not work.'

'Yes, it will. Because if it doesn't, I am telling them everything. Who we were. What we did.'

The other man summoned a contemptuous laugh, but in it Peanut heard weakening.

'They would shoot you as well as me, Huasheng.'

'But they won't find me.'

A pause. Peanut tightened his grip still further. Wen Jinghan was trying to maintain his balance, some semblance of control, but it was bleeding out of him.

'We are going back into business, Jinghan,' said Peanut.

The other man tried to wrench himself away, hissing now.

'Get away from me!'

Peanut held him easily and walked him to the temple wall, pushed him hard up against the faded vermilion, a thick forearm against his throat. Wen's eyes were blank, flecks of white spittle at the corners of his mouth. He'd stopped speaking. With his free hand, Peanut reached inside the overcoat.

'I have two letters here. One is to the head of the Launch Vehicle Academy. It says only that an employee was an agent for British Intelligence. No names. It'll take them a while. If I send it, you've got time to get out.'

Wen Jinghan mouthed something incomprehensible.

'The second one is addressed to the Ministry of State Security and it denounces you by name. If I send this one, you'll have no time.'

The professor sat on the pine needles. Wen Jinghan had shouted a little and then cried a little. He had implored, and babbled about his wife, his child. Which had led Peanut to a loss of temper, because, as he informed the professor, he had neither wife nor child, because he'd just spent two decades in a labour reform facility in the Qinghai desert, where marriage and joyful conjugal relations were not readily available. Peanut had relayed this forcefully and then delivered a thump to the distinguished solar plexus and an open-handed, but still formidable, blow to the side of the silvered head. The professor had writhed on the ground for a while and then sat up, his silver hair awry, laced with pine needles, the tears flowing, snot hanging in strings from the distinguished nose.

Peanut stood, hands on hips, over him.

'This will go very fast. In a week, maybe two or three, it'll be over. And you'll never see me again.'

Silence. Laboured professorial breathing.

'Now you'll return to your car. You came by car, yes?'

A pause and then a nod. And Peanut knew he had him. And the future unfolded in Peanut's mind.

'You'll go back to your car and you'll drive to the Launch Vehicle Academy, and you'll get something good – something good, as a proof – and you'll bring it to me tonight.'

The professor was looking down now and a strange mewling sound escaped him. Peanut knew to move on fast.

'What have you got in your office, Jinghan?'

The professor shook his head. 'It's all changed. It's all on computer now. Classified networks.'

'You will find something on paper. What do you have on paper?'

'I knew you'd be back. I always knew you'd be back.'

'What do you have on paper?'

The professor pawed the pine needles, picked up a handful and let them trickle through his fingers. Then sighed. 'Some reports. Two or three. But they're all individually numbered. I can't give them away. They'll know.'

'Go to your office. Take one of the reports. The best one. Bring it to me tonight. Seven o'clock. At the corner of Jianwai Avenue and Dongdaqiao. Just north, on the left side of the street, there's a big place with photocopiers. Bring it to me there. We'll copy it and then you'll take it back. It'll be out of your office for three hours.'

Wen Jinghan had closed his eyes and sat still.

'Are you back in contact with them?' he said.

'Yes,' Peanut lied. 'And one other thing. Money. Bring me whatever money you can. As much as you can. Now get up.'

*

They walked back down the hillside in silence, skirting the temple, Wen Jinghan leading. Peanut smoked a cigarette, and spat. At the edge of the car park Peanut took the professor's arm again. Wen Jinghan looked away, on the verge of tears.

'One more time. Seven o'clock, Jianwai Avenue and Dongdaqiao. I don't need a huge pile of documents, just a proof. Go straight to the academy. Do not talk to anyone. Get this done and things will go fast. A week or two and you're free and clear.'

The professor was unresponsive, looking into the middle distance.

'And remember those letters.'

The professor pulled away and walked across the car park, took his keys from his pocket, held them up. A whoop, and the lights flashed on a sleek blue Japanese sedan with darkened windows. Peanut stared, then jogged across the asphalt, catching the professor as he opened the car door.

'Is this really yours, Jinghan?'

Wen Jinghan forced a watery smile. 'Yes.'

Peanut breathed out, looked around, and, seeing no one else in the car park, dealt the professor another vicious slap to the side of the head. The professor groaned and staggered against the side of the car.

'Don't be late.'

The sedan pulled away. Peanut made a mental note of the licence plate. Then he walked to the bus stop, where he waited, disgusted, angry, ashamed and triumphant, for the number 931 bus.

Lunch with the Foreign Ministry, and a chewing-out, polite but loud and clear. Mangan and Harvey were summoned to an enormous circular table at the Golden Peak Seafood Village, on the twenty-second floor of a marbled block full of telecoms companies.

Silent girls glided across red carpet to bring them hot towels and Eight Treasure Tea. Across the table sat three suited minions and the Foreign Ministry's deputy spokeswoman, coiffed, who quietly cleared her throat.

'So. Mr Mangan. Mr Harvey.' Her English was excellent. 'We do appreciate your coming today. It's a pleasure to see you. And of course we follow your reporting very closely.'

'Thank you for inviting us, Madam Wang.' Harvey, massive in his suit, was trying to look ingratiating, which, thought Mangan, gave him the air of a scolded teenager.

'Now, let us be very frank with each other. We know you must report, and you are free to report in China. Of course.'

A pause and a knowing half-smile, as if to say, we all understand what that means, don't we? 'But other departments are sometimes rather quick to judge, let us say.'

Mangan couldn't resist. 'Which other departments would those be, Madam Wang?'

The half-smile again.

'Well, perhaps you encountered some of their representatives in, where was it now, yes, in Jinyi. Those departments.'

Mangan liked Deputy Spokeswoman Wang. He thought he sensed an ember of irony glowing somewhere in there, behind the façade. Now and then, speaking privately, she might actually tell you something, if you could break her code.

The silent girls brought bowls of fine, soft crab in a clear broth, shrimp sautéed in pepper and a flaking carp steamed in ginger and scallions. Madam Wang merely lifted her chopsticks and touched the food. Harvey loaded his bowl and ate voraciously.

'Those other departments, Mr Mangan, Mr Harvey, felt that your reporting of the authorities' efforts to safeguard good order at Jinyi was not entirely fair. And they felt that you were not . . . straightforward with them. And on the basis of that, they have suggested a review of your accreditations as Beijing-based foreign correspondents.'

Oh, shit, thought Mangan.

Harvey stopped chewing.

'But we in the Foreign Ministry have suggested that would not be appropriate. At this time,' said Madam Wang. See? We protect you, for now. Don't do it again.

After another half-hour of excruciating small talk Madam Wang and the minions took their leave. Mangan and Harvey stood, and thanked them gravely for the lunch. Mangan pledged full cooperation and begged the Foreign Ministry's continued understanding. The restaurant staff escorted Madam Wang's party out of the restaurant. Harvey turned to Mangan. They looked at each other for a beat and burst into laughter, and Harvey ordered beers.

8

Beijing

Stillness is the enemy. So Peanut walked.

The evening turned chill and clear. Sunset, coming early now, shards of purple cloud strewn to the west. Jianwai Avenue was fraught with traffic, long queues at the bus stops, *Beijing ren* all motion, heading home to the dim, overheated apartment, the mug of tea, the rice bowl, the pork sizzling in the wok.

Through Altar of the Sun Park, up to the Workers' Stadium, where the young boys were busy on skateboards, and with the twilight, south on Dongdaqiao. Peanut laced his movement with stops and sudden turns, crossed the road in heavy traffic, readied himself for a first pass of the photocopy shop.

And there was Wen Jinghan, standing outside the shop, waving at him limply. Dear God, he thought. He crossed the street in sudden, gathering darkness. The professor stood hunched and silhouetted against the harsh neon spilling from the shop window. He held a plastic carrier bag. Inside the shop, assistants in blue shirts and baseball caps worked copiers and faxes.

'You're early,' Peanut said.

'Huasheng, we have to talk.' His voice was weak, tentative.

'What did you bring?'

'Not here, for heaven's sake.' Whining.

'Give it to me, now.'

The professor didn't move.

'Now.'

Wen's hands, Peanut saw, were trembling. He handed over the carrier bag. Peanut took him by the arm and walked him into the copy shop. Then stopped, unsure.

The professor looked at him. 'You have to pay at the counter.'

'You pay. Hurry up.'

Wen Jinghan walked slowly to the counter and handed over yuan notes. The assistant gestured with her chin to a free copier. Peanut looked inside the carrier bag.

A document, thick, ringbound.

On the cover two characters in red, *juemi*, 'Top Secret', the highest level of classification. Then a number: 157.

Also, the title: *A Preliminary Report on Certain Questions Relating to Second Stage Failure in Launch Vehicle DF-41, with Implications for Scheduling in MIRV Experimental Launch Programme.*

And underneath: *Leading Small Group on Military Affairs.*

Peanut felt the dryness coming in his mouth. Dear fucking God.

'Copy it, Jinghan, now.'

'You will get us killed, like this.' His voice little more than a whisper. 'You know that, don't you?'

The professor looked close to collapse. Peanut had seen it before, in the prisons, the sudden shrinking of the spirit, in hours sometimes, utter defeat. Peanut shielded Wen as the professor took the document from the bag. The assistant was looking at them. Wen placed the document on the photocopier's glass. Closed the lid. Pushed the button.

Opened the lid. Turned a page. Closed the lid.

Pushed the button.

Peanut saw the copy of the cover page spill smoothly from the bowels of the copier, and reached for it quickly. Then the second page, a table of contents.

A third page. Closed the lid. Pushed the button.

'For God's sake. How many?'

The professor stopped and looked at him. 'Sixty.'

Peanut looked around, licked his lips. The counter assistant was busy with another customer.

'Well, hurry.'

For twelve agonising minutes the professor copied. Peanut put the sheets in the plastic bag. Then it was done.

Peanut propelled Wen out of the shop and they stood on the pavement, Wen still holding the report.

'How did you get it out?'

'Put it up my shirt.'

'Anyone see you?'

'Would I be here if they had?'

'You take it back tonight. Back to your safe, yes?'

'I can't do this, Huasheng.'

'You are doing it. Give me the number of your mobile phone.'

Wen Jinghan told him and Peanut wrote it on a scrap of paper.

'And the money.'

A wad of one-hundred-yuan notes. A thick wad, Peanut noted.

'Now listen carefully. We are offering a one-time transaction. One time only. What you've given me tonight is the proof. You are in this now, Jinghan, and there is no turning back, do you understand?'

Silence. Peanut wanted to hit him again. 'I'll call you with instructions. It will all be over soon and no one the wiser.'

Wen Jinghan shook his silvered head and looked away, to the muffled figures in the street, the lights of the traffic flaring in the Beijing night.

'It's never over,' he said.

PART TWO

The Op.

9

United Kingdom Secret Intelligence Service (SIS),
Vauxhall Cross, London

The view from the terrace was remarkable. One of the privileges, perhaps, of this work, this place, though God knew the privileges were few enough, once you discounted the sense of the special, the insiderness so cultivated by the Service. Leaning against the railing, she looked across the Thames, squinting against the river's late autumn glitter, the sky a condensate blue. She turned and went back inside.

She sat in her cubicle, her grey cell. The telegram lay on the desk in front of her. Phone calls to Hopko always merited a little consideration.

She reached for the phone, hesitated, then forced her hand to the receiver and dialled.

A soft burr.

'Hopko.'

'Val, it's Trish. Patterson.'

'Good morning, Trish Patterson.' The voice wry, non-committal.

'Well, yes. You'll have seen the telegram from Charteris. I've run the traces. And it's curious. I wonder if we should gather.'

'Well, Trish Patterson, gather we will. My office, say, one hour?'

'Fine, see you then.'

So, an hour to think about it. Perhaps rehearse a bit.

Patterson made notes, went for a cup of coffee in the staff cafeteria, sat alone and reread them. Meetings of the Service's Western Hemisphere and Far East Controllerate were usually conducted on an assortment of chairs in Hopko's sanctum. The air of collegiality could dissipate quickly. Rivalries and resentments turned the conversation spiky. Intelligence Officers who had been in their role for a paltry eight months knew not to make a point too forcefully.

She arrived first, of course. Hopko wasn't there. So she took a chair in a corner – always secure your flanks and rear – and waited. Hopko had Chinese prints on her walls, delicate things from the Song dynasty: a butterfly, a grove of bamboo.

Next to arrive was Drinkwater, Security Officer, suited, hair cropped to grey stubble, meaty, ruddy, the suggestion of inner rancour.

Then, hard behind him, Waverley, Requirements Officer, Far East, who winked at her and sat with exaggerated relief. Waverley teetered on the edge of louche. He had long fair hair, an olive-green linen suit, a smile that failed to reassure.

Silence, as the three of them looked over Charteris's telegram and the traces. Patterson tried to read their faces, but found nothing.

Patterson wondered if Hopko contrived her entrances. She breezed in now, coffee cup in hand, closing the door behind her with a foot clad in a black heel.

Hopko, Valentina. Targeting Officer, China. Visiting Case

Officer, who knew where, though the stories abounded. Hopko placed the cup on her desk and then licked a finger of spilled coffee. Patterson could feel the energy pulsing from her like heat. Stocky, dark Hopko. She was dressed, to Patterson's austere eye, too young for her nearly fifty years, the black skirt riding a little too high, the emerald blouse gaping a little too open, herring-bone stockings. Hair the colour of jet, teased or backcombed or something to give it body. Patterson, for all her army years, felt the stirring of her inner snob. She thought, She looks like a bloody waitress.

Hopko turned, as if she'd heard. Patterson shifted in her seat.

'Morning, Trish.' Hopko fastened that gaze on her. 'Things afoot in the Middle Kingdom, are they?'

Hopko's face had seen a great deal of sun, the skin imperfect, freckled, almost tawny. She wore heavy black-rimmed glasses. Behind them, restless eyes.

Hopko sat. 'Shall we?'

'I would draw your attention to two things.' Patterson could feel her tone of voice slipping into military. Calm down, she thought, it's not a bloody O-group. She cleared her throat. 'Charteris requested traces on keywords "night" and "heron". Those terms are associated with a network known as PAN GLINT. Long defunct. It was an emergency signal, to be delivered by phone or letter.'

Hopko was skimming the papers in front of her with a pen.

'Second, we all know the newspaper Philip Mangan represents, and we all know that its Beijing bureau for a while played host to an officer of this Service, operating under natural cover. PAN GLINT was handled by that officer.'

Silence. Which Patterson looked to fill.

'Hence, perhaps, the contact's insistence he was an old friend of the paper.'

'Perhaps.' Drinkwater of Security, looking at her. 'Sorry, Trish, can we be a bit more specific? When, exactly, was this PAN GLINT network in operation?'

'From 1985 to 1989.'

'Bit of a blast from the past, isn't it? Who were they?'

'PAN GLINT targeted China's aerospace research. They were aerospace engineers. Five of them. All graduate students at the big academies in Haidian. Rocketry, telemetry, metallurgy. The lead agent, and cut-out for the rest of them, was codenamed WINDSOCK. The "night heron" code was WINDSOCK's emergency signal. He handled the product and contacts with the case officer.'

'Officers, plural, surely,' murmured Hopko.

'And do we know who that officer was? Or officers?' said Drinkwater.

'No.' Initial traces had taken Patterson no further than cover names.

Hopko turned to Drinkwater, took off her glasses. 'But I'd warrant, Simon, it was Sonia and Malcolm Clarke.'

'Really? Good lord.' Drinkwater seemed wrong-footed. The temperature in the room had risen a notch, but Patterson had no idea why.

Waverley, of Requirements, began. 'Obvious question, what happened to PAN GLINT?'

'PAN GLINT fell apart in late eighty-eight and into eighty-nine,' said Patterson. 'Less and less active. No contact reports after March eighty-nine. WINDSOCK was reported disappeared in mid-eighty-nine. One of them killed himself. The others stopped responding.'

Hopko swivelled on her chair. 'After the demonstrations in Tiananmen Square and June fourth, everything came to a halt, I think. The Clarkes left that year, a few months after the shootings. So.'

'And Mangan. What do we know about him?' This from Drinkwater of Security, impatiently.

'Not much.' Patterson gave herself a mental kick for not having a biography. 'You'll have seen his copy. Reliable journalist. Some way from greatness in his profession.'

'But decent, though, isn't he?' Hopko leaned forward, looked expectant. 'I think his stuff is rather good.'

'Why, Val? Why's it good?' said Drinkwater.

Hopko sat back, dangling her glasses. 'Because he's thoughtful. Some investigative pieces of his in the paper told me things I didn't know. And those arrests in Jiangxi, all those poor bloody Followers. He was the only journalist who got himself there, I think. Rather resourceful of him. And the pictures were extraordinary.'

'No previous with the Service?' said Drinkwater.

'None,' said Patterson.

'All right, everyone. Can we go round, please?'

Hopko's Fancies, they called her insistence on hearing every possible explanatory narrative, no matter how far-fetched, wringing each one dry before throwing it away. 'Trish?'

'Well, let's take this man at face value,' began Patterson. 'Let's say he was an asset, twenty years ago, more. He's back. We don't know where he's been, what he wants or what he's got. But the approach to the bureau and the recognition code tell us he's real.'

Hopko was jotting notes. 'But twenty years?'

'Any number of reasons. A new opportunity. New needs. Middle age.'

Hopko looked at her. 'So age makes traitors of us, does it?'

'No. He was a traitor already,' said Patterson. 'Age makes us want to revisit. Doesn't it?'

Hopko nodded. 'Point. Tom?'

Waverley, Requirements Officer, would write up and distribute the product from any operation, Patterson knew. R officers stripped away the nonsense, the delusions, deflated the grandiosity of the agent, the credulity of the agent runner. She watched him balance sceptical with collegial.

'I'll go for nasty,' he said. 'It's Ministry of State Security. They've found out about PAN GLINT. Or maybe they knew all along. They've sweated WINDSOCK for his tradecraft, and now they're pushing someone back at us.'

'What for?' said Patterson.

Waverley shrugged. 'Mischief-making. Disruption. Distracting us from other things. Why does anyone ever run a counter-intelligence operation?'

'And why would it be someone else, Tom? Couldn't they have just turned WINDSOCK? They could be pushing *him* back at us,' said Hopko.

'They could indeed. But normally they just shoot them, don't they, rather than try to turn them. MSS tends to feel they're trouble, double agents.'

Hopko was silent. Waverley cocked his head at her.

'Val, I have the worrying impression you would like to pursue this,' he said.

Drinkwater snorted. Hopko turned to him and crossed her legs.

'Simon. Please. Save me from myself.'

Drinkwater shook his head and adopted a tone of patient explanation.

'It's just the usual. The locals are trying to flush out natural cover officers among the foreign journalists. Or at least they're looking for links between the journalists and the local stations. Smoking out freelancers or whatever. So they throw out a marker – some cute little recognition code, for example – to see where it goes.'

Hopko was poker-faced and said nothing. So it fell to Patterson, who abhorred a vacuum.

'That doesn't really explain the fact that the recognition code was valid, though, does it?' she said.

Drinkwater didn't look at her, spoke directly to Hopko. 'Well, I dare say it's like Tom said. They got something out of WIND-SOCK. Years ago, probably.'

The meeting dragged on. If Security Branch had its way, thought Patterson, the Service would not run operations because all operations were by definition threats to Service security. Drinkwater was like a man trying to drown a kitten. Patterson decided not to give up.

'We have nothing to lose,' she said. 'Let me at least establish the identity of the contact. In any case we can't approach him. He'll come back to Mangan in his own good time.'

Drinkwater, speaking past her again, shook his head and smirked.

'Val, can we just put this out of its misery, please? Security Branch will not sanction Beijing Station chasing around after some MSS dangle.'

Hopko looked at her notes. Then, ignoring Drinkwater, turned to Patterson.

'Might I suggest we issue them both P numbers, Mangan and the contact. Put them in the system. Charteris to pay attention, signal us if the contact reappears. Let's see what develops.'

Hopko shuffled papers and looked about her brightly. 'Thank you so much, everyone.' Dismissed.

It took until late afternoon for Patterson to apply herself to WINDSOCK, or whoever he might be. She applied to Registry for two five-digit P numbers.

P77395: MANGAN, Philip. UK citizen. Age thirty-six. Beijing-based journalist as of current date. Holds a foreign correspondent's accreditation with the Beijing authorities.

Reports approach, contact unidentified, suspected BEI 72. Reference: P77396; PAN GLINT; WINDSOCK.

P77396: UNKNOWN. Presumed PRC citizen. Age unknown, reported late forties. Approached P77395 with offer of information. Possible BEI 72. Reference: P77395; PAN GLINT; WINDSOCK.

Into the system. Seeds planted.

10

Beijing

Peanut bided his time in Beijing's grey chill. He found a second-hand bookshop off the third ring road, on the ground floor of a brick apartment block. It was little more than someone's living room. A handwritten cardboard sign pointed to it from the street. The proprietor was a bespectacled elderly man, bald, in *zhongshanzhuang*, the blue cotton jacket buttoned up to the throat, a throwback to socialism. Yet he was, it appeared, a man who read classical Chinese and valued the eclectic. In piles, in boxes, the *Shi Jing*, the *Analects of Confucius*, Ming dynasty novels. An electric heater in a corner lent the room a smell of scorched dust. The old man looked up at Peanut, a dim smile, then returned to the *People's Daily*. A ginger cat sat on his lap and watched Peanut shuffle amid the musty classics.

He found what he wanted: a copy of the *Chu Ci*, the Songs of the South, in a blue paper cover stitched with cotton thread. An old friend, Qu Yuan. The ancient thinker, strategist to kings, rejected and tortured by exile. Killed himself in a river. Scraps of the poems floated to the surface of Peanut's memory.

In spring, the orchid; in autumn, the chrysanthemum;
Eternally thus, till time's end.

Peanut handed ten yuan from operational funds to the old man, who took it in a veined, quivering hand. Then he gestured, as if to make Peanut wait a moment.

'This is good. If you like a challenge.' The bookseller's voice was a dry rustle. He reached slowly for a brown volume and held it out. 'I was given a whole box. Take one, if you like.'

Peanut took the book. *Tai Bai Yin Jing.* The Hidden Book of Venus. No, not smut, military affairs, a Tang dynasty treatise. Peanut nodded, faintly disappointed.

'Well, thank you.'

'It's quite a work.' The old man was regarding Peanut intently, and now made an effort to stand, palms flat on the desk, pushing himself up. 'Forgive me, but do I know you?'

Peanut turned away, flustered, then was gone, back on to the street. He looked back just once. The bookseller was at the window, watching. Peanut moved quickly in the twilight.

To a photo shop. Where he paid fourteen yuan and posed against a white background, and an acned, spike-haired boy told him to hold still.

'Is it for a passport?'

'You could say that,' replied Peanut as the flash died in streaks of colour across his retina.

Then back to Fangzhuang, and the department store, where, tentatively, Peanut bought a mobile phone, the cheapest one he could find. Just as Yin had briefed him, he queued at a newspaper kiosk outside the Metro station and bought a little blue coupon to cover fifty yuan's worth of calls.

By the time he arrived back at the Blue Diamond, trade was picking up, and Dandan Mama greeted him wordlessly with open palms, as if to say, where have you been? Yin sat before a mirror, brushing her hair. Peanut walked, unhurried, to the store-room, took off his coat and dropped the two books on the mattress. Then he took up his position, on the stool by the beaded curtain. He lit a cigarette. Yin brushed past him, avoiding his eye, a young man in a baseball cap shuffling behind her.

And so on, into the night. The girls lounged in the salon or sometimes walked for a moment or two along the tiled steps outside, their breath steaming on the air. The rattling television showed a soap. A chiselled tycoon in a tuxedo argued passionately with his simpering, ringletted lover, mouth like a rosebud, the set a Shanghai mansion with Grecian statues and high gates.

Peanut, silent, watched the migrant workers slouch through the curtain. Some were in twos and threes, reeking of sorghum spirit. More of them were alone.

Peanut composed, in his mind, another letter.

And later, when he'd locked the front door, turned off the neon lights and cleaned the ashtrays, he watched Yin insert the battery and plug the phone in to charge. Slowly, as if to a recalcitrant child, she explained to Peanut the significance of the coupon, how to activate his account. She looked disdainfully at the little device.

'You're not going to impress anyone with *that*,' she said. He took notes as she told him how to make a call, how to answer one.

It was Sunday morning and Mangan spooned coffee from a tin. The 'bureau' was silent and chilly. Pyjamas, again, and he sat at the desk looking through the Xinhua News Agency copy, pawing the papers, wondering if anything might do for his Monday edition. *Top Chinese official urges transformation of economic development mode!* Or perhaps *Vice Premier urges Gansu cadres to stress stability!* No?

A key rattled in the front door and Ting bustled in, red-cheeked. She wore a silvery padded jacket and long leather boots with heels.

'It's almost winter, Philip! *Dongtian, a!*' She set down a shopping bag and stood breathing heavily, smiling. She always took the stairs. 'I smell coffee?'

He pointed to the kitchen. 'Fresh. Why are you here? It's Sunday.' Ting studied Kunqu, classical opera, on Sunday mornings, a big, gossipy class of socialites wrestling with *The Peony Pavilion*.

She wagged a finger at him as she went to the kitchen. 'I'll tell you.'

She came back and perched on the edge of the desk, hands wrapped around a steaming mug. 'Go and put some clothes on.' She pointed at the wall, then her ear, mouthed just in case.

Mangan put on a hideous dressing gown decorated with giraffes, and they went out on to the balcony. It was cold. Ting took out her diary, spoke quietly. 'I was at a party last night and there was a journalist in from Yunnan. Surnamed Ma. *Yunnan Daily*. He said he knows a village that is all Followers, some little lost place in the mountains, whole families who gave everything to the movement.' She tapped a page of hastily written notes, some phone numbers.

'Anyway, the police came and took away the young men, all at once. He spoke to some families, and the men are being held in some sort of camp. They've been there for months now. He told me where. I have it written down. He can't use it, of course, so he said he'd put us in touch. As long as we keep him out of it.' She looked at Mangan, expectant.

Yunnan. A long way away. But this little scrap of hearsay had an urgency to it. It was a story.

'Better rip that page out of your diary.'

'Do you like it?'

Her look was searching.

'Of course I like it. I really like it.'

She tore the page out, handed it to Mangan as if awarding a prize, then turned away from him and went back into the apartment, arms raised in victory, fists clenched.

'But, Philip, you'll have to make the calls on this one, yes?' She bent to gather up her bags. The sunlight caught her black hair and Mangan thought he saw other colours, greens and blues, flecked through its blackness.

'Of course,' he said.

She was reversing towards the door. 'You should come to Kunqu. It's fun. Lots of rich girls. And the glorious culture of China, obviously.'

'Why would I want lots of rich girls?'

Ting gestured to the room, its shabbiness.

'Because, in the end, poverty is not very sexy, Philip.'

Mangan smiled and made a *Go!* gesture, and heard the door slam and her feet clattering down the stairs. Silence again.

The knock, when it came, was soft.

Mangan stood and crossed to the door, pulling his dressing gown tight. Through the peep hole he saw a man dressed in dark-blue coveralls splashed with paint. He carried a pot of paint and a brush, and had his back to the door, so Mangan could not see his face. Mangan opened the door and the man turned.

'Mr Mang An. Sorry to trouble you. You remember me?'

Mangan took in the bulk, the bristled hair.

'I believe I do.'

The man went into Mandarin. He smiled and made deferential movements, the half-bow, the open hands.

'Sorry again to trouble you. I would like to speak to you very briefly. May I come inside?'

Mangan stalled. 'I am afraid we don't really have anything to talk about. I am very busy.'

The man's eyes flickered quickly downward over the absurd dressing gown, the bare, enormous feet.

'Of course. I am sorry. But Mr Mang An, events are moving very fast. It's important you know what is happening. This affects you.' With this the man straightened up and pointed at Mangan. 'These events affect you, Mr Mang An.'

'What events are you talking about?'

The man took a half-step forward and gestured to the inside of the apartment. 'Inside, please.'

Mangan reluctantly moved to one side. Oh, mistake, he thought.

The man moved quickly into the apartment. Mangan closed the door. The man took a white envelope from inside his coveralls. His hands were smeared with black paint.

'Mr Mang An. I am giving you an envelope.' He spoke quietly, barely above a whisper. 'Inside is one letter, one photograph and a document, two pages. The letter will explain everything. Please read it. And understand, Mr Mang An, that I deal only with you. Nobody else.'

'You are not dealing with me. I cannot accept anything from you.' Mangan held his hands up. 'You must leave now.'

The man just smiled. He walked across the room and put the envelope on the desk. Mangan had the sense of having lost control. 'Leave now, please.'

The man was already at the door, and then was gone. The entire exchange had taken under two minutes, yet Mangan felt manipulated, almost physically, as if the man had picked him up bodily and turned him around. Annoyed, he turned, and went to the balcony. He saw the coveralled figure with its powerful, rolling gait, carrying its paint pot, moving fast towards the north gate, walking past the guards and back on to the street. How did he get in?

On the desk was the envelope, a smear of black paint on it.

Mangan picked it up and dropped it in the waste bin. Then bent and took it out. The envelope was blank and sealed with tape. Are there consequences if I open this? he thought.

He held the envelope to his nose and smelled it. Paint.

Yes. I will know something that I do not know now. That is a consequence.

He waited. Then opened a desk drawer and took out a pair of scissors.

One letter, on thin grainy paper, squared, of the sort children might use to practise their characters. In handwritten Chinese, but the characters clearly drawn, each stroke separate and particular. A letter written for a foreign eye. One photograph, passport size, full face against a white background; the face that of the old friend of the paper who spouts nonsense about birds and who arrives unbidden on Sunday mornings and who, we are almost certain, does not work as a painter.

And one document, two pages. Photocopied. On the first page, in the blocky, spiky typeface that screams Communist Party, two characters. *Juemi.* 'Top Secret'. At the bottom of the page, a number: 157. And in the middle of the page, a title. *A Preliminary Report. Certain Questions. DF-41.* The other characters demanded a technical dictionary, but Mangan was not of a mind to consult a technical dictionary just now, to go digging for radicals and phonetics and scrolling through hundreds of unfamiliar terms. *Leading Small Group.*

On the second page a table of contents. *Background. Explanation of April 16th Incident. Actions and Policies Related to April 16th Incident. Criticisms of Responsible Cadres. Implications for Launch Schedule.*

Mangan ran a hand through his hair and wondered if he'd left any trace of himself on the page. A fingerprint? *Annexes. Key Personnel. Timeline of Key Events. Minutes of Leading Small*

Group Discussions of April 16th Incident. His Chinese was fairly good, in its way. Good enough to know that he was looking at a document whose origins lay deep in the secret heart of China's ballistic missile programme. Good enough to know that he was looking at a death sentence. For someone.

He locked the documents in a desk drawer, and dialled.

'Charteris.'

'David, it's Philip. Sorry to call on a Sunday.'

'Not a problem. Something exciting happening? You're so assiduous, Philip, always the first to know.'

'Well, not this time. You remember my telling you about that, um, encounter I had. Birds.'

'Careful.'

'Well, another encounter. Bit perplexed, to be honest. Where are you?'

'At the gym. Come here. Now.'

Dear Mr Mangan,

I am an old and dear friend of your country. I have served your country in the past. There are many in your government who know of my service. I would suggest that you or your colleagues in the UK government contact Mr and Mrs Clarke if your government needs to be reminded of my service to your country. I enclose a photograph so they may easily identify me.

I now stand ready to serve your country once more, one last time. I suggest an exchange. I can provide access to very valuable items. In return, I seek help with travel, the means and the opportunity. I may be reached at this number: China country code, 196 447 3349.

I would prefer to deal only with you, Mr Mangan. The fewer entanglements the better, I find. You will, of course, need reassurance that my offer is genuine, and is not orchestrated in some way. Please be assured that my offer is utterly sincere and I make it of my own volition. Anything I can do to persuade you of this I am very happy to do. I enclose a sample of the kind of material I am able to deliver.

You will also wonder why I do this. I will refer you to a passage of ancient Chinese poetry:

I cut water chestnut and lotus a garment for to make,
And gathered hibiscus to girt myself about.
I regret not the loss of place.
I shall hold to the purity of mine own heart.

I am sure Mrs Sonia Clarke will know who the author is.

We must conduct this business quickly, so I hope to hear from you very soon.

Your friend.

Mangan took a cab to Dongzhimen. The sprawling compound of 'villas', a pastiche of a northern European garden suburb, was flanked on all sides by skyscrapers. On the wall surrounding the compound, a graffiti artist – he was all over Beijing, an anti-hero, infuriating the authorities – had stencilled his signature image in black: a figure, this one a dog, wearing goggles. Underneath it one word: THREATEN. Mangan paid the taxi off and walked into the compound.

Charteris waited at the entrance to the clubhouse, a towel round his neck. He said nothing, just beckoned Mangan into a damp, grey room filled with exercise machines. Televisions suspended from the walls were playing Korean music videos. Charteris turned his mobile phone off, removed the back cover and took out the battery and memory card, and put all the pieces in his gym bag. Mangan, making a wry face, did likewise.

Charteris put the bag down in one corner and walked over to the far side of the room. Mangan found himself leaning into the corner, his face only a few inches from that of Charteris, who murmured.

'Where did he approach you?'

'He came to the flat. Why all the bloody drama?'

'How did he get into the compound?'

'I don't know.'

'And what did he say?'

'He gave me documents, a letter.'

Mangan could feel Charteris tensing. 'Where are they now, the documents?'

'They're where I left them in the flat, locked in a drawer. What are you not telling me, David?'

'We're going back to the flat. Now. Don't say anything.' Charteris walked quickly across the exercise room, picked up the gym bag, took Mangan's arm and walked him out of the club-house to the car.

Minutes later Charteris's black BMW was parked in the Jianwai compound and the two of them were in the lift, silent, Mangan embarrassed, Charteris businesslike. Mangan entered the flat first, but Charteris was quickly to the desk, waiting for him to open the drawer. Charteris pointed to the desktop computer and made the slicing gesture at his throat. Mangan sighed and shut the computer down. Then he unlocked the drawer and took the letter, photo and photocopies out and laid them on the desk with a mock-dramatic gesture. *Ta-da!*

Charteris looked around him and took a piece of paper from the printer and wrote, *Is this all of them?* He pushed the paper across the desk to Mangan, who was trying to signal indignation, hands on hips, head to one side. Charteris just pointed at the note.

Mangan nodded.

How long have they been here?

Forty minutes now, about.

Charteris breathed out.

Anybody else been in the flat?

Mangan shook his head.

Come with me.

Charteris picked up the letter, the photograph and the document, eased them back into the envelope and put them in a pocket, along with the printer paper. Mangan stared, mute, testy now. But Charteris was already out of the apartment at a near run and Mangan followed him down the stairs.

'David, it's polite to ask before you walk off with other people's secret documents.'

'Philip, shut up.'

'No. What's going on?'

They were outside now, in the bright morning, the cold almost metallic. Charteris stopped and faced Mangan. He spoke in little more than a whisper.

'That letter and that document are extremely dangerous. I'm taking them from you and I'm giving them to the Embassy Security Officer, who, I imagine, will destroy them the minute he claps eyes on them.'

'Just hang on there, David. This man is communicating with *me*.'

Now Charteris looked irritated. 'Philip, grow up. If those documents were ever found, you – and Ting – would be in Qincheng Prison for twenty years. Or worse. Dangle or no dangle, it is my duty to take them from you, which is what I'm doing.'

'Your *duty*?'

'Or whatever you want to call it.'

'But, wait. Think for a moment. If you take them, I'm doing exactly what this man wants me to. I'm passing them to the UK government. If this is a dangle, I'm incriminating myself even further.'

Charteris said nothing, just shook his head again. He was in his car now, slamming the door.

'Do not tell anybody about this, Philip, and if he approaches you again, let me know immediately.' Charteris had backed the BMW into its parking space and now pulled straight out, fast.

Mangan was left standing, shivering. What the hell just happened?

Qu Yuan, the ancient, doomed adviser to kings, had supplied the verse for Peanut's letter. Peanut wondered if they'd pick up on the code he'd agreed with them all those years ago: lotus – *I am operating of my own free will. I am not under duress.*

Qu Yuan had, indeed, supplied an entire framework for Peanut to think about his situation and his appallingly dangerous bid to contact British Intelligence.

But it was the other book, the brown volume given him by the old man in the store, which now absorbed him. For the *Tai Bai Yin Jing*, the Hidden Book of Venus, had much to say about agents and how they should comport themselves.

> Be as the hawk entering the deep forest, or the fish plunging
> deep, leaving no trace.
> Be as a swirl of dust arising. Subtle! Subtle!

Peanut sat in the storeroom, the air a fug of cigarette smoke, feeling his way through the text, the ancient, complex characters. The author, Li Quan, about whom Peanut knew nothing, had written a treatise balanced somewhere between strategy and philosophy. His was the metaphysics of the baggage train, the siege engine, encirclement. And of intelligence.

Writing thirteen hundred years ago, Li Quan referred to those who gathered intelligence as *xing ren*.

Xing: to walk, to move. *Ren*: person, man. Moving man.

Spy as moving man. Stillness is the enemy.

Later Peanut stood ladling out the vegetables in their cumin broth, steam rising in the cold bright air, black paint still under his nails. Yin, covername Beautiful Peony, deep dark circles under her eyes, was holding out her rice bowl. And the spiky, hatchet-faced, orange-haired girl, covername Pavilion of Softness, was pressing the peppers into the rice with her chopsticks, swirling the broth. Moving man, spy.

Peanut wondered how much longer, here.

11

SIS, Vauxhall Cross, London

The date. A reference number.

FM CX BEIJING

TO LONDON

TO TCI/29611

TO P/64815

FILE REF C/FE

FILE REF R/84459

FILE REF SB/38972

TO: CABINET OFFICE 771

TO: RESEARCH DEPT 864

LEDGER UK S E C R E T

LEDGER DISTRIBUTION: CABINET OFFICE JIC ASSESSMENTS STA

PRIORITY

/REPORT

1/ BEI 2 received a telephone call from Philip MANGAN P77395. MANGAN said he had been approached for a second time by unidentified Chinese male P77396. The contact came uninvited to the flat in which MANGAN works and resides. The contact deposited documents with MANGAN. The documents included what appeared to be photocopies of official materials at the highest level of classification.

2/ BEI 2 met MANGAN immediately and took possession of the documents. BEI 2 advised MANGAN his continued possession of the documents endangered his own security and that of his staff. MANGAN allowed BEI 2 to remove the documents.

3/ The documents are as follows:

A – Photocopy, two sheets, title page and table of contents taken from report on experimental launches of DF-41 missile. Numbered. *Juemi*/Top Secret classification.

B – Handwritten letter, one sheet. The writer, presumed to be contact P77396, appears to make an offer of service.

C – Photograph, one. MANGAN confirms the subject in the photograph is contact P77396.

Documents are scanned and attached. They follow by bag.

4/ BEI 2 advises that Document A may have CX value, advises immediate assessment.

5/ Grateful for traces on PAN GLINT, WINDSOCK, confirmation that P77396 is identical WINDSOCK.

/ENDS

Patterson's phone rang. It was Hopko.

'You will get to those files. At once, please.'

Patterson left her arid little cubicle and walked the silent corridor. She took the lift to Central Registry.

A matronly Registry bee stood next to a pile of files. She was wiping what looked to be dust from her hands with a tissue.

'There you are. Eighty-four to eighty-nine. The lot.'

Patterson ran her fingers over a tan cover.

She signed the files out and carried them back to her cubicle.
That afternoon she made a start, and stayed at it into the night.
She moved chronologically, making notes, building the narrative,
fighting her way through the Service's long-abandoned paper
system, the memoranda known as minute pages, white for sub-
stantive, pink for ephemeral, the tally sheets, an obsessive record
of who saw what, when, festooned with the self-important signatures of officers long gone. Audit trails. Telegrams. Malcolm
Clarke's pungent contact reports. Requirements. Assessments of
product. The short life of a forgotten network, frozen in dusty,
bureaucratic amber.

Patterson found the Clarkes' reports working on her, drawing
her in. There was a persuasiveness, a vividness to them. PAN
GLINT was made up of five agents, she read. WINDSOCK was Li
Huasheng, born 1960 in Beijing, to a family of intellectuals. The
father was a geologist, Professor at the Institute of Mines. The
mother taught Chinese literature in a high school.

She turned a page.

The family, wrote Clarke, was stable, intellectuals building
New China, watching their step in the volatile Mao years, getting
by, caring for their children. Little Li Huasheng went to primary
school in 1966.

And then things started to go wrong. The Cultural Revolution
was underway. Red Guards were all over the campuses and one
day they were at the door and the father got it in the neck. The
Red Guards threw things out of the apartment windows, hurled
pot plants to the floor, smashed pictures. They branded the
father a capitalist roader. They locked him in a maintenance
room in the Academy of Mines for four months in the summer
and autumn of 1966. When they remembered, the Red Guards

pushed rice or bread through the door. He nearly starved. They took him out for struggle sessions. Sometimes he was made to kneel on a stage, a sign around his neck, as a crowd shouted abuse and denounced him. Sometimes mother and son were forced to attend the sessions. The father was beaten twice, but the real damage was psychological.

Patterson stopped and rubbed her eyes.

When the father was allowed out of the maintenance room, he came home, but he never worked again. He died a few years later. The mother supported the family. They lived in a single room. Things died down. The Red Guards were reined in, but they were still around, posturing and glowering, keeping track, waiting for next time. Li Huasheng forged on through high school. He took the university entrance exams and won a place at Tsinghua University. He was bright. He read physics and went on to the Aerospace Institute, where he specialised in ballistics. And it was there that the Clarkes recruited him.

Patterson picked her way through the recruitment process, watched the Clarkes deftly place their agent at the centre of a network. She scoured the protocols, the tradecraft, for clues. She looked for duress codes.

Patterson was exhausted. She left the building for twenty minutes to walk quickly in a freshening wind off the river, clear her head. She bought a kebab and sat on a bench on the river bank in the chill dark and ate it, and returned to her cubicle reeking of onion.

At two in the morning she turned the page to find an encounter report the Clarkes filed early in the operation. They'd picked up WINDSOCK in their car, at night, driving slowly through Beijing's darkened streets, had spoken with him for eighteen minutes.

'WINDSOCK remains preoccupied by the fate of his father. He

speaks of his father as a gentle man reduced by the depredations of the Cultural Revolution to a shadow who spent his days in a darkened room, starting at noises, venturing out seldom, weeping often. He died in 1972. The posthumous rehabilitation of the elder Professor Li came in 1979, as it did for many of the victims of the Cultural Revolution, but for WINDSOCK the sense of monstrous injustice was only the greater for it. The proximate cause of death was a heart attack, but WINDSOCK insists his father died of fear.'

Patterson imagined the Clarkes probing their new agent, feeling out his motivations, calculating how far he'd go for them.

'WINDSOCK may hold limited access for now, but a combination of anger, ambition and acquisitiveness may render him a highly exploitable asset in the long term.'

By three she had moved on to the sub-agents. The first to come on board was TANGO, one Gu Hua, a metallurgist at Tsinghua University, a friend of WINDSOCK's. Then COPPER. He was at the Aerospace Institute. His field was Materials and Precision Tools. Clarke described him as 'larcenous'. Then came CURTAIN. He's the truly clever one, wrote Clarke, destined for great things. Wen Jinghan. He'd already gained his Ph.D. in rocketry and telemetry. The last was NEPTUNE, an electrical engineer. Deceased, said the file, a suicide. WINDSOCK was cut-out. The Clarkes only encountered the others a handful of times.

The next morning, on three hours of sleep, Patterson briefed Hopko, who ate an eclair at her desk.

'And what year was it they first met him, Trish?'

'Nineteen eighty-four.'

'Ah. Interesting moment.'

Patterson sighed inwardly. 'Why interesting?'

'Oh, China really started to change that year. The Cultural

Revolution trauma was fading. Those big beautiful reforms were starting to take hold. In the villages the peasants had been allowed to grow what they wanted. No more horrid communes, or fewer anyway. In the cities they started to think things were possible. And that October was the thirty-fifth anniversary of the People's Republic. Big parades, lots of looking forward. Something new in the air, some sense that you could start to push boundaries, transgress.'

Hopko dabbed her mouth with a napkin.

'So, WINDSOCK. Mr Li Huasheng. Clever, furious, missing his daddy, has resurfaced after all these years. He's turned up on the doorstep of what he thinks is the Service, because that's what he knows. To encounter a bemused journalist. Is that what we think?'

'I think it's a real possibility. One worth pursuing,' said Patterson.

Hopko was silent for a moment, weighing it.

'I'm constantly amazed,' she said, 'at how many agents have fathers who are missing, either physically or emotionally.'

'Shouldn't we talk to the Clarkes before we make diagnoses?' said Patterson.

Hopko looked surprised.

'Oh, Malcolm Clarke died years ago. But Sonia's still alive.'

'And will that help us?'

'Do you know, I think it might.' Hopko beamed. 'Because the word was that Sonia did all the work.'

He could have used his new mobile phone, but something in Peanut understood the function of the cut-out. And that something – call it tradecraft – told him one phone for Mangan, another for the professor.

So he took a bus, and then he walked, to Beijing South Railway Station, the morning frigid, the colour of ashes. He stayed with a crowd, where he could. Three times he cut abruptly on to quiet side streets. He found no one on his back. But the sense of precariousness was growing in him.

He made his way through the murmuring crowd, migrants most of them, with their cheap luggage, string bags of fruit, cigarettes, to find the station a shining silver dome, sparkling lights affixed to nests of white steel. He saw a train that looked like something from the science comics he hoarded as a child, sleek, white, sculpted. It looked like a missile. He stared at it, wondered at its shimmering modernity, and had to tear himself away.

No one was using the public phones. He dialled slowly, using the card Yin had given him.

'Yes?'

'It's me. We're going out for dinner. You're paying.'

Silence.

'The Oasis. In Qianmen. Six o'clock.'

Nothing.

'Do you hear me, Jinghan?'

'Yes.'

A long day, spent weaving through south Beijing. He'd been tempted for a moment by the Revolutionary History Museum on Tiananmen Square, but caught himself. The thought of the plain-clothes men made his stomach lurch.

So he followed the railway tracks south for a time, and then west, into a district of light industry. He walked into a sharp wind that howled between silent, still factory buildings. Weeds sprouted through the asphalt. A strange whitish dust had settled on roofs and car windows. Then through broad tree-lined streets, north to Taoranting Park, where he sat for an hour listening to a knot of old men singing Beijing opera to each other. They had set up their operational base in a concrete pavilion by a lake. They had laid newspapers on the stone table, a bag of fruit, a thermos full of tea. One played an *erhu*, its two strings mournful in the grey cold over the lake, the green water. The men ignored Peanut. There was no one else. A few flakes of snow fell.

Another round of Hopko's Fancies, this time for the benefit of higher orders. Roly Yeats, Head of Western Hemisphere and Far East Controllerate, now sat in Hopko's sanctum beneath the fine, fragile leaves of bamboo and waited for the conundrum to be placed before him. He was once a lecturer at Manchester, Patterson knew. He was impish, ginger-bearded and elusive, Patterson thought. He rubbed his hands together.

'Yup, okay. So what have we got, Val?'

Hopko had assumed the advantage by placing herself behind her own desk.

'Well, it's a poser.' Hopko looked over her glasses and smiled.

'Fire away, then.' Yeats had a northern twang, for authenticity, thought Patterson.

Hopko turned to Patterson and looked expectant. Patterson swallowed, and began.

'Well, we've all seen the latest from Charteris. The contact has turned up unbidden at Mangan's flat, handed him a fragment of a white-hot document and left. We have a photo of the contact. And a letter with a phone number.'

Hopko said, 'Charteris was clumsy, but at least he got hold of the material.'

Drinkwater of Security was tensed, ready to leap.

'Could we please have a *bit* more bloody detail? Where did Charteris and Mangan meet? Under what circumstances? Was anyone watching their backs? This feels slipshod, frankly.'

Yeats looked benign. 'Perhaps Charteris was improvising, frankly.'

'He bloody well *was* improvising, I'd say.'

'Is that a sin, in the circumstances?' said Patterson.

Drinkwater leaned forward and for once talked straight at her.

'In Beijing improvising *is* a sin,' he said. 'In Beijing we plan. We consult. We do *not* improvise, unless we want to be eaten alive.'

All present regarded Drinkwater for a moment, then Yeats turned to Waverley.

'Tom.'

'Well, the document changes things somewhat, doesn't it?' he said, evenly.

'Tell us why, please.'

Waverley cleared his throat. 'Charteris is right. Even this, the table of contents, reaches the CX threshold. This is useable intelligence.' He ran a hand through his hair. 'The consensus was really pretty strong that the DF-41 programme was dormant, or abandoned. Not just us, the Americans, too. And the Japanese. But this, just this, seems to tell us that it's alive. And how. Mobile, long-range ballistic missiles built for multiple thermonuclear warheads, in testing, if this is to be believed. Why don't we know about it? And what the hell is the April sixteenth incident? We have no idea.'

'So it's gone for assessment?' said Yeats.

'To Defence Intelligence. And they're already breathing heavily.'

'Why, do you think?'

'Well, they see missile programme, Roly. Major intelligence requirement. Crucial. And the cover sheet and number match known formats for Leading Small Group Documents, though obviously they grumble that it's a photocopy. They'll want the original, and the rest of it, mark my words.'

Yeats stirred. 'Are we not getting ahead of ourselves a little?'

'All the usual caveats, Roly,' said Waverley quickly. 'Maybe it's fake, maybe it's being peddled, whatever. But we need to start looking for collateral, and, reluctantly, I think we must take a closer peek at our mystery man. Poems and all.'

'Yes, what's the poem about, anyway? Lotus? What is it?' said Drinkwater.

Hopko looked over her glasses.

'It's an excerpt from a work called *Li Sao*. It's very ancient. Written by a man named Qu Yuan. A reflection on loyalty and rejection and exile, told through a shamanic journey.'

Silence for a moment, while the notion of ancient Chinese shamanic journeys was digested.

'Well, what does he mean by it?' Drinkwater sounded offended.

'He says he quotes it by way of explaining his motivation,' said Patterson, in the hope of offending Drinkwater further.

'Yes, I'm aware of that, thank you. But how does it explain his motivation? I mean, really.'

'I'm not sure it helps us much,' said Hopko quietly.

'And what about the rest of it?' said Yeats. 'Does anybody have a view on his offer of service?'

'Yes, I do, Roly,' said Drinkwater. 'And it's not bloody repeatable.'

'The thing is.' Yeats folded his arms. 'The thing is, this all feels very unusual. And I find I'm less interested in the document – forgive me, Tom – than I am in the notion that this chap wants us to believe he has access. So who is he? What access has he got? And is he righteous? Or is he bad? I think we should take a sniff of him – if, and only if, we can do it at arm's length. No direct contact with Beijing Station.'

The room was silent for a moment, Drinkwater biting his lip, Hopko looking over at Patterson questioningly. What now? Patterson thought.

Yeats put his palms on his knees, elbows out, as if to rise. 'Minute and plan of action to me, please, Val. Assessment to me, please, Tom. And, Simon?'

'Yes?' said Drinkwater.

'Unclench a little.'

They all rose to go. As Patterson walked down the corridor, Yeats slowed and waited for her.

'Good work . . . '

'Patterson, sir.'

'Oh, call me Roly, please. I rather get the sense you'd like to be involved in this operation, if operation there is to be.'

She didn't reply, sensed something in his look, danger.

'Just be sure to keep me apprised, won't you?' he said.

12

Beijing

By six the cold was coming on. Qianmen was thick with people and glittered with winter lights. Peanut, tired and chilled, turned on to a pedestrian street hung with red lanterns. A medicine shop spilled its woody reek into the street. The smell at once comforted him and enlivened in him a powerful desire for something, for a life in an unnamed town somewhere filled with the familiar, a life not yet lived.

Oasis was cavernous and dim. Sour-faced waiters wore beaded waistcoats and embroidered skullcaps. On the walls were murals of maidens, curvaceous and green-eyed, in clothes of revealing gossamer. *The Exotic Silk Road! The Sensuous Desert!* Brash central Asian synth-pop blared in a language Peanut couldn't identify. There was to be a floor show. Peanut took a booth at the back of the restaurant. He ordered lamb kebabs in chilli and cumin, noodles with sweet peppers, salad, bread and beer. He waited.

Twenty minutes later the silver-haired professor eased himself into the booth. He was expressionless.

'So this is what you ate, is it? All those years. Is this why I'm here? A reminder?' said Wen Jinghan.

'No, Jinghan. I ate corn bread for all those years. This is what I didn't eat.'

'For all those years.'

'Don't get petulant with me, Jinghan. You're here because I told you to be here.' Peanut forked a chunk of dripping lamb on to a plate, added salad, and shoved it across the table at Wen, who stared at it.

'Tell me how it works,' said Peanut.

Wen Jinghan took his time.

'Where's your sister?'

Peanut stopped chewing.

'Mei's in New Zealand,' he said.

'She got away.'

'Yes, she got away.'

'Are you in touch with her?'

Peanut sat back.

'What are you trying to say to me, Jinghan? You're not making a threat, are you?'

Wen looked up. 'No. No threat. I just wanted to ask.'

'Because if it is a threat.'

'And your mother passed away, what, ten years ago? While you were away. My mother went to the funeral. Did you know that? Wore a black armband. Did all the bowing, everything. We sent a big wreath.'

'Did you now.'

Wen Jinghan withdrew a cigarette from a pack – Zhonghua brand, Peanut noticed, expensive, the cadre's cigarette – and lit it slowly, collecting himself. Peanut took more lamb, tore off more bread, too quickly, he knew. Wen watched him.

'Clever of you to remember the anniversary of my father's death. Do you think about your own father much?' Wen Jinghan said.

Peanut didn't answer.

'When I saw you looming out of the trees, up there at the temple, I thought you'd come to be my friend again,' said Wen.

'No, you didn't, Jinghan. You started to shit at the sight of me.'

Wen exhaled slowly. 'This little scheme of yours. Is it working?'

'This little scheme of ours. And yes, thank you.' Peanut pushed his plate away from him. He reached over and took a cigarette from Wen's pack, lit it. 'Now. Tell me how it works.'

'How what works?'

'Your access. You mentioned networks.'

The professor just half-smiled, shook his head. Peanut stood up and walked around to Wen's side of the booth. He looked around quickly. The restaurant was full and loud, plates clattering, music thumping. Peanut slid into the booth next to Wen and laid a hand on the back of his neck, applied gentle pressure. Wen had both hands braced against the side of the table now, pushing back.

'Jinghan, do not try to talk your way out of this. You are *in*. And you have a lot to lose.'

Wen Jinghan said nothing, his head forced down towards his plate. Peanut suddenly slackened his grip and Wen's head jerked backwards.

'Tell me how it works.'

Wen stared furiously at the table, breathing hard, his nostrils flaring. A waitress looked, then looked away.

'Networks.'

'They are stand-alone networks. Do you know what that means?'

'Indulge me, Jinghan. I missed the ... the what do you call it ... the digital revolution.'

'It means that you can't get access to them. They are secure. They are not connected to any other network. Passwords and fingerprint scans. And when you log on to them, every move you make is tracked by fifteen-year-old shits from some utterly unnamed security department. So, no, you can't get anything from them for your sordid little scheme.'

The floor show had started. A couple in cartoonish Arabian dress danced on a stage to a pulsing Uighur love song. The man, heavy-browed, a scar on his bare shoulder, took the woman by the waist from behind and ran his hands down to her hips while she writhed. With an extended second finger he made a rotating motion against her skin, as if stimulating some exquisitely sensitive point. She feigned gasps. He stuck his tongue between his teeth and leered into the audience, some of whom were now up and dancing.

'You have printers, Jinghan.'

'You are a fucking baby.'

'Print things out.'

'Every time I print, the system monitors what I've printed. The fifteen-year-olds come and knock softly on my door. So polite. Professor, so sorry to bother you. But have we perchance been printing out these blueprints, those reports. Now, why would we need to do that? I print, I die.'

Peanut exhaled. 'I like the sound of blueprints.'

'Fuck you, Huasheng.'

'So tell me how we do it.'

Wen Jinghan drew deeply on his cigarette and looked down, and Peanut knew instantly that there was a way.

'You will tell me, Jinghan. Really, you will.'

'We must find him first. And then we can take a look at him,' said Patterson.

They were in Hopko's office, talking through an operational framework. Hopko wore kitten heels and a suit of some plum colour. She was standing, holding her glasses by the earpiece.

'Go on,' she said, a note of caution in her voice.

'Well, we can't use Charteris. All station officers are ruled out, Roly says. Drinkwater was close to foaming at the mouth at the thought of it.'

'So?' said Hopko.

'It will have to be a Visiting Case Officer.' Patterson tried to sound nonchalant, looked at her notes. 'We use the telephone number and make a direct approach. Three days max, in and out. Probably best to use the Hong Kong land border and a train to Beijing.'

'And the Visiting Case Officer would be you, I imagine.'

'I know the case as well as anyone,' she said.

Hopko grinned. Patterson went on.

'Val, I have been with the Service now for well over a year. I am experienced. In the army I handled agents. In Iraq.'

'I know you want a run, Trish.'

'But what?'

'But China is a denied area. There will be no VCO.'

Patterson was nonplussed.

'Too dicey to contact him directly, too uncertain a payoff,' said Hopko. 'If P77396 turns out not to be WINDSOCK at all but some MSS thug dangling us, ghastly consequences for all concerned. You'll be picked up and under the lights in no time: thoroughly blown and even more thoroughly embarrassed.'

So how? wondered Patterson.

I will deal only with you, Mr Mang An.

'Val, you're not suggesting . . .'

'Why not?' said Hopko.

Mangan.

Patterson caught herself. The notion of using a civilian grated on every fibre of her military being. She tried not to sound too incredulous.

'Forgive me, but why on earth would Mangan consent to get

involved? He'll run a mile, won't he? Sanctity of the press and all that.'

'He may, Trish, he may,' Hopko said, with what Patterson considered an indecent measure of equanimity.

Hopko had walked across the room and closed the door, using it to punctuate, change the subject.

'So,' she said. 'How are you finding it?'

How am I finding what? thought Patterson.

'Do you miss the army?' said Hopko.

'Do I look as if I do?'

Hopko smiled. 'Just wondered.'

Patterson shrugged. 'It's taken me a while to adjust to the, um, culture.'

'It's just that – and this isn't a criticism, merely an observation – you seem rather distanced from your work. I wonder if you're happy in it.'

Patterson was startled.

'Well, I don't think that's the case at all, Val.'

She thought for a moment.

'I'll admit to feeling on the back foot at times. Some of the older officers . . . ' She didn't complete the sentence.

'Like who? Between us, of course.'

'Do you know what Simon Drinkwater said to me? My second or third day in the P section? He was surprised to see me on the China beat. Thought I might be a bit . . . "conspicuous" was the term he used. Thought I should look to the southern hemisphere.'

Hopko shook her head.

'Drinkwater is a frightful shit. But you're not the first black officer in the Service, even if people like Drinkwater make you feel like you are.'

'It didn't really matter in the army.'

'And we must ensure it doesn't matter here. Are you ready for an operational role, Trish?'

Patterson, thoroughly wrong-footed now, sought to regain her balance, leaned forward on her chair.

'You know I am.'

'Well, then. Fancy a day out?'

13

She took a Service car. By late morning she was in the Chilterns, the motorway snaking past fields touched with frost.

As she drove, Patterson considered Valentina Hopko, her superior officer. Her mentor? Perhaps. She had sought intelligence on Hopko where she could, sought to understand the unlikely alchemy that had produced her. Hopko's father was British, but of an émigré family – Ukrainian, was it? – working in the Gulf as an engineer. Her mother was Lebanese, and little Val spoke Arabic to her, Russian to her father and English to the Filipina maids. Her early years were spent all over the Middle East, Muscat, Sharjah, Basra, soaking up accents, stories, geography, scatological vocabulary.

Then came exile to an English boarding school outside Stoke, where, displaying a mix of Slav doggedness and Levantine flair, dark, stocky Val mastered the sodden hockey pitch, the calamitous diet, the dreary timetable. Her admiring housemistress would have been taken aback when Val had insisted on Leeds University. *Leeds? My dear girl, we were thinking of Girton for you.* No, Leeds. For Val wanted to study Chinese under Skinner, in the Leeds Chinese department, lodged in its little Victorian house adrift in a sea of campus concrete, where languid, incisive Bob Skinner would have taught her to read and immersed her in history and forced her to think about dictatorship, and power.

On weekends she would drive a senile Austin Princess up into the Lakes, it was said, and march for hours across the fells.

And when the Service clapped eyes on her, it fell, no doubt, into a swoon.

Then, of course, the picture went dark. Glimpses of Hopko as an operational officer – rumours of a stint in the Gulf running an agent deep inside OPEC. Negotiating positions. Production quotas. Oil futures. Product that could save the British excheq-uer billions. And where she was rumoured to have recruited a skittish Arab general, who, while screaming in public for Israel's annihilation, played geopolitical footsie under the table with Val and her quiet, predatory Service.

Later a China posting under diplomatic cover. Hong Kong. Then the Middle East again. Visiting Case Officer, London-based. And then, well, something. Something that, if it were known what transpired, might explain why Roly Yeats sat in the seat marked Head of Controllerate and Valentina Hopko did not. Or was Val merely guilty of that very particular offence: serv-ing while female? Patterson did not know.

She left the motorway, drove down a silent, dark back road, hemmed in by beech woods.

Patterson, the little girl from the council estate in Nottingham, had never had a mentor. There had been teachers at her shabby secondary school, good, tired, harassed people, who had pushed her. But hers was not an upbringing in which watchful elders offered grooming and patronage. She remembered showing her parents the university admissions forms, asking them their advice. They'd been in the sitting room, looking at the television.

She remembered them fingering the forms, their blank, almost fearful expression, their eyes skittering back to the screen, her own embarrassment. She'd taken the forms to her bedroom and filled them out alone in ballpoint pen, and was dumbfounded when Coventry offered her a place.

In her second year, she'd started taking courses in Chinese, and surprised herself. The rote learning, the endless study of characters, piles of flashcards teetering on her desk, spilling from her backpack, suited her temperament.

And in her third year an army recruiting team visited the campus, bluff, solid men in polo shirts and fleeces. They showed her brochures and asked her what her plans were. One, a warrant officer, came to watch her at the judo club. She laid it on thick in the *randori*, brought a girl down hard with her hip throw, put her in a choke till she submitted, showed the warrant officer her speed and litheness, her capacity for aggression. When she bowed and left the mat, adjusting her belt, he gave her a round of silent applause. His look said, I'm impressed. They went to the student union bar, sat at a plastic table, and he bought her a shandy. He asked her about 9/11, what she thought, and he listened without patronising her. He asked her if she'd ever thought about Sandhurst. She felt seen.

She emerged from the beech woods on to sudden, open uplands, the frost heavier here, lacing the hedgerows in white. Ahead of her, its tower rising through a stand of trees, gold in low sunlight, an abbey.

She pulled in before a half-timbered cottage in the centre of the village, its thatch low over mullioned windows, stone boxes spilling some flower of searing blue. The village of Brightwell, silent, soaked now in afternoon winter light. Patterson stretched in the crisp air, took it in. A pub – *The Black Boy*, for heaven's sake. A post office, a green. Notices tacked to a telephone pole declared a coming winter festival and choirs at the abbey, and urged Brightwell to compost. She knocked at the cottage door to no response. A piece of notepaper lay on the step.

I'm over at the abbey! The Cloister Tea Room!

She walked to the abbey, negotiating the cobblestones in her heels. The abbey's interior was vast, ancient and plain, filled with hushed activity. A scaffold stood next to an expanse of whitewashed east wall. On its platforms of wooden plank, three women in overalls kneeled or lay on their stomachs. Under light from a powerful halogen lamp, they picked at the plaster with tiny steel implements. Where the plaster had been removed, Patterson could see a faint reddish outline on exposed wall, some ancient fresco revealed inch by agonising inch.

She asked in a stage whisper, 'The Tea Room?'

One of the women, portly, wearing a red headscarf, smiled and gestured to a sign. *The Cloister.*

The Tea Room was quiet, with a scattering of elderly couples dressed in hiking gear, murmuring. It was cool, the air smelled of stone. Patterson, in her business suit, sat before a table spread with fruit cakes, torte, macaroons. A tall, pale matron in half-moon spectacles poured her a cup of tea the consistency, it seemed to Patterson, of a light crude.

'Just take what you like, and tell us what you had at the end, and we'll tot it up. I'll tell her you're here,' said Half-moon. Carrying the teapot, she went to a doorway and lent in.

'Your visitor is here, Sons darling.' And then more quietly, 'She seems very . . . metropolitan.'

Patterson waited. From the doorway came a woman untying an apron. She wore her grey hair clipped short, and a blue cardigan over a white shirt. A hint of stiffness in her walk, Patterson noticed, but elegant. A thin mouth, deep creases to her face, and the watchfulness that never quite leaves those in the trade. Her eyes found Patterson, then flickered to the door and back, before settling on her, taking her in. Then a terse nod.

'We should go back to my place, I think.' She turned and barked through the doorway. 'Vivvy, I'm off.' It came out 'orf'. 'I should be back later on.' Patterson left too much money tucked under a plate. Half-moon watched them walk out into the cold cloister.

Sonia Clarke kneeled and pushed a burning spill into the fireplace. The fire caught quickly. A clock chimed softly in another room. There was more tea on a tray, and Patterson positioned a digital recorder among the china and sat primly on a sofa patterned with roses. She reached into her briefcase and took out a brown envelope.

Sonia stood and turned.

'Hadn't you better show me some identification?'

'Of course, Sonia. Here we are.' Patterson handed over her Service identity card, the real one, with the diagonal red stripe, to be used only with officialdom and nosey policemen. She gave a bright, reassuring smile. 'And you can call your routine contact number if you need to be sure.'

'No, that'll do.' Her eyes were on Patterson now. 'So what's this all about?'

'Well, I want to take you back a little way.' She drew from the envelope a sheaf of photographs, all of them middle-aged Chinese men, some of them images snapped in the street, others passport photos, blown up for clarity.

'Would you mind just taking a look at these? And tell us whatever comes to mind.'

Sonia reached behind her to the mantelpiece for a pair of glasses on a gold chain. She put them on and took the photographs. She went through them, slowly, one by one. And then stopped, held one – a passport photo of a bristle-haired, sharp-eyed character – up to catch the fading light.

'Well, well,' she said. 'Hello, Peanut.'

Peanut stood, mute, fascinated, furious, in the cold neon-lit night. Beyond his own reflection in the glass, a car. *Lambo* . . . a foreign word. Several of them. They were yellow, boxy and spiderish, made him think of whip-quick insects on the desert floor. A salesman held a door open, nodding appreciatively as a woman in suit and shades lowered herself, skirt riding up long legs, into the driver's seat. She gripped the wheel and shook her hair out. An older man looked on, the smile of ownership. Over his arm a coat of silver-grey fur, which he held for her.

Peanut watched it play out, the theatre of the unattainable in the Beijing night. He had taken to coming here from time to time, when trade was quiet and Dandan Mama gave him an evening off, to Jinbao Jie, Golden Treasure Street, to watch China sell itself a new fantasy.

Earlier that cold afternoon, at a filthy underpass in Hepingmen, he had purchased a knife from a ruddy-faced, green-eyed Uighur man. It was a lethal thing, the blade narrow and double-edged, with a fuller for strength. The knife had a rubber handle and a black nylon sheath, military issue.

The Uighur, unsmiling, had taken his money and counted it twice.

'Be careful who sees it.' The man's breath had steamed in the cold air.

'Oh, I will.'

'They don't like it, the cops.'

'I know.'

'Don't use it on anyone.'

'What are you, the Discipline Inspection Commission?'

The Uighur had looked at him.

'Don't be clever. You don't look like you can run very fast.'

Peanut had shaken his head, turned away. As he had walked off, he saw the graffiti again, sprayed on the underpass, the woman in the hideous goggles. THREATEN. The stencil was perfect, the image urgent.

'We encountered him first at English corner.' Sonia Clarke sat back in her chair and looked at the fire as she spoke. Patterson sat still, allowing the memories to come, only occasionally prodding. Outside the winter dusk was setting in, and the room was darkening.

'Beijing used to have these places, in parks sometimes, or just on streets, where people would gather to practise their English. English corners, they were called. Learning English was everything. They'd watch a television programme called *Follow Me* and then go to English corner and practise. It was allowed by then. Encouraged, even. Well, for us, it was a goldmine. A couple of journalists, helping out the locals with their English, chatting them up a bit at the same time. All very above board. There were snitches there, of course, but it didn't matter. It was a way of building acquaintance, you see, which was very hard to do in China back then. I told Malcolm, I said, we'll find people there, targets. He didn't think so, but I told him. And I was right.'

'Which year was this, Sonia?'

'Eighty-four. There was an English corner in Ritan Park. It was just a short walk from Jianwai, where we had that bloody flat. I'd go down there and chat with whoever turned up. We met Peanut in October, gorgeous Beijing autumn. I know that because it was just after National Day, the huge parade that year, through Tiananmen. Thousands of troops, tanks, these ghastly floats celebrating hydro-electricity or sorghum production or what have you. Deng Xiaoping was up there on the gate taking the salute. Anyway, a few days after that was the first time I saw Peanut at

English corner. Li Huasheng. He was sparky, intense. A bit fat, which was unusual. He was trying his damnedest to enthuse about the parade in English. I said to him, "What did you like best? The tanks? The floats?" And he shook his head and wagged his finger at me, and he said, "The students. The Beida students."'

'And what did he mean?'

'The Beijing University students. They were marching in the parade, two, three hundred of them. But no float or anything. They were just ambling along. They were wearing those big green army overcoats everyone wore, and they looked exactly how Chinese intellectuals ought to look – weedy, big glasses, a straggly beard. Tubercular. Suffering for wisdom. They had a few hand-painted banners, black characters on a bed sheet. And one of them read "*Xiaoping, ninhao!*"' She paused, a hand held in mid-air in the gloom as if framing the banner, its blotchy characters.

'Can you imagine? Calling the most powerful man in the Communist Party by his given name? Not Comrade Deng. No. Xiaoping. And *ninhao!*, "hello!" But with the honorific, *nin*, as you'd speak to a teacher, you see? It achieved both intimacy and respect. It said, we understand you. We're with you. And then they did the most amazing thing. As they passed Tiananmen Gate, with the entire Politburo up there watching, they just broke ranks, and ran. They just ran, laughing, their pathetic banners flying around and their army overcoats flapping, all those engineers, and biologists and theorists and economists, just running, all flat feet. No marching, no saluting, nothing. They looked ... unbound. I remember thinking that. You're unbound. Mao's gone. All that intellectual cringing and dissembling has gone. Thinking is back. You're the future. And you know it.' She stopped and sighed. 'Anyway, Peanut loved it. He counted himself in that class, you see, the *zhishifenzi*. The intelligentsia. Oh yes, always telling us how brilliant he was, the technical subtleties of his field. And he was right, he was in the intellectual class, but somehow not of it.'

'Why not?'

'He was ... resentful. Loved the idea of reform, and China resurgent and all that, but he had this gimlet eye for it. Hated the slippery bastards who'd come through the Cultural Revolution intact. The shits who'd killed his father. *I see them every day, Sonia, strutting around campus. Mouthing all the new slogans. Reform and opening up is all tops! Mind out for spiritual pollution!* The same ones as locked his father in a ... what was it, a broom cupboard or something – now saying hello to him in the dining hall. God, Peanut was angry. But he held all that anger in. And I thought, I'll have some of you.'

'Why the name, Sonia? Why Peanut?' asked Patterson.

Sonia Clarke smiled. 'His given name was Huasheng. It means something like China Rising. Just the sort of name you'd expect for someone born when he was. Lots of little East Winds and Red Dawns running around. But if you take those two words, *hua* and *sheng*, and say them on different tones, you get the word for peanut. So we called him Peanut. Which he liked, he said.'

'He seemed to have taken to you.'

'We never really even pitched him.' She turned to Patterson. 'Would you mind turning the lamp on, luvvie.' The lamp was dim and cast part of the older woman's face into shadow, etching the lines deeper. The fire was low, and outside it was nearly dark. 'He just sort of came to us.'

'Why did he do that?'

'Oh, there was a complex bargain, you understand.' Clarke raised an admonishing finger, then let her arm slump back into her lap. 'We offered him the moon. In the shape of a visa. We said we'd get him placed for a doctorate in Britain. Well, the look on his face. The sheer hunger. All he had to do was talk to us, help us understand. Lots of euphemisms, but he knew exactly what we wanted.'

'How on earth did you have these conversations, Sonia? Where? It was impossible to talk to a foreigner without attracting attention, wasn't it? Back then?'

'Isla was still a baby. I'd take her out in the pram, wander around Ritan Park. Peanut would break away from English corner and fall in beside me. We could manage a few minutes.'

'And where was Malcolm in all this?'

'Oh, grandly managing the operation. Liaising with London. Planning. He designed the whole thing. Sold it to Head Office. Nobody expected it would yield much in the short term. But Requirements was mustard for missiles. You see, we all knew rocketry was China's pass to strategic power, Taiwan, satellites, the lot. And we seemed to have stumbled on the next generation of designers. And we wanted to hook 'em. And we did. For a while.'

'And what did Peanut deliver?' said Patterson.

'Well, I assume you saw it in the files. He wrote these letters, by hand. Some of it was campus gossip. Which, in hindsight, we should have paid more attention to, given what happened. And there was quite a lot of self-aggrandising stuff. Peanut's analysis of such and such a Party meeting. Peanut's take on the economy. Guff, really. But there was real meat, too. He wrote these lists. Long lists of names, specialisations, equipment, projects, offices, committees, everything associated with the academic side of the missile programme. The WINDSOCK product allowed us to start building a picture of the structure. Who sat where. Who gave the orders. Who paid. Didn't help us with the military side of it, but we thought, Well, in time that might come.'

'And the others?'

'It was Peanut's idea. He said he thought he could recruit sub-agents. Well, he didn't say that, of course. He said he had friends who he thought he could persuade discreetly to help, if the visa offer were to apply to them, too. There was a lot of hemming and hawing. Head Office didn't like the security risk. But Head Office was liking the product.'

'And?'

'He went to his best friend. Gu Hua, he was called. Sold him some rot about a foreign scientific journal looking for quiet insights into China, in a position to sponsor him for a visa to the UK. Gu Hua signed up with gusto. *Voilà*, sub-source TANGO. He gave Peanut a bloody great inventory of machine tool factories run by the military, which Peanut dumped in the pram. Deadly dull. But awfully secret.' She grinned a hangman's grin. 'I had to stroll nonchalantly to the embassy to get rid of the bloody thing. God, I was sweating.'

'I imagine you were, Sonia. And so PAN GLINT came into being.'

'That's right. Peanut kept adding people. It took a couple of years.'

'How did you service the network?'

'Lovely dead drop at the Summer Palace. Malcolm found it. I'd take the baby and go out there every four weeks or so, wander about, check my back. A chalk mark in one of the pavilions by the lake told me the drop was loaded. And then I just had to reach into one of those litter bins shaped like a panda. So I'd faff around with nappies and what have you and go to chuck them away, and there they'd be. Peanut's lists, snug in a film canister and wedged inside the panda's ear. I'd leave behind instructions. A little cash.'

'So by the end of, what, 1986, PAN GLINT was at full strength.'

'Insofar as it ever had much strength. I mean some of Peanut's early stuff was very useful. There was another chap. Sub-source CURTAIN. His stuff was good. Very technical. But PAN GLINT became unreliable. It would go dormant for months at a time, and then up would pop Peanut with a new clutch of documents, demanding to know when he was off to London. And then something changed. The demonstrations started on the campuses. Late eighty-six, early eighty-seven. It was all rather shocking. They started in Hefei, which is the middle of bloody nowhere if you're from Beijing. And the Beijing students felt shown up by these hicks, so they started their own. New Year's Day eighty-seven. In the snow. They walked all the way to Tiananmen, sang the "Internationale", got arrested.'

She sighed.

'Some bright spark in Zhongnanhai decided it was "bourgeois liberalisation" and there'd better be a campaign against it. So all the kids were packed off to the villages in their summer hols to learn from the peasants. Can you imagine? Peanut got all agitated. *They're going to do it again, Sonia, you watch. We'll all be locked in broom cupboards. Our lives do not belong to us, Sonia. We cannot create.* Fewer lists, more guff after that. Peanut on the nature of true reaction. Peanut on the failure of Chinese civilisation.'

She stopped, took off her glasses and rubbed her eyes.

'It was the summer of the yellow dress.'

There was a pause.

'I don't think I'm familiar with that,' said Patterson.

Clarke smiled. 'There was a market up in Haidian, near the Beijing University campus. And that summer one of the stalls started selling a little cotton dress in bright yellow. And it sat there for a few weeks, no one daring to try it. I mean the girls had moved on from baggy Mao suits by then. They were wearing blouses and sensible trousers. But the idea of a dress that showed your legs, and your shoulders! And in bright yellow! *Scandale!* And then some brave soul bought one and wore it. And before you knew it the campuses were blooming with these gorgeous girls in stunning canary yellow. The stall couldn't keep up with demand. And then someone bought one in red! And the girls started moving and holding themselves differently.' She let her hands weave gracefully through the air. 'They were suddenly *women*, not Communists.'

She paused and gestured to Patterson.

'We work our whole lives, don't we, looking for that shard of information, that secret, which has – what did we call it? – predictive value. A signpost. A precursor to understanding. And sometimes it's staring us in the face. And because it's not secret we ignore it. That yellow dress told us that a whole climate of belief and behaviour was giving way to something new. And the new – when it came – would be bright and sexy and young. But we had *no* idea of its significance.'

She was tiring now, Patterson could see.

'How did it end, Sonia?'

'I hardly know. We saw less and less of Peanut. The others seemed to lose interest. They all watched that television series, *River Elegy*, and it was as if they'd found religion. *We must tear down the walls, Sonia. We are strangled by isolation, suffocated by a cruel and grandiose culture. Stunted by chauvinism. Modernity, Sonia!* They all declared themselves for democracy. Poor loves. I contacted Peanut directly. Late eighty-eight, I suppose. Activated a meeting by letter. We were supposed to prepare for handover to a new case officer. Fat chance. He had the grace to turn up, but it was only to end it. *Go away, Sonia. This is my cause now. You're not relevant.* And that was that. And by the following April he was demonstrating on Tiananmen Square. They all were.'

'What happened to him, Sonia?'

Clarke spoke very quietly. 'I don't know. When the troops moved in to clear the square, June third, we thought he was arrested. But he vanished so completely. No notice of any trial. Word got out about where a lot of those arrested got sent, but no one ever mentioned Peanut. Did he die in custody? His sister said he was in labour reform up in the north-west. But I don't know if it was ever confirmed.'

'He's back, Sonia,' said Patterson.

'I thought he might be.'

'We don't know if he's real.'

'Did he use the word "lotus"?'

Patterson paused, calculating.

'Yes. Yes, he did.'

Sonia Clarke looked towards the window, the gathering darkness.

'Oh, they'd never turn Peanut.'

She drove back to London in darkness, thought of agents she'd run. The little Iraqi boy in Nasiriyah, a runner for the local hoods, stubby teeth, eyes like torches, riding his moped barefoot between insurgent safe houses. Lieutenant Patterson had put a tracking beacon under his rear mudguard, which delivered the exact coordinates of every local nasty, superb operational intelligence. For about three weeks. And when they found the boy, on a rubbish dump outside town, his fingers were gone, and someone had taken to his head with a power drill. She turned the radio on.

At Archway, she let herself into the house. Damian, from downstairs, was in the hallway, checking the mail. He gave her a mock salute.

'Captain Sensible. You're late tonight.' Damian, who worked in an advertising agency, knew that Patterson shuffled paper in an administrative backwater of the Foreign Office. In a moment of Chablis-induced weakness, she had told him of her army background. She brushed past him.

'Night, Damian.'

She could feel him watching her as she climbed the stairs.

'You look tense, Trish. Come in. Have a bowl of soup.'

'Night, Damian.'

Her flat was freezing. She turned on the heat and sat on the sofa. The news showed bombings somewhere, the brown dust, the screaming widows. She put her hand to her chest to calm the sharp-clawed, squirming thing that lived there.

14

Yunnan Province

They left the car and walked the last half-mile, Harvey with the camera and run bag, Mangan carrying the tripod on his shoulder. The track was steep and Mangan broke into a sweat even though the air at this altitude was crisp. To their left, terraced paddy fields swept down to an emerald valley floor, morning mist just burning off. The village clung to the side of the mountain, weathered wooden houses, chickens in mud alleyways, posters warning of HIV, slogans on the walls in white characters a foot high: STABILITY OVERRIDES EVERYTHING. A woman in a faded grey tunic stopped sweeping and watched them pass.

The contact who was supposed to take them into the village hadn't turned up. They'd sat and waited in a peeling hot pot restaurant in Kunming, trying the phone, but it never answered. At Mangan's insistence, they had come anyway, stopping and asking directions, leaving a trail, Harvey shaking his head and following reluctantly. Now they were here, the village closed and silent.

Mangan looked around.

'I'd guess we've got half an hour before someone blabs to someone we're here. Can you just start?'

Harvey said nothing, took the tripod from Mangan's shoulder easily, set it down and clicked the camera into place.

Mangan turned and walked between the silent houses. Up ahead the pinched cry of an infant. Mangan walked towards it. Through a doorway he could see two women kneeling by a fire, a cooking pot suspended over it. One was peeling some sort of root vegetable with a knife. The other held the child. Mangan knocked on the door jamb. The two women turned, startled. The one with the child stood up and backed away into the gloom.

'Good morning,' Mangan said, in slow Mandarin.

The women said nothing, watching him.

'I am sorry to disturb you. Could I come in?'

Still nothing. Mangan gingerly entered the room.

'Are you Followers of the Master?'

The standing woman, holding the child, said something fast to the other in a dialect Mangan could not understand.

The kneeling woman, knife in hand, tipped her chin at Mangan. *Who are you?*

'I am a journalist. I want to find out what happened to your husbands.'

The woman put the knife down.

'Why's it your business?' She was trying to speak Mandarin. Mangan could feel out the sense of it.

'Someone told me your husbands were taken away because they followed the Master.'

The woman with the child spoke again, sharper now. She turned to Mangan, raised her hand and moved it from side to side. *No.* Her eyes were red and crusted – some sort of infection.

'Can you help us?' said the kneeling woman.

'If you tell me what happened it might help,' said Mangan.

'How will it help?'

'When did the police come?' said Mangan.

The woman looked down. 'They told us this is a political problem.' *Zhengzhi wenti.* 'We mustn't talk about it.'

Mangan sensed some of the light disappear from the room, and turned. A man was blocking the doorway, silhouetted against the sun so Mangan could not see his features.

'*Ni ya. Gan ma?*' You. What are you doing? A hard tone, which Mangan didn't like.

'We're just talking,' said Mangan.

The woman with the child started speaking fast, gesturing at Mangan.

The man walked into the room, over to the kneeling woman, leant down and took hold of her arm. She looked at the floor. He pulled her to her feet and said something quietly into her ear, then looked at Mangan. He was broad-shouldered, wore a white shirt. He didn't work in the fields. Or perhaps he had once.

'I'm very sorry to have disturbed you,' said Mangan. He began to move towards the door.

'She's very sorry, too,' the man said.

Mangan stepped out into the sunlight. He could see Harvey, gesticulating. Two other men stood next to him, one had a hand on the camera.

Mangan walked towards him. 'We're leaving, Harv. Now.' Harvey tried to pick up the camera, but the man wouldn't let go.

'You don't have any permit to be here,' said the man.

'We're leaving,' said Mangan.

'You can't leave.'

'We're going to go and get a permit.'

The men both laughed.

'The women here talk shit,' said the other man. 'You shouldn't believe them.'

'They said nothing to us.'

'Let's hope so.' He looked over Mangan's shoulder. Mangan

turned and saw the man in the white shirt emerging from the house, leading the woman. He held her upper arm and her wrist. They walked in the other direction and disappeared around a corner.

Mangan turned back around and held his hands out, tried to speak forcefully.

'Really, she said she couldn't talk to me.'

The men did not reply, just looked at him. Mangan tried again, nearly shouting now.

'Who are you? What's your work unit?'

One of them gave the camera a heave and it toppled over and fell into the dust.

When they reached the bottom of the hill, their car and driver had gone.

They walked to the next village, carrying the equipment, Mangan trembling with anger, Harvey silent. They found a boy in a T-shirt who agreed to drive them back to Kunming in his van at exorbitant cost. Mangan had to sit in the back, on a mat.

It was cool, late evening as they pulled into the city. They paid off the boy, found a food stall near the lake, sat on tiny three-legged stools and ate chicken wings crisp-fried in Yunnan peppers, and noodles in a clear broth, ladled into chipped bowls by a quiet, smiling man who asked them gentle questions about where they came from. He gave them a fiery, clear liquor poured from a bottle filled with ginseng root. Mangan's phone rang.

'So how was it?' Ting, expectant.

'Catastrophe. Busted. We got nothing.'

'Oh.'

'It's not your fault.'

'Okay.'

'Honestly, it's not.'

Harvey gestured for the phone.

'Ting, it's Harv. Not your fault. Nothing we could do. Honest.'

Ting was speaking, Harvey listened.

'No. Nothing to be done, sweetheart. Except for sacking the two of us. Or starting a revolution. Yeah. Yeah. Bye.' He handed the phone back to Mangan. Ting was still on the line.

'There's one more thing, Philip. Check your mail. Some people called from Singapore. They want you to fly there. Some sort of conference? They've sent you an invitation.'

'What people?'

'Um, Pan Asia Institute for International Affairs. But it's short notice, so you must reply.'

'Never heard of them.'

'Me neither. Check your mail. Philip, I'm really sorry.'

'Not your fault.'

They walked back to the hotel in silence, the disappointment weighing on them. Behind it, guilt.

Dear Mr Mangan,

I take great pleasure in inviting you to participate in a small conference we're holding here at the Pan Asia Institute later this week.

The title of the conference is 'China: Stability Hopes, Security Challenges'.

Many at our institute are aware of your groundbreaking reporting on challenges to Party authority of late and would welcome an on-the-ground media perspective.

We hope you would provide us with a short (thirty- to forty-five-minute) presentation, to be followed by a round-table discussion with fellows and scholars.

The institute is able to offer a small honorarium, and we will of course carry the cost of business class travel and

accommodations. We do apologise for the short notice, and
hope very much you are able to join us.

Yours sincerely,

Marissa Leung

Director, External Relations

Pan Asia Institute for International Affairs

Ting had booked his ticket to Singapore for him and then
insisted he accompany her to the theatre. They left the apartment
in a cold, wet sunset of slate and gold, took a cab.

The theatre was in Zhongguancun, an inauspicious doorway
between two computer stores. In the basement, a dark boxy
space with hard wooden seats. Ting led him in by the hand. She
was wearing black boots of mock snakeskin, her silver quilted
jacket, a hat of grey fur with earflaps; all with such ease, thought
Mangan. Three or four people greeted her as she walked in. One,
a tousled artist in a green army overcoat – its own fashion state-
ment in this place, tonight – gave her an exaggerated imperial
bow, hands clasped before him. She smiled, kissed him and
introduced Mangan. The artist feigned amazement. *Foreign journalist, everyone! Quick, prepare to be closed down!* There was
laughter, which Mangan joined in.

'If only I had such influence with the authorities,' he said, in
Mandarin.

The artist smiled. 'Really, it's good to see you. Do you think
you might write something?'

'Not if it will close you down.'

'Well, perhaps just be delicate, yes? The authorities have, well,
noticed us, and we're living on our nerves a bit here. The last
thing we need is to be celebrated in a western newspaper.'

He grinned, and Mangan thought of the woman led away in the
village and felt a hollowness in his stomach, forced a smile. Ting,
only partially understanding his discomfort, leaned in to him.

'Poor Philip,' she said. 'Such noble intentions, yet all China mistrusts you.'

The play was extraordinary. Two performers costumed as Red Guards danced the dances of the revolutionary operas from the high days of Maoism, against a pounding beat. But their heroic posturing degenerated into the hypnotic, angular shuffle of characters in a video game, revolution refracted into digital dream. Above them, on an enormous screen, their avatars danced through a virtual China, rendered in the style of a game, its point of view dipping, twirling through rolling seas of banknotes, vast imagined structures against an ice-blue digital sky, fractured urban landscapes littered with soft toys, superheroes, anime characters. The digital and real dances converged and parted, the performers dwarfed by the virtual dance behind them, and Mangan found something deeply poignant in their disintegrating revolutionary postures, shadows against the screen.

Afterwards they all went to a dim Guizhou place with walls of slatted bamboo. Ting ordered fish in an ochre soup of deep, rich sourness, blindingly sharp pickles. They smoked and gossiped animatedly about Beijing's arts scene, the scandals, the love affairs and, sometimes, the arrests. Mangan listened to the sharp playfulness of it, the Beijing wryness. The tousled artist told a story of an underground exhibition of conceptual art. Its chief exhibit – *event of the season!* – had been a one-day installation of live seafood, crayfish and eels suspended by thread, twirling and writhing in the air. The police, confused, assumed the installation to be subversive and closed it down, ushering Beijing's demi-monde from the gallery.

'What happened to the seafood?' said Ting.

'Well, that's the thing,' said the artist. 'The police confiscated the lot and ate it.'

They screamed with laughter and thumped the table. *Tai bang le!* Too perfect! Mangan ordered more beers and the artist turned to him. He was not drunk, but getting there. He looked hard at Mangan.

'So, that's us. Molluscs, video art, ways of seeing and interpreting. But we're fucked, because everything we see and interpret is at the Party's pleasure. But what are you? What are you part of?'

Everyone at the table was watching Mangan.

'Well, I see and interpret,' he said. 'But I do it for a newspaper, for television.'

'Yes, I've watched television,' said the artist.

Mangan took another swallow of beer.

'Journalists like to say that we're writing the rough draft of history,' he said.

'Do you believe that?'

'Sometimes.'

'Why are *you* writing the rough draft of *my* history?'

'I'm not writing it for you. I'm writing it for people in Europe and America. Anyway, no one owns history, do they?'

'Why don't they want to see my rough draft of history?' The artist was lighting another cigarette. 'I've a sculpture. The Great Wall in mixed media, wire and animal skins. That's rough history. But no one will exhibit it.'

'I'm sure they would in London,' said Mangan.

'Fuck them in London. Have you ever been arrested?'

'Yes.'

'But they let you go.'

'Yes.'

'They let you go because you don't matter. You realise that, don't you?'

Mangan shook his head.

'They let me go because it would be too much trouble to keep me.'

The artist waved a hand dismissively.

'If you mattered, they wouldn't let you go.'

He thought suddenly of the bristle-haired man, his insistence, the weight of his words. Only you, Mang An. Why do I matter to him? he thought.

They waited for a taxi. A few snowflakes swirled in the headlights. Ting took his arm.

'Was that okay?' she said.

'I loved the performance. And your friends are, um, exciting.'

'They are, what do you say, self-involved.'

'No, I admire them. They take risks.'

She looked at him, half-smiling.

'You're thoughtful.'

'I'm fine,' he said.

A taxi came and they drove across Beijing, back to the city centre. Mangan told the driver to go to Ting's apartment block. She took his hand.

'Come up. I'll make you ginger tea,' she said, then kissed him softly. 'And for breakfast, rice porridge with pig's ears.'

Patterson passed Hopko the telegram from Charteris.

'It's brief.'

'Is this all he's got?' said Hopko. She stirred a cup of coffee. Patterson read.

/REPORT

1/ Philip MANGAN is in his mid-thirties. He has worked in Beijing for four years as a freelance reporter. He is accredited with the Chinese government – as all foreign reporters must be – for a major newspaper. He files for other outlets, too, including for a small London-based production house that syndicates news footage to television networks in several countries. His reputation in Beijing among other journalists is that of an independent-minded and original reporter. He has not sought a secure staff position with a major media organisation, claiming to prefer the freedom that freelancing brings.

2/ MANGAN grew up in Orpington, Kent, the only son of a doctor and a housewife. Both parents are deceased. He attended private schools and University College London, where he studied Politics. He took courses in Mandarin Chinese at the School of Oriental and African Studies. His spoken Chinese is proficient.

3/ MANGAN's reporting tends to foreground the political and social aspects of China's development. He reports less on economics or business, and there is little quantitative work in his reporting. He has focused particularly on human rights issues, state repression of religious and ethnic identities, and incidents of social unrest. It may be that, as a freelance, he is merely satisfying market demand for the 'scary China' narrative. But while the agenda he adheres to may tend towards the sensational, his treatment of the material generally does not. His stories are – for the most part – balanced and well-researched, though he can be impetuous. Two years ago he incorrectly reported the demise of a senior Politburo member, an error the Chinese government found hard to forgive, and his editors found even harder. He has been detained by the authorities on a number of occasions, and is ready to test the boundaries of their tolerance. He appears frustrated at the limits of what a foreign journalist can achieve in China.

4/ MANGAN employs a part-time assistant, named ZHAO Ting, a PRC national. ZHAO Ting, who is well-connected and comes from a wealthy Beijing family, provides him with many of his leads and handles administration and payment –

something at which MANGAN is hopelessly inept, by his own admission.

5/ MANGAN works with a freelance cameraman named Paul HARVEY, an Australian national. HARVEY is a well-liked figure in East Asian media circles, and his decision to work with MANGAN lends the latter a certain cachet.

6/ MANGAN is something of a loner. He appears to have no strong roots or links to any one place. He drinks moderately and may use soft drugs. He pays little attention to his personal appearance and gives the impression that he is unimpressed by what others may see as the glamorous side of his work as a foreign correspondent. However, he does have an ego, and while he would never admit it, craves professional recognition.

7/ MANGAN may prove a difficult target for recruitment. He has the finely tuned antennae of the professional reporter and will quickly recognise an approach for what it is. His sense of professional journalistic ethics will militate against accepting, but may not prove an insuperable obstacle. Money may help, since he appears constantly short of it. But his desire for recognition and his sense of frustration at the limitations of journalism may provide a case officer with an avenue to secure his cooperation.

/ENDS

'Money, vanity, frustration. Well, thank you, Charteris,' said Hopko.

Patterson drew her travel documents, passport, credit card. She'd be using the 'Rachel Davies' identity.

Mangan was ironing a shirt. A suitcase lay open on the bed. He heard the door slam and Harvey talking animatedly to Ting. A pause, then a howl. He walked into the front room. Harvey lay slumped on the sofa, pointing. Ting was holding up a copy of the *Trib*.

China's long and controversial campaign to suppress new religious sects has entered a new, intense phase.

Security authorities have established a secret network of isolation camps in which young male adherents of banned religions are detained indefinitely.

It was a good piece, Mangan saw, thoroughly reported. It had satellite images of the camps, their locations, eyewitness accounts, and reaction from the US and Europe. He knew the byline, a Hong Kong-based correspondent who came in and out of the mainland.

'Scooped,' said Harvey. 'Scooped to buggery.'

Ting laughed, but then bit her lip and gave Mangan a wide-eyed look.

'Sorry, Philip,' she said.

He shrugged, tossed the paper over his shoulder, and it landed on the floor.

'There goes the Pulitzer,' he said.

'Get him,' said Harvey. 'The man who didn't care.'

Ting looked puzzled.

'I thought you'd be upset,' she said.

'Nope,' said Mangan.

She looked at him quizzically.

'You are upset, aren't you.'

He rubbed a hand across his face.

'Bollocks. Yes, a bit.'

'Well, I'm so fucking upset, I'm going out for lunch,' said Harvey, and stood up.

He and Ting took Mangan by the arms and marched him out of the bureau, a coat over his head, Harvey kicking the door shut behind him. They went to a little bistro in the Sheraton and drank an absurdly priced bottle of Sancerre.

Later, back at the bureau, Ting dozed on the sofa and Mangan frantically finished packing and then it was time to go to the airport. Ting held him lazily for a few moments, smiling, her eyes closed, and let her lips brush his cheek and then waved him away.

A town car, the driver called it, not a limo. Mangan's mistake. But it was big and black and air-conditioned and waiting for him when he landed at Changi. The passenger in the back was provided with mints and bottled water and a weighty, glossy magazine called *Elite: Excellence in Business Travel*, whose reporters spared no effort in bringing to the demanding reader the very latest in spas, boutique resorts and thread counts. After thumbing it for a few minutes Mangan decided his personal favourite was the 'Happenings' section. *Delors Luxe Global Ambassador Shelley Kwok poses with Lars Nesser of Island Oriental Hotels at Orchard charity fundraiser.* In the photo, a minute and leathery woman of indeterminate age leaned into a heavy, pale man in a cummerbund. They held champagne glasses, and were joyously startled by the camera flash and their own good fortune. *Astrid Van Sittart, co-founder of Luxe Connection Brand Development with friends at Bali Tide launch.* Astrid, lithe and Eurasian, in strapless dress and chunky silver jewellery, was overjoyed to be with her friends. Pages and pages of it. The car hissed through light, quiet traffic, beneath overpasses covered in ivy. Ah, Singapore.

The 'conference' was indeed small, intimate even. Twelve people sat at a long table in fierce air-conditioning. Mangan fought his way through notes he'd scribbled that morning: *The Followers – Rebels or Reactionaries?* Polite applause. Questions, mostly earnest, mostly tinged with sympathy for the Communist Party's legal position if not its methods. 'Surely, Mr Mangan,' came one, 'the exigencies of maintaining stability?' The audience was largely Singaporean, politely distrustful of the western reporter's motives. An Australian worthy was in the chair – formerly, Mangan remembered, he had been something big in ASIO, Australian Security and Intelligence.

At the far end of the table was a quiet woman, British, Mangan guessed. Tall, straight-backed and black, in a severe grey suit. Her eyes, which never left him, were like flint.

When it was over the Australian mumbled his apologies and handed him off to the Brit, who stood patiently, waiting for the after-chat to finish.

'That was fascinating, Mr Mangan,' she said. She introduced herself as Rachel Davies and produced a card that gave her affiliation as United Kingdom Foreign and Commonwealth Office, Research Department. She gave a tight smile.

'I was hoping we might be able to meet for dinner,' she said. Mangan, surprised, heard it as something like an order.

The restaurant was called Du Fu, after the poet. They sat in a discreet booth of black leather and etched glass. The Foreign Office ordered rather well, Mangan noticed. Tiny, trembling dumplings, towers of silky duck and taro root. And then lobster and bamboo in nests of crisp noodles. Eels in ginger.

'Well, it's a pleasure to meet you. I've followed your work,' said Rachel Davies, with the warmth of a steel rail. Mangan mentally put inverted commas round her name. 'Rachel Davies', drinking sparkling water. What on earth does she want? he thought. Is she always this uptight? They talked about the Followers, life in Beijing, pollution levels, press corps gossip. 'Rachel Davies' was doing her best to be fascinated by all of it. Yes, thank you, Mangan would have a second glass of wine.

'Now please forgive me, Mr Mangan, but I'm going to talk shop with you for a moment.'

Mangan waited.

'The fact is, you've caused a bit of a stir.'

'Have I? How?'

'David Charteris is careful. He wanted to be sure about a few things, so he showed that document to one or two people.'

What?

'And, well, a stir,' said 'Rachel Davies'.

'He said he was going to give it to the Embassy Security Officer,' Mangan said. 'He said it was for my own good.'

'Yes, and he did, of course.' A tepid smile. 'The thing is, people who understand these things say that the document appears to be important.'

Another pause. Mangan fought the impulse to respond, and let the silence stretch out. The woman smoothed her hair, sat even straighter.

'We rather assumed you'd want to write the story.'

Mangan felt as if he needed time he didn't have.

'And what is the story?' he said.

She looked surprised. One elbow on the table, she framed a headline with her fingers.

'Oh, come on, Philip. Chinese missile programme far more advanced than thought. DF-41 in testing. East Asia, Europe, America all thrown for a bloody great loop.' She looked expectantly at him.

Mangan spoke slowly.

'Is this really news to the UK government? Or anyone else? I'd be surprised if it were.'

'Rachel Davies', or whatever her name was, leaned in again, serious now.

'Well, that's the thing. It *is* news to us, you see. And we are way off the record now. We haven't seen a blind, bloody thing about the DF-41 for years. We thought it had gone away. And now you come along with your mysterious visitor and his bit of paper.'

Mangan's mouth felt a little dry; he took a sip of water. She went on.

'And as I'm sure you know, Philip, it's more than just a new, shiny toy, isn't it? If it works, the DF-41 will be able to hit Europe. And Los Angeles. It can carry multiple warheads. It's road mobile, which means it's a second-strike weapon. Sounds a bit like a strategic nuclear capability to me. Like what the Americans and the Russians have, and even us. Might this not be China stepping up, Philip? Reaching for superpower status? What do you think?'

She was unsmiling.

'All right,' Mangan said. 'If that's true, if the Chinese are building a missile that changes the game, and we don't know about it, it's a very good story. I would want to write it. But I don't have any means of confirming whether the document is genuine. So no story.'

She nodded.

'Well, exactly. And Her Majesty's Government is in the same position. We don't know if the bloody document is genuine either. So I wonder if we might be able to help each other a little.'

'And how would we do that?'

'It's not uncommon for your kind and mine to collaborate a little.'

Not so uncommon, Mangan knew. Though such offers of collaboration had never come to him. Until now.

'Why would you do that?' he said.

'Because if this story is going to run, we would rather it ran in a way we can live with, at a time of our choosing.'

Here's the rub, thought Mangan.

'So I write the story, but not yet,' he said.

'That's part of it.'

Mangan had the sense of a scene reaching its climax. She went on.

'Like you, Philip, we need to know if this document is

genuine. So we need to know the source. Who is he and where did he get it?' She left it hanging, reached for a piece of duck and glistening taro root.

Mangan blinked.

'You want me to go back to him,' he said.

'How else, would you say?'

'You've got his number. It's on the letter that Charteris stole. Give him a tinkle.'

'Not sure Her Majesty's Government can quite do that, Philip. Easier for you, though. You're a reporter.'

'One minute you've Charteris telling me I'm at terrible risk and prattling about his duty. And the next you want me to go back to him.'

She didn't reply immediately, just rested her dark eyes on him. He returned the gaze. Her expression didn't change.

'Philip, it will be your story, and they'll read it in the Cabinet Office. And Number Ten. And the Pentagon. And the White House. The people who count. It's a scoop, Philip, the sort that comes along once or twice in a career, and it matters. The work of a really serious journalist. And it's yours. If you want it.'

'I can't handle any documents.'

'You won't have to. Just ask him who he is, Philip. And how he got that cover sheet. We'll do the rest, and we'll tell you what it all means, and when the time is right, it'll be your story.'

Mangan felt her eyes on him. He fought to slow down.

'This is . . . a risk.'

'Rachel Davies' was absorbed in picking up a piece of lobster. She cleared her throat.

'I thought you chaps, reporters, took the odd risk, sometimes.'

Mangan could sense her hard, silent laughter.

He walked to clear his head, down past Boat Quay, the music and laughter from the bars clattering into the street, light rippling on the water. Clutches of brokers from the big trading houses stood holding bottles of lager, raucous in the night. He walked to the end of the quay, smelled the sea.

What on earth *was* that? Had he just been pitched? Who was she?

We know who she was, Mangan thought. And, yes, he had just been pitched.

So. 'A little collaboration'. Was the story worth it? Well, yes. It would be a series of front-page pieces for the paper, no doubt, and much more besides. It would be a moody analytical piece in an influential journal; a muscular op-ed in the States. It was hot and cold running interviews on radio and TV and the net. It was a scoop, and everyone loves a scoop.

A little collaboration. Is that all they were offering? She had given him a London phone number. *But best to talk to David Charteris for now. Let him know what you're up to. Tell him when you're going to meet the source, won't you? That's important, isn't it? Don't go to meetings like that without telling someone in advance.*

He searched his feelings, as he stood there, Singapore's warm, wet night against his skin, and turned over all the reasons for gracefully declining. A journalist does not sell his birthright. A journalist is immune to the blandishments of the establishment. A journalist is too busy telling the truth.

Or trying to. And failing.

He looked for a cab, and there was one waiting. Its lights flickered on and its engine started just as he reached the kerb.

Patterson made straight for the High Commission, swiped herself into the station, got on a secure line to London, to Hopko, who was abrupt. She wondered whether Yeats was listening in.

'What did you make of him?'

'I'm not sure, to be honest. Erratic, self-involved. A journalist, in other words. But I think he's tempted.'

'Is he capable?'

'I don't doubt he's capable. He's bright. He knows Beijing, and he has a notion of security, how it works. He could act as access agent, if he were willing.'

'But is he willing? Or will he write about us in the Sunday supplements?'

'That I can't tell you. Yet.'

'I think he'll do it. They usually do, the journalists, can't resist a bit of action,' said Hopko. 'And, Trish, I think it's time to get Granny Poon moving.'

In the P section it was agreed that the All China Moulded Plastics Industry Expo could not have been better timed. And to Patterson, back in the office straight from the airport, fell the task of urging Yip Lo Exports Inc. of Kowloon to attend.

This she had done – a salad by her side on the desk – by leaving a message in an obscure password-protected corner of the company's website. A representative of Yip Lo, closing up the office on Soy Street for the day, made a last routine check and found the message waiting. He read it and knew to act immediately. The protocol was to visit a commercial email provider at a particular time. There waited a second message, placed in the Drafts folder just moments earlier. Attached, a file. Yip Lo's representative opened and read the attached file on a laptop computer that was kept locked in a safe. The safe did double duty as an altar, bearing a shrine to Guan Yin, the Bodhisattva of Compassion, in the Poon family home. The attached file could be read only by using certain software that was not commercially available. The software frequently infuriated the representatives of Yip Lo Exports with its elephantine slowness.

In this case the message was brief. Would representatives of Yip Lo please make their way to Beijing, reside in certain hotels, attend the All China Moulded Plastics Industry Expo, and await contact using prearranged methods. On reading the message the representative of Yip Lo – a small but industrious exporter of plastic flowers, tablecloths and novelties to European retailers – understood that he should move fast, book tickets, reserve rooms and start to check his back.

The representative of Yip Lo closed and deleted the file and replaced the computer in the safe beneath the protective gaze of Guan Yin. He stood, stretched and looked from the window – the Poon apartment was on the eighteenth floor for luck – across to Hong Kong island, where the big Chinese bank buildings paraded in the night.

And then the company representative got to work. For the Poon family – matriarch Eileen, known as Granny Poon, majority stakeholder in Yip Lo Exports Inc. of Kowloon and smoker of small, foul Indian beedis; her sons Frederick and Peter; and a cousin Winston – were a small treasure of British Intelligence. Patterson had read their personnel files repeatedly. The Poons were venal, loyal, quiet and the best street artists in Asia.

They had to be. If they were anything less, China's Ministry of State Security would have found them and shot them by now.

15

Beijing

Evening, and Mangan was in the midst of a ghastly but lucrative commission for an Italian television station via the agency. Some starlet, promoting a fashion and perfumery line launching in China, simpering at a big hotel. Harvey was grinning. An officious little flack in heels pointed them to a spot on the carpet, behind a rope. Harvey muttered obscenities under his breath. Ting carried the tripod on her shoulder, loving it, her evening just beginning. Harvey followed the starlet in, then tilted up and down the dress – aquamarine, taffeta, said the flack, as Mangan wrote despairing notes – the shoes, the smile. Mangan, in a blue blazer that had seen years of cruel and degrading treatment, waved a microphone at her. She gave her spiel, first in Italian, then English. Her lips were plump and pink and glistening, but her breath smelled of something sharp and chemical.

Afterwards Harvey and Ting packed up in raucous good humour, chiding Mangan for his terrible interviewing. But Mangan left them dealing with the lights and cables, walked out into the street and lit a cigarette. He took out his mobile phone.

'Charteris.'

'I've a bone to pick with you.'

'Philip! Welcome back! Let's pick it over together.'

'Where do you suggest? For the picking?'

'My dear chap. Hyatt. Rooftop bar. We'll pick in comfort. Does right away suit?'

Midnight. The hotel was a marble air-conditioned nowhere. Charteris was in a corner of the empty bar on a leather banquette. He sat in shadow, so Mangan could not make out his features. He flapped an arm as Mangan loped in.

'I'm drinking vodka. Lots. Have one?'

Mangan nodded assent. The vodka was cold, shot with lime.

'So, David. I've been to Singapore.'

'Fascinating chaps down there at the Pan Asia Institute, I hear,' said Charteris. 'Terribly on the ball.' A sardonic smile.

'Odd, David, that a Foreign Office type – a close associate of yours, I got the sense – should show up like that.'

Charteris said nothing, smiled.

'You took those documents and sent them back to London, didn't you?'

'Yes.' Charteris affected a patient expression.

'I rather get the impression that they ... I mean, this is not what I do.'

'What's not what you do?'

'They want me to try to establish the source.'

'But that is exactly what you do, isn't it? If you're going to write the story, you must establish the source, mustn't you? Philip, this is an ever so slightly precarious topic for discussion in public.'

'I won't be used.'

Charteris leaned forward, the humour gone.

'Oh, come on, Philip, don't be so bloody precious.'

'I'm not being precious. I do not want to get mixed up in something.'

'Oh, really. Well, what can I say, Philip, that will stiffen your nerve a little?' Charteris was speaking fast now, urgently, quietly. 'You have made an impression on them, Philip. They have decided to let you inside the wire a little. Rashly, I recommended they do so. That doesn't happen often, Philip, and it's a two-way street. Get a little, give a little. Don't fuck it up.' Mangan, startled, made to speak but stopped himself.

'When are you going to call him?' said Charteris.

Mangan still said nothing.

'Do not meet him without telling me. No phones. Tell me in person.'

Charteris was formal, cold almost. Then he stopped, and relaxed. The smile returned.

'Look, Philip, you'll have a big one in the favour bank if you do this. And if you do it soon. It will work for you. Just let me know, okay?' And then he was gone, his jacket slung over his shoulder, and Mangan sat alone, staring through the glass at the shimmering glow over Beijing.

Peanut lay awake. The storeroom was cold. He had dozed for a while, sunken in the half-place between sleep and waking, where memories of his father floated. A summer morning in the Fragrant Hills, the forest, a rocky path. Dappled light, the pulsing whirr of the cicadas. His father's pale hands held out a frond picked from a bush. A finger run down the stem made all the leaves curl and close.

He felt the thrum of the mobile phone before he heard it. The phone lay next to his pillow. The glowing screen cast a silver light around the storeroom. Peanut reached and clicked the answer key.

'Yes?'

'This is the journalist, the British journalist, you spoke to.'

'I know.'

'I need to speak to you again.'

'Yes, you do.'

'Where can we meet?'

'The Zhihua Temple. Tomorrow. Four in the afternoon. I'll find you.'

Silence.

'Have you got that?'

'Yes.'

Peanut turned, pulled the blanket up.

'Do my friends know I'm here?' he said into the mobile phone.

'What?'

'Do they know?'

Then just the digital *pip* and silence.

Patterson stumbled into the kitchen, searching for her shrieking phone.

Three-thirty in the morning. Saturday. Christ.

'Trish? Val. Office. Now.'

She ran on to the Holloway Road in jeans and trainers and her green Intelligence Corps sweatshirt, her breath steaming in the pre-dawn air. And, miracle of miracles, found a taxi, emptied by some late-night clubbers spilling on to the pavement.

She made the driver drop her on the Embankment. She jogged across the bridge, towards the angular greenish glow of headquarters. By 4.17 she was swiping her pass, the tall green gates closing behind her, hurrying past the bicycle racks and little trimmed box hedges and into the building.

Hopko was already in the operations suite. No make-up, hair tied back in a scarf; was that a tracksuit? On one screen, Charteris, coming in on a secure video link from Beijing Station.

On another, a map of east-central Beijing, with points plotted in red. On a third, a list of telephone numbers, matched to code-names GODDESS 1 to 4. On a fourth, the T2 IOP visualisation software. Patterson logged on and started working her way through the telegram traffic. A round-shouldered technician was playing with incoming telephone lines.

Then Yeats was there, in a T-shirt and fleece, all questions and rubbing of hands.

'C'mon then, Val, what do we have?'

'The meeting is in three hours.' She pointed to the map. 'RATCHET has to walk from his apartment here to the temple, here. About half a mile. The surveillance will make an initial pass of the temple in a while. Granny Poon will go in and have a look around. Two of the boys outside, one back-up ready to roam. Afternoon there, nice weather, sunny cold day.'

'So the main thing is just to get a sight of him, yes, the contact?'

Hopko looked fixedly at the screen.

'Well, more if we can, I think, Roly. If all's clear, Granny Poon and the boys will try to pick him up and go home with him. See where he bunks. But they won't overdo it.'

'Comms?'

'Pay as you go mobile phones, Roly, newly bought, one use only, then we'll get rid of them. They call the local number, we encrypt and route through fibre.'

'Right, right. Absolutely. And RATCHET? Up for it, is he?' said Yeats.

Hopko looked at the Beijing screen. 'David?'

'He said he would do this for us, but only this. Very earnest.' Charteris's voice was thin, the encryption lending it a digital tinnitus. 'But I think he's fine. It's not like he hasn't met a sensitive contact in Beijing before. He'll be fine.'

Yeats thought for a moment.

'Does he mean it, when he says this is all he'll do for us?'
Charteris looked to camera.

'No.'

Yeats smiled.

'Good, good. Right, then. Who's for coffee?' He bustled out.
Patterson watched him go and then caught Hopko and Charteris
frowning at each other down the video link. Hopko held up her
hands.

'Don't ask me, David, I don't know why he's here.'

'But, Val.'

'I don't know, David.'

Charteris could be seen shaking his head. Then he got up and
moved out of shot.

Hopko grinned at Patterson.

'*Carpe diem*, Trish. What *is* that horrible bloody sweatshirt
you're wearing?'

In a grey-walled alleyway of east-central Beijing, an elderly
woman moved through the bright, cold afternoon. She wore a
long quilted winter coat of nondescript colour and ancient vin-
tage, and a blue woollen hat pulled low over her brow. Her scarf
rode up, obscuring her jawline and the lower part of her face.
What could be seen of her features revealed a complexion a little
more sallow than that of the pale *Beijing ren*. A southerner, perhaps. Or a face from the emerald hills and rivers of central China.
Hunan? Somewhere damper, more lush than this dusty north
China plain, where the grit gets in your rice, under your nails,
between your teeth. Her eyes were dark and narrow, preoccupied. Of short stature, this lady, but erect, wilfulness in her walk.
She carried a plain canvas bag, with a little shopping perhaps, a
change purse, diary, tissues.

At the gate of the Zhihua Temple the woman lingered for a
moment, apparently considering something, a change of plan.

The temple, the elderly lady knew, was no longer a functioning place of worship, the monks long gone. The brass plaque at its gate informed her that it was now administered by the Cultural Relics Bureau. The temple had been saved, the woman remembered, from the wrecking infants of the Cultural Revolution by Prime Minister Zhou Enlai himself. Now it was home to a troupe of earnest, impoverished musicians who spent their days reconstructing the haunting ritual melodies of ancient China, to the annoyance of those who lived in the neighbourhood. Opening hours: ten a.m. to five p.m. Admission five yuan.

The woman stepped back a pace. She looked at her watch and placed a finger to her lips, considering. She reached into her canvas bag and withdrew a small purse, from which she took a five-yuan note. She paid the attendant and stepped into the first courtyard.

The elderly woman wandered round the temple for perhaps fifteen minutes, through the Drum Pavilion, the Ten Thousand Buddha Pavilion. A marvel! The strange black roofs sweeping skyward, the sculpted dragons and owls atop them. No other visitors today. She was alone.

After a while she sat on the steps and took out her mobile phone.

On the screen a green sphere next to GODDESS 1 began to blink. The technician leaned over and tapped it, the click of fingernail on plastic in the silent suite.

'Connected to GODDESS 1.'

Hopko leaned towards the console.

'*Wei?*'

'*Wei? Wo lai le. Lai chi feng le ya! Tianqi zhen hao. Tiangaoqishuang.*' Mandarin, with a southern clip to it. I'm here. I'm taking a stroll! The weather's lovely. Crisp and clear.

I am telling you that I see nothing to indicate hostile surveillance.'

Her breathing. A distant siren in the background.

'*Hao. Xiexie.*' Good. Thanks.

The technician tapped the screen and the line went silent.

Hopko stood, hands on hips, looked questioningly at Yeats, who nodded.

'David?'

Charteris looked into the camera.

'I'm happy.'

Then, the wait.

They sat, silent, in the suite. Their dishevelled clothing lent them a weird, uncomfortable intimacy. After what seemed to Patterson an interminable period of time the green sphere next to GODDESS 2 began to blink.

'*Wei? Keren laile.*' The guest's arrived.

RATCHET has entered the temple.

'*Xiexie.*' Thanks.

Stillness is the enemy.

Peanut approached the temple from the west, moving quickly, reasoning it would be easier to spot a tail if he progressed from busier to quieter streets. He stopped twice, once in a medical supply shop, where he absorbed himself in the study of wheelchairs and commodes, and once in a reeking public toilet, where he lingered for twelve minutes. In his right hand he carried a plastic bag. His left remained in his pocket, cradling the knife.

He walked straight past the gateway to the Zhihua Temple. In the ticket booth, one attendant, female, listening to a radio, drinking tea from a pickle jar with a screw-on lid. He headed on, away, turned south down a narrow alley with soaring walls, then eastward towards the second ring road. One parked car, silver, no occupant. One street sweeper, male, dressed in grey, wearing a surgical mask. One purveyor of fried noodles, female, rotund, red anorak, pushing a cart. Atop the cart a gas ring and a wok; beneath it a propane tank, in a configuration not unlike that used by Chef in the early morning, and from which a migrant who sounded like a Beijing native purchased greasy dough sticks dusted with sugar six weeks, or a hundred years, ago. One passing jeep, blue, Beijing plates.

When he reached the second ring road, he stopped, stood beneath a plane tree. His fingers, he noticed, had turned numb, so tightly were they clenched around the handles of the plastic bag. He lit a cigarette, inhaling on a stream of icy air, massaged his hand. Three minutes to four.

Move.

GODDESS 2 again.

'*Wei? Pengyou laile.*' Our friend is here.

'*Xiexie.*' Thanks.

He paid with a five-yuan note. The attendant did not look at him. The radio was playing a *xiangsheng*, long-winded comedy, and she was listening and grinning as she handed him a ticket.

He walked through the first courtyard. The Englishman was standing there, hands in the pockets of a green windbreaker, gawping at him. He walked on towards the rear of the temple, through deepening shadows. The Englishman followed like some dim-witted animal. The temple was all but empty. One other couple, an old woman and her son, took pictures of each other with a mobile phone before the Hall of Wisdom and Cultivation.

The Pavilion of Ten Thousand Buddhas was almost dark inside now. Peanut inhaled its woody, resin smell, ancient incense smoked into the timbers. The little niches, each with seated Buddha, thousands upon thousands of them, disappeared up into the dark eaves. Peanut turned right and made for a wooden stairway. He sensed the Englishman behind him. The stairs were narrow and rickety, the wood blackened and smooth, leading to an upper chamber. Light streamed in from a balcony. The altar held Sakyamuni, seated on a lotus, his *foguang*, Buddha-light, aglow from copper skin. At his side the Buddhas of past and future. No one else, just the divine. The journalist was coming up the stairs. He emerged, stooping, into the chamber. Peanut gestured and stepped behind the altar. A low doorway into the eaves, some sort of storage space, lit by a single bulb.

Peanut squatted. The Englishman, bent almost double, entered the space behind him and closed the door. They sat close. Peanut could see the Englishman had not shaved, could smell his foreign smell; butter, fat.

'So, Mr Mang An.' Peanut, whispering.

'We don't have very long before this place closes,' said Mangan, in Mandarin.

'We have about half an hour. That's enough. We can speak in Chinese?'

'Yes. And I have questions.'

'And I have conditions,' Peanut responded.

The Englishman blinked.

'All right. What are your conditions?'

'You'll tell them this.'

'Tell who?'

Peanut cocked his head to one side.

'Do not fool around with me, Mang An. You have contacted the relevant departments of your government, yes?'

Mangan was silent.

'And they saw the proof, yes?'

'The proof?'

'The document and the letter I left in your office.'

Mangan gave a tight nod.

'So, tell them this,' said Peanut. 'A one-off transaction. Access to stand-alone networks in the General Armaments Department and the Launch Vehicle Academy. One time only, but superb access.'

The journalist was holding up both hands.

'Wait. Just ... wait.'

'What? Why?'

'This is not why I'm here.'

Peanut leaned forward now and took Mangan's wrist. He spoke in a rasp.

'I will tell you why you are here. And you will tell them. A one-off transaction. Access to stand-alone military networks. In return a passport – a polite nationality, please. Maybe Australia. Or Singapore. And fifty thousand dollars, and a ticket out of here, however that works. This is truly a reasonable offer. You will tell them. They know me, and they know I will deliver.'

Peanut felt himself becoming annoyed at the Englishman's pained, pale stare.

'I cannot make any such arrangement. I am a journalist,' said the Englishman.

'Screw journalist. You just tell them, Mang An. That's your job.'

'Christ.'

'Tell them.'

'Listen. I have questions.'

'All right. Ask your questions.'

'The document you left with me. The cover sheet and table of contents.'

'What about it?'

Mangan licked his lips. God in heaven, he thought.

'Right. Where does it come from?'

'It said on the cover sheet. It's a report for the Leading Small Group on Military Affairs, a technical report. It's very secret. It's so secret it'll break your balls. Here's the rest of it, by the way. A show of good faith.'

Peanut reached into the plastic carrier bag and pulled out a pile of photocopied pages, and thrust them towards the Englishman.

'Oh, Christ.' Mangan had his hand on his forehead.

'What do you think of that, then?'

'Just. Stop. For one minute.'

Peanut said nothing.

'Where did you *get* this document?' said Mangan.

'Who's asking? Who cares where I got it? There's more and I can get that, too.'

'I'm asking.'

'You don't—'

Mangan spoke over him. '*They're* asking. Understand? They want to know the source.'

Peanut looked at the Englishman, his flaming hair, flushed face, green eyes. He looked like a piece of fruit.

'Tell them I have a sub-source. Like before.'

'A sub-source.'

'He is ... collaborating with me.'

'And you got the document from him?'

'Yes.'

'And who is he, if I may ask?'

'I'm not telling you. He'll get some of the money.'

'But this sub-source has access to the documents?'

'Yes. And to the networks.'

The Englishman took a breath. He seemed to be calming down.

'And who are you?' Mangan asked.

'What do you mean who am I? They know who I am. I gave you a photograph, for heaven's sake.'

'But *I* don't know who you are.'

Peanut breathed out. God, for a cigarette.

'Perhaps better you don't know.'

'Do you have a name?'

Li Huasheng. Counter-revolutionary spawn. Night heron. Traitor. Peanut. Prisoner 5995. Song Ping.

'Quite a few.'

'Give me one I can use,' said Mangan.

'They called me Peanut.' The 'Peanut' in English, carefully pronounced.

'Peanut,' the Englishman repeated, looking levelly at him now. 'Do you have a family?'

For a moment Peanut was unable to respond. He looked at his hands. Was it rage? This tide rising in him?

'No, I do not have a stinking family.'

The Englishman said nothing, gave a questioning look.

'I have not been in a position to have a family,' said Peanut.

'Why?'

'I was in a fucking labour reform facility. Next question.'

'Why were you in the labour reform facility?'

'I hit someone.'

'You must have hit them pretty hard.'

'I did.'

'When was that?'

It was when everything ended. It was when our hopes proved as easily crushed as the skull of that little soldier.

'*Liu si*,' said Peanut. The fourth of June, 1989.

'Where do you live now?'

'Never you mind.'

'How long ago were you released?'

'Never mind.'

'Had you served your sentence?'

'Let's just say my path to this point has been unorthodox,' Peanut said.

The Englishman thought for a moment.

'You're on the run, aren't you?' he said.

What? Peanut thought. How the hell did we arrive here quite so quickly?

'That's enough—'

They froze.

Feet on the stairs. Peanut grabbed the Englishman's arm, held up a silencing hand.

Light footsteps. Slow.

Coming towards the altar now. Peanut could hear the Englishman's shallow, fast breathing.

The footsteps stopped. Muttering. Peanut felt his own blood pulsing in his clenched jaw, behind his eyes. Hello, fear. You're back.

Then a voice, a woman.

'*You ren ma?*' Anyone there?

Silence.

'*You ren ma? Kuai guan menr le ya.*' We're closing soon.

A longer silence. Then the footsteps receding, back down the stairs.

'*Kuai guan menr le ya.*'

The Englishman had his hand over his mouth and exhaled slowly.

'I'll leave first,' Peanut said. 'Remember what to tell them.'

He made to get up, then stopped, looked hard at the Englishman.

'You're a clever bastard, Mang An. Do not let me down.'

The technician ran the video GODDESS 3 had shot on the mobile phone. Granny Poon waved inanely at the lens, then a quick move away to glimpse the contact walking across the temple courtyard, the rolling, aggressive gait, the brush cut, the frown. A slight pan, and the shot fell on RATCHET, stooped, in jeans and a green waterproof, a few yards behind the contact, matching his pace and direction. Following him, in other words. The two disappeared into the second courtyard and the shot returned to Eileen Poon, looking over her shoulder, then went to black.

'The contact was holding a bag.' This from Yeats. 'I thought it looked like documents in it.'

'Could have been, Roly,' said Hopko, who sat, her legs stretched out and her arms folded, eyes fixed on the screen showing the incoming lines.

Mangan sat hunched under the eaves. He ran his hand across the wooden floor. It was smooth. He imagined generations of cloth slippers with straw soles lending the floorboards their patina, centuries of monks, devotees, scholars in silks, ladies of the court, eunuchs, merchants of tea and opium, fortune tellers, hucksters, the sick, the lame, the panoply of traditional China.

The photocopied report lay by his feet. The man who mumbled about birds and who had black paint on his hands and called himself Peanut had left it there, gesturing briefly to it as he'd left.

Never accept classified documents. Read them? Fine. Take notes on them? Just about okay. But don't take possession.

Nimble, that man, for his bulk. Something fluid and muscular to his movements. He was a man used to physical work. But his eyes ticked with calculation. How did he live? Where did he get his money? How did he buy that atrocious blue jacket with the shiny buttons?

The photocopied report still hadn't moved.

In the gloom Mangan could make out the characters in the title at the top of the first page.

DF-41 Intercontinental Ballistic Missile Programme: History, Objectives, Parameters.

What if he just left it lying there? Someone would find it. The ticket collector would be interrogated. The authorities would pull the footage from the cameras on all nearby intersections. And there would be Mangan, on a jerky, digital path to a Chinese prison, while the diplomats wrangled for years over his fate.

He was cold. A sliver of sunlight appeared between the wooden door and its frame, slicing through the murk. He watched the dust motes float through it.

And then Philip Mangan shed his illusion that he was working in the name of journalism, of a story, of a little collaboration, and became operational. He picked up the pile of photocopied pages, opened his windbreaker and placed the pages under his sweater, tucking them into the top of his trousers.

He zipped up the windbreaker, crawled through the doorway and moved quickly towards the stairway.

'GODDESS 1 on the line.'

'*Wei? Keren zoule. Wo ye yao zou. Keren geile liwu.*' The guest has left. I'm leaving, too. The guest gave a gift.

Hopko sat forward.

'*Shenme liwu?*' What gift?

'*Geile huar.*' Flowers. Meaning documents.

'*Hao. Xiexie.*'

Hopko turned to the Beijing Station screen.

'David, RATCHET's carrying.'

Charteris looked up, startled, then was gone.

Mangan was clammy, despite the cold. The heat rose up his back, into his neck and cheeks. It was nearly dark. He came from the alleyway almost at a run, forcing himself to slow, on to Jinbao Jie, snarled traffic, blinding headlights. A woman stood at the street corner with a cart, selling *baozi*. A taxi slowed, the driver gesturing at him from the window. The pages dug into his stomach. The flat? Could he take the document pages back there? Walk through the gates into the compound, past the guards and the

State Security hoods in the little gatehouses? To his bugged flat? Could he call Charteris? Should he? He turned north, away from home, and walked fast.

'GODDESS 4 on the line.'

'*Wei? Pengyou bu hui jia li qu. Dao biede difang le.*' Our friend's not going home. He's going somewhere else.

'*Hao. Ni pei ta qu ma?*' Are you going with him? Hopko, biting her lip.

'*Dangran. Yihuir zai shuo.*' Of course I am. We'll talk again in a while.

'Translate, please. Where are we?' Yeats sounded tense.

'Granny Poon is staying with the contact. But whatever the contact was carrying when he went into the temple, he no longer has, so the assumption is he's given it to RATCHET, who's now carrying.' Hopko stood, dangling her spectacles in one hand. 'And RATCHET is not heading back to his flat, he's heading elsewhere, so one of the boys is staying with him. Charteris will track him down, won't he, Trish?'

The elderly woman boarded a bus. She wore a green scarf now, and thick glasses. The target had made some sorry and revealing attempts at dry-cleaning – some hammy business in a shoe shop, a public toilet, again – but nothing to trouble her. The target now sat, six rows in front, staring from the filthy window as they ground eastward down Jianwai Avenue. So noisy, so cramped these buses! So slow! The woman would believe in China's economic renaissance when public transport approached the silken speed of Hong Kong's. Not till then. Two seats behind her GODDESS 3, eyes half-closed beneath the brim of a baseball cap, sat with a shopping bag on his lap, the leaves of a cabbage visible. Still all clear.

So who was he, this man? She liked to play guessing games

with her targets, spin out her own versions of the stories she'd never know. He was educated, but down at heel. A crudeness to him, but fiery. No congruence in his appearance and his bearing. He wore a smart jacket but walked as if he meant to tear someone's lungs out. No congruence. And that, to the woman's practised eye, made him conspicuous. He needed to change.

And his efforts at counter-surveillance, dear God. She'd put a stop to *that*.

The bus began to empty as it left the city centre. The elderly woman descended at a poorly lit intersection and made her way into the back streets of brick and neon as if she had lived there all her life. Here, in snatches of talk on the night air, she heard less of the soft Beijing speech and more of the choppy, sibilant south, her own speech. Anonymous, this place. She kept the target on the edge of her vision, reeling herself in a little closer when he twisted and turned. She could sense more than see her boy, GODDESS 3, behind her.

And then, as she turned a corner, the target was gone. She kept her pace steady. There he was. Yes. In the window of, what was this, a beauty salon? He was speaking to an orange-haired girl, who put her hands on her hips, leaned forward to him. He was taking off his jacket and seemed to be laughing. Was he a client? No, something else. Proprietor?

And at that moment Granny Poon's mobile phone rumbled. She reached into her bag fussily and pulled it out, staring at the screen. No number. She keyed answer. But there was only silence.

What was that?

She moved thirty paces further, then abruptly crossed the street. She turned and looked for, for what? A flicker, a hint. Movement out of the flow. Some tension of gait or look, fleeting as a shadow, visible only to one who had spent decades on the streets of China. They were good, these people, when they tried. Were they out there tonight? Were they on her?

The street was quiet.

And here was GODDESS 3, coming in for a second pass of the target's destination.

Some beauty salon. Pervert.

Mangan, walking hard towards Dongzhimen, felt the stirring of panic. His mobile phone rang.

'Philip, good lord, where on earth are you?'

Mangan reached for a biting response to Charteris's languid tone, couldn't find one, and told him.

'Keep walking, I'll pick you up.'

It was eight minutes before a taxi drew up. Charteris was slumped low in the back, wearing a baseball cap and a scarf. Mangan got in, made to speak, but Charteris shook his head and gestured to the front of the vehicle. A microphone protruded from the dashboard. The driver looked straight ahead and pulled out into the traffic. Mangan gave a questioning look. Charteris returned a sardonic smile and settled back in the seat, eyes half-closed. He had a blue backpack on his lap.

'Let's go and have a drink,' he said.

They got out at the mouth of a *hutong* near the Drum Tower. Charteris paid the driver, while Mangan turned and avoided the driver's look. The street was crowded with students, some tourists. The bars were warming up.

'Slowly does it, Philip. Just walk.'

They walked in silence past the junk art shops and noodle restaurants. Charteris stopped outside a bar, put a hand on Mangan's arm.

'This one's loud.' Red lanterns hung against the grey *hutong* brick. Pink neon spelled out the name, Funky Time. They went in. Charteris took a booth at the back. The music was Shanghai synth-funk, screechingly loud. Charteris took out his phone and gestured with it. Mangan took out his own and, under the table, removed the battery. Charteris leaned across the booth.

'Are you carrying something, Philip?'

Mangan nodded, looked down at his stomach.

'Leave it for now. What happened? Keep it oblique.'

Mangan told him. 'Well. We met. He told me to call him Peanut. Just Peanut. No other name. He has an offer, he says. One time. Like in the letter. Access to networks. David, I . . .'

'Slow down. One thing at a time. Did you ask him where the proof came from?'

'He has a collaborator. Like before, he says. He got it from this collaborator.'

'Say who?'

'I asked. He wouldn't say.'

'But you asked him.'

'Yes. He called it a . . . a what . . . a sub-source.'

Mangan saw Charteris's blink. A waitress came to the table, ponytailed and sullen. She wore a dress plastered with the brand name of a famous beer that hugged her figure. Charteris ordered a Coke, Mangan a vodka.

'And what about him, Philip? Did you ask about him?'

'He's on the run. Been in a labour reform facility since eighty-nine, the demonstrations. He said he assaulted someone. I think maybe he killed them.'

'How do you know he's on the run? Give me everything he said, Philip.'

'He said he used unorthodox methods to get out of prison. I asked him, are you on the run? and he looked surprised, like I'd rumbled him.'

'But he didn't say so.'

'He might as well have done. For Christ's sake, David.'

'Don't get agitated, please. What else?'

'He wouldn't tell me where he lived, or his circumstances. He just wanted to talk about this offer. He said you already knew him, knew he'd deliver.'

'And the offer, tell me quickly.'

Mangan placed his hands palm up on the table, shook his head.

'David.'

'Tell me.'

Mangan looked down. And Charteris waited for him to take another step.

'Come on, Philip, you're nearly done. Tell me what the offer was.'

Mangan shook his head, rolled his eyes. It was, thought Charteris, a gesture intended to convey resigned acquiescence. Take the step, he thought.

'Stand-alone networks at the General Armaments Department and the Launch Vehicle Academy,' he said.

An offer of access to China's secret heart.

Charteris nodded, gave nothing away.

'All right, that's enough. For now. You've a ticket booked for Seoul tomorrow afternoon. Do not take your phone. Go to the Plaza, wait for a contact.'

Mangan gaped. Charteris ignored him.

'Now take the backpack. Go to the lavatory and put whatever you're carrying into the pack. Go.'

Mangan stood up slowly, his gaze not leaving Charteris. The lavatory was next to the bar's entrance. The music was pounding. Two girls in tight halter tops and glitter eyeshadow sat at the bar drinking cocktails through little straws. They watched him and whispered. He stopped by the entrance to the men's lavatory and looked over to the front door. Out in the street a western family was strolling past the shops. The shopkeepers gestured and smiled at them, cooing over the blonde kids. Diplomats? English teachers? Mangan had a sense of the world receding. He turned back. Charteris was resting his elbow on the table, chin in hand. He nodded, and gestured with his eyes towards the lavatory.

Mangan pushed open the lavatory door, the reek of piss. He entered the stall and lowered the lid of the toilet, sat. He pulled the pages from under his clothing. They were damp. He pushed them into the backpack. Philip Mangan, observer of events from a careful distance, becomes participant, meddles in history. *Jesus Christ, I am out of my mind.* He rubbed the back of his neck.

He stood, flushed and walked out of the lavatory, back to the table.

'You really are a shit, David.'

'I'm a shit in a good cause. And now you are, too.'

Charteris reached under the table for the backpack, stood and leaned in one last time to be heard over the music.

'That was very, very good, Philip.'

'Piss off, David.'

GODDESS 3 – Winston Poon, the wiry cousin – entered the Blue Diamond at about nine p.m. He was greeted by a rotund woman who simpered a little and offered him tea and the weeknight special. She gestured to the girls who sat amid the salon clutter with fixed smiles. GODDESS 3 selected a short pale girl, with protuberant teeth, whose name was given as Beautiful Peony, though in GODDESS 3's judgement this was a work name. The two of them stood and Beautiful Peony took GODDESS 3 by the hand and led him towards a beaded curtain, next to which, on a stool, sat the target. The target had changed into a pair of blue shorts and a white vest. He smoked as he sat. He was, in GODDESS 3's view, providing security for the salon. The others in the room seemed to treat him with respect, the reason for which became clear a little later.

GODDESS 3 proceeded through the beaded curtain and was shown into a small room with a bed. There he was asked to disrobe, which he did. GODDESS 3 then pleaded an inability to perform and sat with the girl for a decent interval, before dressing and returning to the salon. In conversation with the girl, GODDESS 3 asked discreetly about the target. The girl replied that 'Uncle' was there to help with the running of the business.

When GODDESS 3 re-entered the salon, the target was standing, in conversation with three men, all of whom GODDESS 3 judged to be migrant workers. They appeared intoxicated and were behaving in a boisterous fashion. One of them reached for the girl known as Beautiful Peony as she passed and placed his hand inappropriately on her bosom. The target, moving surprisingly quickly, administered a blow to the man's lower back. He then took the man by the throat and propelled his head into the wall several times, leaving the man stunned but not seriously injured. The target ordered all three men to leave the salon, which they did. GODDESS 3 noted that at no time during this incident did the target appear to lose his composure. GODDESS 3, himself no amateur in these matters, concluded that the target was possessed of a considerable capacity for violence and had the physical and mental resources to match.

Ting had left a message. *Philip, we'll be at Neo Lounge.* He needed company, and more to drink. She was at the bar, which glowed pink, with Milam from the *LA Times*, Harvey, and a cluster of press corps interns and hangers-on. As Mangan approached, Harvey eyed him, then reached down the bar for a cold, misty bottle of vodka. Harvey poured and held out the glass to Mangan.

'What you been up to?' he said.

Mangan shook his head.

'Are you all right, Philip?' said Ting.

Milam was watching.

'We wondered where you got to, Philip. Busted again?'

Mangan looked at him.

'What?'

Milam blinked.

'Last week. In Yunnan. You and Harv. No?'

'Oh. That.' Mangan took a mouthful of vodka.

'You should be careful,' said Milam.

'Thanks. Cheers.'

'You got to watch out.'

'Yup, thanks.'

'*And* Ting tells me you've been in Singapore. Nice hotels, business class. Mm-hmm. How can I get me one of those gigs?'

'Yes, right. Ting, I've got to go and do another one. Tomorrow. Same people, Pan Asia thing. In Seoul.'

Ting looked up at him, the surprise on her face.

'Tomorrow. They don't give a lot of notice, do they?'

'They're using me as a sort of fill-in, I think.'

He took another sip of vodka. Something was fluttering in his stomach. Nervousness, a measure of shock. Hard-bitten journalist finds himself caught up in matters that offend his professional sensibilities. Professes indignation.

Feels something else entirely.

Anticipation?

'Anyway, tomorrow afternoon I'm flying. So we might need to do some rescheduling.'

Harvey feigned choking on his vodka.

'Scheduling? Philip, since when do you have a schedule?' he said, and Ting put her hand over her mouth and laughed.

'Well, I'm flying tomorrow,' he said.

'Tomorrow. Rescheduling. Okay, Philip, I'll do some rescheduling,' Ting said.

Mangan was surprised at how easily the lies came.

Even later, with Ting lying in the crook of his arm, her skin against his, her breath on his neck, he wondered at how easily they came.

16

Patterson had been home to Archway, showered and eaten a fried egg sandwich, before heading straight back to headquarters. She took the stairs from the Tube to the street two at a time and dodged traffic.

Just opposite the headquarters of the Secret Intelligence Service, to Patterson's perennial amusement, stood the Pyramids Sauna. Catering exclusively to men, and open for business twenty-four hours a day, Pyramids enjoyed an ancient Egyptian theme. Its façade featured images of oiled boys in white shifts and golden headdresses, King Tut-style. *London's raunchiest venue! Weekend parties!* In the cafeteria she had once joked that the Service was surely the mirror image of its steamy neighbour, 'full of overheated men trying to stab each other from the rear'. It hadn't gone down well, and she had made few jokes since.

She was in the lobby now. She inserted her pass and stepped on to the pressure pads. She was due in Hopko's office in forty minutes. The telegram traffic had come through: contact report; a version of the product – Charteris had been up half the night scanning and encrypting; surveillance report from the GODDESS team, encrypted by Winston and dropped, for seconds only, on the Yip Lo website. She was to collate them and have them ready for the meeting and Hopko's Fancies and sod the weekend. Though weekends, Patterson was finding, were largely deserts of silence relieved only by television.

Hopko was still in her tracksuit. Roly Yeats had managed a discreetly checked shirt and a jacket and was stroking his beard. Tom Waverley, of Requirements, had been hauled in from the golf course.

'So,' said Hopko. 'Poons seem happy that no one's watching. We can, perhaps, rest a little easier that we are not being played. Trish flies to Seoul tonight. She will have meetings with Eileen Poon, and Mangan.'

Hopko turned a piece of paper and looked at it over her glasses.

'I must say I think they did awfully well, the GODDESS team. Don't you, Roly? I do hope there's nothing wrong with Winston, not being able to perform like that. What do you think, should we encourage him to see a specialist? His insurance will cover it, won't it?'

She turned to Yeats, as if expecting an answer. Patterson found Hopko's ability to deadpan terrifying. Yeats said nothing.

'Perhaps it just needs a pill, Roly, what do you think?'

Yeats was deep in the telegrams. Hopko turned to Patterson. 'Men's problems.' *Don't drag me into this, Val.*

'So, Mangan steps up,' said Hopko. 'Thought he would, didn't I, Trish? And in the course of about, what, twelve minutes in a cupboard upstairs in a temple, speaking in Chinese, he elicits an astonishing amount of information. Man's a bloody natural.'

'Information that is not readily confirmed, though,' said Waverley.

'That's true,' said Patterson. 'But the pieces fit together. Our man was WINDSOCK. He assaulted someone during the Tiananmen uprising in eighty-nine, he was arrested, went to labour reform like a common criminal.'

Waverley smiled regretfully.

'But it's circumstantial,' he said.

'Well, I think we can check the prison part,' ventured Patterson.

'Oh?' said Yeats. The whole room was looking at her now.

'The Taiwanese have acquired a lot of inmate lists, over the years. Not complete, but extensive. Court records, too. But it would mean handing them a name, of course.'

'You'll be handing out no names for the time being, thank you,' said Yeats. 'Now, Tom, the product.'

'Well, it seems to match what he gave us before. I've struggled through a few pages, Roly, and it seems to be very significant CX. We've given it an initial rating of C2' – 2 designating a report of likely reliability; C designating a source of suspect or unproven reliability.

'C2? That's not going to set anyone on fire, is it?' said Yeats.

'Just to start with, Roly. It's already gone to Defence Intelligence. They're going to handle translation. They're all in a tizzy, bringing in staff. We'll write a preliminary assessment and, if it all stands up, we could break it out to consumers as early as next week.'

Yeats looked disconsolate.

'But C2? Can't we gin it up a bit?'

Hopko had her stony look on. 'Roly, we need to find collateral. Though as usual, there may be none, because we may have stumbled on a genuine secret. Always tricky that, isn't it?'

She peered around the room, looking, thought Patterson, in her scarf and bangles and tracksuit, like some sort of unemployed new age priestess.

'But if our man's to be believed,' said Patterson, 'the main event is still to come.'

'All right, I'll bite. Go on,' said Yeats.

'In the initial account we have of the meeting the contact used the words "sub-source" and "collaborator", and said it was "like before".'

'So we have a reporting chain,' said Yeats.

'He's doing what he knows. And he's been in prison. So he has nothing to sell, but he's getting it from somewhere. So who's the collaborator?'

'I am hoping you have an answer, young Trish,' said Yeats.

All right, she thought, here we go.

'Well, I've tried to find him through the T2 Operating Platform,' said Patterson. 'Our contact wasn't on screen much, as you might expect. Our man simply doesn't figure – no addresses, no bills, no passport, no phones, no web presence, no nothing. A few mentions in scientific journals from the eighties, that's all. Nothing after June eighty-nine. Very consistent with being in clink for two decades.'

Yeats was listening closely. He loved technology, preferred it to his own officers, thought Patterson. She forged on.

'But his old friends, the other sub-agents from the original PAN GLINT network, are a different story. COPPER's at the University of Alberta, very visible. Great strings of information. I can tell you how much he earns, where his kids go to school, the brand of shirt he wears. No, really, I can, I've got credit card receipts.'

Laughter.

'But nothing there points us back to Beijing, let alone into the General Armaments Department. He has a few ageing relatives in a small town in Hebei Province, that's all. He seems to have pretty much made a clean break. There's no way the collaborator is COPPER.' She paused, took a sip of coffee. 'And NEPTUNE's dead, we know that.'

'All right. And the rest?' said Hopko.

'TANGO, again pretty visible, gave up academia altogether in the early nineties. He went into business, "jumped into the sea" as they used to call it. Anyway, he did very well. He owns a shopping mall in Shanghai and does villa developments up and down the coast. Drives an Aston Martin. The T2 had good visibility on him, lots of reporting in the business media, photos, charity stuff, but again no string that led towards the military.'

The room was quiet now. Patterson had spent many hours with the early versions of the T2 in the army. She was, she knew, one of the few officers who could really use it.

'But then there's CURTAIN. Real name Wen Jinghan. Professor. Age fifty. Not much there, but what there is ... well. He's tagged in scholarly journals, and everything points to involvement with launch technology. He's had, and presumably still has, a position in the General Armaments Department. His main job is at the Launch Vehicle Academy down at Nanyuan. We don't know what he does, but he's senior. And I found multiple strings flying off into the military and the defence industry. A private firm in Washington was doing targeting for CIA a couple of years ago and they actually identified him as "of interest". There's one photograph: a press clipping, he's in the background.'

She forced herself to stop.

'So he's missiles,' said Yeats.

'He certainly is.'

'And, perhaps, he's networks.'

'Yes.'

Yeats had steepled his fingers and sat back in his chair. Patterson saw the smile spreading on his face.

It was late afternoon. Patterson was parched and had a headache forming behind her right eye. The light from the greenish windows in Hopko's office – polymers on the glass to prevent electromagnetic leakage, thermal imaging – was dimming. She suddenly remembered she had agreed to go to the pub with Damian, and perhaps on for a curry, a rare evening out. They'd talk about the football and his job at the advertising agency.

But now it was time for Hopko's Fancies.

'Let's go round,' said Hopko. 'Tom. Where's Requirements?'

'Well, if there's one thing guaranteed to stir the pot more than missiles, it's networks,' said Waverley. 'Architecture, capacity, content, the lot. Chinese cyber. Priority requirement, right there in the Red Book. If this character can deliver access to the networks he says he can ...' Waverley left the sentence hanging.

'But?' said Hopko.

'But how? Even with a friendly body inside the General Armaments Department. What do we plug in, and where? And, of course, there's the one-off problem. We just don't like one-offs.' He looked directly at Patterson. 'We like a track record, as you know. A one-off, you never quite know what you're getting, do you?'

'Quite. Trish?'

'I assess we have the beginnings of a reporting chain. But Mangan needs to be made fully conscious for it to work,' said Patterson.

Hopko, making notes, smiled.

'And Mr Yeats, sir?'

Yeats paused for effect. Then nodded sagely.

'I'm prepared to take this another step. We'll need advice, especially on the technology. It'll have to go right up the chain, Director, Permanent Under-Secretary. We all need to be ready for that. We need to consider the role of Mangan carefully. Let's have a plan quickly.'

'Right you are, Roly. Oh and Trish, you have one last thing, yes?'

'The contact, who we now presume to be Li Huasheng, has been issued with a codename. He is GENIUS.'

'Is he, indeed?' said Yeats. 'Well, let's bloody hope so. You will keep me personally informed, young Trish Patterson, of his every move.'

17

Seoul, South Korea

Mangan, a few years earlier, had put together a quick and cheeky feature on Seoul's new international airport at Inchon. He had likened its architectural form to a giant armour-plated slug. A South Korean diplomat had written to him to tell him of 'all Korea's disappointment'. On arriving amid the dazzling white steel and glinting marble, Mangan half-wondered if they'd let him into the country.

But the passport officer waved him through. He took a train into a cold city, grey as granite, and a taxi to the Plaza, where, once, Mangan had sat in the coffee shop watching the rioting. The hotel overlooked a wide grassy circle that served as a great spot for a riot. And when South Korea's furious students took to the streets over beef imports, or Japan, or the plight of rice farmers, or just because it was Tuesday, the foreign press corps could watch it over coffee, and avoid the tear-gas.

And now he sat in the lobby bar, with a beer and some nuts and a copy of the *Herald Tribune*. Awaiting contact.

*

Patterson was at the Service safe flat out east in Gangdong-gu with a cup of green tea, under neon strip lights in a tiny kitchen. Granny Poon famously ignored all rules concerning smoking and had lit a beedi, the stench of which now filled the flat.

Granny Poon eyed Patterson, this new, tall, stony-faced Englishwoman. Trying too hard, she thought, needs to relax into it.

They had gone over every minute of the operation at the Zhihua Temple, the collective Poon memory bringing it to life in granular detail. The target's briskness, verging on recklessness, his sense of intention.

'He's dangerous,' Granny Poon said. 'He needs to be cautious. It's Beijing, Trish. Where spies die, yes?'

They talked about the brothel, the target's calm ruthlessness.

'And tell him,' said Granny Poon, 'tell him to stop counter-surveillance. Terrible! All the time he ducks, dives. It's too much. Anybody from MSS sees him, they know. He may as well write on his forehead, I Am A Spy. Not Very Good One.' She lifted a crabbed finger to her forehead and made writing motions.

'We'll tell him,' said Patterson.

'Really, he must stop. Also the cameras, they see it. They have software now. Watches you walk, sees if you walk funny.' Behavioural tracking systems. She waved a finger, rarely this insistent.

'He puts the operation in danger. Tell him.'

She described Mangan's artlessness, which was maybe not such a bad thing. 'In Beijing no tradecraft lives longer than bad tradecraft,' she said.

They had agreed on two more tranches of surveillance in the coming week. Where did Peanut go? Any meetings? Any entry to official buildings? The boys were resting up, dry cleaning, building cover. Granny Poon would go back to oversee.

They got up, Patterson to leave first. But Granny Poon stopped her, hesitant.

'What is it, Eileen?'

'I did not put it in the report.'

'What?'

'It's just. There was . . . something.'

'What was it?'

Granny Poon made a pinching movement with her fingers, as if trying to pluck something from the air.

'I did not report it because I think it's not important. Outside the salon, the target already gone in, I just felt something, and then my phone rang. No one on the other end. No number. So I check, but nobody on my back, nobody on the target's back. Winston, he sees no one. We're clean, I'm sure.'

Patterson was looking at her, waiting for more, tension on her face.

'This was not Chinese surveillance. I know them, I can see them. You know, right? I've been spotting them for thirty years. This was not MSS.'

'Who, then?'

'Who knew my phone number?'

'Me, you, the London team, Beijing Station,' said Patterson. Eileen shook her head.

'Nobody. It's nobody. Just a feeling.'

Patterson said nothing.

'Maybe a junk call. Some advertising, something,' said Granny Poon.

'Did you change your phone?' said Patterson.

'Yes. We change every day, anyway.'

Patterson considered.

'Do I need to make this official?'

'Tell you what. I go back to Beijing. All this week I keep an eye out, okay. Then we talk again.'

An awkward embrace. Hopko had sent shortbread from Fortnum's, which Granny Poon loved.

Mangan, installed in the Plaza's Italian restaurant, had finished the carpaccio and was wading into the linguine with seafood in a clear broth, when a young man in suit and overcoat approached his table.

'Mr Mangan?' He was blond, young.

Mangan swallowed and wiped his mouth.

'Yes.'

'Oh, good evening. I'm very sorry to disturb your dinner. My name is Backhouse. I'm from the embassy. I just wanted you to know I'll be picking you up in the morning. Would nine be all right? Downstairs?'

'Nine.'

'Wonderful. See you then.' And he was gone.

So that was contact.

18

Seoul, South Korea

It was 'Rachel Davies' again. Sitting on a vile black leather sofa, in a flat in some godforsaken corner of the city. She wore a black turtleneck and jeans. She was alone. Were there others lurking unseen? She stood up when he walked in, her face a mask.

'Hello, Philip. Thank you for coming. I know it was short notice, but things are moving quickly.'

'Are they?'

'Yes. But let me just ask you, any problems on the way here?'

'No,' he said, blankly.

'At Beijing airport did they ask you any questions at passport control?'

'No.'

'Anybody contact you here in Seoul, apart from the embassy?'

'No.'

She walked him through his plan for the rest of the day, his return trip to Beijing. She told him what they should do if they were interrupted. Mangan listened, mystified.

'Well,' she said. 'You've done it again.'

'Done what again?'

'Created a stir.' Mangan felt her warm a little. The way to her heart, he thought, lay through the provision of secret intelligence.

'And how's that?' he said.

'Well, you got a good deal out of our man in a very short time. And you had deft footwork with that document.'

She sat down, crossed her legs.

'But you're a reporter. So you know how to do these things, right?'

Do I? he thought. He wondered if that was sarcasm he was hearing, running beneath her words.

'How reliable do you think he is, Philip? Now you've talked to him?'

'I don't have the first idea. How good was his information?'

'Oh, first rate, if it's true. If it's not some horrible plot to ruin us.'

'Might it be?'

'Yes. But we don't think it is.'

'Why not?'

She's opening a little, talking about what she knows, he thought.

'Well, deception operations often feel slick, well-thought-out. And then you find a gaping hole.' She paused. 'But with a genuine operation, there's a rickety feel to it, constant improvisation. A human feel.'

Operations, now, thought Mangan.

'May I be very frank with you?' he said.

'Of course,' she said, but Mangan saw the flicker of concern.

'You need to tell me exactly what my position is now.'

'I'm coming to that, Philip.'

She opened a folder on her lap, consulted something. This is punctuation, thought Mangan; a semi-colon in my life. Then she spoke again.

'As I'm sure you realise, you're talking to British Intelligence.'

'Is Charteris an Intelligence Officer?'

'Yes.'

Mangan bit back a response.

'Which part of British Intelligence?' he said.

'The Secret Intelligence Service. SIS.' She was trying to gauge his reaction, he sensed.

'And I'm now part of an operation?' he said.

The woman spoke quietly and with great seriousness.

'Philip, at this point I must impress upon you – though I think you understand – the need to remain utterly discreet. For everybody's sake, including your own. We need to be very, very careful now.'

Mangan nodded. Every response I make takes me one step further in, he thought.

She continued.

'We would like to come to an arrangement with you. Put you on our books for the duration. There'll be remuneration, of course.'

'You're offering me a job?'

'No. We're offering you an association. This isn't uncommon. People help us out a good deal. Not so common for a journalist to come on board, but there we are.'

'Why? Why do people help you out? Why can't a professional do what I'm doing?'

The woman thought it over. All the time her eyes stayed on him.

'Beijing is, well, you've seen the cameras. You understand surveillance. You've encountered the MSS, the police, the neighbourhood committees. Every old lady on a street corner is a sensor for the state, even if she doesn't know it yet. The web mamas, the phone tappers, the GPS locators, every hotel a listening post, every handheld a beacon. How easy do you think it is for a professional to work?'

'Why is it any different for me?'

'Because you have natural cover, Philip. You've a reason for being where you are, for going where you go. And it's been built up over years. It's quicker and safer to reverse engineer you than it is to build something from scratch.'

She paused. Then spoke again.

'Let's leave that for a moment,' she said.

For the next two hours she took him through the meeting, probing his memory.

Mangan talked, reconsidered, talked again. He found himself using the same mental muscles that he used in reporting; the way of looking, looking at something for what it is, for what it isn't.

At her pressing, he found memories of the meeting he didn't know were there. The man's left hand in his pocket was holding something. What was it? Or the flicker on his face when he spoke of the prison camp, the sense of anger tamped down, doused.

She made no notes. They were presumably recording. She kept returning to the offer.

'But what, in your view, was he actually offering?'

'He's offering you a person, a collaborator. He believes he's got someone on the inside, and he's the middle man.'

'And he wouldn't tell you who this collaborator was.'

'No. As I told you, he just said it would be like before.'

'And the collaborator's motive? Anything at all, Philip. Do think, now.'

Nothing. She frowned.

'When he used the term "collaborator", what sort of tone of voice was he using?'

'It was faintly sarcastic perhaps. He had a half-smile, a know-ing look.'

'So it's possible he used the term in an ironic way?'

'Yes. Yes, I suppose that's possible.'

'Is it possible that he doesn't have a collaborator at all? That whoever's supplying him with material is doing it under duress?'

'Impossible to know.'

She nodded. A pause. Mangan took the leap.

'He's done this before, hasn't he? With you,' he said.

She looked up sharply.

'There are aspects of this that you are going to remain ignorant of. I'm sorry.'

'You already know who the collaborator is, don't you?'

She gave her tight smile. She appeared ready to wind the conversation up.

'I'm not just flattering you, Philip. You've achieved a great deal. And we want to take this further.'

'And if I don't want to?'

'You can walk away at any time. That's understood. But if you do, we'd appreciate some warning, and some candour. And we'll need assurances from you.'

Mangan said nothing. 'Rachel Davies' stood, walked to the window, pulled back the curtain and looked out.

'If we go ahead, we'll meet outside China as much as we can. Nasty little flats like this one.'

'I rather enjoyed the meal in Singapore,' said Mangan.

'Treasure the memory,' she said, absently. 'Doesn't happen often.'

What was she looking for?

'We have in mind a project for you,' she said. 'A book. The Pan Asia Institute publishes a series called *Topics in Asian Studies*. Nice glossy little numbers. There'd be lots of trips, meeting editors. Interviewing. How does that grab you?'

Mangan was nonplussed.

'Is it a real book?'

'Oh, yes. Publication guaranteed. Might even do you some good. And it will give you mobility. A reason for being out of the country.'

'I see.'

'Charteris will be there, in Beijing, but he'll have to keep a distance. You're good at working alone, aren't you?'

Silence.

'The important thing, Philip, is to keep things normal. Carry on reporting. Maintain your friendships. Go out, stay in, succeed, fail, do what you normally do. But you're writing this book. Choose a topic. Write a summary. Do this as quickly as you can. Approach the institute. They will commission it, I'm assured.'

'What will you want me to do? I mean, really do?'

'You will meet our man perhaps three or four times, no more. Once or twice you'll have to carry a small item, something that's normal, natural for a journalist to have. That's it. We'll keep it very simple.'

'How long will this last?'

'Impossible to say. I think it will be weeks, a few months at the most. And then it'll be over.'

'And why should I do it? What's the purpose?'

She sat back down on the sofa and crossed her legs.

'The purpose.' She let the words hang in the air.

'The point of it,' said Mangan.

She looked surprised at the question.

'Well,' she said, 'most of us tend to think that in the digital age we have all the tools we need to know the world, don't we? We think our search engines and our satellites and our data-mining programmes and our sensors allow us to know the world. But it's an illusion. All that digitised information is a sample, nothing more. And in the case of China, the sample we see excludes the most salient facts, because the most salient facts are kept secret. And the Chinese are good at keeping secrets. That's one little bit of Leninism they haven't forgotten. Keep your mouth shut. Keep everybody guessing. Knowledge is power. Knowledge of what gets said in the Politburo meeting, who says it, what the Party leaders think, what they feel. What animates them. What their intentions are.'

She paused, then spoke again.

'If you think that reform and openness and networks have rendered China terra cognita, Philip, you're wrong. It's terra very bloody incognita.'

'So you spy,' he said.

'So we spy. We have to.'

She paused.

'Good enough to persuade you to act?'

Mangan exhaled. To act. To cease observing from a distance, through a lens.

But writing is acting. Reporting, constructing narrative is acting. Isn't it? To inform is to influence.

'I will need an answer,' she said.

19

Beijing

Yin took Peanut to an internet café in Fangzhuang. She paid and registered and they searched for a vacant screen among rows of silent boys in headphones. Peanut looked at their screens. He saw cars exploding, helicopters, rockets, gleaming silver surfaces, fountains of flame. What was this? What were they doing?

They sat, and Yin showed him the, the what, the browser. He read an article from the *People's Daily* on the screen, and then people commenting on the article. Some of the comments suggested the newspaper article was wrong, or mistaken.

'Can they do that?' he said.

Yin just laughed.

He saw pictures of a South Korean singer – Yin's favourite, a smooth boy with windblown hair – performing on a stage with thousands of people watching.

He lit a cigarette and asked the thing to show him pictures of the People's Liberation Army. There were thousands. Thousands! There were the mobile launchers, on a road somewhere, troops in camouflage milling about. Short-range missiles, these ones. Was that a DF-15? DF stands for Dongfeng, East Wind, he told her. Yin was uninterested. They scuffled over control of the keyboard and Yin brought up a picture of two women barely clothed, doing ... what? He spluttered and reddened while she laughed again.

Later they had lunch at some hamburger place, one bite and it was gone. She asked him how it was he didn't know about computers, mobile phones. He didn't reply.

'Where have you been?' she said.

'You don't tell anyone, Yin. That I don't know about these things.'

'You were inside, weren't you?' She was grinning, leaning over the table.

'You don't tell anyone.'

'Everyone already knows.'

He forced a smile.

'What do they know?'

'Chef says you've "been away", and he and Dandan Mama talk about it.'

'Do they.'

She nodded, eyes wide, enjoying herself.

'Well, you don't talk about it,' he said.

'What did you do?'

'I won't be here much longer.'

Her smile fell away.

'So you won't be able to tease me any more,' he said.

'Are you going away?'

'Yes.'

Her lip was trembling, he saw with astonishment.

'Where will you go?'

'I don't know yet. Come off it, Yin.'

She had dropped her head and was staring at the table. He saw a tear fall on to the red plastic tray. She murmured something.

'What?'

'I said, maybe I could come with you.'

He didn't reply. They left the restaurant and walked towards the subway station. At an intersection Peanut looked up at a billboard. The advertisement showed a woman in sepia, her shoulder, her lips, her shining hair in a twist. The slogan read: *Because it's my time.*

Yin caught him staring at it.

'They do something to fix the picture. They tell you it's real when it's not,' she said.

Beneath the billboard, on a wall, was the stencilled graffiti again. THREATEN. This time it was a bird, a crow, wearing the goggles.

Patterson had decrypted the telegram, and now read it quickly.

GODDESS 4 reports that GENIUS left the salon at 02.42 ZULU/10.42 local. GENIUS was accompanied by a young woman who also resides at the salon and who goes by name BEAUTIFUL PEONY. GODDESS 3 and GODDESS 4 were on rotation. GENIUS and companion walked to subway station. No contacts were observed en route. No sign of hostile surveillance. At Puhuangyu subway stop, GENIUS alighted, still accompanied by young woman. They proceeded out of station and walked three hundred metres to the WANG BA internet café. They entered the café at 03.36 ZULU/11.36 local. They sat at a screen. The young woman appeared to be instructing GENIUS in use of the computer. GODDESS 4 made one pass. GENIUS and the young woman appeared to be viewing semi-pornographic images. GENIUS and companion left the WANG BA internet café at 04.50 ZULU/12.50 local. They proceeded to a fast food restaurant where they ate hamburgers. They appeared to be deep in conversation. The young woman known as BEAUTIFUL PEONY became distressed. They left the restaurant and returned to the Metro, arriving back at the salon at 05.46 ZULU/13.46 local. No further contacts were observed. GODDESS 2 and 4 withdrew. GODDESS 2 and 4 carried out a series of passes over the next six hours. On several occasions GENIUS was visible through the salon window or mopping the front steps. GODDESS 2 and 4 assume GENIUS remained on the premises. At 13.30 ZULU/21.30 local GODDESS 1 took up a static position in the BLUE MOUNTAIN restaurant opposite the salon, and confirmed repeated sightings of GENIUS on the premises until GODDESS 1 withdrew at 15.00 ZULU/23.00 local.

20

Washington DC

The few runners out that morning along the Parkway were hooded and muffled. Winters in Washington DC could be surprisingly sharp, the air, on occasion, streaming down from the Great Lakes, shrouding the capital in dry, bleak cold.

Monroe had strapped his legs before heading out, bandaged his creaking, middle-aged knees. He jogged slowly through trees that stood stark against the sky.

He was back on his front porch now, through the screen door, and enveloped in the aroma of coffee from within. Molly was at the kitchen table with the *Post*. He stood for a moment in the ticking silence, smelling the coffee, the chemical cleanness beneath it, bleach, laundry detergent.

She looked up from the paper.

'It's seven-thirty, Jonathan.'

He took the stairs slowly, walked through the bedroom to the bathroom. He stood under the shower, which was hot but fitful. Limescale in the head? He towelled his lean torso, rubbed a clear spot in the steamed-up mirror, leaned in to clip his beard. The *snick* of the shears. His beard was short and tidy, a dignified frosting that strengthened his jaw, made up for the baldness and the greyness. Naked, he padded to the cupboard for underwear, starched shirt, sober crimson tie.

On the Metro the young man seated next to him read a Bible in Korean. He looked out of the corner of his eye, tried to piece together the script.

At C Street the security was tight. Some visiting Foreign Minister was snarling traffic, the diplomatic police watchful. Once inside he moved, frictionless, through security to his office.

'Morning, Mr Monroe.'

'Morning, Mr Monroe. You have the interagency at 10.30; you have the Assistant Secretary at 11.30. Afternoon is clear. Mr Harman of Liaison has already called and awaits your call back.' The secretary handed him a note with Harman's number. He nodded and entered his true home, the SCIF, the muffled, airless Sensitive Compartmented Information Facility.

On his desk, two packets. The first: collated intelligence, analysis, the Daily Brief. The second: selected pieces of raw intelligence, intercepts, agent reports more or less scrubbed, imagery.

The first packet, then. To be disposed of as quickly as possible. The Daily Brief's charts, headlines and newspapery language annoyed him. And some of the analysis, well. Sophomoric drivel written by some twenty-five-year-old at the Defense Intelligence Agency. *China's principal rival for regional influence continues to be Japan.* Why did they bother? He put it to one side.

The second packet was different. The second packet had TOP SECRET/SCI stamped on it. He went straight to the China folder, which was thick this morning. Decrypted Chinese cable traffic, some of it days old. It would keep. The debriefing of some bankers who'd been in Beijing talking to the Ministry of Finance about currency exchange rates. Transcripts of phone calls made by Chinese diplomats at the UN, some emails. Something that purported to be an internal Party memo detailing unrest in the rust belt, origins unclear. And what was this? Liaison material. In from the jolly old Brits, how charming.

TOPSECRETSNTK//DTELASTIC//TS-UK//NOFORN//ORCON//25X1

He signed the cover sheet and opened the folder. *Certain Questions. DF-41.*

The phone was ringing. Harman, of Liaison.

'Have you seen the stuff from the Brits?'

'Good morning, Grover.'

'Good morning, Jonathan. Have you seen it?'

'I have just this second opened the folder.' Monroe put a throat sweet in his mouth.

'Look at the translation for us, Jonathan. Then look at the original. Give us a view. We need you on this.'

'Grover?'

'Yes?'

'That's what I'm trying to do.'

'Well, good. Do you think you might have something for us, say, at the interagency?'

'I shall try, Grover.'

'Thank you, Jonathan.'

'And, Grover?'

'Yes?'

'We might want to give our British friends a look at the DTWHIPLASH material, might we not?'

A pause.

'The what?'

'DTWHIPLASH.'

'We'll discuss.'

*

The first collateral was coming in. A sharp-eyed American military attaché, based in Beijing but driving through Hebei, had come across a People's Liberation Army convoy. At the centre of the convoy was a six-axle truck carrying a large canister. The vehicle appeared to be a TEL, Transporter/Erector/Launcher. So, in the canister was a missile. A big one. DF-31, thought the attaché. What's that doing here? But then he looked more closely. The configuration of the vehicle was unfamiliar. The canister overhung the front of the tractor. And it looked bigger than usual. And that's not six axles, it's eight. And the hydraulic rams that should raise up the canister to its launch position weren't there. Was this some sort of mock-up? A prototype?

The military attaché snapped some images on his mobile phone as he passed, and, one hand on the wheel as he accelerated away, put a marker in his satellite navigation system. The attaché sent his findings back to Bolling Air Force Base with coordinates and a recommendation that the satellites get busy. Which they did.

The results were now on Patterson's desk in a series of images and reports under the codename WHIPLASH, sent post-haste by some bigwig in the US State Department's Bureau of Intelligence and Research, INR. Something afoot. A new, bigger transporter, for a new, bigger missile. The dimensions of the canister, calculated from the satellite images, came hair-raisingly close to what was described in the GENIUS product. The defence analysts were in a frenzy. Requirements was beaming. It's real, Trish, said Hopko. He's real.

21

This was the moment to keep one's mouth shut. Patterson shuffled the files in front of her on the conference table. Next to her was Hopko, circles under those dark eyes, in a skirt that was, well, hippy, and a necklace that looked like Stonehenge.

At the far end of the table sat the Director, Requirements and Production, engrossed in the briefing papers in front of him, dark suit, one hand on chin, in the other a bulbous fountain pen, with which he made scratchy annotations. Next to him was Yeats, who kept leaning in to the D/RP and murmuring. Opposite Patterson was Drinkwater of Security Branch, taut and steely as a wire brush, and another, more senior Security officer whose name she'd forgotten already.

Waverley entered, locks awry, and winked at her. Everyone waited for the gap at the head of the table to be filled. By C, the Director of the Secret Intelligence Service, himself.

He arrived five minutes late, gave a sterile apology, and the meeting got underway.

Hopko briefed. Hopko proposed. The Director of Requirements and Production was inquisitor in chief. C listened.

'But the sub-source. I'd feel a lot more comfortable if I knew for sure who he was.' The Director laid his fountain pen on the table. 'Come to that, I'd feel a lot more comfortable if we could confirm where GENIUS has been all these years.'

C spoke, drily.

'So would I.'

Drinkwater leaned forward, as if delivering news of a death.

'Security *is* concerned, Chief, that checking GENIUS against the Taiwanese lists *will* constitute unacceptable risk to the integrity of the operation.'

The Director of Requirements and Production allowed his gaze to fall on Drinkwater.

'I appreciate that, thank you, Simon. However, I rather feel that the use of an agent whose entire adult life is a mystery poses a threat to the integrity of the operation.'

Waverley spoke.

'Run up a big list, why don't you? Fifty, sixty names. Drop GENIUS's name in the middle, Li Huasheng in among all the other Li's. Let the Taiwanese check 'em all against their lists. They'll not know which one we're interested in.'

He held out his hands. Simple.

In the end, at Hopko's suggestion, they agreed on a request to the Taiwanese for a list of all subjects, surnamed Li, sentenced to labour reform between May 1989 and June 1994. And the request would go via the Singaporeans. Drinkwater was squirming. C was showing signs of impatience.

'And the gadget?'

'A memory stick, or thumb drive,' said Hopko. 'Stealthed. Won't set off any alarms in the host system. We hope and believe.'

'And what sort of a take would that offer us?'

'These things are up to a terabyte now. We can clone a decent part of a network,' said Hopko. 'It's a little larger than normal, but still small. It'll attach to a key chain.'

A pause.

'It's worked before, Chief,' said Hopko.

'What's the flap potential?' asked C.

'Well, if the gadget is discovered, the sub-source is arrested, obviously,' said Hopko. 'He tells all, and we must assume fingers us as his paymasters. He points them towards GENIUS. But GENIUS is hard to find and resourceful, so we have a cut-out there, which would buy Mangan time to get out.'

'You're telling me it's manageable?'

'It is. I am.'

The D/RP sat back and exhaled. He looked at C, who neither moved nor spoke.

'Christ, Val,' he said. 'I'll take it to the Special Adviser. But only because it's you.'

Wen Jinghan was a study in disbelief.

'Thirty thousand yuan? *Thirty thousand?*'

They were in Tuanjiehu Park, perhaps the only people, the day blustery and frigid. The water in the lake had begun to freeze. They sat on a bench next to the exercise area, the equipment stirring and squeaking in the wind.

'It's a lot of money,' said Peanut, wrong-footed.

'My summer holiday costs more than that.'

Peanut said nothing.

'You're telling me that I'm betraying everything, everything I know, risking nine grams in the head, and you're going to pay me thirty thousand yuan.'

'Well, aren't you the businessman, suddenly?'

Wen Jinghan looked at him open-mouthed.

'This is a farce.'

'I don't have to pay you anything at all. Your reward is my not sending those letters.'

The silver-haired man just shook his head, looked away, raised his hands, then dropped them on his knees, a gesture of despair.

'Jinghan, don't give me your I've-found-my-courage line again. It bores me.'

'Well, don't worry, Huasheng, about boredom. We'll have plenty of excitement soon, when State Security bangs on the door. Oh, God.' He looked down.

A woman, muffled to the eyes, walking a small dog and talking on a mobile phone, passed them.

'I need to know all your security procedures, Jinghan. At both places. At the Academy and at the General Armaments Department. Everything. From the minute you approach the building to when you're looking at your computer.'

Wen Jinghan had his eyes closed. A bird was picking its way across the ice with tiny, inky feet.

The Sings came back. Three thousand six hundred and forty-eight people surnamed Li had, according to the Taiwanese records, been sent to labour reform facilities between those dates. Would you like us to narrow it down a bit? they'd asked. Why not just give us the name? Hopko and a keen boy from Research spent a nervous two hours going down the lists, Patterson looking on.

And there he was. The sentence was handed down in mid-ninety. Li Huasheng. Beijing Fengtai District court. Attempted murder, assault, wounding. Reform through labour. Loss of political rights.

The sense of excitement around the operation was palpable.

Wen Jinghan began to speak with a tone of tired indulgence of the security arrangements at the General Armaments Department.

Cameras outside the building. A static post on the gate. A concrete guardhouse, the *chuandashi*, whose occupants stare and note. Then, inside, metal detectors, like an airport. Peanut pointed out he had never been to an airport. The professor looked at him with something Peanut felt came very close to contempt, so Peanut was obliged to sound threatening, again, to keep the upper hand, and the professor carried on. Bags through a machine, contents of pockets go into a little tray. A once-over with a wand. To get into the offices where he worked, a second sweep. A bag search, in and out. A swipe card opened the doors. The building was a Faraday cage, but the computer itself was not. Logging on required a thumb scan, a network key in the form of a card inserted into a reader, and a password. The system was alarmed against any unauthorised hardware.

The Launch Vehicle Academy was similar, but here security was conducted by a private company, which made it sharper. Security officers would appear unbidden in your office, conduct spot checks. Workers were known to be patted down on their way out, on top of the bag search.

Peanut thought about it.

'How comprehensive is it, Jinghan?'

'Very.'

'You got a sixty-page document out.'

The professor shuddered.

'Hold it together, Jinghan. Not much longer and it will all be done. Now go home.'

'What are you planning to do?'

'I'll call you.'

'No, I mean, how on earth do you think this can be done?'

'We did it before.'

'It's different, now.'

'Why? Because you've got a smart car and your nose in the trough. What the fuck happened to you, Jinghan?'

'A lot happened while you were shovelling shit in Qinghai. Did you notice? We grew up. The Party grew up. The cadres stopped killing the intellectuals and started listening to us. We rebuilt China. We turned our country into a global power. *We* did that. You're fighting an old war, Huasheng. The little shits who killed your father are all gone.'

'I'm going to turn you in just for the fun of it,' said Peanut.

The professor slumped.

'Don't you do that.'

'Go home, Jinghan.'

Peanut watched the professor's retreating back. Dusk was coming down, lights flickering on in the apartment blocks, their pale glitter in the lake's ice. The park was still. He was hungry, should be back at the salon. He lit a cigarette and watched. The woman walked her dog. He could just see her across the lake.

To his right a man in a tracksuit, half-walking, half-jogging, was coming towards him. Peanut watched him. Overweight, breathing heavily, his breath steaming, the man came close to Peanut and slowed. The man looked intently at him. Peanut looked away. The man stopped next to the bench on which Peanut sat, and stood there, breath rasping in the cold. Peanut stood up deliberately, flicked his cigarette into the lake, where it skittered sparking red over the ice, and, hands in pockets, walked away. The man began to follow, staying a few paces behind. Peanut began to move more quickly; the man kept pace. Now the path led away from the lake into a stand of bamboo. Peanut heard the man's footsteps quicken. He turned to find the man almost on him, one arm extended. Peanut took a step back.

'What do you want?'

'You know what I want.'

The man moved towards Peanut, placed a hand on his upper arm.

'Get off me, now.'

'Don't be awkward,' the man said.

Peanut allowed himself to be pushed off the path into the bamboo, which clacked and rustled. It was darker in here. The man was behind him, still holding his arm, forcing him on.

And then Peanut turned, very fast. His left hand, with a *thwack*, was on the back of the man's neck. His right brought up the little knife and laid the blade flat on the man's cheek, its point just below the eye.

'You move, it goes in.'

The man stood stock-still, leaning in slightly to Peanut, his mouth wide, eyes flickering.

'What do you want with me?' said Peanut.

The man could only whisper.

'You know . . .'

'Who are you working for?'

'What?'

'Who are you working for?' A little pressure under the eye.

'I . . . I work for an insurance company. What's that got to do with anything?'

Peanut blinked.

'Why were you following me?'

'I thought . . . you . . . you know. Please don't do this.'

'You thought what?'

'Please.'

'Why?'

'We come here to meet, people.' The pitch of his voice was rising. The man was shaking now, his knees starting to give way.

'I made a mistake,' he said. 'Please let me go now.'

Peanut allowed the point of the knife to break the skin, a tiny blossom of blood visible against the knife's sheen. He could feel the bulge of the eye against the point. The man gasped, then wrenched himself away. His head went down and Peanut felt the knife cut in. The man thrashed and swung open-handed at

Peanut's head, barely making contact. Peanut pulled the knife back. The man bent double and placed his hands over his eye. He was breathing very fast, making an urgent mewling sound with each exhalation. Then his knees went and he was on the ground amid the bamboo stems.

'What the fuck did you do that for?' said Peanut.

Blood was running out through the man's fingers. He didn't speak.

'I'm asking one last time: why did you follow me?'

The man muttered something Peanut couldn't make out.

'What?'

Now the man shrieked, his voice cracking. 'I just wanted to *play.*'

Peanut swallowed. He could smell blood and piss. He turned and pushed his way through the clattering bamboo, and ran.

Ting ordered the bean curd drenched in explosive chilli sauce, and delicate shredded pork. They had spent the day driving around the villages to the north-west of Beijing, looking for sand. The paper wanted a feature on desertification. *Sandy Tentacles of the Gobi! Reaching for Beijing!* It wasn't hard to find. They found villages where houses were almost buried by dunes moving south-east year by year. The villagers pointed to rows of scrawny poplars they'd planted, which did no good. The fields were grey and icy, but the sand was, well, sand.

China's vibrant capital could soon vanish beneath the vast Gobi Desert, according to environmental experts.

Mangan shot some stills of a mournful family atop their roof, as the dune slowly filled up their home, spilling in through the windows. The stills were good, with nice textures, sand, brick, the rough clothes of the toothless grandmother. But Ting pointed out that the family looked as if they were marooned on the roof, as if by a flood, so Mangan made them come down and shot them all over again, the grandmother laughing *mei guanxi!* No matter.

In the car on the way back Ting had spoken of the simplicity, the honesty of traditional peasant life.

'It's very beautiful, Philip. Generations of family in one village. We've lost that, now.'

Mangan had spent enough time in villages – villages with corrupt and brutal local officials, the young men all gone to work on the building sites, villages racked with HIV – to wonder where the sentiment came from.

Now Mangan studied her, as they waited for the food. And she studied him back.

'You seem a bit ... preoccupied, Philip. Is everything okay? How are our finances? Can you still afford me?'

Mangan looked at his beer glass.

'Yes, well, looking up, actually. These people at the Pan Asia Institute. They've made a proposal.'

He stopped. Proceed with care, he thought. Ting looked expectant.

'What sort of proposal, Philip? Marriage? Something more casual?'

'They've asked me to put in a proposal for a book.'

Ting looked astonished.

'A book? You?' She put her hand over her mouth to stifle a laugh. Her nails were painted bronze.

'I know. But they're so floored by my lectures, they want more. So there we are.'

'What's it going to be about?'

'Well, I have to put in an idea, a summary. I was thinking, we could look at some aspect of the Followers. Who they are, how the state has responded to them. God knows we've spent enough time watching them. It would say something about power, challenges to state authority. It's compelling.'

'We?'

And may God forgive him, because he would never forgive himself.

'Yes, I wondered if you might help me with it.'

'Doing what?'

'Helping me get all the materials together. Forcing me to write the bloody thing. You'd get a credit – if you wanted it. There's a bit of money. It could be very good for you.'

The food arrived. Ting spooned bean curd into her bowl. The sauce was a deep red on her rice. She was pensive.

'So is that why you've been preoccupied?'

'Yes, I think so. All in a good cause, you see.' *You see?*

She smiled, and nodded.

'All right, Philip. I'll think about it. The Followers. And thanks.'

They ate, chatted about the rumours swirling around that Harvey was being considered for some big network job in Hong Kong. But there were always rumours swirling around Harvey.

Mangan paid, and looked at his watch.

'Somewhere to be?' said Ting.

'Yes.'

Ting thrust her face forward in exaggerated curiosity.

'Well, where?' she said.

'Nothing you'd enjoy.'

Now she frowned.

'Don't say that, Philip.'

'Sorry. I just meant . . .'

She placed her fingertips on the back of his hand.

'I know very well what I'd enjoy.'

'I'll see you tomorrow.'

He got up and left.

God forgive him.

GENIUS made the contact in TUANJIEHU Park. GODDESS 4 made one pass only of the meeting. The contact was a man aged approximately fifty years old, grey-haired, with the appearance of a successful professional. GENIUS and the contact sat on a bench and were in conversation for seventeen minutes. After the meeting ended GODDESS 4 stayed on the contact. The contact returned to the main gate of TUANJIEHU Park and hailed a taxi. GODDESS 4 lost him in traffic. GODDESS 1 picked up GENIUS as he left the park. GENIUS appeared agitated. GENIUS walked north to scheduled meeting in SANLITUN district with RATCHET.

At the north end of the Workers' Stadium couples waltzed under streetlamps to music from a karaoke machine placed on the pavement. A dozen or so couples, in thick jackets and woollen hats, lifting and turning.

Mangan stood in the shadow from a tree, scanning the bystanders. But Peanut was behind him, breathing hard, pressing something into his hand. Mangan palmed it and put it in his pocket. A voice in his ear.

'Anything for me?'

Mangan's mouth was dry.

'They say you are to stop all counter-surveillance immediately. It makes you conspicuous.'

Silence. He turned, saw Peanut's hard eyes.

'They're watching me?' said Peanut, grinning. 'Ha!'

Mangan looked straight ahead at the dancers.

'Anything else?'

Mangan shook his head. Peanut spoke very close to his ear.

'Tell them I need a commitment. Soon.'

And then he was gone.

Something like a polka came on, the sound rattling across the asphalt, vying with the traffic, and the dancers picked up their pace.

22

Washington, DC

Monroe chose the quiet car. He would use this time properly, to read, as the landscape slipped by. Philadelphia languished in a cold rain, the scrapyards of twisted metal and weeds. Monroe loathed the plane. He took the train for the calm and quiet. Hours still to Boston, where they'd meet him in a big, comfortable car, and drive him to the Charles Hotel. His talk, for the benefit of Harvard faculty, principally, though he had allowed the presence of a few doctoral students, was entitled, 'The Dragon's Crosshairs: Towards a Reframing of China's Defense Priorities'. And there would be dinner at the Harvard Faculty Club, beneath the Canalettos, with a select group. He read. New York came and went. And by three he was in Boston. He asked the driver to go via the Back Bay, where Beacon Street twinkled under snow, and over the river to Cambridge.

'He doesn't step out often. He does his work quietly, and usually reserves his analysis for the corridors of power in Washington. So we're very privileged to have here today the foremost analyst of

Chinese affairs in the US intelligence community, Jonathan Monroe of the State Department's Bureau of Intelligence and Research, known as INR. Ladies and gentlemen, today's session is of course unclassified, but nothing is for attribution. I hope everybody will respect that. Jonathan.' A liver-spotted professor – no stranger himself to matters of intelligence – gestured to Monroe.

Monroe nodded. 'And if I start slipping into the indiscreet,' he said, with a grave smile, 'perhaps Mark will ease me back on to the path of the righteous.' He nodded self-deprecatingly towards the professor.

It was Monroe's stump lecture, with a little secret sparkle added for Harvard. He strode with purpose through China's military modernisation: its scope, its cost; he tantalised with details of China's newest submarines; he danced through the professionalisation of the army's non-commissioned officer corps, in-flight refuelling, anti-satellite capability, and perhaps, soon, a ballistic missile, known as a carrier killer, which could drop out of the sky on moving naval targets at sea.

'Oh, and ladies and gentlemen – and I should be careful here – I'm hopeful that we will soon see developments in our, let us say, understanding of China's launch vehicle capacity.'

A smile and a wink. A frisson in the room.

For the next hour the attendees immersed themselves in earnest discussion of what it all added up to. China's claims to exclusivity in international waters. China as strategic competitor? As peer competitor? As asymmetric threat? How, when China's defence budget did not exceed one sixth that of the United States, could China be seen as any kind of competitor at all? Surely China was really no more than a prudent emerging power protecting her interests?

And towards the end of the session a question from the doctoral student in pink, a pink dress, sort of salmon pink, the one whom Monroe had been trying not to gaze at for the last hour and a half, but for whom he had reserved some of his most confiding glances and knowing smiles. Her question was spoken in the accent of the China coast, leavened and smoothed by the society of America's great universities, spoken softly from beneath a beguiling fringe of bible-black hair. Her question was about what exactly? Something epistemological, by the sound of it.

'My name is Nicole Yang and I am a doctoral student here at Harvard. I'm from Taiwan. Thank you for taking my question, Mr Monroe. I want to ask you about *knowing*. It is your business as an intelligence analyst to construct knowledge, is it not? Knowledge of the geopolitical landscape, knowledge of the threats that face us. Knowledge on the basis of which our nations make great decisions. I wonder when you *know* you know, if you see what I mean. When does uncertainty stop? How do you *know* when it stops?'

What I *know*, young lady, is that I'd like to *know* what's under that dress.

'Well, that is a fascinating question, Miss Yang, and one that, as I think you have shrewdly surmised, bedevils the intelligence analyst.' A pause for reflection, a frown. 'Or it *should* bedevil the intelligence analyst. When it doesn't, well, you get certainty, and Iraq.'

Knowing laughter. Then Monroe put one hand to his chin. Silence in the room.

'But intelligence work, Miss Yang, is rarely definitive. It *tells* you very little. But it *suggests* a lot. So the job of the analyst is to be, I think, less a knowledge-maker, as you put it, and more a *sense*-maker. We try to wrestle form and meaning out of shards of information, and these assemblages are the fulcrums on which our leaders must balance policy, and we must constantly rebuild those assemblages adding and subtracting slivers of information as we go. And we must always, always, allow uncertainty its due.'

Applause. A modest tip of the head.

Afterwards, when he had shaken some hands and pried off the junior faculty, she was waiting for him in the foyer. His eyes flickered down to her breasts, flickered up again.

'That was a wonderful talk, Mr Monroe, thank you so much,' she said.

'It was my pleasure, Miss Yang. And what, if I may ask, is the subject of your doctoral dissertation?'

'Chinese strategic thought, Mr Monroe. Notions of territoriality. A taxonomy, of sorts. There is a great deal I would like to ask you, if the opportunity were to arise.'

Monroe looked at his watch, blew out his cheeks. *Might it be possible?*

'Well, Miss Yang, I have a dinner this evening, but afterwards, at perhaps ten, I may be found in the bar of the Charles Hotel. If you join me there, and you buy me a glass of something warming, perhaps we can look at one or two of those questions in more congenial surroundings.'

She actually lit up. And did she just bite her lip?

'I will see you there, Mr Monroe.'

The Permanent Under-Secretary was still in his cycling gear, lurid shorts that hugged his crotch and thighs, a T-shirt and a helmet. The Director of Requirements and Production, known for fastidiousness in his dress, wondered how the man could bear to be seen like this every morning, sweaty and exposed before his staff.

'Morning, morning,' said the Permanent Under-Secretary. He made a saluting gesture with a small bicycle pump. 'I'll be right with you. We're meeting in room four.'

The Foreign Office Special Adviser was already seated. He motioned a hello as he leafed through his file. They sat in silence. The Director of Requirements and Production fidgeted.

The Permanent Under-Secretary hurried in, suited now, his

hair wet. The D/RP readied himself to brief, sat up in his chair. The Permanent Under-Secretary wasn't interested.

'Okay, right then. Seems to me this is a risky op. We're using a UK citizen on a freelance contract, and we're fiddling with some serious Chinese stuff.' He ran his finger down a page. 'But I must say, the reaction to the first tranche of product has been very, very positive, hasn't it? My word. Commendations from Defence. Thank-you notes from Langley. Collateral flying in from those clever chaps at INR. Doesn't get much better than this, does it?'

The Permanent Under-Secretary raised a warning finger. 'But. We are proposing a whole new level of complexity, are we not, in the next stage of this thing? The potential for a flap seems pronounced. What happens if the civilian, this RATCHET, screws up?'

'RATCHET has a high degree of deniability built in. He is very flexible, very mobile. He's a freelance. He has no dependants, no serious ties to China. If he has to up and leave in a hurry, he can. I'm not too worried about RATCHET.'

The Permanent Under-Secretary looked at him.

'Oh, really? What *are* you worried about, then?'

'GENIUS is also sound, we have a high degree of confidence.'

The Permanent Under-Secretary waited.

'My concern is with the sub-source. He has been issued a codename, now, I believe. Yes, sub-source CRATER. We have one sighting, which seems to confirm his identity as that of our former sub-agent. But we know little about him. The reliability of CRATER is perhaps the area of greatest uncertainty.'

'And?'

'Well, as of now, this is planned as a sale,' said the D/RP. 'There will be no defector in place, just a one-off transaction, access in return for reward. There'll be mutterings over the quality of the product due to its being in the form of digital files, and so susceptible to forgery. And, of course, a one-off operation does not allow us to find collateral and build an agent's track record over time.'

'Absolutely. Taken on board,' said the Permanent Under-Secretary. Meaning, yes, your arse is covered.

The Special Adviser spoke now.

'If I may, to what extent might the arrangement – this one-off transaction business – be open to review at a later stage, do we think?'

The Director of Requirements and Production nodded.

'These things are of course always open to review.'

'It's just,' said the Special Adviser, 'the attraction for me in the operation, and I think the Foreign Secretary would agree, is the degree to which it may allow us a look at the Chinese network itself. Quite apart from what's stored on it. A number of consumers come to mind who possess considerable appetite for this category of intelligence, both inside and outside government.'

The thought hung in the air of room four for a moment. The Permanent Under-Secretary nodded his agreement.

'Cyber, yes. I like cyber very much. Cyber is hot. And cyber is, as we know, gentlemen, *funded*.'

She ordered, to Monroe's astonishment, very old, very expensive Scotch. She didn't ask what he wanted, she just handed it to him without a word, its gorgeous amber shining in the soft light. Then she went to a quiet table with leather chairs, sat with her legs angled to one side, ankles crossed, like a fifties movie star. He followed. She'd changed out of the pink and wore a cocktail dress of deep green silk, her shoulders bare, and a single string of pearls. Still she said nothing.

'So. Tell me again. You are writing your dissertation. How can I help you?' he said. For want of anything better.

'Well, there really is so much,' she said.

*

GODDESS 1 was pulling out, for now. She would be heading quietly to the airport, the mobile phone wiped and dumped in a rubbish bin, the memory card just that, a memory, the boys already gone. Eileen Poon waited for an elevator with her luggage, a little suitcase on wheels in plain black. She would not miss this hotel, with its cracked floors of fake marble tile, its peeling gilt fittings, its thumps and screeches in the night. Though she knew she'd be back, if not to this hotel, then to a hundred more like it. This operation was going ahead, she could feel it. The target was dry as a bone. Nothing even resembling contact with in-country counter-intelligence; no dodgy little meetings, no unexplained absences. She'd rarely seen a man so *insulated*.

And yet.

Granny Poon, during thirty years on the streets of China, had developed instincts that she half-trusted. Those instincts now told her of something hovering just out of reach, out of her field of vision. Not any corporeal presence – she'd spot that in seconds – but an *interest*. She had hinted of her unease to Patterson, and afterwards reproached herself. *Stupid old woman, jumping at shadows, losing her touch.* The elevator hissed and rattled.

She walked through reception. The girl behind the counter looked at her. She walked on, and as she reached the revolving door, looked back. The girl was on the phone, dialling. A porter in a stained red coat stood on the pavement.

'Airport?'

'Yes.'

'Which terminal?'

She said nothing.

'What time's your flight?'

'I'll get a taxi on the street.'

'No, no, get one here.' The porter blew on a whistle and gestured into the dark. Headlights came on.

Eileen Poon turned and walked to the street.

The porter was shouting after her and another man was with him. She turned a corner, quickened her pace and let the darkness wash over her.

Operation STONE CIRCLE came into being with a flurry of paperwork, authorisations, briefings, clearances. A stingy budget received speedy, if grudging, approval. Yeats hovered, and disappeared for hours at a time. He would leave the building, but quite where he went was hard for Patterson to ascertain. Hopko was a blur. She spent hours with the technology – the 'gadget' – closeted with technicians in the basement, and making lightning dashes to Cheltenham, where in the huge, chill GCHQ building, she was briefed and briefed again on the new mechanics of cyber-espionage. And she spent an almost equal amount of time with the Service lawyer, cajoling and reassuring, explaining how the use of a UK citizen as freelancer posed no insurmountable legal challenge.

Patterson sat in her cubicle sorting the paperwork and writing an operational schedule. Hopko had ordained the operation to be done and dusted in four weeks. Charteris came up with local procedures, meeting places, protocols. Mangan was eased along with occasional calming words from Charteris and was dispatched to Singapore for a 'meeting with his editors'. The editors – bemused by this unknown newcomer to their authorial stable – quietly commissioned a book, as they had been politely asked to do by one of the Pan Asia Institute's most important donors.

For Patterson, yet another plane.

In Singapore, at a white, cool villa not far from Phoenix Park, once the residence of British army officers, she talked Mangan through what they knew, what they thought they knew, and what they had planned. The night before he left, they sat on the veranda, in the tropical night, the frogs chirruping. Mangan lit a cigarette.

'How do you feel?' Patterson asked.

Mangan tilted his head one way then the other, as if to say, okay.

'Is there anything you need?'

'Don't think so,' he said.

'You feel ready.'

He just nodded.

'Stay sharp, Philip. Stay aware. Please,' she said.

Peanut's fingers traced the characters on the brittle paper.

A swirl of dust arising!

Subtle, subtle!

Spy as moving man.

They are watching me. We are back together.

He turned out the light, pulled up the blanket. Not long, now.

2 3

Beijing

22.40, by a frozen canal in Liangmahe. Mangan was surprised. This part of the city was full of foreigners, with the attendant surveillance, cameras affixed to every building like gargoyles. But here he saw what Charteris had seen. The path by the canal led under a bridge. It was very dark and the traffic noise was intense. Explaining on the phone to Peanut had been a trial and had made him nervous.

Peanut was late, came bustling down the path twelve minutes after the appointed time. He wore a red anorak with a garish brand name printed on its back, its hood up. Mangan smelled cigarettes and the sorghum liquor.

'This is a stupid place to meet. I couldn't find it,' Peanut said.

'I didn't choose it.'

'Better we make our own arrangements next time.'

'Our next meeting will be in two days, at oh-six-forty at the east gate of the Temple of Heaven Park. If you cannot make it, then one day after that, and again the day after that. Do you understand?'

'Yes, yes.' He sounded bad-tempered.

Mangan pushed on, the way he'd been told.

'You are to prepare the sub-source for the delivery of an item and instructions.'

'What item?'

Mangan looked at him.

'I don't know what item.'

'How can I ready him for the delivery of an item if I don't know what the item is?'

'It will be something small and everyday. I think they're going to pass all the instructions at our next meeting.'

'You *think*?'

Mangan paused.

'Well?' said Peanut.

'I have a commitment for you.'

That got his attention.

'Go on,' said Peanut.

'They agree in principle to your fee. These are their words, not mine. They undertake to pay you as long as the material turned over is deemed sufficient. In cash. It will be waiting for you in a destination country.'

'What do they mean, "sufficient"?'

'That's just what they said.'

Peanut spat.

'And the travel?'

'They agree in principle to helping you leave the country. They will provide travel papers and expenses. They say leaving the country will be up to you, though they will suggest to you ways out. They will not undertake to find you citizenship of another country, but they undertake to find you legal status abroad, a visa, residency, something.'

Peanut was staring fixedly down the path.

'Did they say where?'

'No.'

'Somewhere warm, maybe.'

'Maybe.'

Mangan closed the door to the flat. The *clack* of the lock echoed around the room. He took off his down coat and poured a vodka, left the lights off, went to the window. He took his binoculars. Not much to see tonight, most of the windows were already dark, the little theatres closed. But, there, a woman wearing red stood at a sink. She shook the water from her hands and turned as if someone had called her name, and walked listlessly from the room. There, two floors up, a man sat bent over a low glass table. He was examining something closely, but the audience could not know what. And over there, the *wujing* on the gate turned up the collars on their green overcoats and tied down the earflaps of their fur hats.

The cold was deepening and the dusty smog muted the city's lights, spun halos around the cars' headlamps.

A flicker of movement. Mangan turned his binoculars to it. A muffled figure, wearing a white surgical mask against the freezing, particulate-sodden air, made its way from the main gate along the path that wound between grey arid flowerbeds, walking carefully on the ice. The figure stopped. Mangan watched. The figure raised a gloved hand, pulled the surgical mask down to the chin and turned its face upwards, towards Mangan's window. Towards him. The figure stood still, its gaze fastened on the window. Mangan stepped quickly back into shadow.

He stood in the darkness, listened to his own breathing.

The woman, 'Rachel Davies', would want to know that Peanut had accepted. Charteris was due to call him tomorrow, and he'd say, the proposal's been accepted. And Charteris would congratulate him. And then he was to wait. 'Rachel Davies' was very big on that idea, that this racket, as she called it, was all about waiting. Waiting, and keeping it light. Keep it light, Philip, as light as possible, she'd said. A good operation is a whisper.

He ran his finger along the base of the window frame, felt the fine grit between his fingers.

Mangan did not have to wait long. There was a short hold-up while alternative operating systems were installed on the gadget, just in case, and the logo had to match that of the professor's car, of course, but these things were done quickly, at Hopko's persistent urging. And when they were done the gadget was dispatched by secure bag, couriered to Beijing Station.

A London winter twilight, a misty stillness drifting with smell, a sudden rush of roasting and herbs, a tiny twist of perfume on the air, above dank leaves. The smell of steaks in passageways, thought Patterson as she walked.

Hopko's house was in Canonbury Square. The houses here were of grey brick, their understatement a guarantee of their opulence. How the hell, she thought, on a Service salary, but bit the thought back as mean-spirited, even for her.

She knocked at a black door. It was opened by an elderly Asian man in a white waiter's jacket and a bow tie, who gestured her in. A heavy in a black suit and earpiece reviewed her invitation, murmured, frowned and lingered over a list before checking her name. She took off her coat and handed it over. Dressing for the evening had been traumatic: her one good dress, short, of white crushed silk, left her sleek and, well, muscular. She walked up a flight of stairs. The entire first floor was a reception room with cream walls, green curtains of some heavy embroidered cloth sweeping from ceiling to floor, and leather benches before a slate fireplace. At one end of the room a baby grand piano, at which a young man with Chinese looks was playing something jazzy and clever, and an enormous Christmas tree. She felt eyes on her as she walked in. The crowd was Whitehall, mainly secret, some diplomatic and liaison services, many wives. There was the Permanent Under-Secretary, tieless, in a very good suit. There was Yeats, rumpled and flushed, explaining something slowly to the Japanese liaison officer. She took a glass of red wine from a waiter. It was hot and had things floating in it. No matter, move to secure position. She made her way to the fireplace, where she towered over the men sitting on the leather benches. They looked up at her and she pretended not to notice them. She felt a hand on her arm. Hopko was in a layered black chiffon thing and half the silver of China. Patterson was glad of her approach.

'Trish. My god, you're fabulous. Who knew?'

'Val.'

'You're wasted on us, my love. Come quickly now and meet an air vice marshal.'

He was the wry type, grey eyes and sensible haircut, young for his rank, much cleverer than he was willing to let on. He was something big in Information Operations.

'Val tells me you're army,' he said. 'How on earth did you make the transition?'

'Not sure I have,' she said.

'Do tell,' he said, smiling.

'Well, that's the thing, I can't. Tell.'

'What, not even someone like me?'

'I could tell you, but then I'd have to eat you,' she said.

He laughed at the old line. She looked down.

'I'm not sure I believe it,' he said. 'Val Hopko's protégés always seem to do just fine.'

'Is that what I am?' she said.

He looked startled.

'I'm sorry. I didn't mean to be presumptuous.'

'No,' she said, trying to row back. 'It's just . . . I'm not anyone's protégé.'

He blinked.

'Of course not. Please don't take it that way.'

An awkward pause.

'Val has sorted a place for smoking cigars,' he said. 'Shall we go and have a look?'

They went up another flight of stairs, to where French windows opened on to a roof terrace with wrought iron furniture. Gas heaters threw out a tent of warmth. They selected cigars from a divan, Patterson's long and slender.

'You smoke like a pro,' he said, and put his jacket around her bare shoulders. They eased into conversation with some people from Five. She shook hands, said hello. They all sat and puffed under the gas heaters. One told an absurd story from Belfast days, something about burgling a Provo house to bug it, dogs in the garden, a drugged sausage that they wouldn't eat. Patterson tried to think of something to contribute but got stuck outside Nasiriyah in the heat, the eyeless corpses.

She got up and mouthed, bathroom. The air vice marshal, Liam was his name, half-stood as she went, and smiled at her.

She went up another two floors. She passed a half-open door and glimpsed low light and bookshelves. She stopped and pushed the door open further. The room was a study. The bookshelves were floor to ceiling, many of the books in Chinese. Opposite, beneath a sash window, stood an open bureau, its desk covered with papers. Patterson walked over to it. On top lay a dictionary of classical Chinese. Next to it a book of what, poetry? Patterson puzzled through the characters. *Poems of Bai Juyi*. And a page of translation, handwritten, scarred with crossings out, corrections.

Mourning Peony Flowers
Heartsick, there by the steps, for the red peonies.
By evening time, there were only two stems left.

When morning comes the wind will rise, and surely blow
   them away.
In the night I mourn the waning red, and take a lamp to
   look.

'Are you spying?'

Patterson jumped, put one hand on the desktop. Hopko stood
in the doorway.

'I'm sorry, I shouldn't ...'

'Oh, Trish, don't worry. It's fine. You've discovered my little
pastime.'

Patterson looked down, tried to gather herself under Hopko's
gaze.

'They've all been translated many times before, of course,'
Hopko went on, giving Patterson time, 'but there's something
elusive to them, so I always want to try again.'

'My Chinese doesn't run to classical poetry, I'm afraid,' said
Patterson, realising as she said it how curt it sounded.

'No reason it should,' said Hopko. 'How are you finding them,
downstairs?'

'Well, you know. I'm just a junior officer.'

'You probably have more experience than most of them put
together,' said Hopko.

'Few successes.'

'Well, perhaps we're on the verge of something this time.'

'Do you think?'

'I think it's possible. But I have a feeling things are going to
become a little ... unpredictable.' Hopko made a wry face.

'Something I should know?'

'If I knew for sure, I still wouldn't be able to tell you. But this
brings me to a delicate request.'

Patterson waited. Hopko was leaning against the door jamb.
She spoke in a very level tone, and quickly.

'I'm thinking contingencies, Trish. And I want you to famil-
iarise yourself with a contingency operation that we have
available to us *in extremis*. It's on file as CALIPER. I've cleared you
in. But perhaps we can keep to ourselves that this is a part of our
operational thinking, for now. Would you do that?'

'Can I ask what CALIPER does?'

Hopko thought for a moment.

'I'd rather you read the file.'

Patterson nodded.

'Now come on, if you don't fancy the air vice marshal, there's
a rather dashing covert operations chap down there. He's got a
little moustache that we won't hold against him.' And she took
Patterson by the arm, the height disparity between them ridiculous, and led her back down the stairs.

The purpose of the invitation had been served, and
Patterson left a short time later. As she took her coat, Liam
gave her a card with his number on it and made a regretful face
as she turned away. She walked out into the square, the night
air chill against her skin. Her heels clattered on the pavement.
Somewhere a blackbird started up, reedy and solitary in the
darkness.

January. After a few days' rest in Hong Kong, GODDESS was back
in position. Beijing was foul with smog and early dust. Eileen
and Frederick Poon made a trip to a factory in Tianjin. They
ordered a consignment of orange whistles, wind-up penguins
and miniature skateboards. The latter item was particularly
sought after that season on the playgrounds of the eastern
United States, and would be good business. Winston Poon,
happy in his hotel room in front of a Cantonese movie channel,
signalled, 'Awaiting instructions'. Patterson signalled back,
'Standby'.

She sat at her desk alone, late in the evening, and brought up the file labelled TOP SECRET/UK EYES ALPHA/CALIPER, and read it again.

Charteris had booked the room, a musty box with stained quilts in a backpacker hostel off Nanluoxiang. Mangan turned on the television, took the battery from his mobile phone. Peanut arrived late, jumpy.

'Why a hotel, Mang An? This is not good.'

Mangan put a finger to his lips, motioned to Peanut's mobile phone. He took it, disabled it and left it on the bed next to his own. He took Peanut's arm and pushed him into the tiny bathroom, turned on the taps. They squatted on the tiled floor.

Mangan handed him the gadget and watched the smile spread over his face. Mangan made him practise and repeat back the instructions three times.

'This is good, Mang An,' said Peanut. 'Very, very good.'

Mangan just nodded. Peanut stowed the thing in an inside pocket.

'What else do they say, Mang An?'

'About what?'

'About me. About this thing.'

He will look for reassurance, 'Rachel Davies' had said. *You must convey to him that he's being taken seriously, that his work is about more than the money.*

'They know exactly what you are doing. They respect you. I can hear it in the way they speak.'

'And they have watchers out, yes?'

'I'm sure they do.'

'Who's in charge? Can you tell me that?'

'Best not. I don't even know their real name.'

'Yes, best not.'

We want him to feel loyal to us. We give stability and purpose, and a future.

'But they are very senior officers, and they want you to succeed,' said Mangan.

'This has become quite a big operation,' said Peanut.

'Yes, it has. Let's make it work,' said Mangan.

'Oh, I will.'

Mangan watched Peanut pull the scarf up over his face against the smog and slip out of the door. The landing was empty and Peanut made quickly for the stairs and was gone.

Mangan settled down to wait for an hour before he left. He lay on the bed, lit a cigarette. One more of these meetings and it was done. The entire weird episode would be over.

24

Beijing

The sky over Beijing was a filthy grey brown in daylight, orange at evening. One's fingers and lips cracked, grit in the mouth. And the dust had a dry mineral odour that Peanut would forever associate with the *hutong* homes of elderly relatives, where it worked its way into cupboards and linen year after year. It lingered on books.

He remembered his father on his knees in their apartment, picking up the books that the Red Guards had hurled to the floor. He had bent to help. They put the books into a brown trunk. After a few minutes his fingers were grey with the dust. His father had wiped his nose with the back of his hand. His mother had been in the next room, kneeling over an electric ring, trying to cook cabbage in a little oil.

Yin stood at the salon window, cold, clutching herself. They had shut up shop, bolting the doors. Each morning the sinks, the hairdryers were coated with dust. Dandan Mama sat cracking sunflower seeds in her teeth. The television showed the dust swirling across north China, its origins in Mongolia.

He stood.

'I'm going out for a bit.'

Yin shook her head.

'What for? It's horrible.'

'Just some business.'

He unbolted the door.

He lingered at the end of the thoroughfare, his hood up. The smog was a bitter shroud, wiping the features from the tower blocks. The streets were all but empty.

He had chosen a rattletrap cinema in Fangzhuang, a late-afternoon showing of a risible action film, its shirtless star in a jungle somewhere, oiled and subtitled into poor Mandarin.

The professor was sat exactly where he'd been told, high up at the back, no one behind him. Peanut climbed the steps, sat beside him, leaned in and whispered.

'I could do better than this,' said Peanut. Wen Jinghan stared at the screen. 'What do you think, Jinghan, you and me, with our ill-gotten gains. We'll produce a movie. A spy story.'

The professor said nothing. Peanut looked at him, shook his head, then reached into his pocket and took out a small pouch of a suede-like material. It was sealed with a drawstring, which Peanut pulled open. Inside was a car key, its head black, plastic and boxy, a key of the sort that might permit a driver to open or start a vehicle from a distance.

'Look at me, Jinghan.'

The professor turned, his gaze blank.

'It's a car key,' said Peanut. 'For your shiny Japanese car. You put it on your key chain.'

The professor looked, expressionless.

'But,' said Peanut, and, his thumb exerting pressure on the shoulder of the key, a *snick*. The shaft came away, revealing a rec-tangular plug protruding from the black plastic head, a plug of the sort one might insert into a port on a computer.

The professor looked away.

'Very clever,' he said.

'It is, isn't it?' said Peanut.

'The system's alarmed,' said the professor. 'It's alarmed against any external hardware. I told you this. When I plug that in, the alarms go off. And security puts an electric baton up my arse. Or in my mouth. They do that, you know. It doesn't leave marks.'

Peanut leaned in very close now.

'Do not tell me about electric batons, Jinghan.'

The professor shrank away.

'You do not tell me about electric batons, do you know why? Because electric batons have featured in my life the way that shiny Japanese cars have featured in yours. In that I encountered them frequently. Do you understand?'

'I didn't mean . . .'

'Shut your fatuous, condescending mouth and listen.'

The professor closed his eyes, then opened them and turned, not meeting Peanut's gaze. He pointed at the key and spoke in a furious whisper.

'This will not work. It cannot work.'

'Listen. This is what they have told me to tell you. They understand alarmed networks. And this will not set off any alarm. It's . . . it's, what . . . stealthed.'

'You haven't the faintest idea what you're talking about, have you?'

'These are clever people.' Peanut could feel the poverty of his responses. The professor was meeting his gaze now, and there was a sneer.

'Jinghan, this is what you will do. You insert the plug in the port. Then you watch this little green light here.' Peanut pointed to a diode on the key's head, his chipped, dirty nail against the plastic.

'The light will start to flash. After about five or six seconds it will stop flashing and will show a continuous green. When it does that, you pull it out, immediately. Then you wait thirty minutes. Then you do the same thing again. Insert it, wait for the green to stop flashing. It will take longer this time, maybe twenty or thirty seconds. When it goes to continuous green you pull it out again.'

The professor was still silent.

'So just remember, when it goes to continuous green pull it out.'

Silence.

'That's all. And then you just reassemble the key.' The *snick* as the shaft locked back into place. 'Take it, Jinghan. Practise opening it up.' He held out the key.

Wen Jinghan sighed.

'Look, let me find another way, all right? I mean, this is crazy. This is just ... it's crazy. I'll think of something different.' He patted the air, as if to calm Peanut down and to indicate the conversation was closed. He turned back to the screen. Peanut could see something fiery out of the corner of his eye. The cinema rumbled to the movie's explosions. Peanut sniffed.

'No, this is how it's going to go. And then it's over.'

'Do you believe that, Huasheng? I mean, really?'

'When it's done, Jinghan, call me at this number and leave a message. Any message, doesn't matter.' Peanut handed the professor the little bag and a piece of paper with the Blue Diamond's number written on it.

He had chosen the restaurant for its reek of Washington, of power, of quiet murmurings in panelled rooms. It was in Georgetown, and its middle-aged waiters would bring you mounds of fresh oysters on crushed ice, good champagne. She took his arm lightly as they went in. Monroe tried to stifle the adolescent thrill he felt. They sat. She ordered a champagne cocktail, for heaven's sake.

'Taiwan,' said Monroe. 'Do you know I've never been?'

She considered.

'It's more cosmopolitan than you might imagine these days,' she said.

'I'm sure it is. You seem *very* cosmopolitan.'

'So I've been told,' she said.

'But as an employee of the US government, I have to get authorisation to go. Isn't that a shame?'

'We'll have to get you invited,' she said. 'I'm told that can be done.'

'Oh, *really?*' said Monroe.

She giggled, held a hand up to her mouth.

'Oh, I know a few people, Jonathan. My family is old army, old KMT. Taipei is a village.'

It surely was. And Monroe had run her name past a couple of the village's wiser inhabitants, just to make sure, to be told, *she is exceptional, Jonathan. Father was an aide to the Generalissimo at one point. Grandmother related to the Song sisters, a distant cousin. Aristocracy, really.* And the databases had nothing recorded against. She was just what she said she was – a doctoral candidate at Harvard, with very good connections.

'And what will be your role in that village, do you think?' he said.

'After my doctorate? Oh, I don't know. Washerwoman. Whore.'

Monroe must have let his shock show, because she was laughing again, a little incredulous.

'I've embarrassed you. Jonathan! We'll have to unbutton you a little.'

Unbutton me? he thought.

'But let me answer you,' she said. 'I am thinking about diplomacy. Or perhaps something less formal, something in international affairs. We Taiwanese depend on quiet, informal friendships, don't we? We depend on them for national survival, even though we are not deemed a nation.'

'You surely do. I must say I admire the way you exist there, in China's shadow, the way you comport yourselves. You are very, very effective,' said Monroe.

'But you seem to feel things are about to get more complicated for us. With China.' She hesitated, then spoke. 'I felt you hinting at this, in your talk at Harvard. You mentioned the launch vehicles. Do you mind if I ask you what that was about?'

Monroe loved these moments.

'What will you do with my answer?'

'Keep it very, very quiet. Just for me. Or perhaps, with your say so, I may share it informally with one or two friends in Taipei, friends who are equally discreet.'

Monroe affected deep contemplation for a moment, then deep seriousness.

'On one condition, Nicole. You will tell me how your friends respond.'

She nodded, gave him her half-smile. He spoke very softly and she craned her long pale neck to hear.

'We have indications that China is moving ahead with the DF-41, and that it will have MIRV capability.'

He paused for effect, took a morsel of bread.

'Now, they're having technical problems. In April a prototype second-stage blew up on an underground test stand, killed eight technicians, two senior engineers. They're calling it the "April sixteenth incident". But they're unperturbed. So.'

She nodded, considering, her eyebrows raised.

'That, I think, will be news to my friends,' she said. Then she looked straight at him, and reached over and touched his hand.

'Thank you, Jonathan. Really, thank you.'

And later, in the car, she confessed to being a little drunk, and, her perfume enveloping him, kissed him in such a way –

suddenly, hard, nails in his shoulder – as to leave him in absolutely no doubt.

He left it until Saturday, reasoning that there would be fewer people in the office. Now he stood, retching, in his bathroom. Lili was banging on the door.

'Jinghan, are you all right?'

'Go away.'

She was silent. He could sense she was still outside the door.

'I've just eaten something.' He was shivering. He splashed water on his face. 'I'm all right.'

He opened the door and brushed past her. She watched him put on a coat and pick up his keys. He turned.

'I have to go to work for a little while.'

'Oh.'

'I'll be back late this afternoon.'

She said nothing. Wen Jinghan walked out of the house. His house. His new house, in a barren development on the edge of the city, white-walled, an iron fence enclosing a lawn, even. Some of the other houses in the development remained unoccupied; some were unfinished, grey and skeletal. The professor unlocked his car with a *blip*, and pulled away.

He followed the fifth ring road for a while, then cut into Beijing. The smog and dust rendered visibility poor, the traffic sluggish behind ponderous buses, overloaded trucks. It was more than an hour before he arrived at the main gate, where he showed his pass and was waved through. He parked and left his hands on the wheel for a moment, breathing deeply.

As he approached the building his throat caught, and he felt the urge to retch. His breath hissed through his teeth. The foyer was empty but for two security officers in grey uniforms. They waved him forward towards the barrier. The professor took off his coat, bundled it and dropped it on the belt. He took his mobile phone and his keys from his pocket and dropped them in a plastic tray, which he also put on the belt. One of the two guards sat on a stool and watched the scanner's screen. The other guard beckoned to him. He put out his arms and the guard casually passed a wand over his legs, his waist.

As it approached his hips the wand squealed.

The guard gestured wordlessly to Wen Jinghan's trouser pocket.

The professor looked down, as if to say, what could that be, Officer?

The professor reached in his pocket and pulled out a small framed photograph. It was no bigger than a matchbook, the frame of intricate silver filigree. The professor smiled and shook his head.

Sorry, Officer.

The guard looked down at the photograph. It showed a girl, nineteen, perhaps, in a mortar board, her head back, laughing.

'My daughter,' said the professor.

The guard smiled and nodded. The other guard came from the scanner to look.

'I want to put it on my desk,' he said.

'Is she at university?' asked the guard.

'Yes, she is. In America.'

'Harvard,' said the guard.

'No, no. She's at a college in California. A small place. Nothing special.'

'You're very lucky.'

'Not so lucky to be working on a Saturday to pay the fees!'

'All of us!' said the guard. They laughed.

The professor went to the scanner to pick up his coat. The plastic tray was next to the coat on the rubber belt. He reached down and took his mobile phone and his keys.

'Mobile phone on the rack,' said the guard.

'Of course.'

He walked to a wire mesh rack bolted to the wall, laid his mobile phone on it.

'Better get to it,' he said.

The guard gave a wave, friendly and dismissive at once, then sat heavily and reached for a newspaper.

The professor swiped the card that hung from a lanyard around his neck and went through a set of double doors. He walked down a long corridor, to the men's lavatory, where he stood in a stall and retched again and again.

He placed the photograph on his desk. It stood there, reproach and talisman both. His office was a glassed-in cubicle. Outside the glass lay a larger open-plan space that was mercifully empty today. From his desk he could see across the space to the door.

He unlocked a drawer and took out a file, something related to personnel and budgets. He strewed papers around his desk and placed a yellow pad of paper atop them. Paperwork! The price of leadership! His computer was on. He took a second card hanging from the lanyard and inserted it into a reader. Then he placed his thumb on the keyboard scanner and typed a password. The screen brought up a menu. People's Liberation Army General Headquarters. Do not proceed unless authorised to do so. Do not attempt to access areas for which user is not cleared. Report unauthorised access.

Wen Jinghan scrolled down to General Armaments Department. He clicked through to Comprehensive Planning Department, brought up some personnel lists. Then he waited, a riot in his belly.

They came fourteen minutes later, two of them, opening the door at the far end of the office tentatively, scanning the empty desk spaces. Then one saw the lights on in Wen's office and pointed. The other smiled. They walked across the open area to the professor's office, knocked on his door. He waved them in.

'Good afternoon, Professor. Sorry to disturb you. We're from Network Security.' He was young, spectacled, in a short-sleeved check shirt.

'Yes, yes. Here's my ID.' He held out the card on the lanyard.

'Thank you, Professor. So.' He gestured to the papers. 'What are you busy with on a Saturday?'

'I'm behind.'

'Behind with what, if I may ask.'

'My work.'

Silence.

'Look, it's a complex movement of personnel through the testing areas out in Shaanxi. I'm trying to piece it all together. It's difficult. Now, please.'

The man's eyes flicked to the screen, the papers on the desk. 'Of course. I'm sorry to have disturbed you.'

Check Shirt looked for a moment as if there were something else he wanted to ask. But he just nodded and turned to leave, ushering the other man before him.

Wen Jinghan waited another hour and a half, tinkered with the personnel lists on screen. He left his office and walked. The corridors were silent. In the men's lavatory he stood in front of the mirror and ran the tap, then cupped his hands and let the water pool and spill over his fingers. He bent and dashed the water on his face.

At the canteen he took a styrofoam cup and filled it with hot water from an urn. He opened a sachet of green tea and poured it on to the water, watched it balance on the surface tension, move lazily in a circle.

Check Shirt was there, with his companion. They sat at a table on the far side of the empty canteen. Check Shirt was opening a metallic lunch box carefully, peering into it as if the contents might pose a security risk. Wen Jinghan gestured to them, a backward tip of the head. Check Shirt raised and lowered a pair of chopsticks in faint acknowledgement, then returned to his lunch box. The professor turned and left the canteen, walking back to his office, quickly now.

He sat at his desk and unclipped his key ring, withdrawing from it the black, boxy car key. The *snick* as the shaft came away. His breathing, he realised, was shallow and fast, like a sprinter preparing for a race. His fingers were leaving damp prints on the plastic. The computer tower was at his feet. With a last look towards the door, he leant, probed with his fingers for the port, and pushed the drive in.

25

Hong Kong

They often made her wait. They would say, so sorry to keep you, Miss Yang, so sorry. Or sometimes they wouldn't. And now she stood at the window, looking from the twenty-eighth floor down across Mid-levels – the apartment blocks were slender as pencils, or incense sticks – to Hong Kong harbour. She had been waiting for two hours now in this miserable safe flat, its mid-century air-conditioning moaning, spatters of rain against the window.

It was, of course, part of their power game. Their intent was to instil in her a mix of fright and reassurance. Nicole understood this perfectly. But it annoyed her, and made her less, not more, amenable. And she had her onward flight to catch to Taipei.

So who would it be today? The beetle-browed one, with the thinning hair and the Hunan accent? Or the athlete, tall and angular, with his condescending Beijing demeanour? Or her favourite, whom she had named 'Gristle', for his leanness, the tautness of the tendons beneath his skin, and his air of scarring, survival. Gristle was sixty if he was a day and had been around the block, clearly. He spoke quietly, played fewer games, asked good questions.

And when the knock on the door came, it was, to her relief, Gristle, with a younger one she'd encountered only once before. New generation, clearly. Pop-eyed old Gristle might hack and spit, suck on a Great Wall cigarette held peasant-fashion, claw-like between second and third fingers; this one smiled, wore fashionable boxy black shoes and slick eyewear, stared at his handheld device a good deal. He looked like a Hong Kong kid, but he spoke the Mandarin of the far north. Such a giveaway. But that was the point, wasn't it? We are from Beijing, said the accent. And when you're talking to State Security we want you to know you're talking to State Security. Wireless, she'd call him. They didn't wait for her to open the door, they just walked in.

She was seated, cross-legged in jeans and cowboy boots, wait-ing. Wireless bobbed his head. Gristle gave her a tight smile, and sat.

'Miss Yang,' he said.

She just nodded. Wireless opened a laptop and placed a small digital recorder on the table.

'You're looking, prosperous,' said Gristle.

'I've been waiting two hours.'

They both looked at her, let a beat pass. Gristle sat back, left it to Wireless.

'Please do not be upset. We have a very full schedule,' he said.

'I have a flight to catch.'

Another beat.

'Should you miss your flight, we will ensure you get another one.' Not as toothless as he looked.

'Tell us first, please, of your current situation,' Wireless said. 'You flew in from the United States yesterday evening?'

'Yes.'

'Did you notice anything out of the ordinary as you left the United States? At immigration?'

'No.'

'Were you asked any questions by the airline or by any officials?'

'Aside from the normal security questions, no.'

'And when you arrived in Hong Kong did you go straight to the Mandarin Oriental?'

'Yes,' she said. Gristle was smirking at mention of the fancy hotel.

'Have you seen anyone you know since you have been in Hong Kong?'

'I met a group of friends last night.'

'Where?'

'At the Calypso Club, in Happy Valley.' She saw Gristle mouthing the word, Calypso.

'Name them, please.' Wireless tapped on the laptop as he spoke. Gristle lit a cigarette, coughed, looked at her. She named them: the broker, his young socialite wife, her Taiwan friends who ran the design company, the lawyer she knew from Harvard.

'Why do they think you are in Hong Kong?'

'I'm breaking up the journey home, doing some shopping.'

'What did you talk about with them?'

'Gossip. Money. Houses. They're not interested in what I do.'

Gristle sat forward.

'Everyone's interested in you,' he said.

She didn't reply.

'They are, though, aren't they? Have you told anyone about your, what shall we call it, your *relations* with Monroe?'

'No.'

'Has anyone found out about them?'

'I don't think so. We are very discreet.'

'Discreet? My people saw you sucking him off in a parking lot.'

'No, they did not.' She tamped down her anger.

'Oh, I'm sure they did.'

'Your people are making things up. You should keep a tighter grip on them,' she snapped.

Gristle smiled, sat back, drew on his cigarette. Wireless veered off on another tack. They went back to the States, through contacts at Harvard and around Boston; the Chinese students on campus, who was doing what, who had got a job where, which kids were going into biotech, processing; who might be heading out to work at the big Massachusetts weapons factories; the American Chinese; new names on faculty.

That was exhausted soon enough, as she knew it would be. Gristle stared at her.

'So get on with it,' he said.

'I've seen him four times now. I would say he's hooked.'

'Why do you say that?'

'I can tell.'

'How?'

She looked at the ceiling.

'How do you think? Because he looks at me like a teenager. Because he calls me and whispers. Because he can't keep his hands off me.'

They went through each meeting she'd had with Monroe. They wanted the physical details, but she stayed sketchy, stringing them along, which annoyed them.

'Stop being so coy. We need to know what stage you're at with him,' said Gristle.

'Consider it foreplay,' she said. She looked at Wireless. 'Do you know what that is?'

Wireless did not respond. Gristle slowly lifted a finger and pointed at her.

'You've got something, and you're not telling us,' he said.

'Do I?'

He lit another cigarette.

'He said—' but Gristle cut her off.

'When?'

'Ten days ago.'

'Where?'

'When I flew down to see him in Washington. At the restaurant in Georgetown.'

'What was his mood like?'

'He was excited, all lit up. Dangling his secrets at me, like he does.'

'And?'

'So I asked about the launch vehicle reference at the talk.'

'What did he say?'

'He said they had indications, that was his word, indications, that China was proceeding in the development of the DF-41 missile. And he spoke about an "April sixteenth incident", an explosion, ten dead.'

Gristle was looking towards the window, exhaling slowly.

'Never heard of it,' he said.

'Well, he seemed to think it was important.'

'Never heard of the missile, never heard of the incident.'

'Well, he has.'

'He wants to screw you. He'll tell you any shit. And you believe it.'

'No. He thought it was important.'

'How do you know that?'

'Because he was entrusting me with it. He thinks I'm going to back-channel it to people in the know in Taipei. He wants collateral. He wants to know what the Taiwanese know. So he wants me to get an ever-so-quiet response. And he wants to be my mentor.'

'What do you mean, mentor?' said Gristle.

'He has some fantasy of leading me into important, dangerous places. He wants to reveal truth to me, show me the real workings of power, explain it all to me beneath the duvet.'

Gristle was very still, listening.

'He is my mentor and lover, my fierce, illusionless guide; I am the gorgeous Asian naif, waiting to have my creativity and power unleashed and shaped by him.' She made a mock-theatrical gesture.

There was a moment of silence.

'The eternal white man,' said Gristle.

She put her head back and laughed. Gristle smiled, twinkled a little.

'You wouldn't believe it,' she said, smiling.

'Oh, I would,' said Gristle. 'But he's not going to lead you into those places, is he? You're going to lead him.'

She cocked her head at him.

'Tell me why I should.'

He smiled, reached for another cigarette and lit it slowly, the grainy scratch of the lighter once, twice.

'Well, I could say money. Because you are costing us a fucking fortune. But that's not it, is it?'

He paused, drew on the cigarette.

'I could say pressure, couldn't I? Those old aunts and cousins of yours in Shanghai. We threaten to make their life miserable, but you don't give a shit.'

He looked out of the window. Rain was starting to fall in earnest, long, steel rails of it. He looked at his watch.

'It's because, Miss Yang, you are interested in power. And power flows to us now. And you want to be with us. Where the power is.'

It was as good an explanation as any she could think up herself.

*

Wen Jinghan counted off the seconds. Five. Six. Seven. Eight. The diode stopped flashing and turned to a continuous green. He leant and wrenched the drive out of the computer tower, almost overbalancing on his chair. He clenched his fist around the key and sat still, listening. Could one hear the alarms they talk about? Are there bells? He looked across the office. Everything was still. He looked at his watch and noted the time. Nothing to be done now. The tension in his back and neck was a hot pain, his head pounded. He forced himself to breathe. He clipped the key shaft back on to the head and reattached the assembled whole to his key ring. Nothing to see here. Nothing at all.

He looked at his screen. Nothing had changed. What was it doing now, in there? The drive had, presumably, downloaded some sort of application that was busy in the guts of the network. Thirty minutes.

Another walk. Yes, some tea in the canteen, a certain cure for a mouth this dry, a stomach this turbulent. He forced himself to his feet, his knees weak and threatening to disobey.

The canteen was empty. No sign of Check Shirt or his silent partner. He resisted the impulse to go and find them, engage them in conversation, stay with them while the alarms rang and the lights blinked red and people screamed into telephones, and the corridors filled with pounding feet and electric batons. And dogs, probably.

He filled another cup with hot water, dropped another sachet of leaves into it, then placed it on a table and simply stood there.

Eight minutes gone.

Nine.

Voices in the corridor outside the canteen. His stomach lurched and he turned, his feet, he noticed, doing something like a little jig on the floor. His body was behaving childishly. He reached for the cup and took a sip, the sodden leaves smooth against his teeth.

And then, the door. He flinched.

The door was pushed hard from the other side and flew open. Two security guards in grey uniform walked in. They were talking together, something about Guo An, the football team, transfers.

They walked towards the professor, who stood, his feet melded with the floor. They approached him and then stopped. One of the guards gestured with an open hand just past him. Wen looked dumbly in the direction the man had indicated. The urn. The urn! He took a step back and the guards reached for cups, tea. He felt his eyes begin to moisten, some incontinent sense of gratitude welling up. He felt himself raising his own cup in their direction as if in a pathetic toast. Get a grip, he thought. The two guards ignored him. He turned and walked woodenly from the canteen, back into the silent corridor.

Twelve minutes gone.

His screen still had not changed. He leant down. No sound came from his computer except for the usual hum and click of the hard drive. He sat, laid his hands on the desktop, tried to stop the shaking.

Only once before had he felt like this. And it was then, as now, Li Huasheng's doing. The *bastard*. It must have been, what, 1987? The first protests in the universities had begun and the authorities were apoplectic. The police were all over campus, lingering amid the cherry blossom. Behind them you could see the State Security people, quiet, sitting in cars, watching you walk by. There were conversations in faculty offices. And if you were working in a sensitive area, defence technology, for example, perhaps rocketry and telemetry, you were called in for a chat. How did you feel about all this? Were you sympathetic to the demands of the protesters? Had you by any chance participated? Just a little?

He'd decided a measure of frankness was sensible. Well, it

would be nice to have better conditions, better food, some light at night in the dormitories, and I think you should not limit the students' ability to express themselves in peaceful demonstration. And no, I did not participate. The State Security officer opposite – he wore a white shirt, had the skin and hands of a fighter – made notes. His faculty adviser sat, paralysed with fear.

And any contact with foreigners, the source of the bourgeois liberalisation that was infecting so many young minds?

No.

Which was, strictly speaking, true. Because it was Li Huasheng who met the British journalist woman and passed on every scrap of privileged information they could lay their gullible, idiotic hands on. In return for which they had received a nebulous promise of a visa to that distant, damp country, a promise that somehow never came good.

When he sat there beneath the fighter's dead gaze, and in the days following, he knew this same bowel-loosening, retch-inducing fear. Nothing that came later had been as bad as that.

Eighteen minutes gone. His phone rang.

'*Wei?* It's me. Get something to eat on the way home. Get something from Xiao Wang Fu. Get that lamb thing with the coriander.' Lili, in her dressing gown probably, the soap operas on in the background.

'All right.'

'Is your stomach better?'

'Yes.'

'You sound weird.'

'I'm just tired.'

'Well, come home.'

He clicked the call away. He wanted to talk, but he sounded weird. Where was their daughter? What was she doing? She was asleep now probably, in that little apartment outside San Diego that she'd told him about, with the highway outside, the cars flashing past in the darkness.

He took the key from the ring, opened it. A deep breath, and as he exhaled he heard himself producing a strangled humming noise in the back of his throat, the sort of noise one might make when lifting an object of great weight, or anticipating pain.

He slid the drive back into the port and the diode began to flash. He counted off the seconds. Ten. Twenty. Thirty. Still it flashed. Forty. *Dear God, stop.* A minute, for heaven's sake. And just as he reached to pull it out, it turned to a continuous green. He yanked it from the computer, clipped the key back together, his fingers rigid and fumbling, and reattached it to the key ring.

All business, now. He cleared the papers from his desk, locked them in the drawer. Logged off the network. He stood up, made himself straighten. Down the corridors towards the main entrance, holding the key ring, letting it jangle. Nothing to see. A janitor watched him pass. He turned towards the double doors and the main entrance hall.

'Professor.' The voice came from off to his left and was accompanied by rapid footsteps. Wen did not slow down.

'Professor, a moment, please.' It was Check Shirt. The professor felt his throat constrict. Fear was sickening. It really was.

Check Shirt came towards him, making an effort to be quick, breaking into a moderate jog.

'Professor, sorry to keep you. May I ask, have you had any problems with your computer terminal this afternoon?'

Have I? he thought.

'No. Not that I noticed.'

'Oh.'

'Perhaps it was running a little slowly.'

'I see. Well, you were looking at a great deal of data, weren't you?'

Was I?

He shrugged.

'It's just, well, no matter, it all seems fine now,' said Check Shirt.

Wen Jinghan nodded and gave a tight smile.

'Have a good weekend, Professor.'

From a dark, silent perch deep inside himself, Wen wondered if he would make it to the front desk, or whether his legs would go and he would sit on the floor, absurd, a silver-haired charlatan.

They held. He walked across the parking lot, started his car and pulled out into the street, tears running down his cheeks.

2 6

Beijing

The signal from Hong Kong was marked URGENT. It arrived in Beijing at the intake station of the Ministry of State Security's 2nd Bureau, Foreign Operations, towards evening, at a moment when the setting sun poured through the Bureau's windows, and the frosted trees and lakes of the Summer Palace were washed in indigo and tangerine. It arrived as the night watch was coming on, and the corridors were filled with the smell of food, pork with garlic bolts, potato shreds in chilli.

The signal concerned an agent debriefing that had taken place in Hong Kong that same day and appeared to have been written in haste. It called for immediate evaluation of the agent's product by personnel in the 7th Bureau, Circulation and Analysis.

The signal, numbered and marked *juemi*, Top Secret, found its way to the desk of a young man surnamed Ouyang who hailed from Liaoning Province, China's icy north-east, and who had trained as an electrical engineer. Analyst Ouyang, a gentle, spindly young man with an abiding love for Japanese graphic novels, knew missiles. He knew who made them, how, and where

China needed to look to acquire missile technology. And he knew, or believed he knew, how to distinguish between real intelligence, even of the most technical kind, and dross.

But this, this was something different. The DF-41, well, everyone would know about that sooner or later. But the April 16th incident? What was that? An asset operating in the United States had heard mention of it from an American intelligence analyst. How did some American intelligence analyst know all about it, when Analyst Ouyang did not? He sat back in his chair, reluctant to read further, and bit his lip. *This* was not a matter for Ouyang. The signal smelled dangerous. It smelled of a foreign operation. This was a counter-intelligence matter, and the signal needed to be directed, speedily, to the 9th Bureau, Anti-Defection and Counter-Surveillance, a region of the Ministry that Ouyang preferred to avoid, where possible.

In this case, however, it was not possible. And, at three o'clock in the morning, Ouyang found himself sitting across a table in a conference room from a granite-eyed investigator of the 9th Bureau.

'Have you mentioned the contents of this signal to anybody?' said the investigator.

'No,' replied Ouyang.

'Has anybody spoken about it to you?'

'No.'

'Are you aware of anybody in the 7th Bureau who knows the contents of the signal?'

'Well, it was routed to my desk from the intake station, so someone there must have read it and responded to its contents.'

'Why must they?'

Ouyang was stumped.

'Well, they must have read it to know where to send it.'

'Must they? Is that an assumption or do you know that someone on the intake station read it?'

'It's ... it's an assumption.'

The investigator was middle-aged, with a skin of tanned leather and his hair combed over his head from a parting an inch above his left ear.

'Is it also an assumption,' said the investigator, 'that no one in the rest of the 7th Bureau has read it?'

'Well, I can't know for sure.'

'You don't know for sure? I'll ask you again. Did you show it to anybody?'

'No.'

'Analyst Ouyang, why are you presenting me with assumptions dressed up as facts?'

'I ... I ... that was not my intention.' Ouyang was beginning to feel his grip on the situation loosen.

'Why did the intake station send the signal to you?'

'Well, I am the duty officer on the Science and Technology Desk.'

'But why to you? Why not to the Americas desk?'

'I ... I don't know. You must ask them.'

'Must I?'

A pause.

'Analyst Ouyang, why did you send an alert to the 9th Bureau?'

Ouyang swallowed. The investigator was watching his every move, his every tic, he could feel it.

'Because I judged this to be a counter-intelligence matter.'

'Why?'

'The signal suggested that an asset operating in the United States had unearthed state secrets from China in the hands of an American intelligence analyst. I assumed you ought to know. I mean, I thought you ought to know.'

'Why?'

'Well, because, could it not be possible that we have a leak?'

Oh, God.

There was a silence. Then the investigator spoke again.

'Analyst Ouyang, are you suggesting that some unidentified person is giving China's state secrets to a foreign power?'

'I don't know, I ...'

'That is a very serious accusation.'

'I'm not accusing ... I just thought you should *know.*'

'Analyst Ouyang, thanks to your ... intervention, this is now a counter-intelligence investigation. You will remain in this building until our investigation is complete. You will be escorted to quarters where you will remain for the duration, and you will be monitored by officers of the 9th Bureau. We will be speaking again.'

Ouyang gaped. The duration? He felt a hand on his shoulder, pressuring him to move. He stood up shakily, tried to summon the nerve to protest, but the investigator was looking down at the file, making notes. Ouyang turned and walked to the door.

The investigator watched him go. Frightened shitless, he thought. How are we raising such spineless children these days?

The investigator sighed. Four in the morning, and this. He would go now and have a cigarette, some tea, think about his next move.

The little twerp was quite right, of course. Spineless, but smart. The revived DF-41 programme was common knowledge across the military-industrial establishment. No surprise that was out. But knowledge of the April 16th incident, the investigator reflected, was closely held. And the investigator knew exactly how closely held, because he himself had been instrumental in ensuring that no one shot their mouth off about it, and that it never made its way into the press, or into any document with a classification lower than *juemi*. Weeks out in dreary Shaanxi, reminding, cajoling and finally threatening the families, the staff, anyone who knew anything.

So how in hell did an American know all about it?

There were official reports, of course, which had been circulated in six areas only: the Central Military Commission, the PLA General Staff, the Launch Vehicle Academy, the General Armaments Department, the Leading Small Group on Military Affairs, the Second Artillery.

But.

Most of that reporting did not mention casualties. The casualty numbers were sequestered in a series of numbered reports with a much more limited distribution. They went to two places only: the Central Military Commission and the Leading Small Group on Military Affairs.

The investigator, whose name was Han, and who had spent seven years now working security and counter-intelligence on the missile programme, made for the canteen. At this time of night it was half in darkness. A canteen worker in a white cap and an apron sat at one of the tables, leaning forward on the tabletop, asleep on her folded arms. She slept next to a stainless steel pan of *baozi* covered with a cloth, another of noodles and vegetables.

He sat in a corner and pulled a packet of Tiananmen cigarettes from his jacket pocket, took one out, threw the packet on the table with a cardboard *plock*. The canteen worker stirred and looked up for a moment, then let her head fall again. Silence, but for the hum of refrigerators, a vending machine. He lit the cigarette, felt its warm, fibrous wash in his throat.

Now, the Central Military Commission. Senior Party officials, very senior, and military top brass: the sort of people who don't get investigated, at least not by Investigator Han. The Leading Small Group on Military Affairs, ditto. But advisers and support staff to the Leading Small Group, that's a different story. Some wobbly characters in there, scientists, intellectuals, what have you. And we know which of them had access to those numbered reports.

So that's where we'll start.

Early Sunday morning, cigarette smoke curling through the grey light, the smell of frying meat. Peanut sat in a fetid café in Fengtai. He had been woken by Yin, her hair awry, bleary, banging on his door at five. A phone call, she said. He didn't leave his name. Said you'd know.

He sat with his back to the wall, faced the door.

The professor, when he came, wore a facemask, a blue fleece hat pulled low. He sat at Peanut's table, arms, neck rigid, fear dripping from him.

He pulled down the facemask.

'Did you tell them who I am? Where I live?'

Peanut dragged on his cigarette, regarded him.

'Did you tell them?' repeated the professor, his voice taut as wire.

'Why would I do that?' said Peanut.

Wen Jinghan gave a tight shake of the head.

'Because I think someone's there.'

'Where?'

'Near the house. There's a car,' he hissed.

'What do they look like?'

'I don't know. Not State Security. I don't think. It's a silver car. They just drive past, then go.'

'So give it to me,' said Peanut.

The professor's face was crumpling.

'Who are they? Huasheng, help me.'

Peanut spoke quickly.

'It's nobody. I have told no one, and it's not police and it's not State Security. Now give it to me.'

The professor reached into a pocket. An envelope. Peanut felt the boxy shape of it through the paper.

'So it worked? Like I said?'

The professor gave an exhausted shrug, then nodded.

'I'll be in touch, Jinghan.' Peanut stood, stubbed out his cigarette. The metallic scrape of the chair against floor tile. The professor watched him, his face drawn, eyes feverish, hyper-alert.

'Is it finished?' he said.

But Peanut had left the café, walked fast. The street was quiet, the shop fronts still shuttered. He turned abruptly. Behind him a silver sedan pulled away from the kerb, turned into a side street.

Investigator Han sat at a trestle table covered with green baize cloth. He was snappish and very tired. To his right a mug of tea. To his left an ashtray. Behind him the Deputy Director of the 9th Bureau plus acolytes, silent and watchful. And all around him the *dang an* – personal files – of three hundred and seventy-six people, each one of whom was known to have received a copy of a numbered report. *Certain Questions.*

Investigator Han's personal system of triage, administered savagely through a long, stale night, had prised the files apart and reordered them in teetering stacks. Before him the stack of utmost urgency: files containing the lives of fifty-seven people whom Investigator Han deemed the most wobbly: academics; those with foreign contacts; those – only a handful, but still a number that surprised Investigator Han – with a history of anti-Party activity. If a full interrogation were authorised, well, the villa in the Western Hills, a team on standby.

Twenty-four officers of the Ministry of State Security's 9th Bureau, Anti-Defection and Counter-Surveillance, had been seconded to the investigation group and now sat on metal folding chairs around the room. Investigator Han had split them into two-man teams and was assigning interviews. The Deputy Director spoke into his ear.

'Speed, Investigator Han. Speed,' he said.

'Yes, Deputy Director, speed.'

Officers were putting on coats, leaving the room. Investigator Han imagined the black cars pulling out of the Ministry, fanning out across Beijing.

27

GODDESS 2's line was blinking. The technician tapped the screen. Hopko stood, leaning against the console. She looked like a predator scenting, thought Patterson.

'*Wei? Women de pengyou laile, zhunbeihao le.*' Our friend's arrived and is ready. Meaning: RATCHET's in position.

'*Hao. Xiexie.*' Thanks.

The map screen showed a red indicator where the encounter was to take place, and the route to destination. GODDESS 2 was at the encounter point, the rest of the team sweeping the route as best they could. The encounter point was in a narrow alleyway behind the Landao department store, not far from the Workers' Stadium, dead to surveillance. The alleyway served as a cut-through between larger thoroughfares, and shoppers frequently used it. It was mid-evening in Beijing, dark. The smog had lessened, but scarves and surgical masks were still commonplace.

Yeats stood, arms folded, at the back of the suite. The Director, Requirements and Production, had been in earlier, made some comment about 'the action' and left. Patterson

277

shifted in her seat, took a mouthful of a sandwich – mushroom and pesto – and waited.

Mangan had spent forty-five minutes inside the Landao department store. He had gone first to men's clothing, where he surveyed jeans. He tried on a sweater, a blue zip-up thing of the sort Ting would laugh at. He looked in a mirror. The sweater's sleeves were short on his lofty, gaunt frame, his winter pallor, his red hair flattened by a winter hat.

The store was busy and raucous. He walked past rows of sleek televisions. They all showed the same demonstration video of European girls in bikinis, lounging on decks, spreadeagled on river rocks. Knots of men stood and watched the videos. Staff in bow ties hovered and gestured.

In the household goods department Mangan engaged a member of the sales staff in conversation on the subject of toasters. The girl was very young, a school leaver, Mangan guessed. She wore her hair pulled off her face, gathered in a long ponytail, and she wore silver-framed glasses. Her little blue waistcoat fitted poorly, and her black bow tie was loose on her collar, which Mangan realised he found poignant. These Japanese toasters, she said, are very good but they are very expensive. Mangan found it in himself – he was struggling – to agree, and to ask whether, perhaps, there was a Chinese-made toaster available. The girl smiled, yes, of course. This Chinese toaster, she said, is made in the city of Qingdao, and is the equal of the Japanese toaster in every way, and is a good deal cheaper. Mangan bought the Chinese-made toaster. The cashier gave him a flimsy receipt, stamped with a little red chop. You speak Chinese very well, said the girl. Mangan said *nali*, modestly.

With the toaster in a plastic carrier bag in his left hand, his right hand free, Mangan descended two storeys by escalator. It cascaded down the central atrium of the store, sleek and silvery.

He looked at the huge backlit advertisements for lipstick, lingerie, the models impossibly willowy, pale, their blue-black hair. Mangan was tempted to look over his shoulder, but he resisted the urge, as Charteris had told him to, because hyper-vigilance, Philip, is a very noticeable trait. And you will not be carrying a mobile phone, Philip, now will you? No, David, mobile phones leave spoor. They betray our location and broadcast our words; they make us targets, kill us.

At exactly seventeen minutes past eight he left the department store. He turned to his right, raising his carrier bag and turning side-on to move through a clot of people. It was cold. The store had loudspeakers attached to its frontage that broadcast a distorted stream of promises and exhortations. The frontage was floodlit and festooned with balloons and banners. A man touched him on the sleeve, tried to ask him something. He walked on. The mouth of the alleyway was dark and partly hidden by a builder's skip. He stepped slowly into the gloom. And as he did so the large figure with its rolling, aggressive gait was almost on him. He raised his right hand slightly, opened it, to feel the man's fingers fluttering around his, then pressing the key into his palm. Mangan took it, closed his fist around it, and walked forward quickly. As he approached the far end of the alleyway he put the key into his coat pocket and switched the carrier bag from his left hand to his right. You may feel relief at this point, Philip, that the brush pass has worked as planned, Charteris had told him, but that relief is misplaced. You are now carrying.

'GODDESS 2 on the line.'

'*Wei? Hao xiaoxi! Women de pengyou shoudao xin le. Ta hao gaoxing a!*' Good news. Our friend received the letter. He's very happy. The transfer has been effected. No sign of hostile surveillance.

'*Hao jile! Feichang gan xie.*' Excellent. Thank you very much.

Yeats made a small pumping action with his arm. Hopko stood, hands on hips, chewing her lip. The technician smiled.

'Not over yet,' said Hopko.

Investigator Han paced the corridor, smoked, murmured into his phone. The interviews were going slowly, the officers too thorough, too cautious. Kick some fucking doors down, he told them. Frighten them. Stir the pot. Don't look for evidence, look for signs.

Still nothing.

But it wouldn't be long.

28

Beijing

Mangan went south on Dongdaqiao, in the direction of the embassy. He walked quickly, keeping his gaze straight ahead, the carrier bag, in his right hand, swinging at his side. The traffic was stalled, the buses packed in the darkness, their occupants swaying, dead-eyed. There would be snow tonight, supposedly, but the air was dry, thick with dust and fumes. Mangan wondered if there were any moisture in it at all. He passed a vast new apartment and mall complex, its surfaces glinting, tessellated in the night. Where its silvered walls met the pavement, the graffiti artist had been at work; the crow again, with its bulbous, grotesque goggles, the stencil a little imprecise this time, smeary, as if the artist had rushed his work beneath the surveillance cameras. Mangan stayed in shadow where he could. To every lamppost, a camera. Half a million of them in Beijing, he'd read.

And then, walking towards him as he rounded the corner on to Guanghua Lu, Charteris.

Mangan made to extend his left hand, the gadget wrapped

inside it, but Charteris's hands remained in his pockets, and in his eyes, a warning.

Mangan peeled away immediately, made to cross the street. Glancing back, he saw Charteris turning the corner. Behind him, nobody. A taxi was grinding slowly along the kerb, looking for fares. Mangan hailed it and got in. He gave the driver the name of a hotel. He looked down at his hands to find them trembling, damp.

'I have GODDESS 1.'

'*Wei? Xin meiyou dao.*' The letter hasn't arrived. The pass has not taken place.

Patterson stood, felt the spike of adrenalin in her gut. Hopko leaned and spoke into the microphone.

'*Weishenme?*' Why?

'*Haoxiang mei you ji.*' It seems he didn't post it. Officer aborted.

Hopko, speaking urgently now, '*You wenti ma?*' Is there a problem? Have you identified hostile surveillance?

'*Yinggai mei wenti ba.*' I don't think there's a problem. But the voice sounded defensive.

'*Zai shi yi shi.*' Let's try again. Move to fallback.

'*Hao.*' Moving to fallback.

'What the hell is that about?' said Patterson.

Charteris's line came up on the screen. The technician brought it in.

'It's me. Sorry I didn't turn up. I wasn't feeling well,' he said. I believe I may have detected hostile surveillance.

'I see. Well, everybody else was fine,' said Hopko. No hostile surveillance reported.

A pause, just the sound of Charteris's breathing hissing on the line. Patterson reached over, closed the microphone.

'Fallback, Val,' said Patterson.

Hopko considered.

'Yes, fallback,' said Yeats. 'Now.'

Hopko closed her eyes for a moment. Patterson saw her jaw clench. She opened the microphone.

'We'd like to move on,' said Hopko. Proceed to fallback.

Another pause on the line, the rustle of Charteris's movement.

'Well, okay.' Officer proceeding to fallback.

Mangan sat in the lobby lounge of the Crowne Plaza, watching the doors, wondering about cameras. A smiling waiter approached, gestured at the menu. Mangan ordered sparkling water, left money on the table so he was ready to move.

Then Charteris was striding across the lobby, nonchalant, hands in pockets. He made for the men's lavatory, went in. Mangan watched the door close behind him. He waited ten seconds.

Up and moving now, past the check-in desk. Two hotel security goons with earpieces stood self-importantly by the main doors, running their gaze across the lobby. Mangan tried to ignore them. Do something with your hand, she'd told him. Look occupied. As he walked he checked the time on his wristwatch, patted his pockets for his mobile phone, pulled it out, looked at it, even though it was switched off. He pushed open the door to the men's lavatory. Charteris was standing at the basins, rinsing his hands. No one else. Charteris took a towel, dried. As Mangan approached him, he let one hand fall to his side, palm out. Mangan pressed the key into it and spoke quietly.

'What happened?'

'Outside the embassy. I thought there was a watcher, in a car. I was wrong. It's nothing.'

And he was gone.

Mangan leaned against the countertop, breathing.

Dao le. The letter's arrived. Officer has re-entered the embassy.

'Hao. Hai you shi ma?' Anything more?

283

'*Meiyou biede shi.*' Nothing more. No sign of hostile surveillance.
'*Na, ni hui jia ba.*' Go home.
'*Xianzai jiu zou.*' We're leaving now.

And with that, Hopko authorised the GODDESS team to disperse and return to their Hong Kong base as quickly and quietly as they could. And Patterson went down to the cafeteria for coffee, and they made their way slowly back to the P section, where she and Hopko sat in silence for a few minutes, before Hopko stood suddenly and went off to find Yeats, to tell him that the principal operational phase of STONE CIRCLE had been completed.

Granny Poon peeled off from the target and walked south. As she rounded the corner on to Jianguomenwai Dajie she took the phone from her pocket. She removed the SIM card, bent it double between her thumb and index fingers till she felt the plastic split, then she dropped the two halves in two separate rubbish bins, the battery and phone in a third. She hailed a taxi. She opened the door and climbed in slowly, one hand atop the open door to steady herself, an elderly lady, a little rheumatic perhaps, taking her time. And as she lowered herself into the seat, she glanced back at the passers-by. And a man smiled at her. A man in his thirties, with a baseball cap, a short black jacket, perhaps a golfer's jacket, jeans of a light colour, and white training shoes bearing the mark of a famous brand in red. She sensed, more than saw, his lingering look and she fastened the image of him in her mind. She sat in the back seat, closed the door and asked the driver to take her to Beijing South Railway Station, where she would take the express to Tianjin, and from there a flight to Hong Kong. Winston would take the bags.

She sat in the back of the taxi in a stale cigarette reek. The taxi ground slowly through the Beijing night.

Someone was watching, probing.

Who?

PART THREE

The Product.

29

GCHQ, Cheltenham

The gadget, wrapped in polythene and placed in a plastic container impervious to dust or water, went by secure bag. The bag – a large black briefcase of the sort lawyers might carry – remained handcuffed to the wrist of the courier for the ten-hour British Airways flight to London.

At Heathrow a van waited to transport courier and bag to the town of Cheltenham, where, in a basement of the enormous doughnut-shaped structure that housed Government Communications Headquarters, the exploitation team waited. Patterson sat against one wall, chilly in the air-conditioning, and eyed them. Six linguists, three computer technicians, eight analysts. They sat at terminals arranged on a horseshoe table in a secure computer lab. A cryptographic team was on standby. Late afternoon now, the flight was on time, the courier due any minute.

Hopko, of course, charmed them, flitting from terminal to terminal, asking questions, being interested, perching herself on the table, leaning in to hear explanations of software, databases, digital dictionaries. She spoke at length to one woman – a BBC, she called herself, British-Born Chinese – who would be the lead translator and who seemed to have absorbed an astonishing vocabulary of Chinese military terms. Hopko tested her playfully on missiles. Throw weight, drawdown curve, midcourse phase. But the woman wanted to know context, please, Val. What sort of material are we expecting? Hopko just shrugged and smiled and said she had no idea what would be on the drive other than, well, 'a largish chunk of a very secret Chinese network'. This prompted grins around the table. The analysts looked at one another and raised their eyebrows, shifted in their seats. One boy – a technician – overweight, his hair gelled, adopted a mock frown and spoke up to Hopko.

'So we might be here a while, then?'

Hopko played along.

'Oh, definitely. All leave cancelled, I'm afraid.'

Patterson watched Hopko stand and walk purposefully to a man who had remained silent throughout, brow furrowed, concentrating on the screen before him. Middle-aged, this man, thinning fair hair on a pale pate; the moist patina of one who spends many hours in windowless secure rooms. And the dress sense, too. Ill-fitting, pleated trousers, a light-blue shirt, square spectacles.

Patterson looked at the man's identity badge. It read, 'McGovern, Mike'. The green strip with the word CONTRACTOR in white. Beneath it CALTRON APPLICATIONS INC. So McGovern, Mike was private sector, brought in by GCHQ from a corporation. A very big, very quiet corporation. To do what, exactly?

Hopko reached out a hand.

'Mike. Hello. Val Hopko.'

He looked up and regarded her, a weary look, one that braced for criticism. He shook her hand, said nothing.

'And to what do we owe the pleasure?' said Hopko.

McGovern held up his hands in surrender.

'They tell me to be here, I'm here,' he said. A faint Irish accent.

Hopko waited.

'I'm on the exploitation team because you will be using applications that were designed by Caltron,' he said slowly. 'Security applications. Applications that will ensure your networks are not all blown to bits by whatever is about to be brought into this room. Figuratively speaking.'

A pause.

'Consider me tech support. I'm here to help.'

Hopko seemed about to say more, but the door opened with a hiss and two uniformed security men escorted in a courier in a rumpled suit. The courier looked around, questioning, and Patterson, as holder of the relevant codes, stood to meet him. She uncuffed him and then entered the combination that opened the case. The room was quiet now. Hopko, on tiptoe almost, watched Patterson pull out the watertight box, open it, unwrap the gadget. The technicians crowded around making approving noises. There was business with signatures, and the courier, clearly relieved, left the room. The lead technician, wearing rubber gloves, took the car key, opened it up and inserted the drive into a terminal.

Patterson watched Hopko, saw in her dark eyes sheer, joyful venality.

Once McGovern and the techs had pronounced it clean, the team worked their way through the drive trying to discern what they had, explorers in a pixellated tomb.

They had a lot. They broke the product out into serials. WOODWORK to cover hundreds of documents related to China's missile programme; the DF-41 was there, so was the carrier killer, so were anti-satellite weapons still on the General Armaments Department's drawing board, and policy papers that projected the capacity of China's strategic missile forces twenty-five years into the future. Analysts pretended to fall off their chairs and rub their eyes in shock. They ate sandwiches at their desks until the techs objected because of the crumbs, and nobody minded the overtime. QUILTER to cover naval procurement files, which would need the creation of a special analytic cell with draftees from DI Strategic Assessments, Naval Intelligence and more specialists from the corporations who joked about being 'pressganged'. DRAWBRIDGE to cover product related to budgets and accounting practices, STEAMER to cover a tranche of personnel files; God only knew when they'd get to them. Patterson was alternately madly busy channelling samples of product to Waverley of Requirements and stunned with boredom as the translators haggled over some minute distinction in the vocabulary of phased array radar. She ate miserably, slept fitfully in visiting officers' quarters and washed out her underwear in the sink, her overnight bag having proven woefully inadequate.

But the serial that created most excitement in the room, especially among the technicians, was GAMMA, which was to cover product describing the Chinese military's information operations. A slender file, GAMMA, but tantalising. Here were maps of the network infrastructure. Here was China's military telecommunications backbone. Here was the chain of command leading from China's new cyber warfare units to the General Staff. And that, there, said the lead technician, a balding man in his fifties wearing a blue cardigan and rubber-soled shoes, gesturing to the screen, that is a list of exploits we've already found in the operating system.

'A tiny bit more explanation, please,' said Hopko.

'They don't have their own operating systems, you see, Val,' said the technician. 'All their software was written, originally, in the west. But because they're a secure network, they're not connected to the internet. So they don't receive the updates that the writers of the software send out. So their operating systems are full of holes, which they should have patched. But they never did, did they?'

There was much joking among the technicians about the state of the operating system. 'It's like a Swiss cheese,' one said. 'Some of it looks like pirated software. Honestly, ripe for the picking.'

And wherever material appeared that seemed destined for the GAMMA serial, there was McGovern of Caltron Applications Inc., purveyors of cyber expertise and intelligence support systems and services to a number of very quiet agencies. McGovern listened to the translators, offered occasional advice to the techs, pointed out a new approach, a new route. He spoke modestly, and was self-effacing in his manner, and allowed others to take credit for his successes. Then he withdrew to his own screen, or sometimes left the room for half an hour.

And, Patterson noticed, McGovern of Caltron Applications Inc. became as close to animated as was possible for him to be when it was discovered that the gadget had unearthed, from deep in the Chinese network, a series of files detailing contracts awarded to a Chinese corporation, China National Century Inc. CNaC, as it was known, China's brave new telecoms warrior. CNaC fibre stretched from Tibet to Manchuria, its wireless from Korea to Angola, its processors everywhere, from alarm clocks to spy satellites to weapons systems in one hundred and thirty countries.

Patterson watched as McGovern leaned in, the glimmering screen reflected in his smudged spectacles.

Later, on her way to the canteen, Patterson saw Hopko standing in an office and speaking on a secure phone, gesticulating.

The conference room, deep in the Ministry of Defence, was panelled with rich dark wood. At one end, an assortment of comfy leather armchairs, of the sort one might find in a gentlemen's club, arranged around a fireplace. Along the length of the room ran a mahogany table, a file with a tan cover at each seat, each classified to a level of secrecy appropriate to its contents. The contents of the files would not leave the room, nor would they be discussed beyond the room with any degree of specificity. Mobile phones, laptops and any other consumer electronics – the bane of security – were to be relinquished upon entry. Coffee and croissants on a side table lent a wonderful morning smell. And at vantage points throughout the room were positioned, delicately and invisibly, a number of cameras and microphones, so that the proceedings might be closely monitored in adjoining rooms.

Hopko sat in an adjoining room of meaner appointment. Before her were six screens and a keyboard equipped with a little joystick.

Patterson clattered into the room, accidentally slamming the door behind her. Hopko looked her up and down sympathetically.

'Trish. You look hot and bothered,' she said. 'Sit you down.'

Patterson exhaled and sat.

'What exactly are we doing here?' said Patterson.

'Security. Simon Drinkwater is supposed to do it, but I volunteered to do it for him and he accepted with an indecent degree of alacrity.'

Patterson looked mystified.

'We listen and ensure the briefers don't say anything they're not supposed to,' said Hopko.

As she spoke a smart MoD functionary holding a clipboard opened the door to the conference room and a procession of men entered. Patterson and Hopko watched them on the screens. The men were tailored in the manner of senior executives, some affecting a classic masculine authority in navy blue and grey pinstripe, others alluding to current fashion in black, cut snug and narrow.

The men wore visitor passes on dangling cords with a contractor stripe and national flag. Most were British, but here and there Patterson saw an American or a Canadian. Beneath the flag was printed their corporate affiliation: Such-and-such Systems Inc. Such-and-such Mission Solutions. Such-and-such Kinetic Applications. Shiny, hard-edged names, evocative of movement and power, yet elusive in their lack of specificity. What, thought Patterson, do they actually do at TRSI Risk Dynamics?

'See this one?' said Hopko. She touched the joystick and the camera moved in on a silver-haired American, suited in black with a simple red tie. He had poured himself a cup of coffee and sat unspeaking at the end of the table.

'Who's he?' said Patterson.

'He's ex-CIA, Trish. He used to be Deputy Director of their Clandestine Service. But he retired. Now he has a very comfy billet at Shady Creek Group.'

Patterson wondered if the name was supposed to mean something to her. Shady Creek. A name suggestive of small beginnings, roads less travelled, dappled sunlight, authenticity.

On the screen Hopko and Patterson watched the executives open the files, all of which, Patterson could now see, were stamped with GAMMA/TOP SECRET.

'So these are all corporations and we're briefing them on the product?' said Patterson.

'Or those bits of the product that we think they need to know about,' said Hopko.

'Why do they need to know any of it?'

'So they can design things, services, capabilities, that we will buy from them,' said Hopko. 'Here's China's network, we say. Now go away and build something that will penetrate it.'

The briefer was talking now, taking the executives through the early read on the GAMMA material and what it revealed of China's telecommunications infrastructure, its cyber future.

'Though I can't imagine our friend from Shady Creek is going to learn much he doesn't already know,' Hopko said.

'Why?'

'Why? Because Shady Creek is private equity. It owns Caltron, among other things. And you can't move for Caltron people at GCHQ. Remember that pasty fellow during the exploitation? McGovern? He was Caltron.'

Hopko paused for a moment and leaned forward to look more closely at the screen.

'So I imagine that our Shady Creek friend here has already been briefed on everything that was on our drive,' she said.

The door opened again and another figure entered the conference room, hurriedly. Not so well-suited this one, Patterson noted. The figure pulled up an extra chair next to the silver-haired American and murmured in the American's ear.

'Well,' said Hopko.

'What's he doing here?' said Patterson.

'Making sure,' said Hopko, 'that Shady Creek Group has everything it needs.'

And, as she spoke, Roly Yeats, Head of Western Hemisphere and Far East Controllerate, looked straight into a camera, as if locking eyes with Patterson and daring her to question him.

Later, Patterson took the Tube home to Archway and walked home in darkness suffused with a rain so fine it was almost mist. She unlocked the front door and stood in the still hallway, listening for a sign that Damian was at home. She heard nothing but the city's low frequency whisper-roar, climbed the stairs to her flat and let herself in. She changed into jeans, heated lasagne in a foil tray and poured herself a glass of red wine.

She sat at her laptop, eating. She searched Shady Creek Group. The firm's headquarters, she read, sat not on a creek of any sort, but a river, the Potomac, a short distance from the White House and the Pentagon and Langley.

And there Shady Creek had designed the private equity strategy that had brought them to their illustrious position at the most secret conference tables. First the big ramping-up a decade earlier: the acquisition of translation and security and logistics companies. The recruiting of the hard men, ex-Delta and SAS, and the field operatives. At one point the director of the CIA had to ask Shady Creek to stop recruiting in the cafeteria at Langley.

But then, just as the wars were at their height, and with them the tide of United States federal dollars and the endless contracts, Shady Creek pivoted. It started buying clever little cyber start-ups, muscular network systems and intelligence support outfits. And recruiting Chinese speakers, not Arabists.

Patterson looked at the websites. *The Shady Creek Group, through its wide portfolio, offers deep industry expertise and critical mission support across multidisciplinary intelligence operations.* A photograph depicted a uniformed American soldier in helmet and black ballistic glasses, next to a smiling elderly woman wearing a robe and headdress, which, while generic, signalled ethnic otherness. A third man holding a clipboard gestured into the distance, into the sunlight, towards a city on a plain, and the soldier and the woman followed his gaze.

Patterson couldn't sleep. She lay holding herself, staring at the shadows on the ceiling, listening to the city's vibrational hush, its surging and its falling. She thought of the suited men in the conference room, their lack of affect, the sense of deracination that surrounded them. What was their mission, these quiet men? What was her role in it?

She thought back to certainty she had known. Her last day in theatre. She remembered the dawn, and the thudding and chattering of the helos. She had stood on the flightline, drinking tea from a styrofoam cup. The helos came swinging in to land in great washes of dust, the pale sun behind them. She watched the shadowed figures on the tarmac, hunching beneath the rotors, the *whump whump whump* and the gentle, balletic lift, tilt and turn into the sky towards the mountains. Jenkins had been with her, and Rashid, the snarly little staff sergeant from Bolton, pride of the battalion for his Pashtun, his blizzard of Waziri dialects.

'So we're losing you, ma'am,' Jenkins had said.

'Losing you to the funnies,' said Rashid. 'You won't like it, ma'am, all those fast cars, Martinis, whatnot. You'll miss us.'

'I'll miss you like a sucking chest wound,' she'd said, and they'd laughed. Her flight had been called, and she'd hefted her bergen and her weapon, and waved, and turned and jogged towards the helo.

She threw the duvet off and padded through the flat, checking the front door and windows.

She thought about Granny Poon, the woman's unease, the unexplained probing of her phone. Someone was trying to beacon her.

Who?

30

SIS, Vauxhall Cross, London

The Director, Requirements and Production, had a mouthful of brioche when his phone rang. He swallowed quickly and reached for his handkerchief to wipe the crumbs from his mouth. He took a quick swallow of coffee. He'd arrived late this morning and the overnight telegram traffic lay on his desk untouched.

'The Permanent Under-Secretary would like you to come straight over, please. Your car's waiting.'

They were there when he walked in, the Permanent Under-Secretary, the Special Adviser and minions.

And C, the chief of SIS.

Nobody had told him that C would be at the meeting, but there he was, with his rimless spectacles and thinning hair, folded into his chair like some spindly, dark-eyed predator in its lair, poised for ambush.

The Director of Requirements and Production tried to collect himself.

'Extraordinary,' the Permanent Under-Secretary was saying.

'Quite extraordinary.' On his desk a folder marked TOP SECRET/UKEYES ALPHA/GAMMA.

The Special Adviser was beaming.

'Cheltenham's in paroxysms,' he said. 'Listen to this. *A formidable penetration, sure to yield unique and priceless insight into China's information architecture, cyber warfare capability, and the geography of its military-industrial complex.* Honestly, they're like teenagers discovering pornography.'

Laughter. The Director of Requirements and Production waited.

'But seriously,' said the Permanent Under-Secretary, 'everyone's impressed. I mean the missile stuff is fascinating and important, but the cyber stuff, well. The sheer scale of it.'

He paused.

'And. *And* we now know what those duplicitous shits at China National Century Corporation are doing. Did you see that bit?'

He looked up and peered round the room, a picture of injured innocence.

'They are, apparently, manufacturing corrupted processors and pushing them towards certain American importers. With the intention – the active intention, mark you – of getting them into important bits of American military kit. And they've succeeded. Dodgy CNaC chips, gentlemen, with who knows what on them, appear to have made their way into America's shiny new littoral combat ship. Deliberately.'

Another pause.

'Wait till we tell the Yanks. I'll enjoy that. Oh, and even the addled cynics at MoD seem to feel the product is not forged. It's "internally consistent", they say. And there's too bloody much of it. You must pass on our congratulations to Roly Yeats.'

'I shall, of course,' the Director of Requirements and Production said.

C was quiet. Now the Special Adviser spoke.

'Might I just bring us straight to the central question here? Given the extraordinary scope and importance of this penetration, there's obviously a hope it may yield more. Lots of questions, obviously. And so we wonder what expectation we might realistically have of STONE CIRCLE going forward.'

We do, do we?

C spoke for the first time.

'I have given assurances that we can and will review the basis on which this operation was conceived, and we will review whatever arrangements were put in place. I'm sure we're all agreed that this is an appropriate course of action.'

'I'm sure it is,' said the Director of Requirements and Production. Except, he thought, I will have to tell Hopko that whatever deal she made with her agent is off.

C was there before him, though, working like a scalpel.

'Now we appreciate that assurances were given to those involved, and Roly Yeats has made clear that changing an agent's expectations at this stage of the game might present problems for the case officers and for the access agent. So I accept the logic that a change in the operational modalities is desirable.'

Modalities?

C continued, looking straight at the Director of Requirements and Production.

'From this point onwards, with regard to the control of Operation STONE CIRCLE, we feel it's appropriate that other resources, external resources, be brought to bear.'

The Permanent Under-Secretary was nodding. The Special Adviser was looking at some notes.

External resources.

The Director of Requirements and Production, for a fraction of a second, sought to compute whose interests C might be serving, but no answer presented itself.

'When should the handover take place?' he asked.

'I rather think it's already underway, actually,' said C.

The migrant labourers came to the salon earlier now, in the freezing darkness. They wore heavy coats over clothes they didn't change for days at a time, and which accumulated layers of dried, crumbling mud of a tan colour. Their hands were hardened, chapped and split in the cold. They took nips from bottles of sorghum liquor and smoked. Sometimes they left the salon and went straight to work on a night shift, some floodlit construction site, its grinding machinery and whistles going through till dawn. Sometimes they lingered in the salon, silent, reluctant to leave.

Peanut watched the migrant labourers from his stool by the beaded curtain. Though these two men looked less like migrant workers, more like locals, didn't they, the ones bantering a little with Dandan Mama, winking at the girls, handing round cigarettes. Quite the performers. They seemed to be enjoying their surroundings, taking them in.

Then one of them, the taller one, with a very full head of hair and an enormous, sculpted jaw, turned towards Peanut with a look of recognition. The man smiled, waved a hand. He wore a light-coloured coat that came down to his thighs and carried on its chest the motif of a foreign cigarette brand. The coat had a leather collar and looked expensive. The man was tall, but lean, with the angular, hard look to his shoulders and elbows, and the swiftness of movement, that Peanut knew to be dangerous.

The second man was smaller, but also lean. He was less expansive, a quiet, flat look to him; he wore a grey leather jacket, which looked to Peanut's eye too slight to keep out the winter cold, and slacks. So they had driven here.

Who drove to the Blue Diamond?

Lantern Jaw was moving across the salon now, towards Peanut, his outstretched hands proffering a cigarette packet.

'*Lai! Chou yi gen!*' Come on. Have a cigarette. The man's Mandarin was northern, educated.

Peanut took one. Lantern Jaw lit it.

'It's good to see you,' he said.

Peanut remained seated, said nothing. *So this is it.*

'We've got things to talk about.' The man was towering over Peanut now.

'Lucky us,' said Peanut.

'Let's go outside for a moment.' The man nodded in the direction of the door. 'Put a coat on, won't you. It's cold.'

Peanut looked around. Just Lantern Jaw and Flatface. No sirens, flashing lights, screaming uniforms. When did they start arresting people discreetly?

'Should I bring my things with me?' His voice had gone quiet.

Lantern Jaw leaned down. He was actually smiling.

'That's not what's happening. Come outside. I just need to talk to you and then we'll leave you to your charming companions and your business.'

Peanut stood, took his anorak from a hook and followed Lantern Jaw to the salon's front door. Flatface smiled at Dandan Mama and made a *we'll be right back* gesture. Dandan Mama's simpering had given way to a frozen look.

They stood on the steps. Lantern Jaw looked up and down the street, and faced Peanut. Flatface stood behind him.

'You're a very successful man,' said Lantern Jaw.

'Really,' said Peanut.

'Yes, very.'

Peanut narrowed his eyes, searched the man's face, found nothing.

'Who are you?'

'We're your friends.'

'I don't know who the fuck you are.'

'Night heron,' said Flatface, from behind him.

Lantern Jaw nodded, smiled, pointed towards Flatface.

'There you are, what he said.'

Peanut exhaled.

'You're under new management,' said Lantern Jaw.

Peanut looked down for a moment and stroked his chin.

'I don't know what you're talking about,' he said.

'Of course you don't. That's okay. Just listen for one more second. Don't contact anyone, and I mean anyone. Don't go near the British journalist. Don't go near the professor. We're dealing with him directly. You just stay put. You'll receive further instructions.'

Lantern Jaw stooped a little, bringing his head level with Peanut's, looked questioningly, as a parent might wait for a child's acknowledgement of some unpalatable instruction.

'*Hao ma?*' Okay?

Peanut shrugged, looked away.

Then, from behind, a hand hard on the back of his neck, a surprising sensation, and Flatface's voice in his ear.

'What he means is, things have changed. You will get what you are owed, maybe more, but not yet. And you'll do exactly what we fucking tell you, when we tell you.'

Flatface's thumb had found a spot between shoulder and neck that was the source of what Peanut could only understand as a sort of primal pain. The pain shot downwards into his middle back, and upwards into his head and eye, in a way he had never experienced before.

So. Relax. The lesson learned a hundred times at the hands of the thunders. When they've got you, relax.

He allowed his shoulders to slump, his head to loll back. The pain lessened a little. Peanut allowed his knees to bend, let his centre of gravity fall.

And then Peanut made a claw with his right hand as it dangled by his side and bent back his hand a little at the wrist, so that when he brought it up very fast, and simultaneously snapped his knees straight, the thrust had the force of his body behind it, and the heel of his hand rammed into that enormous jaw making contact just under the chin. Lantern Jaw's mouth snapped shut – his teeth made a hollow *sneck* sound – and his head went back. He didn't go down and Peanut wasn't surprised, but he did stagger back, disoriented and groping for balance. Peanut was already bringing the elbow down, again very fast, and turning hard to his right, so the elbow made contact at speed with a spot just below Flatface's sternum. Flatface made a *dugh* sound. His mouth worked, but no further sound came out. For good measure, Peanut now raised his elbow, and moving with the weight of his entire trunk brought it down at a point where Flatface's shoulder met his neck. Flatface was on one knee now, but still there. Peanut took three quick steps and placed distance between himself and the two of them. He had the knife drawn, palmed.

Lantern Jaw had one hand out, gesturing. He didn't look hurt, or even very shaken.

'That was unfortunate,' he said.

'I still don't know what you're talking about,' said Peanut.

Lantern Jaw had a finger inside his mouth. He brought it out, looking for blood.

'Just do what I told you to do,' said Lantern Jaw. 'I know you will.'

Peanut circled as Lantern Jaw walked carefully around him, staying out of range of the knife, and took hold of the lapel of Flatface's leather jacket.

'Off we go. Let's leave him to it,' said Lantern Jaw.

'You cunt,' said Flatface.

31

Beijing

A book. A concise and timely portrait of the Followers, and a trenchant analysis of the state's response. For publication.

For cover.

Ting sat at the laptop, spooling through, translating as she went. Mangan mentally edited and typed. Hours and hours of interviews with Followers going back two, three years, the fragility and tension in their voices growing with each passing month, with each mass arrest. The bureau phone rang. Ting paused and reached for the receiver.

'*Wei?*'

Mangan could hear the caller, male, strident. Ting was bemused, held the receiver an inch from her ear. She looked at Mangan.

'It's for Mr Mang An.'

'Who is it?'

'He doesn't say. But he's insistent.'

Mangan took the receiver. Ting smiled *good luck.*

'This is Philip Mangan.'

'What the fuck is going on?'

Mangan tensed.

'What do you mean?'

'With my management. What's going on?'

'I don't know what you mean.'

Ting was watching him.

'They say I have new management.'

There was a silence. Then Peanut, angry.

'Meet me, Mang An, now. Same place, by the dancers. Now.'

The line went dead. Mangan replaced the receiver, felt himself touching his hand to his cheek.

'What was that?' said Ting.

'It was, I'm not sure.'

'You knew him.'

'It's nothing.'

She shook her head.

'No, it's not nothing. Is there some trouble?'

'Really, it's fine. I might have to go out for a bit.'

Mangan stood, picked up his mobile phone and walked on to the balcony, closing the door behind him. He dialled Charteris in his office, but got only voicemail.

There were no dancers that grey, late morning, just relentless, lurching traffic.

Mangan waited by the north gate of the Workers' Stadium. He stood behind a plane tree to get out of a bitter wind. Peanut arrived four minutes later, stood by the gate looking around. Mangan stepped out, gestured with his head. Peanut walked over.

'They went to the sub-source.' Peanut spoke quickly, his eyes flickering, scanning the pavement.

'What? Who did?'

'These fucking people. I don't know who they are. The same ones that told me I was under new management. God in heaven. New *fucking* management.'

'All right, all right, calm down,' said Mangan.

Peanut turned and fastened his eyes on Mangan.

'Mang An, if you ever tell me to calm down again I will rip out your liver.'

Mangan closed his eyes, exhaled.

'How do you know this? Did the sub-source call you?'

'He called me at two this morning, weeping down the fucking phone. Accusing me. "You said it would be a one-time job. You said it would be over soon."'

'These people, what have they told him to do?'

Peanut shook his head.

'They gave him another gadget, Mang An. Another drive. Told him to go back and do it again.'

'Wait, do what again?'

'What do you mean do what again? Go back and stick the drive in the fucking network. Only this time at the General Armaments Department.'

Mangan swallowed.

'Will he do it?'

'This is not a very robust individual, Mang An.'

'What did you say to him?'

'I told him not to do it and to give me the drive.'

'*What?* Why, for God's sake?'

'I went and got it. Got a cab to his house.'

Peanut pulled his hand from his pocket. He opened his fist. A drive lay in the palm of his hand: black, bulbous, undisguised.

'Jesus Christ. What are you going to do with it?'

'I'm going to shove it up your arse. I want my deal, Mang An. Get it for me.'

The black car arrived in the early evening. It drove once, slowly, past the house, then turned and came back. The car pulled into the driveway.

It was the professor's wife who'd answered the door, an enquiring smile, friendly woman. They'd asked to see him. She'd said, come in out of the cold. Wasn't much warmer inside. Huge house, one of those winding staircases. He was hovering in the background, a shadow, and when they walked into the reception room, he was already leaning against a wall, all trembly. And when they said they had some routine questions, he found it hard to reply, his mouth twisting and working. His wife had looked at him as if he might be ill, walked over and put a hand on his arm, which he pushed away, his eyes still on them.

So they'd waited a bit, slowed things down, just to see what would happen, sat down, took out notebooks, files. He wouldn't sit, said he'd stand. He was desperate. And then when they said could he confirm he had such and such a document in his possession, numbered 157, that was his copy wasn't it and where was it please, he was wide-eyed, terrified. He managed to get out that it was in his safe, in his office at the Launch Vehicle Academy. And then they just left it for a bit longer, didn't say anything. And he started asking, is there a problem? And when they ventured, well, perhaps you'd better tell us who you've been showing it to, his legs started to shake, and he was holding on to the big fancy fireplace for support. And by this time his wife was in tears, saying, what is it, what is it? And they said, well, perhaps you'd better come with us, and he just crumbled, started weeping.

Investigator Han, still at the trestle table, sat back, looked at the ceiling. He reached forward, took a celebratory cigarette from the pack and lit it. He took out his mobile phone and dialled the personal number of the Deputy Director of the 9th Bureau.

'You wanted speed, Deputy Director.'

'Has the search team gone in?'

'Yes, Deputy Director.'

'And the suspect?'

'On his way to the villa, Deputy Director.'

'When will the interrogation begin?'

'We will let him stew for twenty-four hours. So tomorrow. In the night.'

'Investigator Han.'

'Yes, Deputy Director.'

'If the interrogation yields evidence of espionage, you will make an early determination as to whether he can be turned.'

'Yes, Deputy Director. I think he is, perhaps, too fragile.'

'If he cannot be turned, then break him.'

Professor Wen Jinghan, aeronautical engineer, specialist in launch technology, recipient of numerous academic honours, longtime Party member, trusted servant of the state, naked, with his hands behind his head, his thin, hairless limbs crimped into a squat, his penis dangling. The pain in his thighs and groin had grown slowly through the first hour, until it was impossible to ignore. Now it was all-consuming, a red-hot burn that had him clench-jawed and close to sobbing. He shifted his weight from foot to foot, looking for relief.

'Stay still,' said the guard, quietly. He wore a police uniform.

The room was bare but for a chair and table. It was lit by a single neon strip light and was very cold. A heavy brown curtain covered the window.

They had said nothing in the car, so neither had he. He'd sat in the back, between two of them. They drove around the ring road and out into the Western Hills. They slowed and passed through heavy steel gates, pulled up at a villa, and he was gently handed out of the car. And when he couldn't stand up, they put their forearms in his armpits and walked him over gravel. It was late, very dark, quite clear. He could see some stars. You had to come to the Western Hills to see stars. He smelled pine resin and earth.

The villa was low slung and white-walled, fringed by shrubs.

He had affected a normal tone of voice, or what he thought to be one.

'You may be assured of my complete cooperation,' he said.

They didn't respond, walked him in through the front door, into a hallway of brown tiles. There was another man waiting, older, balding, a look tinged with understanding, not unkind. One of the men from the car went over to him and whispered into his ear. The older man nodded, then spoke to the professor.

'My name is Investigator Han,' he said. 'Professor, I must tell you this now. You must confess straight away. If you confess, you can expect lenient treatment. If you do not confess, you may expect us to be very severe.'

The professor was retreating into himself and the man's words seemed to come from a distance, and to bring with them a sense of parody. *They really say that? When you are arrested?* They really do.

'You may be assured of my cooperation.' The words left him of their own accord.

The investigator was talking again.

'I am going to leave you now for a little while, and then we will talk.'

The professor nodded. I understand.

And that was a cold lifetime ago. Now he squatted on this icy tiled floor. The tendons in his thighs and groin were racked, the pain spreading into his stomach as a dull nausea. Such a simple device!

The door opened. The guard turned and stood. It was him, the investigator. Might the situation now change? It might. The investigator was sitting at the table, pulling the chair in with a dry scrape. Now he was speaking.

'Are you ready, Professor?'

Wen Jinghan nodded, swaying now.

The investigator gestured to the guard, who walked over, placed his hands under the professor's arms and lifted him forward, into

309

a kneeling position. A flood of relief. The professor kneeled with his hands on his knees, and began to shiver.

'What is your name?'

'My surname is Wen. My given name is Jinghan.'

'And what is your position?'

'I am a professor of aeronautical engineering. I hold a position at the Launch Vehicle Academy and a position at the General Armaments Department.'

'Is it also true that you hold a position as Technical Adviser to the Leading Small Group on Military Affairs?'

'It is true, yes.'

'And in your position as Technical Adviser, you receive copies of classified reports detailing developments in all aspects of military-industrial development. Is that correct?'

'Yes.'

'Do you, or did you, have in your possession a copy of the report entitled *A Preliminary Report on Certain Questions Relating to Second Stage Failure in Launch Vehicle DF-41*, with the cover number 157?'

'Yes, I have it in my possession.'

'To whom did you show the report numbered 157?'

The professor took a deep breath, and the words again seemed to leave of themselves: thin words, without weight, fragile.

'I want to be clear how all this came about. It is, perhaps, not what it seems. I think I should start from the beginning.'

The investigator nodded to the guard again. The guard bent over and rummaged in a small light-green haversack at his feet, lifting out a black baton, fourteen or sixteen inches in length, with a loop attached to one end. The guard flexed his hand, passed it through the loop and took hold of the baton. He came and stood behind the kneeling professor. Wen Jinghan felt the end of the baton placed firmly against his lower back.

The sensation that followed resembled being kicked very hard at the base of the spine. But the impact of the kick grew and surged through his entire body, a hot *whump*, forging up his back and into his head, his eyes. He felt as if suspended in the air for a moment, then an impact as if he had fallen from a height on to the floor. He felt himself gagging, saw his hands jerking spastically in front of him. He lay on his side.

The investigator was speaking again.

'To whom did you show the report numbered 157?'

'Forced. Of it. Forced.' The words felt like leather twisted tight.

'To whom did you show the report numbered 157?'

'Knew. Of it. Huasheng huasheng.'

'Say the name again.'

'Li Huasheng huasheng huasheng.'

They left him. His limbs stopped the involuntary jerking over the course of what he thought to be about a quarter of an hour. He crawled to a corner and vomited noisily.

They came back.

'Explain quickly now, Professor. Why did you show the document to this Li Huasheng?'

'He forced me to. He wanted to sell it.'

'All right, who did he intend to sell it to?'

The professor was breathing hard. He had, he realised, bitten the inside of his cheek and there was blood around his mouth.

'We will go over all this in detail, many more times. But you must tell me the essentials now. It is very important. Who did this Li Huasheng intend to sell the document to?'

Silence. Not a conscious strategy to resist, no, simply a realisation that the moment he uttered the word everything was finished, gone.

The guard was standing behind him, leaning over, the baton was higher up on his back this time.

'No. No. No.' The words came out on a rising tone, the professor's vocal cords tensing for the shock. He was arching, curling away from the baton, one hand in the air, like a schoolchild seeking to answer a question.

'It was the British.'

'British? Who?'

'He had contacts with the British. He knew a journalist.'

'Who's the journalist?'

'I don't know.'

'He wanted to give the document to a journalist? So the journalist could report its contents? Is that what you mean?'

The professor was silent.

'You must answer, Professor. Really, you must.'

'It wasn't for reporting.'

'So what was it for?'

The professor had leaned forward, his palms flat on the floor. His silver hair hung around his face. He spat something out, listlessly.

'The journalist works for British Intelligence,' he said.

There was a short pause.

'Tell me now, Professor, quickly, how you contact this Li Huasheng.'

'There's a number.'

'Where?'

'Look in my writing desk. At my home. Drawer on the left. Taped to the underside.'

3 2

Beijing

Just before dawn, soaked in sleep, Peanut heard the banging on the salon's front door, loud raps, rattling the door in its flimsy aluminium frame. He stood and crept out of the storeroom. One of the girls, barefoot, in a long T-shirt, was walking up the corridor and through the beaded curtain. She pushed a loose strand of hair behind her ear. There was shouting, now, too. Open. Police.

He ducked back into the storeroom and pulled on trousers, jacket, thrust his feet into shoes. He emptied the contents of the little basket by his mattress into a carrier bag. *Shenfenzheng,* money. He ripped the phone from its charger. It was turned off. He stuffed it in his pocket. His books, a few papers, he left. He felt in the pocket of the coat, the knife's hard outline. The voices were louder. *Where are the exits? How many people in the building?* Police voices. The girl – was it Yin? – stammering her replies. He was almost out of the rear door, into the alleyway, when he stopped. Back into the storeroom – footsteps in the corridor now – and reaching under the mattress, fingers fluttering until they fell on the bulbous form of the second thumb drive. Then he was gone.

Charteris spoke in tight, clipped tones. They were outside, in the grounds of the embassy, just after eight in the morning, barely light, a lowering sky. He didn't have a coat on and hunched his shoulders against the cold.

'Philip, the operation went extremely well. Your part in it is over. It has moved to a new phase.'

'I thought there was only one phase, David. He coughed up, we paid him. Done.'

'These things often change.'

'For Christ's sake, David, someone's turned up with another drive.'

Charteris blinked.

'He contacted you?'

'Yes. He contacted me. Unsurprisingly, he wants to know what's going on.'

'When?'

'Recently. What the fuck *is* going on, actually, David? Who are these people giving out drives?'

Charteris looked at him, seemed to be considering.

'I can't, Philip. Now back off and go home.'

'So I'm just supposed to disappear?'

'There is, I'm told, a plan to contact you and talk through with you your next move.'

'My next move?'

'It's for them to discuss with you, Philip. Not me.'

'Are you no longer involved either?'

'That's not for me to discuss with you either, Philip.'

'You're no longer part of this thing, are you?'

'I'm getting rather cold now, actually, Philip, so I am

going to go inside. Go back to your flat and wait to be contacted.'

The police had sat everybody down in the salon, lowered the blinds. Dandan Mama, Chef, Yin, the other girls. The shouting had been calmed by an older man who spoke with more authority, and smoked.

'There is no Li Huasheng here,' said Dandan Mama, swallowing.

'Who was living in the little room at the back?'

'Uncle. He just helped out. Song, his name. Song Ping.'

'Where is he?'

Dandan Mama looked around, despairingly.

'I don't know.'

'He was here last night,' said Yin.

'Was he.'

Another plainclothesman pushed the beaded curtain aside, came back into the salon. He was waving a piece of paper.

'Receipt for the purchase of a mobile phone and prepaid card.' He showed the older man, pointed something out. 'Here's the number.'

The older man looked at it and nodded.

'Go. Now.'

Mangan left the embassy, walked for a while, to the south, over Jianwai Avenue, past Hot and Prickly, into a neighbourhood with a school, the children in red scarves, Disney backpacks. Two old men sat beneath a plane tree, from which hung caged songbirds, their voices fluting, reedy among the branches. They sing from fear of each other, Mangan thought. Their songs are screams of fear and aggression. The old men sat silent.

When he returned to the flat Harvey was making toast in the kitchen and Ting was lying on the blue sofa, her arm bent across her face, feigning the vapours.

'Christ, what are you putting her through?' shouted Harvey from the kitchen.

Mangan was jangled, confused.

'What do you mean?'

'If I have to listen to another interview of another Follower, I'm going to jump out of the window, Philip. Why can't we do a book on something sane? Opera. Food.'

Mangan could find nothing to say. Harvey came in with a plate full of toast, a jar of marmalade.

'It's cruel and unusual punishment, Philip.' He bit into a piece of toast, then looked at Mangan.

'What's eating you?'

'What? Nothing.'

'He's been like this for a week,' said Ting. 'All, what do you say, surly, yes.'

Mangan just shook his head, went into the kitchen to escape Harvey's searching look. He sat at the kitchen table, pretended to read the paper. He could hear Harvey and Ting talking in lowered voices.

The bureau phone went. He heard Ting's *Wei?* And then she was at the door to the kitchen.

'It's for you.'

He stood and went back into the office.

'Philip Mangan.'

'Mr Mangan. Would you be so good as to come and meet me downstairs? Our mutual friend at the embassy suggested we should chat sooner rather than later.' The voice: controlled, calm, Chinese-American.

Mangan said, 'All right.' And hung up. Ting and Harvey were watching him intently.

He picked up his jacket and gestured *I'm going out.* Harvey made an exasperated face.

'Philip, for God's sake.'

But Mangan was closing the bureau door behind him and taking the stairs two at a time. Outside his block a silver sedan with darkened windows was waiting, its engine running, exhaust steaming in the chill air. A front window hissed open and a hand in a leather glove gestured to him. He walked over. A man, massive, blond, stepped from the driver's side. He wore a black suit and a subdued tie.

'Mr Mangan? Please get in.' His accent – something European. Dutch? Danish? He held the door.

'And, Mr Mangan, if you have a mobile phone?' He held out his hand. Mangan gave him the phone, which he turned off. He took out the battery and shut the phone in the glove compartment.

Another man sat in the rear seat, a small man, in a black overcoat with his hands folded in his lap. The man had Chinese features and grey hair, expensively cut in a buoyant parting. In his sixties, perhaps, the cheeks just a little pouchy but the skin pale, smooth, cared for. Hooded eyes. He was gentle, distinguished, reminded Mangan of a lecturer he had at university, who was studiedly polite and relentlessly oblique. The car pulled smoothly away. The man spoke quietly, America vying with China in the accent, America winning in the idiom.

'Mr Mangan. Thank you for meeting with me. I am genuinely sorry you have been inconvenienced.' He gestured, a soft, regretful chopping motion. His hands were small and manicured, Mangan saw.

'I'm not sure what you mean,' said Mangan. My refrain, he thought. No, my epitaph. Philip Mangan, reporter, spy. He was unsure what you meant.

'I had hoped you would not be further distracted. The phone call from our interlocutor should not have come.'

Interlocutor? Did he mean Peanut?

'In any case,' the man went on, his speech slow and careful, almost ponderous, 'we hope that your involvement is now at an end.'

The man nodded. Mangan did not reply.

'And so,' the man said, 'it just remains to consider your course of action. Might it not be wise for you to leave China for a little while? We thought you might consider a sabbatical in Singapore, while you work on your book.'

'Would you mind telling me who you are, please?' said Mangan. 'Who is the "we"?'

'Oh, I'm sorry.' The man looked rueful. 'Please forgive me. You should consider us to be representatives of your government, just as you did the fine individuals you have dealt with up until now.'

'I have no idea what you are talking about.'

'Of course. I think it would not be fruitful to pursue this line of conversation any further. Perhaps we can agree that there is always much to be learned, and few opportunities to learn it. So we will be carrying on your fine work.'

Mangan felt his anger rising in his neck, his throat, at this smooth fatuous man, his euphemisms.

'Just stop the car,' he said. The man looked at him. The car continued.

'Mr Mangan, it would be desirable for you to have no further involvement in this matter. Your work has been very much appreciated. But we would like your assurances that you will take some time. Singapore would be very suitable, I think.'

'I heard you the first time. Now stop the car.'

The man looked up, caught the eye of the driver in the rearview mirror and nodded gravely, as if it were a great effort. The car pulled over. Mangan got out, closed the door and walked away.

'Mr Mangan,' the driver called, standing on the kerb. He was holding up Mangan's mobile phone. Mangan walked back and took it. The driver gave him a knowing smile, a nod.

Mangan took a taxi back to the flat. He walked to his desk, and sat. Harvey was still there. Ting came and perched on the edge of the desk, put a hand on his shoulder.

'Philip, please tell us what's going on. Who was in that car?'

'It's nothing that concerns you, really.'

Harvey walked across the room and leaned against the wall, by the window. They've planned this, thought Mangan.

'Philip, you know bloody well that's not true,' said Harvey. 'If something is up, you need to let Ting know.'

Mangan shook his head.

'Is it something to do with the book?' asked Harvey. 'Are you getting strife about our last trip? What is it, Philip?'

'Ting, I think I should probably go back to Singapore for a bit. Could you book me a ticket in a couple of days. There's a love.'

Harvey sighed, pushed himself off the wall and went to the sofa. Mangan saw a glance shared between him and Ting.

'I'll be away for about a week or so.'

'Okay, Philip.'

'Okay, then.'

His mobile phone rang.

'Mang An.'

Mangan's stomach lurched. The sound of traffic, rustle and noise, and Peanut's breathing.

'Hello,' he said.

'Are you listening?'

Mangan stood up quickly, went out on to the balcony.

'Yes, I'm listening.'

'Police. Security. They came. This morning.'

Mangan experienced the half-second during which consciousness forms, the fractional delay in understanding. The finger on the burning surface, waiting for the pain. The hiatus on news of a death.

'Police?'

'Yes. Get out. Come to Zhaogongkou Bus Station. Now.'

'But you said, your management.'

'Not that. This is different. I don't know. We're blown. Get out.'

'Wait – are you on a mobile phone?'

'What? Yes.'

Christ. He hung up and pushed the off button.

He swallowed. The temptation was to go back into the bureau, sit, pretend nothing had happened, rely on the foreign correspondent's bubble of protection, the journalist's self-righteousness.

We're blown.

Move.

He walked back into the office, to his desk. From a drawer he took an envelope with some cash in it, two credit cards he seldom used, a mobile phone charger, a notebook and pen. He put these things in a small shoulder bag that had printed on it the device of some economic summit he'd attended in Shanghai. Twenty-First Century Visions, Hopes, drivel. He checked he had his wallet.

Ting and Harvey were both watching him. He turned to them.

'Ting, something has blown up. I'd like you to go home, please.'

'At last,' said Ting. 'Tell us, Philip.'

'A contact of mine, a source, is in some trouble.'

Ting frowned.

'Which contact?'

'You don't know him. Please go home, Ting, and don't come back into the office before I tell you it's okay.'

Mangan saw her expression change to alarm.

'What have you done, Philip?'

He walked around the desk, kneeled down beside her.

'I don't know,' he said.

She raised her hand and ran her fingers through his hair.

'Can I help?'

'No. No. Please go home. Stay there. For now.'

She drew back, the hurt on her face. He looked away.

'Harv, I need you to do me a big favour,' he said.

'And what would that be, Philip?'

'I need you to drive me somewhere and wait for me.'

'Take a bloody taxi.'

'It's important.'

'Not to me.'

'I need this.'

'Need away.'

'I just need a pair of eyes, that's all.'

Harvey didn't reply, just stared.

'Harv, this is very important.'

Harvey sighed, picked up his jacket, reached in the pocket for his keys.

'Ting, go home,' he said.

She was on the verge of tears, sitting at her desk, holding herself tight, looking fixedly at the desktop. Mangan walked to the door, Harvey followed. Mangan stopped, turned, walked back to his desk. He opened the drawer again and pulled out his passport.

'I'm so sorry.'

She wouldn't look at him.

'Tell me what you're sorry *for*, Philip.'

Harvey pulled his jeep out of the compound.

'So where are we going? Or is that too sensitive to share as well.'

'The bus station, Zhaogongkou.'

'And why are we going there?'

'I just have to see someone, very briefly, make sure they're okay.'

'And you want me to wait.'

'Yes. Please.'

Ting sat that way for another ten minutes in the silent flat. She had a sense of something ending, her little set-up here, the three of them. The trust had gone, quite suddenly. She and Mangan had worked together for three years, more, they had lately become lovers – gentle, casual, for sure, but lovers – and now he wouldn't return her look.

She stood and went for her coat, the silvery quilted jacket. She put it on, and the funny hat with fur earflaps that made Harvey laugh. Really warm, though. She went into the kitchen, took her lunch box from the fridge, put it in her backpack. She went back to the laptop. The screen showed a frozen image of a woman in a village in Heilongjiang, walls covered in newspaper and a bowl of rice and bean curd on the table. She had been in mid-flow, some-thing about the Master's way of communicating through a stellar plane. Ting had been there when they filmed that. Harvey, she remembered, had pinned blankets over the windows so no one could see in. She turned off the laptop and closed it. Phone, keys. She walked towards the door and reached to turn off the light.

The knock was hard and clattered around the flat.

Then silence. Then again.

She stood still, her hand in mid-air, still outstretched towards the light switch. What sort of a knock was this? Not a friend's knock. Not Philip back with his diffident shrug and slow smile, or Harvey to pop a cork, spirit her off somewhere, flirt with her. Not one of the others, the Americans or French or Germans, each from their little paper, magazine, radio station, each with its own earnest identity, come in to lounge and chat and quietly pick her brains because Ting knew people, knew where to go, who to ask, how to ask, how to get the paperwork done.

The knock came again. And this time a voice, speaking official. '*You ren ma? Kai men.*' Anyone there? Open up.

She let her hand drop from the light switch. She knew what kind of a knock it was now.

Breath, posture. Big, big smile. She opened the door.

They drove south in silence, the traffic sluggish, twilight coming on. It was a full half-hour until Harvey turned on to the approach to the bus station, and almost dark. The pavements were full with clusters of travellers. Huge two-decker buses halted and hissed through the traffic. Taxi drivers lounged by their cars in lines, hunched against the cold, bought *baozi* from stalls lit by hurricane lamps. The air reeked of exhaust and fat. Water in the gutters had frozen, and people walked tentatively, clutching luggage, holding each other's elbows in the shadows.

Harvey pulled over, pushed the jeep up on to the kerb. 'I think it's about time you really tell me, Philip, what's going on,' he said.

'Stay here, please, Harv.' Mangan opened the door, stepped out. He walked towards the main entrance to the bus station, veering through the crowd. He looked around. Nothing.

He took his mobile phone from his pocket and turned it on. One message. He called his voicemail, listened. It was Milam, his languid tone replaced with something else.

'Phil, hey. Look, is everything okay? I'm here in the compound and I just saw Ting walking out with two guys, like, heavy guys. And, man, did she not look happy. Just call me, okay? It did not look good, Philip, really. Call, like, soon, okay?'

He pushed a knuckle to his forehead, closed his eyes.

He stumbled through the crowd towards the station, searching faces, looking for the powerful, insistent gait amid the shadows, the headlights. A bus pulled out spattering slush, its gears shrieking.

He turned to go back to the jeep, but someone gripped his arm.

'This way, quickly.'

They walked past the jeep. He saw Harvey watching from the front seat. They walked away from the bus station. The crowd thinned a little and the street got darker. Peanut cut abruptly to the right, towards a shop selling videos, a soundtrack blaring from speakers above the door, gaudy posters in the window. Next to the shop a very narrow, very dark alley. Mangan turned and looked for the jeep, which was closer. Harvey had pulled down the street in their direction, following them. Peanut was pulling him into the alley. It was barely wide enough to walk through, and it was a dead end. Why ... but now Peanut had taken hold of his coat at the shoulder and was shoving him through a doorway.

'Up,' he said.

Mangan climbed. The stairwell was dark and reeked of piss. He trod on something soft, pulled away. Peanut pushed him again from behind. He emerged on to a rooftop, littered with empty bottles, styrofoam boxes. They were on a flat roof now, above the video shop. At one end a metal walkway carried over to the next building, and on. Peanut squatted, gestured to Mangan to do the same. Mangan could see him breathing heavily, felt the tension coming off him.

'What have they told you?' Peanut said.

'Nothing. They told me to stop. I'm no longer part of it.'

Peanut spat.

'You broke our agreement.'

'I—'

'You fucking tell them, Mang An. I want my money and papers. That was promised to me. Wasn't it?'

'Yes, it was,' said Mangan.

'This entire thing is now gone to shit.'

He was breathing hard, the skin on his face damp, reflecting the glow from the streetlamps.

'Look, what happened this morning?' said Mangan.

'What do you mean what happened? State Security turned up, and they were looking for me. By name. That's what fucking happened.'

'But how ...'

'I don't know how.' His voice was a furious whisper. 'But if they're looking for me they're looking for you too, Mang An. So why don't we make a call to our handler and politely inform him that on top of his fucking around with my deal, State Security is now all over us as well.'

'I think they're at my office,' said Mangan.

Peanut looked at him, his mouth open. He pointed to the mobile phone Mangan held in his hand.

'Call them, now.'

'I'm not calling them, and not on a mobile phone.'

Peanut looked like he was about to shout, leaning forward; Mangan saw the whites of his eyes, the straining jaw.

'Just call them!'

Mangan shook his head. There was a shout in the street, two storeys below them.

'Mang An!' said Peanut, his face twisted with anger. 'We might have minutes here. *Minutes!* Do you fucking understand? I was in prison and I am not going back. Do something.'

But Mangan was on all fours, crawling through the rubbish to the edge of the roof. He looked down, blinking into the darkness. Three black sedans had pulled up in the street. Two were some distance away from the video shop, blocking traffic. The third was immediately opposite, stopped on the pavement, its engine running. Next to it a man stood. He held in his hand

325

some sort of electronic device, which he was studying. His face was illuminated by the glow from its screen. Four more men were walking towards him from the other two cars. One of the four had his hand inside his jacket, resting it there. They all wore plain clothes, jeans, running shoes. A few onlookers had gathered, standing on the icy pavement beneath the streetlamps, craning their necks, their breath steaming.

The man with the device put one hand up, as if to signal *standby*.

Peanut was now at Mangan's shoulder, looking down, too, and Mangan could feel the jolt of fear in him. Then he was gone, a herky-jerky crawl through the rubbish and shards of filthy ice towards the metal walkway at the far end of the roof. Mangan looked again, quickly. The man with the device was pointing, tentatively, towards the video shop. One of the men was jogging over towards it. He held a walkie-talkie.

Mangan looked back up the street towards the jeep. Harvey had got out and was standing next to the vehicle, hands on hips, looking down the street towards them. Two more of the men were now jogging towards the video shop, and the man with the device was speaking into a radio. Mangan turned and, running at a crouch, followed Peanut to the walkway.

It was a flimsy affair of aluminium struts, galvanised sheeting. Peanut was already on it, crawling. The walkway bounced with his movement. Mangan went on to all fours, crawled the fifteen feet or so to the adjacent roof, the ribbed metal cold against his hands.

A siren, now.

Mangan ran to the front of the building. They were sealing off the street, police in short grey uniform overcoats, balaclavas under their stiff caps; they moved jerkily under the flashing lights. A knot of people was in front of the video shop. Eight or nine kids – they looked like the shop's occupants, T-shirts, spiky hair – were kneeling in the road with their hands on their heads. The man with the device stood, hands on hips, waiting for something.

And then Mangan saw Harvey. He was walking away from the jeep towards the video shop and the police. A uniform was walking towards him. Harvey had something in his hand. It was his blue journalist's card. He was holding it out. And now one of the plainclothes men saw him, ran towards him. Two more followed. The plainclothes man pushed the uniform aside, snatched at the card. The two others went behind Harvey. The plainclothes man waved the card in Harvey's face, shouted something. Harvey held his hands up, conciliatory. The plainclothes man shouted it again. Harvey shouted something back and Mangan saw him turn away, try to shove past the two behind him. The plainclothes man had pulled something from his waistband. An umbrella? No, a baton, telescoping out to three or four times its original length with a *snap*. Mangan could see the heft of it in the man's hand, the nasty little weighted sphere at one end. The man brought it down hard on Harvey's shoulder. Harvey bent sideways and twisted away, one hand up, pointing to the plainclothes man, who brought the baton down again and hit Harvey on the wrist. Harvey doubled over, put his wrist under the other arm. The plainclothes man just stood and watched. The others were moving in on him now, but Harvey was big, and with his good arm gave one a hard shove in the chest. Mangan kneeled up, a shout rising in his throat. But Peanut had wrapped a huge hand around his upper arm and wrenched him back down to his knees.

'Don't you fucking dare,' he hissed.

So Mangan watched, silent, from a distance.

Harvey was clearly in pain, his head still angled over, and now he made a break, running for the jeep. The plainclothes men jogged easily behind him, then slowed, as if to stand back and watch how it all turned out. A siren whooped, then the gunning of an engine. A black sedan came down the street at speed. The driver, practised, dipped the wheel towards Harvey as he passed. The offside wing caught Harvey at the hip and he went up, clean into the air. The momentum was all with his legs and lower torso and he flipped, almost a cartwheel. He seemed to land on his head and shoulder, rolled to one side and lay still. A leg was broken, maybe the pelvis, the feet at wrong angles.

The sedan stopped and the plainclothes man was talking into the radio. Someone was examining the blue journalist's card and signalling *no* with a wave of the hand.

Peanut was tearing him away, dragging him back towards the walkway. Mangan felt as if the nerves in his body were ringing, a metallic toll through his spine, hands, head.

They crawled further along the walkway, to a third rooftop, a little distance now between them and the video shop. The walkway ended at a stubby tower laden with mobile phone repeaters. A ladder was bolted to the wall. They took it, Peanut first, his knuckles white on the rungs as he climbed down to the street. Then they ran into the cold night, Peanut relentless, lumbering, Mangan behind him.

The date. A reference number.

FM CX BEIJING

TO LONDON

TO P/64815

FILE REF C/FE

FILE REF TCI/29611

FILE REF R/84459

FILE REF SB/38972

LEDGER UK T O P S E C R E T

URGENT URGENT

/REPORT

1/ Operation STONE CIRCLE has been compromised. BEI 72 is reported at RATCHET's residence. Situation continues to develop.

2/ Embassy press officer received a telephone call from correspondent for the *Los Angeles Times*, Spencer MILAM, US national, asking for comment on the arrest of ZHAO Ting. ZHAO is paid assistant to RATCHET. Press officer replied he had no information.

3/ Whereabouts of RATCHET, GENIUS as of 11.00 ZULU are unknown.

4/ Status of CRATER unknown.

/ENDS

33

SIS, Vauxhall Cross, London

They were in Yeats's office; the first time, Patterson realised, she'd ever been invited in. An ornate lamp stood on the desk and, on the wall, photographs. Yeats with a Prime Minister, shaking hands, looking down the lens; Yeats in some far-off place, in a bush jacket; a river, tropical foliage. Now he was standing, leaning on the back of the chair behind his desk. Hopko sat, legs crossed, arms folded. Yeats spoke.

'Well, technically, this is no longer your responsibility, Val. So perhaps we can dial down the indignation a little.'

Hopko tilted her head to one side and smiled.

'Roly, Philip Mangan works for us. Or he did.'

'As you point out, the locus of operational management is now elsewhere.'

The what? thought Patterson. She stood up.

'Which locus would that be?' she said. 'The one that's driving around Beijing in a silver bloody limo, holding agent meetings? That one? Or the one that's handing out hard drives?'

Yeats narrowed his eyes at her, his tongue working in his mouth.

'What is on that drive?' she asked.

Yeats waited a moment.

'The situation will be brought under control. I think we should end this meeting now,' he said.

'Will it? Be brought under control?' said Hopko, quietly. 'This, Roly, is what they call a flap.'

Hopko stood and walked out of the room. Patterson could feel Yeats's eyes on her as she followed. In the corridor Patterson, feeling the fury rising in her, turned to Hopko. But Hopko just shook her head.

The bus, a big two-decker thing, the heaters on full blast, took them to Tianjin, eighty miles distant, some two hours in freezing rain. Peanut had flagged it down and to Mangan's astonishment the thing had stopped and the door opened with a hiss. Mangan had paid the driver and they'd sat upstairs at the back, Mangan hiding his face as they passed more police cars heading towards Zhaogongkou.

On the expressway Peanut had handed him a cigarette, and they sat silently and smoked. Peanut seemed to be collecting himself, calculating.

'So, Mang An,' Peanut said, very quietly. 'I am inclined not to stay with you.'

'I don't know what to tell you,' said Mangan.

'Well, you'd better think of something to tell me soon.'

'I have to get out of China,' said Mangan.

'We all have to get out of China.'

Mangan exhaled.

'I have a number to call.'

'But back in Beijing.'

'No. In London.'

Peanut raised his eyebrows, looked very hard at Mangan. He had taken off his coat and wore only a T-shirt. Mangan saw his bulk, the hardness of it, smelled the reek of cigarettes, sweat, stress.

'What will you say to them?' said Peanut.

'I don't know. They must meet us, get us out.'

Peanut shifted in his seat.

'Some plan,' he said. And then, after a pause, 'Is there a chance?'

Mangan sighed, shook his head, said nothing.

'They'll shoot me, you know,' said Peanut. 'They won't shoot you, because you're a foreigner, and they'll work something out.'

Peanut turned and faced the window, which was streaked with rain.

'But they'll shoot me.'

They got off outside a railway station in the west of Tianjin. Peanut stayed outside, shivering in the shadows. As Mangan walked away, Peanut said, 'You will come back, won't you?'

And here, of course, the cameras. Nothing to be done. The ticket hall was quiet, echoing. A scattering of travellers, standing, looking up at the screens. Mangan walked the length of the hall to a bank of telephones. At the far end one had a sign: international calls. He went to it, took one of the credit cards, swiped, dialled the number.

Patterson was running down the corridor. The call had come through on a live line for 'Rachel Davies', and the operators had put it into a suite and notified the P section.

She barrelled past Drinkwater who was emerging from a lift. He said something about the Grand National, and whoever he was with laughed.

She crashed through the door to the operations suite. The technician was already there.

'Ready?' he said.

She nodded, trying to calm her breathing.

'Bringing them in now.' He tapped the screen.

She leaned forward to the microphone.

'Hello?' Noise of, what? Chimes, echoing announcements. An airport? A station?

'Is that Rachel Davies?'

'This is Rachel Davies.' He remembered that clipped, hostile tone, the dark eyes. He was wrestling a notebook from his pocket.

'Where are you?' she said.

'We've left Beijing. We need to know what to do.' He was cupping his hand round the mouthpiece.

'You say we. How many of you?'

'Two. Me and ... our friend.'

There was a brief silence, as if she were making up her mind about something.

'All right. Listen very carefully. And tell me if you understand. You will go to Fuzhou City, in Fujian Province. Do you understand?'

'Fuzhou, yes.'

'Then to Xiao'ao Township. On the coast.'

'Xiao'ao. Yes.'

'Look for the Golden Crab restaurant, south of the town by the water.'

'Yes.'

'Behind it there's a breakwater. Be there at oh-two-forty tomorrow night, or the night after.'

'Oh-two-forty.'

'There'll be a recognition—'

A hand, hard on his shoulder. He turned. Peanut, eyes hard, teeth bared, looking down. 'We go. Now.'

'Wait.' He pulled away from Peanut's grip.

'Do you understand?' came the voice on the line.

'No, wait, say that again.' Pushing Peanut away. Peanut hissing at him.

'For recognition, use the Chinese word *shichang*, "market". They'll reply using the word "riptide".' He wrote furiously.

'Do you understand?'

'Yes. But they are—' Then the pip as the line went dead.

Patterson held her head in her hands. A hundred and thirty-three seconds on an open line. The technician looked sympathetic.

'Happens to the best of us,' he said.

She looked at him, aghast.

'*What* happens to the bloody best of us?'

'Oh. I didn't mean to give offence ... I ... '

But she had stood up and was out of the suite, striding back to the P section, wondering if hers would be quite one of the shortest careers the Service had ever seen. CALIPER had been Hopko's idea, she'd seen from the file. Set up a few years back, topped up regularly. A useful contingency, whose use, the file told her in stentorian tones, required authorisation at very, very high level, due to the 'exceptional sensitivity of the operational modalities'. Service speak, Patterson knew, for high probability of mayhem and international incident. And as for the authorisation, well, Patterson had somehow neglected to obtain it.

Would it work?

Mangan hung up. Peanut was rigid, had his fingers twisted into Mangan's jacket. Mangan looked the length of the ticket hall, saw nothing and turned to Peanut.

'They're outside,' said Peanut. As he spoke, at the far end of the ticket hall the large silver doors opened and four police officers walked in, with a couple of plainclothes. They were moving quickly, scanning the hall. To the right of the bank of telephones, perhaps fifteen feet away, a swing door with 'No Entry' stamped on it in red, a window in the centre of it, with wire mesh in the glass. Peanut still held Mangan's jacket.

'Walk slowly,' he said.

They made for the door. Then Peanut was through it and running, Mangan close behind. A corridor, a freight elevator. Peanut's thumb stuttered on the call button. Mangan looked behind him. Through the glass in the door he could see the policemen moving past the telephones. The lift juddered to a stop. A soft *ping*. They waited for the doors to open. The doors stayed closed. More uniforms now, closer to the glass. Peanut raised his hands and let them fall, exasperated. The doors didn't move. Mangan pushed Peanut aside, grabbed what appeared to be, recessed into the metal of the door, a handle. He wrenched it and the door groaned open. Manual doors.

Peanut lurched into the elevator. Mangan slammed the doors behind them. The elevator smelled of garbage. Its control panel offered six floors.

'Where? Up? Down?'

'Down,' said Peanut. The elevator shuddered downward. Peanut leaned back, shook his head.

Two floors down the elevator stopped. A bleak passage with pipework running along its ceiling, cream walls. And, in dribbling red spray paint the length of the passage, anarchy signs, the circled letter A, again and again.

They clattered down the passage to double doors. Peanut thrust them open and propelled himself through and Mangan saw a mop and a bucket and a small elderly man sat on an upturned crate with a metal lunch box in his hand, chopsticks halfway to his mouth, eyes wide, frozen. Peanut couldn't stop and went straight over him, crashing to the floor with man and crate, the lunch box clattering, rice, onions, some fatty pork spattered on the floor.

Peanut was up, fast, and had his hands on the old man's lapels, lifting him, shouting.

'How do we get out of here?'

'Wha—?' The man was terrified, on his knees, pawing at Peanut's arm. Peanut screamed at him again.

'How do we get out?'

The man pointed back the way they'd come, to the freight elevator. Peanut shook him.

'Not that way. Another way.'

The old man was gasping now. He pointed, again, the other direction.

'There's stairs.'

'Show us.' He lifted the man and set him on his feet. 'Now.'

The man started to walk stiffly. Peanut put a meaty hand on his back and propelled him forward. The man grunted and grimaced.

'God in heaven. Move, you imbecile.'

The man went forward at a pained trot. They rounded a corner and another. The light was dim. The red anarchy signs bled down the walls. Ahead of them were double doors with a crash bar.

'There,' said the man.

'What's on the other side?' said Peanut.

'Stairs,' said the man.

Peanut had him by the throat and up against the wall.

'Where do the stairs go?'

'Up,' said the man, his breath rasping under Peanut's grip. 'Up to the rubbish bins and there's a loading dock.'

Peanut let him go and he slid to the floor. Peanut pointed a warning finger at him.

'You do not tell anybody you've seen us. If you do, I'll be back and I'll deal with you.'

The man just looked up at him, on the verge of tears, said

nothing. Peanut dealt him a savage kick that took him in the chest, and he whimpered and cowered. Mangan hit the crash bar on the doors and suddenly could smell the night. They ran up the stairs; Mangan peered around a corner. It was raining hard. The loading dock was empty. A truck stood there, no one in the cab.

'They said we have to get to Fuzhou,' said Mangan.

'Why?'

'I think we might be met.'

'Fuzhou,' said Peanut.

Mangan took a breath, hurried out past the loading dock, through the gate, on to the street. The whoop of a siren came from the other side of the station. There were taxis, waiting their turn to go to the rank.

'How much money have we got?' Peanut said.

They had three and a half thousand yuan between them.

'Trucks,' said Peanut.

Mangan hailed a taxi.

'I'm a foreign journalist,' he told the driver, speaking too quickly. 'I want to interview truck drivers. About the cost of fuel. Could you take us to where there are many truck drivers? A truck stop, perhaps.'

The driver frowned, thought about it, then turned the cab around and pulled away. Mangan sat low, rested his head against the seat. The tiredness in him was gathering in his limbs, in the sourness in his stomach and chest, a desire to do nothing now, to go no further.

And, at some point, he would have to think about Ting and about Harvey. Because he hadn't thought about them yet, but what he knew was welling up at the outer edges of his mind like water against a fragile dam, torrents of guilt and despair awaiting release. But he could not think about them quite yet, because to do so would result in his incapacitation. So he would think about them later.

He thought of becoming angry with Peanut. *Why did you drag me into this?* But his complicity, his own titillation – *an agent! A joe!* – rendered the impulse stupid and dishonest. He looked over at Peanut, who was looking keenly from the window, his breath steaming the glass.

'*Ni kan shenme?*' he said. What do you see?

'*Wode shenghuo.*' My life.

The Tianjin streets went past in a sodden blur of neon and rain.

34

The truck stop was on the southern edge of the city, asphalt crumbling into ice-frosted mud, a restaurant of sorts – Mian Wang, 'Noodle King' – in a low prefabricated hut, steam drifting from vents on its roof. A dozen or so trucks idled by the highway. The first driver Peanut tried wouldn't open the door of his cab. The second was heading the wrong way.

Now Peanut stood on the running board of a white, spattered eighteen-wheeler, pushing a wad of cash up against the glass. That got the man's attention. Peanut climbed in the cab, which was rank with cigarette smoke and dirty blankets. The driver was a wiry thirty-something man in a stained bright-blue sweater, his hair lank and falling across a pinched, narrow face, small, close eyes. He chewed on a toothpick, his jaw working.

'Where you going?' Pinchface said, looking at the money.

'South,' said Peanut.

'South where?'

'South as far as you're going.'

339

The man regarded Peanut, looked at the big shoulders. He held the toothpick, made a sucking sound.

'I'm going to Taizhou,' said Pinchface. 'I'm empty so we'll be quick.'

Taizhou. More than halfway.

'Some things you should know,' said Peanut.

The man looked away, through the windscreen into the darkness.

'Costs more, knowing things,' he said.

'There's two of us. The other one doesn't speak. And nor do you.'

Pinchface smirked.

'Who are you running away from, just so's I know when not to stop.'

'Local people. Nothing for you to worry about.'

There was a silence, while the man considered.

'How much?' said Peanut.

'A thousand.'

Peanut counted out the notes.

'Each,' said the man.

Peanut waved through the window to where Mangan stood in the shadows. Mangan ran to the cab, his coat collar turned up, climbed in. Pinchface jabbed his toothpick at Mangan's white skin, his red hair.

'That's a foreigner,' he said.

'You're observant,' said Peanut.

'I don't like that, not one bit,' said Pinchface.

Peanut rounded on him.

'You took the money, now drive the fucking truck.'

Pinchface, recalculating, muttering under his breath, started the engine. Peanut pointed Mangan to a space behind the seats, where a slab of filthy foam rubber lay on the floor of the cab. Mangan pushed past him and lay down. Peanut sat next to

Pinchface, took out a cigarette and lit it as the truck gathered pace on the highway.

They took the expressway south, shadowing the coast, through China's economic resurrection. Peanut hadn't realised. The glittering cities, mile after mile of factory, warehouse, high-rise, drawn in concrete and neon; beautiful young girls on billboards, curvy, beckoning, imploring. The traffic on the highway flashed past. Sometimes he saw oil derricks out in the fields, floodlit, their great weighted arms heaving in the night.

When he went into the camp, he had left an unsmiling country of low brick, its grey cities drifting into village, railways that wound past somnolent factories, through silent, emerald fields to a yard with a red star over the gate, a mountain of coal, a rooster. Now this.

Just after five Pinchface spoke.

'I need to stop and sleep for a while.'

Peanut caught an edge in his voice, wondered.

Pinchface said, 'I'm pulling over.'

A scabrous rest stop somewhere short of Laiwu, little more than a concreted field, a stinking toilet block. The truck slowed, almost came to a halt. But Mangan, kneeling, looking over the seats, saw them first; some distance away, flashlights probing the length of a bus, blue uniforms rousing its occupants, the driver gesticulating to the uniforms. Mangan leaned forward, cast around. Plainclothes men, standing smoking. Another group of uniforms by the road, waiting.

'How the fuck,' said Peanut.

'Keep going,' said Mangan.

'I'm stopping,' said Pinchface.

'No, you're not,' said Peanut.

'I am. They're after you. I'm stopping.'

The knife, now, small, glinting under the sodium lamps, hovering just in front of Pinchface's eye.

'Keep driving,' said Peanut, quietly.

The driver swore, gunned the engine; the truck picked up speed, pulled out on to the highway. After a few moments he said, 'You can have the money back.'

'Keep driving,' said Peanut.

Mangan sank back on to the foam rubber. Four, five miles further, another clutch of police, another bus by the side of the road. This time they'd taken the luggage off and a dog was going through it.

'Roadblocks soon,' said Mangan.

'They know we're here,' said Peanut.

'Yes, they know you're here,' said Pinchface. 'Look, I won't say anything, you just get out.'

'Shut up,' said Peanut.

Mangan blinked, snapped upright.

'Do you have a mobile phone?' he said.

Peanut nodded absently.

'Is it on?'

'Yes.'

'Jesus Christ.'

They pulled over about a mile further on, Peanut with the knife to Pinchface. Mangan climbed out of the cab. The night air stung him with cold. He was in the emergency lane. A little further on he could make out an intersection, secondary roads peeling off the highway. He jogged along the hard shoulder in the darkness, ran down the exit ramp. Sparser traffic on the secondary road. And a petrol station.

He ran towards the station forecourt, breathing heavily. A man walked away from a small blue truck with an open bed. He was going in to pay.

Walk boldly, it's less noticeable.

He strode into the light, made for the blue truck. It was full of ladders, sheets, pots of paint. A decorator, then, getting an early start. As he walked past, he took the phone – still turned on, perhaps three or four hours of battery life left – and dropped it among the decorator's equipment. He veered away from the truck and walked in a wide circle back into the shadows, started to run again, back up the exit ramp, towards the highway.

A few miles on they passed another three police cars moving fast in the opposite direction, flashing lights on.

Nothing after that.

But it wasn't enough for Pinchface. Perhaps an hour later Mangan lay awake on the foam rubber and felt the truck turn and slow. He sat up. Peanut's head was lolling against the chair. He was asleep, the hand holding the knife in his lap. Mangan saw the driver's face in the mirror; he was biting his lip. The truck was juddering to a halt now. They were on the outskirts of a town, in a grey dawn, the traffic heavy, new buildings of white tile rising out of the fields.

'What are you doing?' said Mangan.

Peanut came awake, sat forward.

Pinchface said nothing. The truck hissed and stopped. He reached for the door handle, got it an inch open.

'Wait,' said Mangan, but Peanut had Pinchface by the collar, wrenching him back into the cab. The knife was in Peanut's left hand, blade out.

'Where are you going?'

'Please, I just want out of this. I need to stop. You go on. I won't say anything.' He looked sullen, dispirited.

'Not possible, now,' said Peanut.

'But you have to let me go sometime,' he said.

Peanut said nothing. Mangan could sense he didn't know what to do.

'I have to stop. I've been going all night. I need to eat, piss,' said Pinchface.

Peanut leaned towards him, tightened his grip on the man's collar.

'You'll drive us to Fuzhou,' he said.

Pinchface looked nonplussed.

'I'm not going to Fuzhou.'

'We'll bring you some food. You can sleep for a bit. Then you drive us to Fuzhou. We'll pay you more.'

'That's not what you said. Before.'

'That's what I'm saying now.'

The man shifted against Peanut's grip, then sat still.

'All right,' he said.

Peanut considered.

'I'll go for food. You don't move.'

The man nodded. Peanut held out the knife to Mangan, who shook his head. Peanut pushed it into his hand.

'If he moves, cut him,' said Peanut. Mangan felt the weight of the knife, heavy for its size. A dense thing. He was kneeling behind the driver. Peanut opened the door on the passenger side and climbed down.

'I'll be back in a minute,' he said.

The door slammed shut. Pinchface sat still, Mangan right behind him.

'Just don't move, all right?' said Mangan.

But the man's right hand was feeling for something in the well between his seat and the door.

'Don't,' said Mangan. But Pinchface had found what he was looking for and there was a metallic scrape as he brought it up. Then he was turning fast in his seat and bringing whatever it was over his head. Mangan jerked back, away from the seat. A tyre iron. Pinchface's swing was vicious but the iron caught on the roof of the cab as it arced over. It came down on Mangan's shoulder, hitting muscle, not bone, a deadening pain. Pinchface was pulling back for another strike. His tongue was out in concentration. Mangan lashed out wildly with the knife, caught something with the tip of the blade, wasn't sure what. Pinchface sat back, swore, lifted the back of his hand to his mouth. The knife had found his cheek and laid it open, and his lip, too. Blood was already running down his chin and dripping on to the seat. He took a short breath and with an *ungh* sound launched himself over the seatback, both hands on the tyre iron, thrusting it forward in a stabbing motion. Now he was falling on to Mangan. The iron made contact with the side of Mangan's head, lacerating the scalp. Mangan felt it as a hot iron ploughing a furrow in his skull, then felt the weight of the man coming down on him. With his right hand he brought the knife upwards to meet the falling man. The blade seemed to glance off something hard and then sink into something of its own accord. Pinchface bucked, dropped the tyre iron and put both hands down on the foam rubber mat, taking his own weight and holding himself over Mangan, and looked down at his chest. The handle of the knife protruded from the blue sweater in the region of the solar plexus, the blade nowhere to be seen. Pinchface pushed himself up to a kneeling position, looking at the handle, then steadied himself with one hand on the seatback.

'Fuck,' he said.

Then he sat, leaning back against the wall of the cab, and looked at Mangan. His mouth was smeared with blood.

'What should I do?' he said.

Mangan swallowed, said nothing.

Pinchface looked down again. He touched the handle of the knife gingerly.

'It's not bleeding,' he said.

Mangan didn't move, sank his fingers into the foam rubber mat. There was silence for a moment.

'You'll have to get a doctor,' said Pinchface. 'You can get one.'

His face was in shadow now. Mangan could hear his breaths coming shallow and fast.

'I think, something, inside,' he said. He made a weak gesture. Then tried to lift his torso off the floor of the cab with his hands, making a ticking noise with his tongue.

'Starting to hurt, now,' he said.

He sat back down on the floor of the cab and leaned forward, his face in light. Mangan could see he'd gone shockingly pale, his skin shining. He reached out one arm towards Mangan, then let it fall.

'Help me now?' he said, the words feathery.

Then silence again, just his fast breathing.

'I want my kid,' he said. 'My little boy.'

But his eyes had lost their depth, had gone flat and glassy. Mangan had seen it before, that death look, seen it in an Aids victim lying on a bench in a filthy rural clinic, seen it in a little girl he'd helped pull from the rubble after a quake.

Pinchface slumped to the side and lay with a *mnama* sound. What felt to Mangan like minutes passed. Pinchface said, quite plainly, 'Oh, there you are.' And then nothing else.

Peanut had walked a quarter of a mile by the side of the highway. He was colder than he should be, he thought, the hunger and lack of sleep starting to tell. A café was selling rice porridge and eggs and *doujiang*. He bought full styrofoam boxes and put them in a plastic carrier bag and carried them back down the cold roadside. It was starting to get light. He opened the door to the truck and climbed in. The Englishman was sitting in the corner holding his knees, like an unhappy child. The driver was lying, asleep? No. That was a knife in his chest. The knife. My knife.

'What the fuck have you done?' Peanut said.

The Englishman just opened his mouth and shut it again. He

turned his head, and Peanut saw black, matted blood in the red hair.

'He attacked me,' Mangan said, turned his head away again.

Peanut closed the cab door behind him, rubbed his chin.

'You'll have to drive,' he said.

Mangan said something Peanut could not make out.

'You'll have to drive us to Fuzhou,' Peanut repeated.

'I said, I don't think I can.'

'Mang An, I don't know how to drive. They didn't teach us to drive in labour reform. You will have to drive.'

Mangan rubbed his eyes, shook his head as if to clear it.

Peanut, lips curled, pulled the knife out and wiped it. They covered the body, first with a blanket and then with the foam rubber mat, bumping into each other in the narrow space. Mangan stood, swaying a little, gestured to the truck's dashboard.

'I can't drive this,' he said.

Peanut climbed from the cab and walked away from the truck, crossing the highway towards a cluster of low buildings. A warehouse or factory, didn't matter. In the parking lot he squatted and waited, perhaps eight or ten minutes. A white car pulled in, a Volkswagen, one of the ones made in Shanghai. Peanut, all business, walked over to it, waving, smiling. The driver, a woman in a catering uniform, got out.

'No, no, get back in the car,' said Peanut.

'What?' she said.

'Back in,' said Peanut. She saw the knife, and did so.

'Now drive over to where that white truck is,' said Peanut.

She turned on to the highway, had to go some distance and make a U-turn, Peanut yelling at her to hurry up, her knuckles white on the wheel, eyes wide, the tears coming.

At the truck Peanut got her out and forced her into the cab,

347

made her lie curled up under the steering column, her head by the pedals, and he tied her with what he could find, a length of twine around her throat and twisted on to the brake pedal so she couldn't move for fear of choking herself. Mangan didn't say anything.

Mangan wore the woman's green woollen hat and drove south. He ate some of the rice porridge and egg, but threw it up. He pulled over and slept for an hour in the late morning, woke to find Peanut changing the licence plates on the car, working at the screws with a coin. He'd swapped the plates with those of a car on a second-hand dealer's lot.

The highway broadened on the approach to Shanghai, but they skirted the city and kept up a reasonable pace through the trucks, Mangan weaving, trying to stay alert. He pulled over again in the afternoon and slept more, Peanut shaking him awake at dusk and feeding him *baozi*, which he ate ravenously. Then on into the night, the temperature rising a little as they headed south.

They crossed the Hangzhou Bay Bridge in darkness and Peanut looked back at the lights of Shanghai.

'I would like to have seen all that,' he said.

Mangan said, 'We'll never be able to come back.'

'Not such a blow, for you,' said Peanut.

'And for you?'

Peanut thought for a minute.

'Mang An, do you know the story of Qu Yuan?'

'Some of it. But tell me.'

'Well, ancient China. Two thousand three hundred years ago, more. The Warring States period. All these little kingdoms battling each other year in, year out for resources, influence. One of the kingdoms was called Chu. A mysterious place, Chu, all mountains in the mist and shamans and tigers in the forest and apes hooting through the trees.'

Mangan, listening, pulled into the left lane to pass an eighteen-wheeler groaning under a load of timber. The *tick tick* of the indicator, its greenish light on Mangan's face in the darkness.

'And the king of Chu had an adviser named Qu Yuan. Loyal and wise and brave, this Qu Yuan. He loved his country, feared for its future.

'And Qu Yuan pleaded with the king to stop fighting the other kingdoms and to forge an alliance with them. Because the real enemy out there was the state of Qin. A brutal bunch in Qin, forever expanding, pillaging, burning books, murdering scholars.'

Rain on the windscreen, the highway a halogen blur.

'Anyway, the king rejected Qu Yuan's advice, and the other advisers told lies about him and he was banished from the court. So he wandered in exile and studied the country he loved so much and wrote poetry. Beautiful, Mang An, but mournful.

'Well, Qu Yuan was right, of course. Qin troops attacked Chu and the capital fell. And when news reached Qu Yuan he was heartbroken, wandering along the river, haggard, filthy, muttering lines from his poetry. In the end he threw himself into the water, drowned himself.

'Didn't matter to the Qin leadership of course, just one more crying poet out of the way, what did they care? And Qin set about doing what it did, burying scholars alive, burning libraries, imposing order, rubbing out culture. And eventually Qin unified all the kingdoms into one empire, China. You with me, Mang An?'

Mangan nodded in the darkness.

'All that difference, all those ways of living and being, just gone. And the super state, Qin, triumphant. Imposing standards, weights and measures and axle widths, laws and punishments, aggrandising itself at every turn with slaves and monuments and palaces and great tombs. Sound familiar, Mang An?'

They were moving away from the sprawling conurbation around Shanghai, the traffic thinning.

'I suppose,' Peanut said, 'what I mean is that, no matter how much we want to belong, Mang An, Qin makes exiles of us.'

By ten, Mangan was unable to continue. They turned off some way past Ningbo, drove the car on to a back road, parked up under trees, and Mangan lay in the back seat, wondering how much he'd lost, and falling into a racked sleep.

35

Off Route G104

Mangan woke in darkness, his jaw clenched, Peanut leaning over him, hissing. He felt cool night air on his face.

'Get up. Now.'

Mangan lay, thick with sleep, blinking up at him.

'What?'

'They're here.'

Peanut pulled him from the car and Mangan sat heavily on damp earth and leaves. Peanut had hold of his arm now, starting to drag him, spoke in a rush.

'I walked up to the main road. There's a car there. Three of them. Two are walking down towards us.'

'But that's . . . who?'

'I didn't fucking ask them, Mang An.' Peanut turned him bodily and pointed. Torchlight through the trees, still some distance away. 'Now *move*.' Peanut wrenched at his coat and the two of them stumbled into the undergrowth away from the car. They pushed through scrubby bushes and low trees in the darkness, Mangan breathing hard, the branches snapping against his coat with a *thwock* sound. They came on a small clearing, refuse piled at its centre: a charred mattress, plastic bottles. Peanut stopped and turned and looked past Mangan. The torchlight was just visible, close to the car. Mangan struggled to think.

'They're tracking us? Now?' he whispered.

Peanut just shook his head and let his hands fall. Voices came, faint, from the direction of the car.

Mangan licked his lips, pointed to the road.

Peanut nodded and they cut off to the left, back into the undergrowth, as quietly as they could. Underfoot was dry, their footfalls rustling. The hum of traffic from the road grew louder. The torchlight was still behind them. Then a voice, a dry echo in the trees.

'We can see you.'

Mangan froze.

'We can see you. And you should probably just stay where you are and we'll come to you.'

A pause.

'*Hao ma?*' Okay?

Peanut was shaking his head, his eyes wild. They stood at the base of a steep bank, studded with saplings. At the top of it the main road, the traffic rushing past in the night. They were up and scrabbling in the earth and leaves and rubbish, on their knees now.

Another shout.

'We can see you. Really, we can. And we're following you. And you have something of ours, don't you? So let's just stop all this.'

Silence.

'Please?'

Peanut reached the top of the bank first, emerging on to the roadside, the traffic yards away. He pointed. Mangan looked thirty, forty yards, perhaps, to their left, where a white car was pulled over. Mangan made out a figure at the driver's seat, illuminated by a glow. Peanut stopped, held up a hand, crouched, then crawled along the verge, approaching the car from behind. He turned.

'Mang An. Go to the right side and bang on the window. And pray the driver's door isn't locked.'

Mangan stood and walked quickly to the passenger side of the car. The figure in the driver's seat balanced a laptop against the steering wheel. The glow lit the interior of the car in silver. Mangan thumped on the window. The driver looked up from the laptop, startled, squinted towards him, leaned over to see him more clearly. But then the driver's side door was open, Peanut's arm around the man's neck. The man, eyes wide, moved quickly to break the headlock, ramming one hand into the hold and twisting, but the laptop constricted his movement, and Peanut was dragging him from the car, falling backwards on to the verge. Mangan ran around the car. Peanut was on his back, holding the headlock. The man lay on top of him, writhing and twisting in the manner of a wrestler seeking a way out. Peanut was grunting and hissing through his teeth, spittle on his chin.

'Knife, Mang An.'

The stubby knife, Mangan now saw, lay on the ground about four feet away. He lunged for it, brought it up. He pointed it at the struggling man, whose eyes followed the blade, but who still tried to break the hold.

'Stop moving,' Mangan shouted. The man worked harder. He had one hand well inside the hold now, between his own neck and Peanut's iron grip, to the wrist, but his eyes were bulging and he wasn't breathing.

Mangan moved closer, held the blade to the man's face. Still he fought. Peanut rasped, his voice high and tight.

'Cut him, Mang An.'

Mangan hesitated. The man's eyes were on him. Then he pointed the blade upward, raised the knife high in the air and brought it down fast, ramming the heel into the man's face. It found the bridge of the nose, and the man grunted and stopped struggling, closing his eyes tight. Mangan was surprised at how quickly and copiously blood began to flow from the nostrils. Blood everywhere, in seconds. Mangan stood, his knees threatening to give. He looked down and saw a spatter of blood on his sleeve, felt his gorge rise. The man had his hands raised in front of him, palms outwards. He was trembling, Mangan saw. Peanut loosened his grip and the man took a long shuddering breath, and then slowly raised his hands to his bloodied face. His eyes were still tight shut, as if he were about to cry. Peanut slipped out from under him, breathing hard, grabbed the knife and held it to the man's throat, and leaned on to him.

'How are you tracking us?'

The man said nothing.

'How are you doing it? Tell us or I'll cut you.'

The man spoke from behind his hands.

'On the laptop.'

Mangan darted to the car, reached in. On the laptop screen was a map with a purple arrow at its centre. Above, GPS coordinates.

'They're tracking us. But what can they see? What are we carrying?'

Peanut gripped the man's jaw with his left hand, forced the blade closer to the man's neck.

'Tell us.'

Still the man said nothing, just the sound of his breathing from behind his hands, the blood running through his fingers.

Carrying, thought Mangan.

We are carrying.

He stood shakily, dropped the laptop on the ground, and stood on it, grinding his heel into the screen, stamped on it. The plastic casing shattered and Mangan kicked it into the road, into the wheels of the passing trucks. When he turned back he saw torches bobbing through the trees.

'Get the keys from him.'

Peanut screamed at the man, who just said, 'In the car.'

The keys were in the ignition. Mangan started the engine and yelled at Peanut, who was already running for the passenger side door. The man lay on his side now, was starting to prop himself up with one elbow. Mangan saw movement in the rearview mirror. Two men were emerging from the scrub at the side of the road, running towards the car. As the headlights washed over them Mangan glimpsed a tall, powerful figure with parted hair and a jawline so pronounced it suggested deformity. In one hand the man carried a torch, and in the other Mangan thought he saw the dull glint of a sidearm.

We have something of theirs.

We are carrying.

The drive.

A beacon on the black, bulbous second drive.

And what else was on the drive?

Mangan stamped on the accelerator and felt the car lurch forward, wheels spinning. He jerked the steering wheel over and took them out into the traffic, horns blaring as the trucks veered past him.

What else?

Just after dawn, a turnoff for somewhere called Linhai. He took it, Peanut looking at him, frowning.

'Why are we doing this, Mang An?'

Mangan said nothing.

'How does this help us, Mang An?'

'Shut up. Look for an internet café.'

Low cloud, grey light, street sweepers arcing their straw brooms through pooling rainwater. Mangan drove them slowly between white tower blocks, past a stadium, down Lantian Lu, Blue Sky Road, scanning the storefronts.

The Net Queen café was open, empty, foul-smelling. A girl with a pierced lip sat, rocking back on her chair, thumbing messages on a mobile phone. She stood and thrust a clipboard at Peanut, who signed in as Song Ping. A camera, mounted on the wall, watched them. Mangan hovered in the background. The girl looked at him, then gestured to a row of mouldering terminals.

'Number thirty-six,' she said.

Mangan sat and logged on, Peanut leaning in.

ME: Frog, you there?
ME: Frog?

A pause.

ME: Talk to me, Frog. Now.

Nothing. Just the blinking cursor.

'He's not fucking there, Mang An. He's eating dinner or playing games or jerking off. Let's go.'

'Wait.'

He clicked over to his email account.

Philip Mangan – if you are receive this message, please know we must talk with you. We require you contact us immediately. Please call this number. We wait your call.

A mobile phone number. No signature, the sender a generic address. Dated two days previously. Then another.

Philip Mangan – you are in grave circumstance. Your friends in grave situation. Please be contact us immediately. Call this number.

Four more messages, the same. Mangan swallowed. Then one more, dated six hours previously.

> Philip Mangan – if you use this account, we know. Wait for us where you are.

'Dear fucking God, Mang An. We leave, now.'

'No.'

'*Yes.*'

'Who the hell is sending them?'

'Who cares, we go. Now.' Peanut was gripping him by the arm.

'Even if they can see I've used the account, they can't get here that fast.'

Then, a muffled *pip*.

> TREEFROG: Yo MANGMAN. Where u bin? Frog in da house

Mangan exhaled, Peanut shaking his head.

> ME: Listen to me. I have a thumb drive. Can you read what's on it?
> TREEFROG: Duh
> ME: wtf does that mean can you read it or not. Serious now.
> TREEFROG: OKOK chil.n I can read. Wot on it?
> ME: Don't know. Govt stuff, spook stuff.
> TREEFROG: say what now?
> ME: A thumb drive from govt – has spy stuff on it.
> TREEFROG: apps?
> ME: What? Say again

Peanut had his head in his hands.

TREEFROG: SO COULD BE APPLICATIONS YES? PROGRAMS? EXE
FILES? THINGS THAT DO THINGS? CLEAR ENUFF FOR U?

ME: yes shall I plug it in

TREEFROG: NONONONNONODON'T PLUG IT IN

ME: why

TREEFROG: DO NOT PLUGIT IN. You kno wots on it? No?
Fucksake mangman could start world war fuckin three. or
four. or six. chill. froggy telling you do not repeat not plug it
in. Where dyou get this thing?

ME: I cant say. Butits sposed to be targeted at China.

TREEFROG: Sposed by who?

ME: govt/security.

TREEFROG: so classified?

ME: very very

TREEFROG: ok youre frightnin froggy now a lil bit

ME: Ffs frog can you read it or not?

TREEFROG: Affirmative mangman. But on wot basis we talkin here?

ME: i need to know whats on it. just look at it and tell me whats
on it.

A pause.

TREEFROG: why?

ME: ive been set up. i think it's a weapon or a spy program or
something.

TREEFROG: w w w wait a goldarn sekkin. how you got this,
mangman?

ME: long story

TREEFROG: fuck you bin up to?

ME: will you help me?

TREEFROG: if it is wat you say mangman that some v v dngerous
shit. made by v v dangeros people

ME: tell me about it

358

TREEFROG : froggy averse to life thretnin situations, kno wot im
    sayin
ME: must happen fast frog.

Another pause.

TREEFROG: where you get it?

Mangan shook his head, exhaled. Peanut was looking at the
door.
    'Hurry up, Mang An.'

ME: Can't say where got it. really cant.
TREEFROG: SHEESH
ME: THIS IS VERY VERY FUCKING IMPORTANT
TREEFROG: ok ok OK jeez frog will take a lil looky look
ME: How do I get iot to you if I cant plugit in?
TREEFROG: ok jes listen i take control of yr terminal so i can
    reasd the drive, download it without whatever shit's on it
    cranking up and blowin us up. go here.

A web address, a fast download, an install.

TREEFROG: let go yr mouse

Mangan lifted his hand from the mouse. The cursor began
to move of its own accord, barrelling through a series of settings.

TREEFROG: OK mangman I got it now. plug the sucker in. oh and
    hope. Hahaha

They left the café. At the door the girl waved Peanut over, wanting payment. Peanut argued, and the girl shook her head and

tapped her fingers on the counter and watched him slowly count out yuan notes. And while she watched Peanut, Mangan, his back to the surveillance camera, lifted the girl's phone from the counter and slid it into his pocket, next to the drive.

They were back in the car, Peanut watching the mirrors.

'How far now, do you think?' said Mangan.

'We should be there by evening.'

They pushed on under a sky of moving cloud coming in off the East China Sea. They stopped to fill the car up and to buy water and food. Peanut stood by the petrol pump and a police car pulled up next to them. The officer got out, stretched, said something to his companion in the car. Peanut turned his back, fiddled with the hose. Mangan looked down. The police officer regarded him for a minute, then turned and walked across the forecourt. Peanut rammed the hose back into the pump and they left.

'Are they still following us, do you think?' said Peanut.

'The police? No,' said Mangan.

'No, not the police. The others. Whoever they are.'

'They want their drive back,' said Mangan.

'We give it to them,' said Peanut. 'It'll be over.' Mangan heard a flicker of desperation.

Mangan shook his head.

'They want us, too.'

Mid-morning Mangan pulled off the highway and parked next to a field. He took the stolen phone from his pocket and logged into the secure chatroom.

TREEFROG: you there?

TREEFROG: you there now?

TREEFROG: FROGGY GETTING A LIL BIT TENSE HERE

ME: here

TREEFROG: where u BIN?

ME: what have you got

TREEFROG: wot I GOT? dunno mangman. this ting is fuckin
huuuuge. take years to even read it

ME: but what is it?

TREEFROG: DUNNO

ME: CHRIST FROG GIVE ME SOMETHING

TREEFROG: it is loaded

ME: WHAT? HOW/

TREEFROG: feel like i seen bits of it before

ME: frog what does it do?

TREEFROG: mangman im just scratchin the surface. its many
layers, many. rootkits, cloaked surveillance pckages. Infect
yr network, read yr keystrokes, clone it, find ways of getting
the info out. Itll turn on the camera on yr desktop an dfilm
you. shit thers a thing will turn on all wireless apps of entire
network,every handheld, and start sendin shit out on the
airwaves. ha. Jeez if you tell it to, im guessin it will go up
like nuke and kill whole network.

Mangan rubbed his eyes, Peanut was outside the car smoking,
watching.

ME: I don't get what does that mean

TREEFROG: mean? it means this one EPIC fuckin spy machine.it
will spy the shit out of you and you never kno. it will take yr
network and wring it fuckin dry. it will collapse yr systems. it
will expose you, make you weak. it is a weapon silent
stealthy and very very dangrous. and it means some very
srious people – govment if yr lucky, corporate if yr not
lucky – involved.

A pause.

TREEFROG: And it means froggy done with this shit now. And it means mangman watch yr butt. cos Im guessin some angry fcukers be wanting that drive back soon

ME: theyre after us

TREEFROG: shit

TREEFROG: nice knowin ya mangman

The highway was slow, gorged with trucks. As they passed a town called Rui'an, an accident, something burning and acrid smoke in the air. A woman in a pink jacket sat by the side of the road, her face in her hands, and next to her a shape under a blanket.

And later, as Mangan tried to overtake, a tanker pulled deliberately over into his lane, its mudguard touching the side of the sedan. Mangan, wrongly, braked as he swerved and the car began to spin. They came to a halt on the central reservation, horns blaring as the cars behind flashed past. Mangan was stiff-arming the wheel, rigid with fear. Peanut just pointed.

'Move, Mang An, don't stay here.'

36

Nearly midnight. The building was silent, but for the occasional lonely officer in an ops suite, waiting for something, someone.

Patterson stared at the email. It had been sent half an hour earlier to Charteris on his personal email account, to her horror. Charteris had encrypted it and sent it on securely. Now it lay spread across her screen and she felt the acrid falling in her stomach, an operation collapsing in front of her, an agent panicked, running. Hopko had a hand on her shoulder, leaned in to read.

This message is for you, David, and it is for 'Rachel Davies'.
Please forward it to her immediately. It is apparent to me that
your service has abdicated responsibility for this operation
and some other group – I have no idea who they are – is trying
to run it. But this operation is now over. Tell whoever is hunting
us to stop. They must stop now. Tell them that I know what is
on the drive, that it is a massive cyber attack on China,
propagated by corporate interests with the collusion of
government. Tell them that if they do not stop hunting us, I will

make public the contents of the drive. I will send them to every hacker, every security firm, every researcher, every privacy and secrecy activist and I will expose the authors of this cyber attack to public ridicule and legal sanction. I will do this. It is time to get us out of here. Philip.

Hopko read over her shoulder.

'Clever boy,' she said.

Patterson had her hands to her cheeks.

'Who?' A voice from across the office. 'Who's a clever boy?'

Hopko and Patterson turned. Yeats was striding towards them, between the cubicles, the lights rendering his face pale, shadowed.

'What have you got there?' he said.

Patterson gestured to the email.

'Our boy talking to us, is he?' said Yeats. 'Do share.'

He began to read, then exhaled.

'My, he's bold.'

He paused.

'But I don't react well to threats,' he said. 'Do I, Val?'

He folded his arms, then rubbed one hand over his beard.

'You'll reply,' he said. 'You'll tell him no one is hunting him. Tell him he is ordered to stay where he is. And help will be with him soon, and exfiltration will follow. Do it.'

'You're going to get him out?' said Patterson.

'Oh, yes,' said Yeats.

'How are you going to find him?'

'I have all the information I need, thank you. I assure you this situation is in hand and you may now desist from any further involvement. Do I make myself absolutely fucking clear?'

'Quite clear, thank you,' Patterson said.

Yeats let a beat pass, then leaned down to where she sat, and put his face very close to hers.

'Not keeping anything from me, Trish?'

Patterson said nothing.

Yeats straightened, glared at Hopko, turned and walked away. The two women watched him go.

'Those people. The Shady Creek people. They're tracking Mangan, aren't they?' said Patterson.

'It would seem so,' said Hopko.

'What will they do when they find him?'

'Kill him, I imagine,' said Hopko.

By six in the evening they had turned off the highway short of Fuzhou and were heading east to the coast, on back roads winding through fields of sugar beet. They stopped and asked a woman by the side of the road the way to Xiao'ao. She stood, shaking her head at Peanut's Mandarin, smiling, looking wonderingly at Mangan. She wore a hat of woven reeds, and from the carrying pole on her shoulder dangled two plastic trays filled, Mangan saw, with razor clams.

'Xiao'ao,' Peanut said, writing the characters in the air. A flash of recognition. She nodded and gestured down the road, towards the coast, saying something neither Peanut nor Mangan could understand. As they pulled away she was standing there, still smiling, pulling a mobile phone from her pocket.

As they came closer to Xiao'ao low hills of deep green rose up, rice terraces curling and angling across them. They rounded a corner and there was the township stretching away ahead of them, beyond it the sea.

They made a first pass. The Golden Crab was closed, its paintwork peeling in the salt wind, its parking lot empty. Behind it the breakwater stretched out into the sea, its concrete a dim whiteness in the dark water.

They pulled the car off the road, left it nose out and unlocked in a stand of scrubby trees a little way from the restaurant.

Mangan had wanted to scout the breakwater, but Peanut wouldn't let him. They climbed a wooded hill, slipping on damp leaves, and sat looking out over the deserted restaurant and the road and the breakwater and glittering lights out to sea that belonged, Mangan realised, to the Matsu Islands, those tiny, defiant scraps of Taiwanese territory, bristling with radar and missile bases, just miles from the Chinese mainland.

'Is that where we're going, do you think?' said Peanut. His voice was tense, but Mangan thought he could hear anticipation in it. 'You'll talk to them, won't you, Mang An, about my payment. My papers. All that.'

'Yes, I'll talk to them.'

'We had a deal.'

'Yes.'

A pause.

'They should stick to it.'

'Yes, they should.'

The night had cleared. No moon, but starlight. They sat, waited, smoked. Mangan dozed.

At 1.50 a.m. two cars pulled into the parking lot at the Golden Crab and stopped, their lights off. Mangan, awake now, thought he saw another further back down the road, but couldn't be sure.

At 2.04 a.m. a car door opened and a figure emerged and walked towards the breakwater and stopped, looked out to sea, hands on hips. Then the figure turned around and went back to the car.

'Is that them?' said Mangan.

'Is that who?' said Peanut.

Mangan peered into the night. 'Whoever is supposed to meet us.'

'How the fuck do I know?' said Peanut. 'If it's not ...' His voice trailed off.

'We should go down now,' said Mangan, 'if that's them.'

'No.' Peanut held up a restraining hand. 'If they set a time, they set a time.'

At 2.25 a.m. several figures got out of the cars. Two walked to the breakwater. Another two stayed by the side of the road. There was at least one more, but Mangan didn't see where he'd gone, and Peanut didn't see him at all. They all waited.

At 2.35 a.m. Peanut said, 'All right, we go now.'

Mangan stood, stiff and cold. They slithered down the hill and emerged at the side of the road facing the restaurant. They crossed over the road and made straight for the breakwater. The two figures kept their distance. Mangan heard the hiss and crackle of a radio, a monosyllabic message. Peanut was walking fast, chest out, arms slightly out from his sides, looking for a fight. Was that the knife, palmed in his right hand? Mangan stayed slightly behind him. One of the men had planted himself in their path. The way to the breakwater was blocked.

'What do we do?' The words not his, someone else out there speaking for him.

'Just walk to him and give him the signal,' said Peanut, quietly.

They walked closer to the figure who stood between them and the breakwater.

'*Shichang.*'

There was a silence.

'What?' said the figure, irritation in his voice.

Mangan said it louder. '*Shichang.* Are you going to the *shichang*?'

'Oh, I see,' said the figure. 'No, no, we're not the people you think you're going to meet. You're not going with them, I'm afraid. You're coming with us.'

The man was tall, wore a long leather jacket, had an overly pronounced jaw. Peanut was still moving towards him.

'Now stop there, friend,' said the man. 'Let's have no repeat of last time. You're not quite forgiven for that, yet.'

Peanut stopped.

'You again,' he said. 'Who the fuck *are* you?'

'Well, we're in charge of this operation, and we'd like to talk to you. At some length, I think.' Lantern Jaw held his hands out. 'So let's all be friends, and come and get in the fucking car.'

Five of them were surrounding Peanut and Mangan now.

'The operation's over,' said Peanut. 'I'm pretty sure.'

'Now why do you say that?' said Lantern Jaw, cheerfully.

'Because it's blown. And MSS is all over it like flies on shit.'

'Well, you should probably explain all that to my elders and betters. Get in the car.' He made a theatrical gesture, towards the car idling by the side of the road. In the front passenger seat Mangan thought he glimpsed the elderly man from the silver sedan, the hooded eyes fixed on him.

An engine, a deep-throated growl, coming from the sea beyond the breakwater. It had been growing on the edge of Mangan's consciousness, but he was only now aware of it.

'Get in the car.' A threatening tone now, which Peanut studiedly ignored. Mangan saw a searchlight on the water. Peanut made to push past Lantern Jaw, but the taller man's hand was in his chest. And from behind, a quick, snake-like move from one of the others to take Peanut into an arm lock. But Peanut stepped quickly to one side and with a short jabbing motion did something with the knife that had Lantern Jaw bending over and clutching at his groin. Mangan saw Peanut ripping himself out of the arm lock, spinning his assailant around. Round and round they went, until Peanut tore himself away and began to run towards the breakwater. Mangan lunged forward, arms out, but one of them was there, smiling, even, took him easily and held him. Peanut, he saw, was halfway to the breakwater shouting about a market, and they were after him, gaining on him.

And then something exploded in Mangan's lower back, and

a second time, and white specks danced in front of his eyes and he sank to his knees. Then a vice-like grip on his shoulder, two fingers in his neck like iron bolts.

'Stay still now,' said a voice in Mangan's ear.

Mangan looked towards the breakwater, could make out only shadows flickering in front of the searchlight, shouts. Then a dull *thop, thop* sound, and something in the air hissed past him. The grip on his shoulder loosened slightly, and the man holding him dropped to his knees.

'Oh, for God's sake,' the man muttered.

Mangan heard a cackle of laughter come from the breakwater. The searchlight was blinding.

The man holding him shouted, 'Is that really necessary?'

Another *thop* and a hiss.

Now Mangan could see, waddling out of the searchlight, an enormously fat man, dressed in a hooded top and baggy shorts. He had cropped hair and a goatee and in front of him he held out a handgun with a sound suppressor attached.

'There's only supposed to be two people here, and there's all you,' said the fat man, his Mandarin sibilant and singsong, pure Taiwan.

'Is that the foreigner?' he said.

The man holding Mangan said, 'Look, this has nothing to do with you. Now just run along.'

'Just what?' said the fat man.

'You're involved in something you do not understand,' said Mangan's captor.

'You're right about that,' said the fat man, and shot him in the leg. *Thop.* The man fell, gritted his teeth.

'You cunt,' he said.

'Shut your mouth,' said the fat man, and shot him again.

Mangan tried to stand, but couldn't. The fat man waddled over to him and hauled him up.

'There are others,' said Mangan, though he didn't know where they'd gone.

'Yes, so let's go, shall we?' said the fat man, not unkindly. Mangan leaned against him, felt the world fade, a spinning sensation, then came back a little. An utter weakness took hold of him and a deep, nauseating pain in his back and groin. He'd been hit, where? By what? There were shouts and more gunfire, a revving of engines. The fat man suddenly seemed angry. Mangan saw the white, sloping concrete of the breakwater beneath his feet and was scrabbling and sliding, the grit beneath his fingers and his feet in the water, to where hard hands took him by the upper arms and pulled him into a yellow boat: long, sleek, unsteady. The hands laid him down on the floor of the boat, and someone was shaking him and saying, 'Mang An, Mang An.' And the same voice was shouting, '*Zou! Zou!*' Go. Go. The boat lurched as the fat man jumped in, and someone said something in a dialect Mangan didn't understand and there was more laughter, and more *thop, thop* sounds, and a huge roar and the boat seemed to rise up and the searchlight went out and they were crashing into the waves, spray spattering the boat, and Mangan looked up and saw stars in an obsidian sky, and he felt a hand on his chest, and a voice in his ear saying, Mang An, we did it. We did it.

37

Taipei, Taiwan

The safe flat smelled of cooking grease and cigarette smoke. The blinds were drawn. A minder, in vest and shorts, sat at one end of the table, a mug of tea and a sidearm in front of him. Mangan wondered what would happen if he lunged for the weapon and turned it on the man and the woman who faced him across the table. He thought about the smooth *snick* of the safety catch, the bucking in the hand, the shock on their pale, English faces.

'We have orders from London,' said the man. 'I'm afraid it's essential they be followed to the letter.'

The woman nodded.

'This is for your own safety,' she said. 'Taipei is not secure. You must be moved.'

'Then we can all relax a bit,' said the man.

For two days Mangan had done nothing but move, from the speedboat to a rust-streaked trawler that heaved and wallowed in the Taiwan Strait, to a lonely dock, by night, at the far fringes of some port, where they took him ashore and Mangan smelled salt air, diesel oil and refuse. They put him in one van and took

Peanut towards another, but Peanut stopped and turned around and stood in the darkness, the sound of the sea lapping against the dock. And he just gave Mangan a long look, and nodded, and turned away, and Mangan hadn't seen him again.

They drove for two hours, the fat man sleeping in the passenger's seat, his head lolling, the silenced pistol in his lap. They brought him to this flat, empty but for a table and a rice cooker and a television and tatami mats on the floor. He was somewhere in the eastern outskirts of Taipei, he thought. The rain came down hour after hour. He sat and smoked, watched sitcoms on a satellite channel. A doctor came to examine the contusions blooming on his lower back and probe his internal organs for damage. Mangan was pronounced sound.

The burst of shock and adrenalin that accompanied his flight and exfiltration receded. He began to think of himself as a murderer: the murderer of an unnamed man in a truck stop, a man who, as the life spilled from him, wanted his little boy; the murderer of Paul Harvey, whose death – the cartwheel, the jutting limbs – visited him every waking minute; and, perhaps, the murderer of his delicate, loyal lover. He knew nothing of Ting's fate, and the uncertainty hung like a slough on his mind. The murderer, too, of a time that he had loved, that they had all loved, the three of them.

Now he considered the demise of the two British Intelligence Officers who sat opposite him, as they told him he was to be moved, tonight, Philip, a flight, very quick, very comfortable, and let's get you away from here.

'Explanations will have to wait,' said the man, 'but everything will be explained, and then we'll start thinking about your next move.'

There was a pause.

'But you do understand that it's over now. It's absolutely over.'

He understood what was over, what he had murdered.

The two SIS officers drove him through Taipei's shuttered streets. At midnight he was escorted aboard a business jet at a silent military airport. As the jet taxied to the runway he glimpsed Taiwanese F-16s beneath hardened shelters, their cockpits glowing.

By morning he was in Singapore, at the cool villa near Phoenix Park, where a sandy-haired man of military bearing made eggs and bacon and coffee, and told him politely that he wasn't to leave the villa, though he could walk in the garden.

Patterson checked the recording devices were running and made her way to the villa's living room. She turned to the minder.

'Please bring him in now.'

The minder disappeared and a moment later returned with Mangan, who was barefoot and wore an ill-fitting blue shirt and jeans. Mangan stopped and stared at her. She tried to read him, but couldn't. She looked straight back at him.

'Sit down, Philip,' she said.

Mangan hesitated, then moved carefully to an armchair.

'Are you all right?'

Mangan just stared. Patterson spoke quietly.

'We can repair much of this damage, but we need to know exactly what happened.'

'How?' said Mangan. 'How will we repair the damage?'

'There may be ways to help her,' said Patterson.

Mangan sat forward.

'What do you know?' he said. 'Tell me.'

'The last we heard was that Ting is in Qincheng Prison,' said Patterson. She watched Mangan's eyes close, his shrinking in the chair. 'She is going to be tried, we're told, but we don't know what for.'

The girl matching Zhao Ting's description had been spotted by a doctor in Qincheng, a decent, courageous man who believed he was passing information to an underground human rights network, when in reality he was talking to BND, German Intelligence. Patterson had read the encounter report from German liaison. A car, a night meeting in a village out in the wilds of Changping District, near the Ming tombs. The doctor had smoked and described the girl they'd brought to him. She was a wreck, shaking, blood in her urine, said the doctor, but some strength to her, a glint in her eye. As he palpated her neck, he'd asked her quietly if she'd been tortured, and she just gave a tight shake of the head. One of the prison guards had told the doctor that she had *guanxi*, connections. So you never know, he'd said. You just never know.

Mangan had his head in his hands.

'You must accept that your pursuing her case will hurt her, not help her,' said Patterson.

'How do you work that out?'

'Philip Mangan is a blown agent. There's nothing he can do to help. But it's just possible that with patience and with time we may be able to do things.'

Mangan didn't move.

Patterson took a breath.

'I must tell you, too, that Paul Harvey's family have been informed that he died in a traffic accident. The Australian authorities have accepted that this is the case. And so, I'm afraid, do we.'

Mangan looked up at her.

'Do we?' he said.

'Yes, we do.'

There was a pause.

'And I must ask you, too, if you are still in possession of the drive.'

'Still in possession of the drive?'

'Please give it to me,' she said.

'You are fucking relentless.'

'It's important you give it to me.'

'Where do they make people like you?'

'I was made in a number of places, Philip.'

From Mangan, something that could have been the ghost of a smile.

'Why do you want the drive?' he said.

'Because I want to know what's on it.'

'I told you what's on it.'

'I want to see if you're right.'

'What's your real name?' he said.

She blinked, looked down.

'Philip . . .'

'Tell me.'

She was silent for a moment.

'You may as well know.'

'I may as well.'

'It's Patricia. Everyone calls me Trish.' It felt, she realised, like an act of separation, of rebellion, even. Name as exploit. Truth as vulnerability.

Mangan eyed her, wondering.

'Well, Trish, here you are.'

And he held out a closed fist and dropped the drive into her hand.

For the next two days they walked Mangan through Operation STONE CIRCLE. Patterson was surprised to find herself conducting the debrief, Hopko briskly deferring to her. So she questioned Mangan, while Hopko listened from another room. She had expected to hear recriminations from him, but he seemed passive and reflective. He spoke as if describing a sickness or a wound, she thought. In her rejoinders to him, confident now, she carefully matched his tone and pace of speech, reflected his words back to him, let him change his mind. Every couple of hours she would take him out to walk around the garden, and Mangan would smoke and scuff the grass with his bare feet.

It was when they got to the truck driver that he broke. He was pale and his breath started coming quickly and then turned to great, shuddering sobs.

'Everyone here knows that feeling,' she said. She left the room and the sandy-haired minder went in and sat with him, and put a tattooed arm around him and let it play out.

Hopko made her spend an inordinate amount of time on the phone calls.

'So tell me again, Philip. You took the call on which phone?'

'On my mobile phone.'

'And where were you?'

'In the flat.'

'And what did Peanut say?'

'He said police and security had come. That we were blown, that we should get out.'

'Did he say where they had come to?'

'No.'

'Did you know where he was?'

'No, he never told me where he was, where he lived, anything.' Mangan rubbed his eyes.

'So you're certain he never told you where he lived? Never mentioned it on a phone?'

'I am as certain as I was last time you asked me.'

'And he never told you the name of the sub-source?'

Mangan sighed.

'Why not ask the pampered prick in the limo?' he said. 'The new management? Or one of his thugs. What about them?'

'Believe me, Philip, we will ask them,' said Patterson.

But she thought, Will we? Do we think we'll get an answer?

Mangan turned to her, angry now.

'Who the hell were those people?' he said.

They are our future, Patterson thought. She said nothing.

'Why were we told to go and do it all over again?'

'Because you were very successful the first time,' she said, quietly. 'And people got greedy.'

Mangan raised a hand, let it fall.

'Is that how we were blown?'

We don't know, thought Patterson. Do we, Val?

After a moment, he said, 'How did this happen?' He looked exhausted, hollow.

'That is what we would like, very much, to find out,' said Hopko, later.

Patterson sat with him while he signed the documents. There was some money, there were undertakings, and there were plans, all conveyed by a lawyer, a cheerful, brittle blonde who'd flown out from Vauxhall Cross. The paper, she imparted breathlessly, had lately discovered a desire for coverage of East Africa, and had realised that Mangan was the ideal correspondent. Great stories there, Philip. Plenty of work. And we can help you find a place. Let's get you back to London and we'll get it all worked out. And your stuff from Beijing is being packed up, what's left of it after the security people went through it. And we're going to help you round out your departure from China.

And suddenly it seemed to be over.

The lawyer left, and Patterson started packing up her files. Mangan spent hours in the garden, reading. Patterson watched him from a window, as he lay spread-eagled on the lawn, lean and dishevelled. They ate a meal together, Mangan regarding her across the table. He tried to draw her out, where she was from, where she had been. But she decided he was only trying to distract himself from his own turmoil. And anyway, it was insecure. They finished eating in silence.

Hopko spent most of the night at the station, and then, in the morning, turned up drawn and unsmiling at the villa. She motioned to Patterson and the two of them went to where Mangan lay on the grass. He shielded his eyes from the sun and looked up at them.

'Who are you?' he said.

'She's my boss,' said Patterson.

Mangan got to his feet, and Hopko held out her hand with a jangle of silver bracelets.

'We would not normally meet,' said Hopko, 'but I wanted to thank you in person.'

Mangan raised his eyebrows, said nothing.

'It's been quite the adventure,' she said, deadpan.

He waited a beat.

'You'll understand if I don't see it that way,' he said.

'It was a success. You may not see that, but it's true. So thank you, Philip, and good luck.'

She made to turn away, but hesitated.

'I know you were told it's over, Philip. But it may not be. You need to know that.'

She walked from the room, Mangan staring after her.

Patterson took him to the airport. He got out of the car, and they stood on the pavement for a while in the warm evening and he smoked a cigarette, the planes roaring overhead. He was unshaven, and looked tired and rumpled, but calm. She stood, arms folded, trying not to look like a soldier, or a spy.

'What will you do, now?' he said.

'Back to London.'

'No, I mean, will you stay with this . . . profession?'

'Do you think I shouldn't?'

'You seem, troubled by it.'

'Do I? I thought I was relentless.'

'Yes, you are that.' He paused, tilted his head. 'But you seem as if you do it under duress. You seem as if you're in some sort of exile.'

She didn't reply.

'China makes exiles of us,' he said. He reached out and put his hand on her arm. Her instinct was to pull away, but she forced herself to remain still, forced a smile.

'I hope I see you again, Trish. Next time I plan to learn your surname,' he said. And then Mangan turned and walked through the hissing glass doors into the terminal, and she lost sight of him in the throng of people. She sat in the car, and breathed slowly to stop the tears coming.

38

Singapore

It was dark by the time Patterson got back to the High Commission. She went to the station, swiped herself in. Hopko was waiting for her, and Charteris was there, just off the Beijing flight, red-eyed. Beneath the fluorescent lights he looked exhausted. He stared at Patterson.

'Surprised to see you here,' he said.

She returned his look.

'Can't think why,' she said.

He made to speak again, but Hopko turned on the two of them.

'Save it,' she said.

They made their way into the secure room, closing the heavy glass door behind them. Hopko lowered the blinds. They sat, Charteris sullen.

'So is it official, then?' said Charteris.

'Is what official?' said Hopko.

Charteris gave an exaggerated sigh.

'Is what official? That Yeats has gone. That Yeats's is the

head that rolled. That Valentina Hopko survives. Is that official?'

Hopko smiled, but Patterson saw the hardness in her eyes.

'Roly Yeats has announced his immediate retirement from the Service, David,' she said. 'But I rather think he'll land on his feet. Don't you?'

'And you've made sure that Sancho Panza here' – he gestured idly at Patterson – 'still has a job, too.'

'Fuck you, David,' said Patterson.

He was shouting now, at her.

'Next time kindly give us a little warning when you're about to bring the entire fucking house down, will you?'

Patterson was standing, felt her own anger hot in her temples, let her voice rise.

'I saved the lives of our agents.'

'They were not yours to bloody save.' He was jabbing a finger at her. 'That operation. CALIPER. Exfiltration! Using smugglers! Taiwanese people-traffickers! Are you out of your fucking mind? You could have started a war. You practically did, from what I hear.'

'So where were you?' she yelled at him. 'State Security was all over them, and where the hell were you? I got them out! And trust me, I've had my bollocking already.'

Hopko had taken off her glasses, and watched them.

'I put her up to it,' she said to Charteris.

Patterson said nothing.

'CALIPER was a contingency. But I felt we were going to need it when . . .'

Hopko stopped speaking.

'When what?' said Patterson.

'When operational control was taken away from us,' said Hopko.

Charteris sneered.

'You mean when they outsourced our little show.'

Hopko didn't reply.

'Why did we hand it over so ... so willingly, Val? With such alacrity?' said Charteris. Patterson was listening hard, now. Hopko thought for a moment, then exhaled.

'Why? Why did we give our operation, our assets, to a private corporation to play with?' she said. 'Because the operation wasn't about us.'

Patterson waited, saw how hard it was for Hopko.

'We all sensed this enormous opportunity, didn't we?' Hopko went on. 'To get deep inside China's network. Well, we're not the only ones interested in what's in there. And governments are not the only players in this business any more.'

She held her hands open.

'The US and the UK together spend a trillion dollars a year on defence and security. One trillion. Imagine being able to tell the Pentagon and the Ministry of Defence they can't buy anything made in China, ever. No chips, no routers, no wiring, no noth-ing, not even a transistor. Sorry, General, all that Made in China stuff is dodgy. It's full of back doors and exploits and it'll spy on you, and it'll make your planes fall out of the sky and your ships go round in circles. And we've got *evidence*. Because we can see into China's manufacturers and we know what they're doing. Oh, but don't worry, General, we'll step in and make it for you: processors, fibre, whatever you need. Buy it from us instead. It's called threat inflation. You may have heard of it.'

She stopped, and rubbed her eyes.

'And let's face it, we don't really know what we're doing with cyber, do we? I mean we'll make a decent fist of it – we just did: STONE CIRCLE was a success, wasn't it? But the people who really know what they're doing don't work for us. Why would they? A house in a suburb, kids in state schools? Two weeks in Spain in the summer? Not for them. The people who know what they're doing, the coders, the physicists, the materials people, they work

in the corporations. But we need them. So we give them contracts, and we let them wander the corridors, and we rent their
expertise. And they design things for us and sell them to us, and
help us use them, the computers, software, networks, satellites,
whatever. And, *and*, they learn all our secrets to boot. And grad-
ually we come to depend on them, and then we become
inseparable, and then we become indistinguishable. And *voilà*.
The espionage industrial complex.'

Hopko leaned back in her chair, folded her arms. Patterson
watched her, then spoke.

'But, Val.'

'But, Trish.'

'Who blew the operation? How did MSS get to GENIUS?' said
Patterson.

Charteris was watching Hopko intently. She leaned forward,
her eyes hard.

'Isn't that the question?' Hopko said.

It had been a hotel room, this time, just across the river in
Virginia. He'd left already, and Nicole lay in a tangle of sheets.
On the table an envelope. *Just for you, Nicole, as usual. Love,
Jonathan.*

She pushed herself up on to her elbows and reached for
the envelope. Inside, a document, thirty pages or so, marked
SECRET/NOFORN. *National Intelligence Estimate. The Political
Future of Taiwan.*

She slid the envelope into her bag, lay back, turned off the
light.

First day at the office.

And what an office. A discreet, white Georgian mansion just
off Pall Mall. A private lift to a secure floor, thickly carpeted,
decorated with contemporary art. His own secretary, his own

SCIF, and a staff of very quiet Americans. A dining room, he discovered at lunchtime. He had been on his way out to get a sandwich when he was taken by the arm and guided to a lunch of crayfish salad and iced tea, made to his taste by a silent catering staff.

The salary dwarfed his Service pension, and the welcome given him by the quiet Americans was respectful.

> Horizon Intel Solutions Inc. is delighted to welcome Roland
> Yeats to the London team. Roland has seen many years in
> the service of his country and brings to Horizon a unique
> and profound knowledge of the contemporary intelligence
> terrain, as well as formidable language and analytic skills. As
> a Vice President for Asia, Roland will focus on collection
> solutions and government liaison with regard to the China
> target, and will play a pivotal role in formulating the
> Horizon offer to European governments. He will also be
> available in a consulting capacity as we strengthen corporate
> synergies across the Shady Creek Group. Welcome, Roly! It
> is a privilege to have you with us as we build robust,
> adaptive strategies for clients across the intelligence cycle,
> and strengthen our global operations in a fast-changing,
> challenging intelligence environment.
> Horizon Intel Solutions Inc.
> 'Intelligence for Leadership, for Life'
> A Shady Creek Group Company.

They were sending him to Singapore first, then on to Seoul. He had asked for his flight schedule, but it transpired he would be flying in the corporate Gulfstream. So it was up to him, really.

Peanut knew he had to move fast. The target was slipping through a welter of food stalls, down towards the brown, viscous

Chao Praya river. Would he take a water taxi? That would fuck everything up.

Peanut hopped a railing, on to a boardwalk, the target just in sight, cutting off to the left, disappearing in a shaded passageway, emerging again into the light. So, not the river. A tea house, with golden Chinese characters atop its gables, the Thai beneath. The man disappeared through the front entrance. Peanut stopped, caught his breath, looked around for somewhere to wait. Over there, a stall with tin pots of curry, platters of fruit. A woman waved a fan to keep the flies away. He bought a bowl of shaved ice with coconut milk and syrup and sat at a little table.

Who was this man, anyway? Was this drugs, or something else? For his first two months they'd had him working drugs, as far as he could tell, the Chinese connections spilling down from Yunnan Province, through Burma, into Thailand. Late night surveillance ops in Bangkok's Chinatown, hanging around outside brothels and nightclubs, some listening. There was more to it, he was sure, but when he'd asked they'd told him to concentrate on the job at hand.

And not such a bad job, considering. It paid, for a start. Enough for a little flat over a quiet courtyard. He grew flowers in pots on a balcony. And the woman downstairs – she was a widow, she said – had taken to cooking for him: curries, noodles with basil, mangos dipped in sweet chilli sauce.

She spoke some language he'd never learn, something from the Shan states, and fragments of Chinese. He struggled with the infernal speech of Thailand, and somehow they communicated, and then, well.

She'd bathe him and dry him off and rub him with white powder from a tin that smelled of mentholatum. And she'd lie next to him and punch his arm, feeling his strength, and chuckle, and when they walked out in the street she'd hold on to him. She liked his size, how people stepped out of his way.

He kept his eyes on the tea house. Please God the man doesn't go out the back. He mopped the sweat from his forehead with a napkin. He turned his face towards the river for a moment, hoping for breeze and finding none. He'd wanted warm, and warm was what he'd been given.

They'd left Taiwan quickly, at night, on the smallest aeroplane he'd ever seen. He had run his hands over the leather seat covers. He hadn't seen the Englishman again. It was Singapore first, where he was sequestered in an apartment on his own with two poker-faced guards who refused to speak except to tell him he was 'drying out'. Two other Europeans came with questions each day. They seemed poorly informed, and their Mandarin was atrocious. They tried to walk him through the operation, everything that had happened. *Please, Mr Li, describe the Ministry of State Security operatives. How many? What did they say?* And he sat and smoked and demanded his money and his papers, and eventually they seemed to give up and asked him to sign a piece of paper, which committed him to silence in this life and the next. Then they brought him to Bangkok, gave him a passport after all, and a bank account that contained less than he had hoped for, though perhaps a little more than he had expected, and they introduced him to a group of hatchet-faced Thais, patted him on the shoulder and left.

And so he'd work at this for a while, see what presented itself. And he'd put away a little more cash each month. And he'd see the widow, and he'd go and play *majiang* in that little dive with the thief Lau and the others and he'd forge what looked and felt suspiciously like friendships, fending off their questions about where he was from and who he'd been by cracking some joke and washing the *majiang* tiles with their beautiful *clack clack* sound.

The target was coming out of the tea house. He was carrying a bag that he hadn't been carrying before, a black clutch bag with a strap for the wrist, which seemed to Peanut likely to contain valuable items. He held the bag under his arm. The target stopped and looked about him.

Don't stand still, thought Peanut.

Stillness is the enemy.

Move.

Acknowledgements

My profound thanks go to my agent, Catherine Clarke at Felicity Bryan Associates, who nurtured *Night Heron* almost from its inception with great patience and generosity. I am also grateful to Karen Godfrey, whose insights improved the manuscript greatly. The team at Little, Brown, including editors Ed Wood, Iain Hunt, and Tim Holman, made it something special. I count myself very lucky to work with them. For crucial encouragement given along the way, thank you to Chris Booth, Simon Wilson, Jon Whitney, Kim Ghattas, Paul Forty, Amanda Brookes, Sally Brookes, Richard Lawrence, and the much loved and missed Melissa Spielman. Professor Philip H.J. Davies of Brunel University provided important guidance, as did his extraordinary book, *MI6 and the Machinery of Spying*. I received help and advice from a number of people who can't be named here, one in particular in whose company I remember passing a long, dank night in a certain Texas car park. My thanks go to all of them. I owe most to my wife Susan, whose love and wisdom carry me along, and to my best advisers, Anna and Ned.

ABOUT THE AUTHOR

Adam Brookes grew up in Oxfordshire and studied Chinese at the School of Oriental and African Studies in London. He has spent most of his career as a foreign correspondent for the British Broadcasting Corporation. The BBC posted him to China twice, as well as to Indonesia and the United States. He has also reported from Afghanistan, Iraq, North Korea and many other countries in Asia and the Middle East. He lives with his family in Takoma Park, Maryland.